FINAL
JEOPARDY

FINAL
JEOPARDY

LINDA
FAIRSTEIN

LITTLE, BROWN AND COMPANY

A *Little, Brown* Book

First published in the United States in 1996 by Scribner

First published in Great Britain in 1996
by Little, Brown and Company

Copyright © 1996 by Linda Fairstein

The moral right of the author has been asserted.

A CIP catalogue record for this book
is available from the British Library.

ISBN 0 316 88008 6

Typeset by Palimpsest Book Production Limited,
Polmont, Stirlingshire
Printed and bound in Great Britain by
Clays Ltd, St Ives plc.

UK companies, institutions and other organisations wishing
to make bulk purchases of this or any other book published
by Little, Brown should contact their local bookshop or the
special sales department at the address below.
Tel 0171 911 8000. Fax 0171 911 8100.

Little, Brown and Company (UK)
Brettenham House
Lancaster Place
London WC2E 7EN

FOR

Esther Newberg

AND

Justin Feldman,

Believers

1

I sat on my living-room sofa at five o'clock in the morning with a copy of the mock-up of the front page of the day's *New York Post* in my hand, looking at my own obituary. The headline I was reading had been prepared hours earlier, when the cops thought that it was my head that had been blown apart by a rifle blast on a quiet country road in a little Massachusetts town called Chilmark.

'SEX PROSECUTOR SLAIN – FBI, STATE TROOPERS JOIN SEARCH FOR KILLER'

Mike Chapman sat opposite me as he worked on his second egg sandwich and lukewarm cup of coffee. He had brought them along with the news story, and in the fashion of an experienced Homicide detective he continued chewing even as he described to me the details

1

of the murder scene – bullet holes, blood spatter, and body bag.

'Good thing you've been a source for so many stories at the *Post* all these years. It's a very complimentary obit . . .' He stopped eating long enough for that familiar grin to emerge, then added, 'And a great picture of you – looks like they airbrushed most of your wrinkles out. Your phone'll be ringing off the hook once all those lonely guys in this city realize you're still alive – maybe you'll get lucky.'

Most of the time Mike could defuse every situation and get me to laugh, but I had been crying for so many hours that it was impossible to respond to his lousy cracks or to focus on anything else but the dreadful day that lay ahead. A woman had been killed on the path leading to my country house, driving a car that had been rented in my name. The body of the tall, slender, thirtyish victim was missing her face, so most of the local cops who arrived on the scene assumed that I had been the target.

We were more than two hundred miles away from the crime scene, twenty stories above the noise of the garbage trucks that rolled through Manhattan streets every morning before dawn, in the safe confines of my high-rise apartment on the Upper East Side. Too many years of investigating break-ins of brownstones and townhouses, with rapists climbing in from fire escapes or pushing in vestibule doors behind unsuspecting tenants, had driven me to a luxury building – low on quaintness and charm but high on doormen and rent. My mother had come into town for two weeks to decorate for me when I moved a few years earlier, but the French provincial antiques and lavish Brunschwig fabrics were an incongruous backdrop for this deadly conversation.

'How'd you get the call?' Mike asked, brushing the crumbs off his slacks and onto the carpet, ready to give me his undivided attention.

'One of the guys in the unit is about to start a trial in front of Torres and grabbed me just as I was going to leave the office for the night. His victim is a junkie – she came in to be prepped for court and was so high she couldn't hold her head up. God knows if she remembers anything about the rape. I had to make the arrangements to get a hotel room for her overnight so we could try to dry her out before she gets on the witness stand. By the time we finished it was nine-thirty, and I just called my friend Joan Stafford to meet for a late supper.'

'I didn't ask you for your alibi, for Chrissakes. How'd you hear about this?'

'I can't even focus straight, Mike. You've got to take me down to my office so I can be there before everyone starts to arrive – I'll never make it through all the questions.'

'Just talk to me, Alex.'

Reliving the events of the past few hours as a witness and not a prosecutor was an unsettling role for me. I tried to reconstruct what had happened after I walked into my apartment shortly before midnight and headed to the answering machine to play back the messages as I started to undress.

Beep one: 'Hi, Alex. I'm on the Ventura Freeway, taking the baby to his play group. Tell me more about the case with the therapist who seduced his patient. It sounds fascinating. How many people do you think *he's* fucked up? Speak with you later.' Nina Baum, my college roommate, still my best friend, making her regular phone car call from one of the endless L.A. roadways on which she seemed to spend her life.

Beep two: Just the deliberate click of a hang-up call.

Beep three: 'Yo, Coop. Wallace here. The lieutenant asked me to give you a heads up. The Con Ed rapist hit again today. Nothing for you to do now. Lady's been to the hospital and released, so we put her to bed for the night. You do the same, and we'll be down at your office tomorrow. Behave. G'night.' The deep, familiar voice of Mercer Wallace, formerly of Homicide, who was now my lead detective in the Special Victims Squad, the unit which investigated all of the sexual assault and child abuse cases that occurred in Manhattan.

Beep four: 'I'm trying to reach a friend or next-of-kin to Alexandra Cooper. This is an emergency. Please call me, Chief Wally Flanders, Chilmark Police – Martha's Vineyard. It's urgent – give a call as soon as you get this message. Area code 508–555–3044. Thanks.'

Of course I had known Wally for more than a decade – I had been going to the Vineyard since I had been in law school, and Wally was as much a local fixture as the fishing boats and the general store.

I picked up the phone to dial, wondering why he was looking for a friend or relative at my apartment instead of asking for me. When he got on the line, he expressed how surprised he was to hear my voice. 'Where are you?' he asked.

'In Manhattan, in my apartment, Chief.'

'Well, Alex, there's been a terrible tragedy here. Terrible. Was there somebody stayin' at your house, somebody you let use it?'

'Yes, Wally, a friend of mine is there. It's okay, she'll

be staying there for a week or two. It's no problem, I've arranged everything.'

My mind was racing but I had never connected the Vineyard with any kind of crime problem except the occasional house burglary. That's why it has always been such a refuge for me, a world away from the grim business of investigating and prosecuting rape cases. Someone must have noticed an unfamiliar person coming or going into Daggett's Pond Way and suspected a burglary.

'Not so easy, Alex. Your friend isn't staying for as long as you thought. She was shot sometime tonight, see, and my guys found the body a few hours ago. She's dead, Alex, real dead.'

'Oh my God!' I repeated quietly several times into the telephone mouthpiece. I was incredulous, as people always are when they get this kind of news. And as intimately as I have worked with violence and murder for more than ten years, it had never ruptured the fragile line that separated my personal from my professional life.

'Alex? Alex? Are you alone there?'

'Yes.'

'Can you get someone over to give you a hand with this?'

With what? I thought. What else could anyone do except stare at me while I spun out of control?

Wally continued, 'See, the big problem is that we thought it was you who got killed. That's why we were tryin' to find your family, for notification. The press already thinks you're the dead woman.'

'How did *that* happen?' I shrieked at him.

'Well, it's really ugly. We figure that you – I mean she – was riding in a convertible, top down – and she had turned off the state road onto that wooded path that leads in to your house. Someone must have been waiting in there for you, and – excuse me – just let out a blast which hit her square in the side of her head.'

I don't suppose Wally could hear me but I was sitting on my bedroom floor, crying as he finished his story.

'We had a call during the evening to go up to the Patterson house, out your way. My boys found the body – couldn't tell much about anything from looking at her and she didn't have no ID. They called in the license plate and found that the Mustang had been rented in your name. Hell, it was your driveway, a rented car, and a girl with a similar build and size – it made sense that it was you.'

'I guess so,' I whimpered back to him.

'Well, I'm glad it's not you, Alex. Everyone will be glad to know it's not you. I figured the investigation would be a monster, tryin' to track down every pervert and madman you've sent to jail. That's why I called in the FBI – I figured we'd be huntin' all over the place.'

Wally actually laughed a few times at that point. 'It's a relief, really. I guess the off-island papers won't even bother with us now.'

The chief had no idea how wrong he was and how bad this was going to be for that tranquil little island.

'Can you help us, Alex? Can you give us her name and who to notify?'

I mumbled the name into the phone, but Wally heard it loud and clear. 'Isabella Lascar.'

The news wires were about to explode with the information that the face of the dazzlingly beautiful actress

6

and film star, Isabella Lascar, had been obliterated, and that what was left of her body lay in the tiny Vineyard morgue, with a toe tag mislabeled in the name of Alexandra Cooper.

Mike waited in the den, surfing the TV channels for clips about the murder, while I showered and dressed to go down to my office in the criminal courthouse. There wasn't enough makeup in Manhattan to conceal the puffy circles beneath my eyes, so I just rolled on some lipstick and grabbed my sunglasses from the bedside table.

'You look like shit, blondie,' Mike offered as I headed for the front door. 'Very bad for my image – doorman thinks I spent the night with a broad who looks like that.'

'If you think I look bad now, you're going to love it when the District Attorney gets done with me in a few hours. C'mon, let's get going.'

Chapman is as dark-featured as I am fair – lots of thick, straight black hair – and what people usually call an infectious grin, when he chose to display it. He was tall and lanky, and his years at Fordham University, where he graduated with a degree in history before following in his father's footsteps and entering the Police Academy, left him with a taste for dressing in an almost preppy style – which set him apart from most of his colleagues. When I called the District Attorney after my conversation with Wally Flanders, he told me that he would assign a detective to stay with me for the next twenty-four hours, and I was as grateful for Mike Chapman's jibes as I was for his company.

It was just before 6 A.M. when we walked to the department car he had parked around the corner on Third Avenue. Mike unlocked the door and I got in, kicking aside the usual littered remains of empty cardboard coffee cups, crushed cigarette packs, and a month's worth of tabloids.

'Fill me in, will you? Who'd you speak to last night, after you got the call?' he asked, as he started toward the FDR Drive.

'I began with the easy stuff. My parents first, just to let them know I was alive. My brothers. Next Joan, since we'd just had dinner, and I gave her the assignment of calling friends. Then, armed with a loaded glass of Dewar's, I called the D.A.'

Paul Battaglia, the District Attorney of New York County, believed that your name belonged in a newspaper only three times: when you're born, when you die, and when he announced your indictment at a press conference at a date and time entirely of his choosing. Assistant district attorneys, as the five hundred and seventy-six of us who worked for him were called, flourished best out of the harsh glare of media light.

Battaglia was the only D.A. most New Yorkers remembered, and with good reason. He had been in office almost twenty years and, at the age of sixty-two, had a national reputation for his impeccable integrity and for running the best prosecutor's office in the country.

Like most of my colleagues, I had joined the office immediately after law school, confident that it was the best training ground for trial attorneys anywhere. I had planned to stay the four years that Battaglia required as a commitment when he extended our job offers, and then move on to the more lucrative private practice of law. But like the overwhelming number of young lawyers on the staff, I fell in love with the challenge of the work – trying complicated felony cases to juries, working around the clock with cops in station houses and at crime scenes, and generally being on the side of the angels in the endless battles against violent crime in the big city.

And a major aspect of my happiness was my respect for Battaglia, who had given so much to me in the eleven years since he had hired me. I liked to think that I had not done anything to disappoint him, until last night.

'You know the man almost as well as I do, Mike. The kind of publicity this thing could generate will make him very unhappy.'

'Tell me what Lascar was doing at your country house in the first place.'

Isabella and I first met three years earlier, at the suggestion of Nina Baum, who had been my roommate at Wellesley. Nina was the head of the legal department at Virgo Studios and in charge of all the contract negotiations for the superstars in most of the company productions.

The three of us were about the same age, although

Isabella's official bio shaved a few years off, and she and Nina had become great friends after working together on a number of projects.

Lascar had a few minor speaking roles in some major movies in the late eighties, but it was her love scenes with Warren Beatty in *Delirious* – cast as his mistress, living in the Hotel du Cap, while Beatty played a roguish bank robber working the Riviera – which brought her celebrity recognition.

When Virgo bought the rights to the best-selling novel *Probable Cause*, Nina called me to ask a favor. Isabella had been awarded the starring role in the movie, playing the part of the federal prosecutor who investigated and convicted a powerful senator for the hired killing of his wealthy wife in their Washington, D.C., townhouse. I had tried a number of high-profile rape and murder cases by then, and Nina wanted me to let Isabella spend time with me, in and out of court, to give her some flavor of the work and lifestyle of a woman litigator.

Battaglia and Isabella first met when I introduced her to him at lunch one day, at a restaurant near the court-house. He had never heard of her at that point, and he mispronounced her name, calling her Miss Lasker. She placed her hand on his forearm, leaned into him with a smile, as she made the correction. 'It's Lass-CAR, darling. Accent on the second syllable. It's French.' She had come across the name of a character – a Lyonnaise courtesan – in a De Maupassant short story, Isabella later told me, and had taken it for her own.

I reminded Mike of Battaglia's reaction to my request. 'He was very good-natured about that nonsense. I asked him if Isabella could shadow me in the office and he agreed.

As usual, his instincts were right, though. He insisted that Virgo *not* list us in the credits at the end of the movie, just in case the depiction wasn't too flattering.'

'So the scenes where she slept with her boss, three senators, and one of the jurors weren't based on you?' Mike chuckled.

'Neither were her devastating cross-examinations, Mike. I think the only thing they used after spending three weeks with me was the scene when she left work early to go to a shoe sale at Saks. The rest was strictly Hollywood.'

Mike knew that Isabella and I had kept in touch ever since, and that she often called me when she was in New York. And never had she called without wanting something from somebody. She had developed quite a reputation as a bitch, which did not come as much of a surprise to me.

'Darling, it's Iz,' the typical message began. 'I'm in town, at the Carlyle. Love to see you. By the way, don't you have some little man who can breeze me through Customs when I come back from Milano next week?' or, 'You know that pass you put in your windshield when you go to a police station? Can't I just borrow it for my driver while I'm here for the week? It'll save us getting all those lousy parking tickets.'

Always minor irritants. Improper, but minor.

Then it changed a few months ago, when Isabella had a serious problem: she was being stalked. The first letters went to her home in Bel Air, but whenever she arrived in Manhattan, the stalker knew to send the letters to the Carlyle and the phone calls followed.

This time I really could help her. Six years earlier, Battaglia had promoted me to the position of Chief of the Sex Crimes Prosecution Unit in the Manhattan D.A.'s

Office. I supervised the investigation and prosecution of all cases of sexual assault reported in the county, as well as the more sensitive, bizarre cases like stalkers. The unit had been the first of its kind in the country and we prided ourselves in doing innovative work to better the plight of women who had long been denied justice in the courtrooms when victimized in these traumatic cases.

'Isabella had called me from California to ask what to do about the letters and calls. We opened cases on both coasts, and when she came to New York we set up a sting operation to try to lure the guy in. We had taped all the incoming calls, the phone company "trapped" them for us, and even though most of them were made from a phone booth outside his house in Jersey, we knew exactly where he was.'

Mike asked what the content of the letters had been.

'The usual. Vivid descriptions of which of his body parts he wanted to rub against which of hers, why it would be better than anything she'd ever known before, how she shouldn't be making love on the screen to "wops like Nick Cage and kikes like Harvey Keitel" . . . and if she didn't meet with him soon, her beautiful blond head would be sitting in his bowling bag at the bottom of his closet so no one else could see it again.'

'I remember this case now,' Mike said, signaling for the exit from the Drive to the ramp leading down to the narrow one-way streets of the courthouse area. 'You arranged a special autograph session for the Lascar fan club members – twelve undercover detectives and one fucking whackjob. And your man showed up, bowling bag and all.'

'Yeah, we had a bus in front of the hotel, with a big banner on the side: Operation Screen-Play. We made a point

13

of searching everyone who boarded to be taken to Miss Lascar's secret location. Arthur Piggott got on line eagerly – surrounded by twelve guys from the D.A.'s squad, who had taken to calling him "Piggy" – and they took him down flat when they found a fifteen-inch machete in the zippered compartment of the bag. Not a tough case for the good guys – even you might have been able to solve it.'

'What happened to Piggy?'

'Bellevue Psych Ward, awaiting trial. He's not competent at the moment, Mike. A bit delusional – thinks he and Isabella are married, he just can't find the certificate or the wedding photos.'

'And Isabella's most recent trip, Alex?'

'She called me two weeks ago, shortly after getting into town. And she told me that she was being harassed again. Phone messages and then notes, but she didn't think they were much so she hadn't saved them.'

'Piggy again?' Mike asked.

'Not likely. I checked Bellevue, but the judge had denied him phone privileges and there's a mail screen on everything that goes out. Anyway, two of the guys are working on it, but there isn't a lot to go on.

'So then Isabella called again, with a more familiar intonation: a favor. "Darling, I've heard you and Nina talk so much about that quaint little farmhouse you have on Martha's Vineyard. I'm so sick and tired of being harassed by these crazy characters, and Nina thought you wouldn't mind if I went up there alone for a few days to be a recluse and read a few scripts. Is it a problem, Alex?'

'For once,' I explained to Mike, 'it was no problem – she wasn't asking me to use my government job to get her some stupid perk. I just assumed she interjected a second stalker to let me think she truly needed to get out of town. The end of September is the most spectacular time on the island, and I was delighted to let her use the house . . . especially if I didn't have to hang out with her and listen to all her crap about "the industry."'

'Did you go up there with her?' Mike asked.

'No. Isabella had to be in Boston at the end of the week, so she was going to go down to the Cape from there, and either fly or take the ferry over to the Vineyard. I had reserved the rental car and charged it to my credit card 'cause my car's in storage for the winter, and I didn't want to give the rental agent her name. Once anybody in town knew there was going to be another movie star on the island, she'd have no privacy at all.'

'Any calls from her once she got there? Any problems?'

I thought for a moment. 'She called a couple of times the first day, just to ask where things were in the house, and how to get to the beach, but she seemed quite happy and relaxed.'

I had been talking with a reasonable degree of calm as I brought Mike up to date, but I choked on the fact of Isabella's death, which still didn't seem possible to me, and the circumstances in which it occurred.

'Mike, if I hadn't given her the house and if . . .'

'You can't do the "what ifs," kid. You did what you did and that's not the reason she's dead. If Isabella Lascar was the target, then whoever hit her would have found his opportunity at one time or another. And if Isabella Lascar was *not* the target, then we have a different situation on our hands, a real monster.'

I shook my head in disbelief. 'That's what the D.A. thinks, too. He really thinks someone was trying to kill *me*, not

Isabella. But that's absurd, Mike. I know any prosecutor makes enemies, but it's a hell of a stretch to think I'm likely to be on a country road on the Vineyard in the middle of the week at the end of September instead of right here in town – a simple call to the office switchboard would have confirmed that.'

'Alex, you think we're dealing with someone who's wrapped that tight? All I know is that Battaglia called the Chief of Detectives right after you spoke with him and gave him two orders. First was to send someone to the *Post* offices to stop the presses on the headline that had *you* as the victim – that's the version I brought up to your apartment when I came this morning – and make sure they ran the correct story about Isabella. But most important was to get someone from Manhattan North to babysit for you until this thing plays out and we know who killed her. I got hit with both of those tasks – that's why they sent me up to your place so early.'

'I know. Battaglia told me he was insisting on a body-guard. You've had better assignments, Mike, but I asked him to ask for you. I need a friend to do this, to be with me, so please don't be mad at me. I wanted it to be you.'

'Hey, I wouldn't miss this one for the world. You think I'd rather be stepping over dead bodies in a Harlem crack den or killing cockroaches back at the precinct? This isn't exactly combat duty. Besides, I told the chief I didn't even have to go home – I could go right to your place because I had left some clean underwear there last month.'

'Mike, you didn't say . . .'

'Relax, kid. You can't lose your sense of humor over this.'

He rounded the corner onto Hogan Place and parked a

few feet from our building entrance on the south end of the criminal courthouse – not a lot of competition for spaces at six-twenty in the morning. 'You've got a lot of friends and every one of them is going to help you through the next few days.'

We got out of the car and headed for the steps. 'What does lover boy have to say about all this?' Mike asked, as he held open the door and we moved into the dingy lobby of the District Attorney's Office, nodding hello and showing our IDs to get past a security guard and the metal detectors.

I wasn't even aware that I frowned as I tried to form an answer to that question, knowing that Mike was never short on opinions about guys I had dated over all the years we had known each other. I liked to think that some of it was because he was a little jealous. It was an easy topic for ridicule, so he often took aim at the 'white collar wimps' he met at office parties and courthouse bars. Jed Segal, investment banker, didn't escape Mike's strike, even though he was not in that category. Jed had first had a brilliant career practicing law, which led to a stint in Washington, before he returned home to California to make an unsuccessful run for the Senate last year. To my good fortune, a tempting corporate offer had lured him to New York earlier this year, when I met and started to date him.

'He's not back from Europe yet. I, uh . . . I tried to reach him but, you know, with the time difference and all. I'll tell him when he calls today.'

'That's what you really need, Cooper, a guy who's always there for you when trouble strikes – just an ocean away. Another deal to close. Then he'll come back to comfort you one of these nights and he'll be all wet and slurpy and I'll be keeping you both safe with my trusty six-shooter by my side, sitting in your living room watching reruns of "I Love Lucy" while he gets consoled on your big brass bed. If only the Police Academy gave MBAs – I could'a been a contender, know what I mean?'

'No, then you'd be an investment banker, too, Mike,' I said as we got off the elevator on the eighth floor and turned into the corridor toward my office, '. . . but you'd still be an asshole. Leave me alone on this.'

'I hit a nerve, blondie, didn't I? Maybe even deep enough for root canal, huh? Lover boy's off limits. I understand.'

I unlocked the door to my office, flipped on the light and sat at my desk, while Mike settled himself at the post in the anteroom where my secretary worked. He had indeed hit a nerve. It was one of those moments when I didn't want to be the tough litigator who could solve everyone else's problems and separate the emotional baggage from the realities of any situation. I wanted to stay curled up at home on my sofa, with Jed holding me in his arms, caressing me and assuring me that everything would be all right. But I wasn't at home and it would probably be days before Jed would be there to make love to me, and the best I could hope for was that the business of a hectic day in the office would temporarily distract me from the nightmare that had so suddenly enveloped me.

3

Manhattan's Criminal Courts Building is a massive, ugly, gray structure, the façade of which unconsciously reflects the rumor – not true – that it was built during the Depression as a WPA effort. The usual maxims about the search for truth and justice are chiseled into its exterior columns and above its entrances which stretch the length of several city blocks. But its even more grim interior houses the cramped work cubbyholes of the thousands of worker bees who do the everyday business of the criminal justice system: judges, assistant district attorneys, Legal Aid Society lawyers, and probation officers. The northern end of the complex – the only piece of it to have been remodeled in more than half a century – is named the Tombs, the cells in which prisoners are held before arraignment or during trials, connected to the courthouse by the Bridge of Sighs.

Mike liked to call the prison Landin Lounge, after the federal judge who ordered it rebuilt because of the over-crowded conditions that had prompted riots and lawsuits a decade ago. 'Yeah, build those scumbags a first-class joint. Give 'em private rooms and color tubes and a gym so they can pump themselves up so they can run faster next time I'm chasing 'em. After all, they're killing each other to get in there, might as well make it comfy for them. Oh, and showers, six showers on every cellblock. Remember Devon Cranston? The homeless guy who lived in Riverside Park and stabbed four people to death? How often did he shower in Riverside Park? You bet your ass he showers twice a day now in Landin Lounge. Meantime,' he was fond of saying, 'if I put my sandwich down on *your* desk for a minute, forty-three roaches swarm out of your filing cabinets and devour it. There's asbestos leaking out of your water fountain and lead paint chips falling off the ceiling into Battaglia's coffee cup. But start with the prisoners first. That's a judge who's really got his priorities straight.'

Despite my tenure in the office and my administrative position, the room in which I work is no fancier or larger than that of any of my colleagues. It's a cubicle about eight by fourteen feet with a single window that faces another dreary government building across the narrow side street. My efforts to cheer it up with photographs and prints are outweighed by the drab collection of battered pieces of furniture: a desk, several unmatched leather chairs, one bookcase, and an array of tall five-drawer file cabinets which – like most city-issued supplies, including a very worn strip of stained carpeting – are a dull shade of gray.

Today, like most other days, there is additional clutter which includes exhibits from complex investigations and completed trials. They document the violent landscape of the city over which my colleagues and I have jurisdiction: maps and charts of rooftops, parks, housing project stair-wells, and elegant apartment interiors – waiting to be marked as evidence at trial or shipped to the archives in the basement of the cavernous courthouse for storage until all the defendants' appeals in each of the cases are exhausted.

The top of my metal desk is covered with a bright red blotter, rarely more than a sliver of which is visible because of the accumulation of manila folders and white legal pads that pile on top. They house case files and witness interviews, police reports and memoranda from unit prosecutors, laboratory analyses of body fluids and blood types, mug shots of suspects being sought, medical records and DNA profiles of rape survivors, and every other form of detritus of the world of criminal law.

I walked from my office down the hallway to the conference room to fill the pot for the first round of coffee, while Mike double-checked to confirm that Piggy was still in the nuthouse at Bellevue.

'That would have been much too easy,' he said, 'so let's figure out where to go from there.'

'Battaglia wants us to review every pending sex offense complaint, all of my closed cases that resulted in serious time, and the lists of guys released to parole recently. My paralegals will help you put that stuff together when they get in – the files are all in their office, down the hall near the Appeals Bureau.'

'You've got to think for me, Alex. Things that aren't in

case files, things nobody else could know about, remarks that you've ignored because you've been in the business too long to pay attention to them. Hang-up calls, letters from cranks, goofballs, malcontents.'

'I've been thinking about it all night, Mike. Most of the guys you and I encounter are much too stupid to plan something like yesterday's murder. I'm sure this is going to tie in to something that Isabella did to someone, really.'

'Well, Coop, we still have to go through the motions, so start combing your file folders for ideas. Jesus, your desk looks like the bottom of a birdcage! I want you to go through every piece of paper that's current, and clean up that mess while you're at it.'

I gave Mike the key to the office shared by my two paralegals, where all the unit records were stored, so he could get a jump on the older cases and parole notifications while I thought about how to begin to examine the jumble of papers on my desk.

I picked up the phone, accessed an outside line, and dialed the number for the Ritz, the elegant old hotel Jed favored when he was doing business in Paris. *'Non*, madame, Monsieur Segal is not in at the moment. Yes, madame, of course I will leave him another message. *Au revoir*, Madame Cooper.' It was midday in Paris. Jed was probably sitting in some outdoor café sipping a good Bordeaux with a client, and unlikely to pick up my messages until he returned to his room at the end of the evening.

During the next two hours, I managed to fill several pages of a white legal pad with some obvious candidates for consideration. There were plenty of active investigations to look at – the drama coach who subjected students to sexual abuse, the drug importer who sedated and videotaped models as he raped them, and the gay art dealer who played sado-masochistic games with young men he picked up in leather bars; and there were literally thousands of closed cases – serial rapists, pedophiles, and professionals who didn't look the part of sexual deviants. For once I was delighted when the hour approached 9 A.M. and the corridors began to come alive with the courthouse regulars.

Laura Wilkie had been the secretary for the Sex Crimes Unit even before I joined the staff and, fortunately for me, had stayed on as my assistant ever since. She was almost twenty years older than I – in her mid-fifties – and lived alone in a small apartment on Staten Island where she devoted her off-duty hours to tending her cheerful flower garden and painting imaginary landscapes. Laura was terrifically loyal to me and responsible for keeping the work of the twenty-five lawyers who reported to me in better control and order than I ever could. When Laura came in she was pleased to see me in place and plopped the pile of daily papers in front of me, as she always did.

'Well, somebody besides me really didn't like Isabella, did they?' she offered with a wry expression.

'Don't say it too loud, Laura, or Chapman will add you to the suspect list. What did you have against her?'

'Oh, nothing really, Alex. She just used people like you so much, and she had *no* use for people like me. She wasn't a very nice person, that's it.'

'She wasn't all that bad. I know she could be rude and insensitive, which was inexcusable. But she was also clever and funny and extremely talented, once you got past that artificial veneer. Anyway, let me bring you up to speed on

23

what lies ahead today,' I went on, repeating last night's events to Laura, who would serve as the shield between me and the outside world. On a good day, no one got past Wilkie – on the phone or in person – without her knowing their purpose, except for close friends. And on a bad day like this, she would be impenetrable, if that's what I asked for.

'Mike's in charge – anybody who shows up without an appointment gets cleared by him.' Laura nodded. She knew that Mike Chapman and I had met on one of my first cases more than ten years ago, and even though the constant macho banter was not Laura's style, she enjoyed Mike's friendship and knew I respected his ability as a cop.

'The D.A.'s at a budget meeting at City Hall, which should go a couple of hours,' I went on. 'He's going to call for me the minute he gets back, so that's the big one I'm waiting for.

'Mercer Wallace should be on his way down with a victim. Make her comfortable in the waiting area and let me see him alone first. I want to get the story from him before I talk to her, because it's part of the pattern, the serial rapist we've been looking for. I'll take calls from any of the guys on trial – Gina may have some questions during jury selection 'cause she's got a tough drug issue in her case.

'And *no* personals, not one, not any, nobody.' In addition to the three lines on Laura's desk, I have a private line that rings only on mine, so I knew that Jed and my closest friends could get through when they wanted to. 'Tell everybody that I'm fine and I'll call them later.'

'What about press calls?' Laura asked, as Mike came back into my room with several case jackets under his arm.

'Hey, Wilkie, you want to lose your job? You ever

know her *not* to take a call from a reporter? Get a grip, Laura.'

'He's kidding, Laura. All press calls go into the Public Relations Office. Please tell Brenda I'll give her a full update as soon as I can.' The District Attorney had a well-trained professional staff to deal with media matters, and my friend Brenda Whitney had her hands full trying to keep tabs on the hundreds of thousands of cases that passed through our office every year. She didn't need the complications of our private lives to make her job more miserable, and it was essential to bring her in on details that were likely to surface in the press.

'Alex,' Laura questioned timidly, 'how about people from the office? Everybody's going to come by to check out how you're taking this. Who do you want to see?'

'Uh,' I groaned and tried to make a mental barricade between myself and the real world. But it was impossible to ignore that there were at least three colleagues I would simply have to see during the course of the day.

Rod Squires was chief of the Trial Division, the man who supervised several hundred lawyers responsible for all the violent crime prosecutions in the office, and who reported directly to Battaglia. He was smart and personable, and at forty-five, had come up through the ranks in the office, having tried some of the toughest murder cases the city had witnessed. He had been a generous mentor to me and a great supporter of mine from my earliest days in the office. 'If Rod asks for me, I'll go down to his office as soon as I'm done with Wallace's case.

'And of course I'll see Sarah.' My unit deputy was a terrific young lawyer. She was a few years younger than I, married to a former prosecutor who had just gone on to the bench, and she had returned from her first maternity leave to assist me with the operation of Sex Crimes. Sarah Brenner was petite, dark, and as attractive as she was competent. I trusted her, I liked her, and I selected her to work with me to oversee the complex and sensitive range of cases that included sexual assault, child abuse, and domestic violence. 'In fact, tell her she's got to review everything new that comes in. I'll be out of commission till I know what's happening with the murder investigation.'

Laura screwed up her courage to ask me about the third one: 'Patrick McKinney?'

'Try to keep him as far away from me as you can, Laura,' I snarled. 'He'll be the first one sniffing around here, hoping to find me miserable, and I'll break his fat fucking neck if he says a word to me.'

Mike laughed: 'Whew! Women in the workplace!'

'Listen, Mike, I don't know what happens in parochial schools – most of the guys survive the nuns and come out with a sense of humor – some a little more tasteful than yours, but humor nonetheless. This guy came out like Mother Superior himself, with a stick up his ass that should have punctured his brain by now.'

Pat McKinney was one of Rod's deputies. He was senior to me by a couple of years, and as rigid and humorless as any man could be. I've never figured what made him such an angry person, but something seethed inside him and most frequently found its outlet when directed at the women professionals in the office.

'Laura thinks he blames the crab incident on me, don't you?'

She nodded as I told Mike the story. 'Pat refused to sign off on an extradition request for one of the assistants in the Asian Gang Unit, who wanted to fly in a witness from Los Angeles and put the kid up in a hotel during the trial. McKinney said it was too expensive and that there was a strong enough case without the witness. I told the assistant that Pat was just crabby that day, and if he wrote up a new request I would walk it in to Rod for approval. Rod signed and the jury convicted. You know those fish stores on the corner at Canal Street?'

Our office was smack in the middle of the part of Lower Manhattan where Little Italy overlapped with Chinatown, and the south side of Canal Street was lined with Chinese-run fish stores that daily displayed open crates of live fish on the sidewalks.

'Well, a few days after the trial ended, Pat arrived to find his office door unlocked. He flew to his desk to call Security to come upstairs, and when he pulled open the top drawer, about forty live crabs came rushing over the lip of the drawer onto his lap – frisky little suckers that had been packed in on top of each other all night. I'm surprised you didn't hear his screams on Ninety-fourth Street.'

Mike liked the story. 'You do it?'

'Are you crazy? I assume it was the cops from the case, but he knows that I'm the one who called him "crabby" that time, so he blames me.'

We were interrupted by the appearance of a uniformed cop in the doorway beyond Laura's desk. He looked like a rookie – baby-faced, polished shoes, new equipment, and a sheaf of arrest papers in his hand.

'I'm looking for Mr. Cooper,' he announced to the three of us.

'You got him. Only I'm Cooper. It's Alex – Alexandra.'

'Oh, sorry. I'm Officer Corchado. They sent me up from the complaint room – I've got a new case.'

Laura moved to her desk to start working the phones and I waved Corchado into my office and introduced him to Mike as we seated ourselves.

'I won't be able to write this up for you 'cause I'm involved in something else today, but my assistant, Sarah Brenner, will work on it with you as soon as she gets in.'

'Yeah, but my lieutenant told me I had to see the bureau chief. There's a problem with a cross-complaint and he said you'd know what to do. You're the chief, right?'

'Yes,' I replied. 'What's the problem? Tell me what kind of case you've got.'

Corchado explained that he and his partner had responded to a 911 call shortly after eleven last night. 'Neighbors had called it in – housing project in the two-three.' East Harlem.

I asked if he'd met the victim.

'Yeah, she was a mess. A kid, fifteen. Taken to the rooftop from the elevator on her way home. Put up a struggle. Lots of blood, mostly from her nose, I think, when he punched her to shut her up.'

'Did he rape her?'

'Yes, ma'am. That's what she said. She was crying so bad we didn't talk to her a lot. Ambulance took her to the hospital.'

'How did you get the guy?' I asked.

'Easy. She knew him. Said he had gone to junior high school with her older brother. So when they took her to the hospital my partner and me went to the apartment to get her brother. We told him what happened and that his sister said that it was Otis who did it.

'Her brother, Kenny, was wild, ma'am. He knew exactly who Otis was and what apartment he lived in. Told us the guy's real name was Herman Myers, but they called him Otis 'cause he used to ride up and down in elevators, waiting for old ladies to get on so he could rob 'em. Just got out of jail on the robbery cases a few weeks ago. Took us right to the apartment, we knocked on the door, and when Otis came out into the hallway to talk to us, we locked him up.'

'Nice collar,' I told Corchado. 'Is it your first felony?'

'Yeah, actually it is.'

'Well, congratulations. You can feel good about this one. Laura will send you down to Sarah's office and you'll have him indicted by the beginning of next week.'

'Yeah, but there is a problem. Otis . . . well, his lawyer called the precinct and wants to file a cross-complaint.'

'What?'

'Well, Miss Cooper, Kenny hit the defendant in the head with a baseball bat. Otis is in the hospital – took a bad crack to the head. That's why the lieutenant told me to see you. Do we have to lock Kenny up, too?'

'Christ, how did you let this happen?' I asked, as my pleasure over a good arrest turned to annoyance.

'Kenny followed along with us to point Otis out,' Corchado explained, 'and I guess he was carrying the bat. He just came back from playing ball so I didn't think nothing of it. He was real quiet until we put the cuffs on Myers, then he started to cry and all. He kept saying, "Why'd you do it to her, she's just a baby. Man, why'd you have to do it? She was a baby."

'Right before we got him to the patrol car, me and my partner on each side of him so nobody could interfere, Otis turns back to Kenny and says, "Shit, she was no baby. Her hole was so big I almost fell into it."'

I closed my eyes at the thought of the way that must have stung poor Kenny, whoever he was.

'Miss Cooper, it was so fast I never saw it coming. Kenny just reeled back and landed the bat square on Otis's head, and he fell to his knees like he was a sack of sugar.'

'Give Kenny a medal,' mumbled Mike from his chair in the corner. 'Lucky you don't have to worry about brain damage – it doesn't sound like Otis's elevator went to the top floor to begin with. When *I* came on the job, kid, taking a defendant to be arraigned with his head wrapped in bandages was the sign of a good cop – we didn't have to let civilians do it *for* us – we could whack 'em ourselves. Stand 'em in front of the judge with their heads wrapped in bandages. Turban jobs. "Yeah, Your Honor, he resisted arrest, sir. Put up quite a struggle." Before all the ACLU crap started you could really get some street justice.'

I rolled my eyes as Mike played with the rookie. 'Ignore him, Corchado. Just go see Miss Brenner for the rape arrest. She'll take good care of you. As for the cross-complaint, give me the papers.' I took the package and found the D.A.'s data sheet, the space for the write-up of the case summary. Across the top of the complaint made by Myers for assault, I scrawled in large letters: 'Decline to prosecute. Reason: Interest of justice as per Alexandra Cooper, Chief, SCPU.'

'What do I tell his lawyer, Miss Cooper?' Corchado asked.

Oh, the beauty of prosecutorial discretion. 'You tell him that Miss Cooper said that he hopes Otis's head hurts so bad and for so long that the next time he even thinks about having an erection, it's so painful that he thinks twice and can't get it up.'

'Way to go, blondie,' Mike cheered as Corchado left the room. 'A chance to spend a few days with me, a couple of solid new cases, a murder to solve, and your charming good nature comes right back to the surface. Book 'im, Corchado.'

'What's the name of the Chilmark police chief?' Mike asked, picking up my phone to dial the call.

'Wally Flanders,' I answered. 'Why are you calling?'

'Just to see what they're up to. Any leads, any news.'

I walked out to Laura's desk to check on my messages.

Laura began to recite them to me: 'Your mother called. She expects to hear from you once a day until this is all resolved. She said the rabbi from your old synagogue called to see if you needed any counseling.'

'Call her back. Reassure her that I'm fine. I'm getting all my spiritual guidance from Monsignor Chapman, for the moment.'

'Nina called from L.A. Can you imagine, she was up at six forty-five to make the call?' said Laura, knowing most of my pals well enough to offer editorial comments on the messages. 'She says it's a *huge* story on the Coast. Not you, of course, but Isabella. Nina says Isabella made herself so unpopular since she hit it big two years ago that everybody in Hollywood has a motive . . . except O.J. Simpson!'

'What else?' I asked, seeing a list of names on her pad.

'Sarah's in. She understands the situation and will assign all the new cases. A lot of your friends have been calling – I'm just taking names and telling them to keep in touch with Joan Stafford. Diane Sawyer called and wants to know if you can do "Prime Time" with her this week – nothing procedural, nothing about the case, just reminiscences of Isabella. I referred her to Brenda. Same for Liz Smith, she wanted a quote from you.

'And Detective Wallace is here with his witness. I've gotten her coffee and a newspaper and she's in the waiting—'

Laura was interrupted by Mike calling out to me with his hand cupped over my phone, 'Hey, Coop, you expecting some guy named Spiegel on the private line?'

'You know it's Segal, you jerk. Can't you be civil to him? Now get out of here for a minute – go say hello to Mercer Wallace and tell him I'll be with him as soon as I get off the phone.'

'Oh, Jed, thank God you called,' I gushed into the receiver, unable to articulate anything that sounded less like soap opera dialogue and more like the paralyzing terror that had knotted my stomach. I was talking over his words as he was saying, 'Alex? Alex? I can barely hear you,' through the crackling static of a transatlantic line.

'Do you know what happened, Jed? Are you still in Paris? Have you heard anything about the murder? Are you going to be home soon?'

I kept spitting questions into the phone, and with the awful echoing in the bad connection I was missing the answers that Jed tried to give back.

'Yes, Alex, I know all about it. My secretary filled me in first thing this morning, and the story of the murder is even big news today in Europe. I'm worried about *you* though – it must be awful for you.'

I don't know why I tried so hard not to cry as I talked to him: 'I need you so badly. Please come back – I just want you to hold me. Please let me know when you'll be home.'

'Of course, Alexandra, I'll try to get back immediately. I love you, darling. I'll call as soon as I know when I can fly out. Unfortunately, everyone on the deal came into Paris for these meetings, so it's impossible to break away. Be strong, darling – we'll get you through this.'

I'm so sick of being strong, I complained to myself after exchanging sophomoric farewells with Jed and hanging up the phone. Being strong for victims who can't do it themselves, being strong for weak-spirited strays of all varieties who crossed my threshold, being strong for strangers who truly did depend on the kindness of others. When I had the opportunity to stop and think about it, I was well aware that it was a complete pain in the ass to be expected to be strong for everyone all of the time – especially because no one ever wants to see *me* through a moment of weakness.

I'm tired of being Scarlett O'Hara. In my next life I'm going to come back as Melanie Wilkes, fragile and helpless.

I blew my nose with a tissue from the supply kept on my desk to service the victim population that passed through every day, and called out to Laura that I wanted her to send Detective Wallace into my office.

Mercer and Mike came in together a few seconds later. 'Before you get started,' Mike said, 'Chief Flanders wants to know if you have any idea who Isabella was taking with her to the Vineyard.'

'No one, Mike. That was the point of it. She wanted to get off by herself for a few days and make some decisions about the scripts that had been sent to her for upcoming roles.'

'Well, Coop, I know you hate it when people lie to you, but she wasn't alone in your cozy hideaway. At least not all the time. Looks like she had a playmate.'

'How do they know she wasn't alone?' I asked, trying to hold my annoyance in check. 'Maybe she met some friends on the island and invited them in for a drink, or . . .' Everything was getting to me today. I don't know why it should irk me that Isabella didn't spend her last few days on earth alone, but I assumed that I was overreacting to news of her tryst because I was so lonely at the very same moment.

'The obvious signs. Not only was Lascar sleeping in your bed, Goldilocks, but the other side of it was rumpled up pretty well, too. Coffee mugs in the sink, food in the frig. Flanders says – get this – his wife read in *People* magazine that Lascar was a vegetarian, but there was a big steak bone in the garbage and some hot dogs ready for a barbecue. Right next to the yogurt.'

'Well, tell them to talk to her friends, not to me. She clearly didn't want *me* to know. Now let me talk to Mercer about his case while you show the Chilmark Police how to play Dick Tracy, okay, Mike? If you need to use *People* to solve the case, I'll get you a subscription.'

Mercer Wallace was one of the best detectives in the bureau. When the time finally came to beef up the Special Victims Squad he was handpicked by the commissioner to lead one of the teams. He was big, black, and very smart, with a gentle manner that endeared him to women who had been victimized, and with an equally tough attitude that signaled to defendants that this was not a man who would brook any nonsense. He was so good at working on these matters that most of the big ones were assigned to him, no matter how heavy his caseload.

'Hey, Alex, Chapman told me about the murder and whatever. Are you—'

'Mercer, do me a favor, let's not even talk about it. The best thing for me is to get to work for a while, otherwise I'm out of control.' I knew he'd understand, and so we began to talk about the pattern that had been developing on the Upper West Side.

'This here's our man, Cooper. Fourth hit. Victim's twenty-four years old, freelance illustrator, which could be a big break for us. After you get what you need from her, I've got an appointment at headquarters with the artists. She's pretty sure she can help us with a sketch. She's really good on detail, and that's what the guys need for a good composite.'

I told Mercer I would interview her briefly. It had not even been a full day since she had been attacked, but the same rapist was responsible for at least three other assaults in the last month – based on his distinctive M.O. Mercer and I were certain of two things: he would continue to rape women, and possibly become more violent, unless we found and stopped him; and he was likely to be someone Mercer and I had met before, a recidivist, a sexual predator who repeated his acts with the same language and sexual interests he had used in the past. He was much too accomplished and much too professional to be a first-timer, so Mercer and I were looking for the key, the little slip he might eventually make that would lead us back to him. In reality, as we looked, we were praying for a lucky break, which was the far more likely way the case would be solved.

Laura Wilkie knew that I would not take any calls while I was interviewing a rape victim, but I reminded her that she had to hold everything, as Mercer came back around the corner with Katherine Fryer and ushered her into my office.

I came out from behind my desk as Mercer made the introductions, and we sat on three chairs drawn into a small circle. It was a way to avoid the appearance of formality imposed by a desk between subject and interviewer, and it encouraged the intimacy occasioned by the topic of the conversation. I didn't do it in every instance, but this was a case which needed that rapport established immediately. There was no time to develop a relationship politely.

Katherine Fryer's night had been even worse than my own, so I was struck by her composure and apparent calm.

'Do you understand why you're here today?' I asked her.

'I'm sure Detective Wallace explained it to me, but I'm not sure I absorbed everything. Everybody's been wonderful, but I was at the hospital for hours and I'm a bit dazed at this point.'

'I know that. I just want to explain what's going on. My name is Alexandra Cooper, and I am the assistant district attorney who's going to handle your case. I'll be with you from today through the day Mercer catches your attacker and we convict him. I know he's already asked you a lot of questions, and I'll have to ask most of them again. But from now on we'll be working on this together, and my job is to get you through this as comfortably as I can. Do you want to ask me anything before I begin?'

Katherine Fryer wanted the normal assurances – that her name wouldn't be in any newspapers and that her parents in Pennsylvania wouldn't have to be told about the rape. 'And if there is a trial, will they be able to question me about my personal life, about my sexual activity?'

'No, Katherine, there have been a lot of improvements, a lot of changes in the law. In a case like this, when you've been attacked by a man you never saw before, *nothing* about your sexual history is relevant to the trial. I promise you: this stuff isn't like all those awful made-for-TV movies. Detective Wallace does the heavy lifting in this case – the worst is behind you. Once he finds the man and you identify him, we won't have you on the witness stand for more than an hour.

'Let me just go through the story with you one time, then you can help with the sketch and go home and get some rest.'

'I can't go home, Miss Cooper. I'll never feel safe there again. I'm going to my sister's house in New Jersey. Mercer is going to go with me to the apartment to pack some clothes, but I'll give you my sister's number until I find a new place to live.'

This stuff really sucks. A woman alone in her home, minding her own business, is victimized there – then has

38

to move out because it's so saturated with the memory of that devastating violation.

I asked Katherine what had happened yesterday afternoon, shortly before one o'clock, as she sat alone in her kitchen.

'Well, I was eating my lunch when the doorbell rang and I said, "Who is it?" and a voice outside the door said, "It's Con Edison." I said I wasn't expecting anyone from Con Edison, that I didn't have any problems. He told me, as I looked through the peephole, that the super had called him in because there was trouble on the gas lines in all the rear apartments. So I could see that he was, you know, dressed like a Con Ed workman and I opened the door.'

I already knew the answers to the questions I was about to ask, and I already knew how many times Katherine Fryer had blamed herself for the same things, but I had to ask them anyway.

'When you say he was dressed like a Con Ed repairman, can you tell me more about his clothing?'

'Well, it was just a flannel shirt and jeans, with a work jacket over them, and a hard hat.'

'Did the hat say "Con Ed" on it, specifically? Did it have any lettering on it?'

'No. It didn't say anything.'

'Did he have any kind of identification that he showed you, like any tag on his shirt or anything he pulled out of his pocket?'

Katherine was avoiding eye contact now, admitting, with regret, that she hadn't asked for any ID, she had just assumed he was telling the truth.

'I let him in and he walked right into the kitchen, where my lunch was on the table, and he opened the stove and looked in. And I kept talking to him as he looked, and I said I didn't ever report a problem with my oven even though the gas had been kind of poor. It's an old building – everything needed repairs at one point or other. Then he said, "Maybe you could get your husband to come out here and give me a hand with this."' Katherine paused and winced as she went on, 'So I told him, "I don't have a husband – I mean, maybe I can just help you."'

That's exactly what he wanted to hear, as Mercer and I were well aware. Home alone.

'That's when he stood up from the oven, turned around and faced me. That's the first time I saw the knife.'

'Take a breath, Katherine,' I said, leaning over to put my hand on top of hers. 'You're doing fine. Just take it easy – I know this is difficult to do.'

'It was a long knife – it had a long, narrow blade. I think he pulled it out of the tool belt he had around his waist. It seemed like it was fifteen or sixteen inches – very, very long. He grabbed me and held the knife right in front of my face. He told me not to make a sound or he would cut up my face. Then he said he'd kill me if I didn't do what he wanted.

'So he walked me into the bedroom and told me to undress with my back toward him, to take all my clothes off and get on my knees. That's when he made me do oral sex on him.'

When she stopped, Mercer offered her a glass of water, and as she sipped it I talked softly to her.

'You're doing fine, Katherine. I'm going to interrupt you from time to time to ask for some details. The questions may sound stupid and trivial, but I need to ask them. You may know some of the answers, and you may not remember others. Just tell me what you can, okay?'

She nodded.

'Did he undress himself, Katherine, or did he just expose his penis?'

'He didn't undress completely. But he did take off his jeans and the heavy belt. He kept his shirt on. And he wasn't wearing any underpants.'

'When you say "oral sex," you mean he made you put your mouth on his penis?'

'Yes, yes, he did. He kept saying he'd kill me if I didn't. Then he told me to stop. He picked me up, he lifted me up, and he put me on my bed. He pushed me down on the bed – face up – and he put a pillow over my face.'

'Was he talking during any of this, Katherine, or was he not saying anything at all?'

'Yes, he talked. He talked a lot of the time. But, but . . . I really can't remember too much of what he said. It was disgusting.'

I leaned in to try to get her to look me in the eye. There aren't many honest people who can lie when they look you right in the eye – just the pathological types. I knew Katherine Fryer could tell me exactly what her assailant said to her if I forced her through it.

'Katherine, you *can* remember the things he said to you – you may not want to, but I know you haven't forgotten them. And as unpleasant as it is, and as much as it may make you mad at me, I want you to say every one of them to me. They're part of his signature, Katherine; they're part of what will help Mercer find him, because he's probably said them to someone else and he'll say them again the next time. And there will be a next time unless we stop him. It's what helps him get off on this stuff, so it's one of the ways you can get back at him. Please help us with this, trust us.'

'Do you want me to leave the room, Katherine?' Mercer asked, hoping it might make her more comfortable.

'No, no – it's not you. It's just, well, it makes me nauseous to think about. I'm not a prude or anything, but . . .'

Again, Katherine Fryer braced herself and went on with her story. 'It was odd,' she continued, 'because he kept going back and forth between the sexual stuff and asking me where my money was. When I undressed, he told me I had big breasts – he told me he liked that. Then he went right on saying he wanted my money and my credit cards. I pointed to my pocketbook. Once he had me on the bed with the pillow on my face, that's when he really talked a lot.

'He wanted to know if his prick – excuse me, that's *his* words I'm using now – if his prick was bigger than my boyfriend's . . . Was it better for me? . . . Why did I have such big breasts and a little pussy? . . . Then, in the middle of that, how much money was in my wallet? Then, right back to how good my boyfriend was in bed. And then . . . he kept saying that he would kill me if I didn't make him come.'

Mercer caught my eye as Katherine rested her forehead in her hand. We had more than enough to know it was the same guy as in the earlier cases. He was trying to tell me to wrap it up so he could take her on to headquarters.

Even the ending was identical. After the rape and robbery, he bound Katherine to the bed with an extension cord, stuffed a dishcloth in her mouth, and replaced the pillow over her head. He ripped the telephone cord out of the wall, and she heard him rummage around in her dresser drawers before the final sound of the front door as it shut behind him. It took more than one hour for the determined young woman to free herself from the cord he had wrapped around her wrists and summon help from a neighbor.

I was glad Mercer had signaled me to cut the interview short. Katherine Fryer was running on empty, and I had found an outlet for my own predicament in trying to lose myself in her case.

'Okay, Katherine, we've given Miss Cooper enough to keep her busy for a while. Let's get some fresh air and walk over to headquarters. We'll let you stop talking and start sketching.' Mercer Wallace stood up and opened the office door, determined not to let me wear out his witness.

'I'll call you later, Coop – see if we can figure out where to go from here.'

I thanked Katherine and explained that I would be available to her for any kind of help she needed. 'Keep a pad next to your bed,' I urged her. 'More detail will come back to you. Like it or not, you'll have flashbacks – triggered by conversations you hear or reminders you see on the news or TV shows. Write down anything else you remember, no matter how insignificant it seems to you, 'cause Mercer and I will want to know it.'

We exchanged good-byes and the two of them walked around the corner to the elevator bank. As soon as they were out of view, Laura blurted out, 'Battaglia called from his car. He's on his way back to the building and he wants you waiting for him in his office when he gets there.'

'Great. If I'm not back in an hour, send reinforcements.'

5

The walls lining the corridor into the executive wing of the office were covered with portraits of a century's worth of New York County District Attorneys. Grim-visaged, no-nonsense men, most of whom had held office without ever being troubled by the presence of women lawyers on their staffs. I walked the gauntlet below their icy stares as I headed in to face Battaglia, sure that they would come alive to talk behind my back about the terrible scandal I had visited upon their successor.

I reached the desk of the D.A.'s executive assistant, Rose Malone, a great-looking woman in her late forties, who had started in the office secretarial pool as a high school graduate but had been hand-selected by Battaglia to run the front office and had done so for almost twenty years.

She and I had spent long hours together throughout my tenure in the office, and we were good friends. Rose was the best gauge of the boss's moods, and a great ally on the occasions when I needed one. 'You might want to save that request until tomorrow,' she would say, on a day the D.A. had been criticized on a particular case action by the *Times* editorial page; or, 'Go right in, Alex – he was so pleased with the verdict your team had on that gang rape.'

'Good morning, Alexandra,' Rose said, courteously this time. Cool, it seemed to me.

'That's terrible, what happened to Miss Lascar. Are you doing okay?' she went on.

Once I assured her that I was fine, she told me to go right into Battaglia's office, and went back to her word processor. No chatter, no gossip, no mood summary, no advice. If Rose was cool, then the District Attorney would be frigid.

I braced for the lecture I was about to receive and opened the door. Battaglia was standing behind his enormous desk, barking into the phone as he motioned me to sit at the large conference table at the far end of the room. I pretended to make notes on my legal pad while I tried to figure who the conversation involved, and was a bit relieved to see that this burst of anger was directed at the federal prosecutor in our district, with whom the D.A. was feuding over jurisdiction in a major mob investigation.

He hung up the phone and slowly walked over to sit across the table from me.

'What the hell is going on here, Alex – do you have *any* idea?' Battaglia spoke quietly, as he began his interrogation.

'Paul, I . . .'

45

'Do you know how this kind of notoriety distracts from the serious business of this office? Do you understand how it compromises your ability to get work done?'

As my color deepened and my embarrassment grew, so the D.A.'s voice escalated. There was no point in my responding to any of his questions because he already knew the answers to those he was asking. I was familiar with his technique, and knew that in a few moments he would stop yelling and begin to press for details. The booming jabs didn't bother me half as much as the next phase, when he could make you feel like a complete idiot if you were unable to provide him with the details he wanted. I had watched unsuspecting colleagues present him with information for an impending press conference, confident in their mastery of the facts of the case, to have him come back with questions like, 'Do you know what church the suspect's mother attends?' or, 'Which junior high school did the witness go to?' or some other point that was of potential value to a politician and none to a junior prosecutor.

Battaglia talked at me for quite a period of time before he began to ask for facts that he didn't yet know. And then it was time to give him every shred of detail from the moment Isabella first was introduced to me and spent time in our office through our most recent correspondence and her request to escape to a private hideaway.

The District Attorney waited for my presentation to conclude before he leaned in, eyeballed me, and asked: 'Can you think of any aspect of this, any hint of scandal, that's going to come back to hurt this office, Alexandra?' The unspoken portion of that sentence, I knew, was . . . 'Because if there is, Alex, you'd better start cleaning out your desk drawer and thinking about the advantages of the private practice of law.'

'No, Paul,' I said, shaking my head repeatedly, 'I've been thinking about it all of last night and this morning. There's nothing more that I haven't told you, really.'

He sat back upright in his chair and reflected for several seconds before his mien began to soften and he took on the aspect of the Paul Battaglia I idolized. 'Okay, Alex, how do you come out in all this? What are we going to do about *you?*'

'I'm practically numb today, Paul. I think it's actually good for me to be at work because it gets my mind—'

'Good for you, maybe, but I don't know how good it is for the office. Patrick McKinney thinks I ought to put you on leave for a few months and wait till this all clears up.'

'Oh, Paul, that's ridiculous. What he *really* thinks is that I should throw my body on top of Lascar's coffin and be burned alive. Of course Pat wants me to take a leave – he can't bear having me around in the first place.'

'Well, I spoke to the District Attorney up there in Massachusetts this morning – the one in charge of the murder investigation. He and the police chief would like you to fly up for a few hours tomorrow. They need a lot of background from you, and they have to go through your house so you can tell them what things are yours and what were Isabella's . . . and what belonged to the mystery guest.

'So make your arrangements and, let's see, tomorrow is Friday – I want you to go up and give them whatever they need. And your detective goes with you, understand? Who've you got?'

'Mike Chapman, Manhattan North.'

'Fine. Just keep in touch with me every step of the way. I think you know that I don't like surprises, Alex.'

'Yes, sir.'

'Two other points. You are not to go to Lascar's funeral. No Hollywood, no photo-ops, no way for the press to keep tying this back in to us. She's dead – say your farewells privately. Understood?'

I nodded in agreement.

'And the other thing. You are not a cop, Alex. As I've told you before, you could have gone to the Police Academy and saved your old man a lot of money. You are an assistant district attorney, an officer of the court, a lawyer. Let the boys and girls in blue play police officers and keep your nose out of it.'

I nodded again.

'Oh, I meant to ask you, do you have any idea who was paying her a visit up there?'

'No, I don't, Paul. She never mentioned it and I never asked.'

'Well, when did she get to the Vineyard?'

Whoops, I could feel it coming. I had a rough idea of the answer, but not an exact time. Two 'I don't knows' in a row. Bad form with Paul Battaglia.

'How seriously should we be looking for this second stalker?'

I was about to make the third strike. 'Paul, I just don't know the answer to that – we're trying to evaluate it now.'

'All right, Alex, be sure and let me know whenever you get some answers. Take care of yourself, that's the most important thing right now. Oh – is there any progress on that serial rapist, Upper West Side? I'm getting a lot of crap from that local community board – can't your guys wrap this one up?'

Yeah, and if I have a free hour this afternoon I'm going to go out looking for Judge Crater, too, I thought, as I told the District Attorney, 'We're trying, boss.'

Mike Chapman was sitting at my desk eating one of the sandwiches that Laura had ordered in for lunch when I returned from Battaglia's office. 'How bad did it hurt?' he asked as I walked in, picking up the growing pile of messages from Laura's desk.

'Not too bad,' I replied. 'The mayor must have given him the money he wanted. He's clearly annoyed, but not wild. Have you heard about the plans for tomorrow?'

'Nope. What's up?'

'I'm taking you to Martha's Vineyard – show you how a real police investigation gets done,' I said, chuckling at the thought of Mike meeting the town police. A few house burglaries when the summer people leave after Labor Day, loads of moped accidents in season, and endless cases of Driving Under the Influence all winter long, but I couldn't remember a murder that had occurred on the Vineyard in my lifetime.

'Whoa, an *overseas* trip, and with the Cooperwoman! You know, I think Patrick McKinney is right. This whole thing with Lascar is just a ruse for you to get a weekend alone with me on an island, so we can . . .'

'Detective Chapman, if you don't control yourself I'm going to leave you behind with that needle-nosed prick. It's not a weekend, it's a day trip. I'll have Laura make the plane reservations. It'll save a lot of time if you leave your gun home – we won't have to deal with all that security stuff at the airport.

'And, Mike,' I added, 'Battaglia asked me a question which raised an obvious point. Exactly when *did* Isabella get to the Vineyard? I've got an idea – maybe Chief Flanders has thought of it—'

'Unlikely, unless his wife supplied it to him. He didn't sound like he was into ideas,' Chapman replied. 'Well, there are only two ways to get there. I mean, you're right, we are going overseas. It's not like most places in the country where a killer could just drive to a murder scene and then just drive away. You can only get to the Vineyard by sea and by air.'

'Yeah, Alex, but thousands of people still do it every year, don't they? And they don't need passports.'

I knew that the Vineyard had a small year-round population of about fifteen thousand, which swelled to almost eighty thousand in the summer vacation months of June, July, and August. Then, after Labor Day, the crowds departed and the little island regained its tranquillity, much to the delight of the locals.

'It becomes much more difficult to get to the island after the Labor Day weekend,' I explained to Mike. 'For example, all summer long, there are direct flights to Martha's Vineyard from New York. Lots of flights, several times a day, from both La Guardia and Newark airports. This time of year they've been eliminated. From now until next June, there's only one scheduled airline that flies from Boston – nine-seater planes, a few times a day – and small private or chartered planes.

'Same with the ferry. The ferry goes from Woods Hole,

on Cape Cod, to the Vineyard, but fewer times a day after the holiday weekend is over.'

'Where are we going with this travelogue, Coop?' Mike asked.

'You know what we're looking for,' I responded to Mike. 'Who was with Isabella on the island, and was that guy – or woman – the one who killed her. Or maybe he witnessed the killing and fled, but knows who did it.'

'All right, do you know when she went up to your house?' It wouldn't take much to draw Chapman into an investigation, I knew that from years of experience.

'She told me she was going at the end of last week, when she finished some business in Boston, probably Thursday or Friday. I assume Chief Flanders has already contacted the Ritz and knows when she checked out,' I offered.

'And she told me that if she had enough time, instead of flying, she was going to try to have a driver, a limo, take her down to Woods Hole – it's only ninety minutes by car from Boston – and she wanted to arrive the "old-fashioned" way, by sailing across to the island.'

'Yeah,' laughed Mike. 'Just like the Pilgrims – the limo, to the ferry, to the rented Mustang, to the chintz-lined cottage. The rental agency people should be able to tell us when Isabella picked up the car. Then, the next thing I do, if Flanders hasn't, is to check the passenger manifests for the airline, starting at least a week ago. What's it called?'

'Cape Air. Exactly. And there's a tiny office at the airport for private planes, which all have to register and submit flight plans in order to come and go. The air arrival and departure part of this won't take much time at all. The local police will know most of the names of islanders and regular commuters, you'll have a few honeymooners and golf outings for the weekends, and then Isabella's manager can look at the unknowns for familiar names that he might recognize, but which wouldn't mean anything to us, right?' I suggested to Mike.

'That covers the air, Sherlock,' Mike replied. 'But what about the water? Does the ferry take cars onto it, as well as foot passengers?'

'Yes, it does. Look, the big problem is boats. There are lots of marinas and plenty of little coves. A private boat could come from the Cape or the Hamptons, drop anchor, discharge and pick up a killer with no way to trace it. That's how most of the drugs get to an island, as you know. Anyway, you could even walk onto the ferry with a shotgun inside a Vuitton tote – there's no such thing as metal detectors on the boats.' I was getting a second wind by this point, suddenly thinking that I knew of a way, even though a long shot, of tracking Isabella's arrival.

'But, Mike, if she came by ferry, and she wasn't alone, there's another possibility,' I suggested. 'On a beautiful fall afternoon, most people who travel on the ferries head topside. There are hundreds of seats, a snack bar, binoculars to scan the horizon – the views of the Vineyard, crossing the sound from the Cape, are absolutely spectacular. Isabella Lascar would have been just like every other tourist on that boat, and whether it's a first trip or the thousandth, I don't know anyone who isn't captivated by the beauty of that vista.'

'I'm afraid to ask what's next. You're gonna want us to find and canvas everybody who was on the boat to see if they saw a movie star standing next to them and whether they can describe the person with—'

'No, much easier. Every single tourist, and half of the

regulars, make that trip with a camera, Mike,' I said. 'People are always taking pictures of each other against the boat railing, like it was the *QE2*, or feeding the seagulls or just staring at the view.'

'You think people recognized Isabella and took her picture?' Mike asked.

'Hard to tell.' I had seen her when she wasn't preening for her public. We had gone all over Manhattan together and people failed to recognize her when she was casually dressed, without makeup and a serious hairdo. 'I mean, she looked absolutely beautiful whether or not she tried to hide it. She'd turn heads, even if people didn't know exactly who she was.'

'So, how does that help?'

'Two possibilities. One is that someone did take her picture, recognizing Isabella Lascar, the movie star. The other,' I thought out loud, 'is that she simply was captured in the frame of some photographs – you know, people taking amateur shots of the scenery usually have bodies in the foreground, whether they intend to or not. Even if Isabella was trying to be incognito, she may be in somebody's snapshots – along with her weekend guest.'

'Which might give us a key witness,' said Mike, 'and a motive, and maybe even a perp.'

'Call the chief. While you work the airlines, have him do this angle. There's only one radio station on the island – WMVY – great oldies, lots of Carly Simon and James Taylor, and all the local news, so everybody listens to it at some point. Do a public service announcement, immediately. Urge anyone with film from the ferry at the end of last week, with pictures of Isabella, to come forward, and if it leads to any information about the identification of her killer . . . then we get the police to offer a reward. There's a shot at coming up with something. I'd even check the camera store near the ferry landing – they do developing in several hours, and probably have the names and numbers of everyone who has brought film in to be developed during the past week.'

'I'll make a deal with you, Alex,' Mike offered, as he threw out the remains of his sandwich and pushed away from my desk. 'You take care of these weenie-waggers here in Manhattan, and I'll work with your Chilmark boys on the murder. This isn't a bad way to begin. I'll get started on it in your paralegals' office and you keep occupied on your own cases.'

I sorted through the phone messages that had accumulated and gave most of them back to Laura, knowing they could wait till the next week. I kept the ones I wanted to handle.

Jed's secretary had called. No way for him to leave Paris until the business meetings end on the weekend – he'll call me at home later and come straight from the airport on Saturday. Shit, I thought, not exactly the response I had craved. But I knew my own priorities when I was in the middle of a major investigation which had to come before any personal considerations, so I understood Jed's position – I guess.

Call Congressman LaMella's office. They want to know our position on the legislative package changing the evidentiary requirement for child abuse cases. Better late than never. Gina Hemmings will call back from Part 82, where she's on trial. The judge is about to charge her jury and she wants to know if you can cite any cases on whether the crime of 'sexual misconduct' is a lesser included count in a rape case. Well, I mused as my annoyance grew, once again Gina has avoided the burden of overpreparation.

Ellen Goldman called to confirm tomorrow's appointment. Battaglia had given her permission to do a big story on the innovative work of our Sex Crimes Prosecution Unit for the *USA Lawyer's Digest*, the premier glossy legal journal. I had already spoken with her several times on the telephone and we were ready for the first interview. She's smart and pushy, but I'd have to move her back to next week. I knew she'd try to weasel Isabella's death into the piece so I decided to call her back myself in an effort to show I was still in control. Slightly. I got her machine and left a message kicking our appointment back until Monday afternoon.

Sarah Brenner will wait for callback. Has a witness coming on Monday and doesn't believe the story. Wants help breaking it down. Boy, am I in the mood to do that – I'd love to make someone else cry. Schedule that one for Monday morning.

Pat McKinney called to see if there's anything he can do to help. Translation: he knows I'm miserable and the boss is pissed off, and he wants me to know that he knows. Response: yeah, you can help me – go fuck yourself.

C H A P T E R

The rest of the afternoon passed slowly. I wasn't able to concentrate on the brief I had to submit for the sodomy case I was scheduled to try in three weeks, and I was desperate to avoid unnecessary phone conversations. Sarah stopped by to discuss several new investigations that needed to be assigned, and to cheer me up with chatter about her baby.

The only phone call of interest was from Mercer Wallace. He was pleased about Katherine Fryer's input with the sketch artist. 'It's the best one yet, Coop,' he told me. 'She's really good on facial characteristics. She's firm about the size and shape of the mustache, and you know how they all say he's got bad skin? Well, she actually draws these big pockmarks and a deep set of creases down each side of his

56

forehead. Swears that's exactly where they are. I never had an illustrator as a victim before but it sure helps the sketch take on some definition.'

I knew exactly what he meant. The typical description started with witnesses saying they're lousy at doing this, and that the guy was average height, average weight, average-looking, nothing distinctive about his appearance, and so on. I had a folder full of sketches of wanted rapists who looked like everybody and nobody. Try and display one to a jury and claim a resemblance to the defendant on trial and it was more likely to look like three of the jurors. Not guilty.

Mercer went on. 'Better yet. She also thinks she made out a birthmark. Says she really tried to avoid looking at his private parts, but he kept sticking it in her face and she's pretty sure he had a fuzzy area on his right thigh, 'bout the size of a tangerine, two inches southeast of his equipment.'

Bingo. One of the few advantages afforded a rape victim in identifying her attacker is actually the intimacy of the crime. She gets to see anatomical parts rarely displayed in a bank robbery or mugging. And sometimes there are birthmarks or tattoos or surgical scars that a victim describes the day of the assault, and that a knowledgeable detective photographs the minute he has his suspect in custody. Mercer and I had our fastest conviction on a case when our witness told us the rapist had a tattoo of a spider on his penis. The jury only needed to see the Polaroid of that scorpion for about ten seconds before they voted to convict the defendant. Then they spent the next hour eating lunch, because they didn't want the defense attorney to think they hadn't spent a serious amount of time deliberating about his client's fate.

Once we had a lead on this suspect, Katherine's description of the unusual mark would help sink him, especially if we didn't get lucky with DNA testing.

Mike came back to my office shortly before five-thirty, as Laura was packing up to leave for the day. 'I don't blame you for getting out of here,' he said to Wilkie. 'I bet you never knew how unpopular your boss was. I got a list as long as your arm here of people who'd like to get rid of her, and those are just the guys she's prosecuting, who don't even know her personally. Wait till I start with *that* crew.'

Laura laughed and said good night. 'I won't see you tomorrow, will I?' she asked.

'No, but we'll call you from the Vineyard. Have a good weekend and I'll see you on Monday.'

Mike and I spent another hour going over the list of possible killers he had culled from my closed case files.

'You've prosecuted some sick puppies, blondie,' he mused as he shook his head over the long accumulation of names he had scrawled during the afternoon, with brief case descriptions next to each of them.

'Great cop you are. It took you ten years to reach that conclusion?'

'No, I mean, we mess with some ugly characters in Homicide. But your guys torture people who are alive and looking them right in the eye. And it takes them a lot longer to do it than a shooting or stabbing – a couple of seconds in my cases and it's all over. I never liked working sex crimes, making the victims talk about it in such detail, relive it. Seeing your screening sheets makes me remember why I hated it so much. Murder is easy – you know how it happened, you just gotta figure out who did it. And you got no complaining witness to screw up your case with inconsistencies when you get to trial. C'mon. I'll take you home so you can freshen up for lover boy.'

'You always know just what to say, Mike, don't you? Let's go – Jed's not getting back tonight. He won't be here till Saturday.'

'Whoops. Looks like you, me, and a pizza. Let's go.'

It was almost seven when I shut down my computer, turned off the light and locked the door to my office, almost reluctantly. It seemed to be easier to stay there than to face the emptiness of my apartment for another long night.

One of my doormen held the front door open for us as Mike and I approached the building, while the other one walked toward the package room, motioning that he had something in the back for me. 'Your mail, Miss C., and some lady dropped off flowers for you,' Victor called across the lobby.

Most days my mail didn't fit in the box and had to be held on the shelf with all the other assorted deliveries. It wasn't a lot of personal correspondence, but I'm a magazine junkie, and the regular arrivals of news magazines, fashion books, women's journals that I clipped for topical articles for my lectures, and things I actually read were always bundled up in rubber bands because they were too bulky for the boxes.

Victor handed me the pile and the small bouquet of tulips, then winked as he said, 'My daughter showed me that picture of you in the paper today, next to that dead movie star. You looked almost as good as she did, Miss C.'

'Thanks, Victor,' I replied as the elevator door closed and Mike pushed the button for twenty. 'What an idiot – can you believe there are people who think that *any* reason to have your picture in a tabloid is a good reason? I swear, I think if some guy showed up with the *Post* in his hand and told Victor he was the one who shot Isabella but he had really been looking for *me*, Victor would wink at him and smile and send him right up to 20B to knock on my door.'

'Not between now and Christmas – he might lose a big tip if you got knocked off in the next few months.'

I opened the note that was hanging from the string around the flowers. 'Thanks for your message. This must be awful for you. See you next week – Ellen Goldman.'

'That's nice. She's the reporter for the *USA Lawyer's Digest* who's doing the profile on the unit and me. Very thoughtful.'

'There's no such thing as a nice reporter or a thoughtful one. Oxymoron – isn't that the word? She's just sucking up to you for something . . . probably wants the exclusive on you and Isabella.'

The elevator opened on the twentieth floor and we turned left to walk to my door. There are six apartments on each floor, and as I placed the key in the lock, 20E opened up down the hallway and a large weimaraner came loping at us with her tongue hanging out of the side of her mouth.

As I kneeled to pat Zac and rub her behind her ears, her owner followed behind her to greet us. 'Hi, David,' I said, rising to kiss him and accept an embrace.

'Alex, I just left a message on your machine. Why didn't you call me during the night? I only heard about the murder this afternoon. Do you need anything, any help?'

'David, this is Mike Chapman. Mike works with me. Mike, this is David Mitchell – Dr. Mitchell's a psychiatrist,' I said as I made the introductions, 'and a great friend. No, I'm okay for the moment, thanks. If you're going to be around this weekend I'll fill you in on the whole story. You look like you're on your way out for the evening.'

'After I walk the dog I've got a dinner date. But I won't be too late, if you want to talk.'

'I've got an early appointment, David, so we'll catch up this weekend. Have a nice evening.'

I barely had the door closed behind us and the light switched on before Mike grinned at me and asked, 'Ever do him?'

'Jesus, Chapman, *no!*' I shouted back at him, laughing for the first time in hours. 'He's my neighbor.'

'Well, that's no answer. You did 31C, didn't you?'

'It's my own fault. Why did I ever start playing this game with you? I really asked for it, didn't I?'

'Yeah, you pump me more than I'd ever have the nerve to ask you. But then, I'm a year older than you are, so I probably have a bit more experience.'

'Where did that expression start – *do* somebody? Is it a squad term? I can't believe I even answer you when you ask if I've ever had a sexual encounter with someone. "Did you do him?" It's disgusting, Mike – I'm beginning to agree with my father that I've been at this job too long.'

'So who's Dr. Mitchell? Good-looking guy – didn't he ever ask?'

'As a matter of fact, no, he never did.'

David and I had been neighbors for more than two years. He was in his late forties, divorced, and with a thriving private practice that made him one of Manhattan's most successful shrinks. For someone like me, convinced that psychobabble and therapy are for other people, I had an abundance of free sessions just by having cocktails with David once a week. He listened to my problems, jogged with me on the occasional mornings he could coax me off my treadmill and around the reservoir, and regularly critiqued my social companions.

'I must be losing my touch, Mike. Anyway, I'll get the ice out. You call Steve's Pizza – it's auto dial number four.'

'Who are the first three?'

'My parents, and each of my brothers. And they should consider themselves very fortunate to be placed above Steve's in my list of priority numbers. When I'm on trial, Steve's is my lifeline.'

Most of my acquaintances were pretty quick to learn that one of the things I had never managed to take time to master was cooking. I had dinner out most evenings – it was usually when I spent time with friends – and when I was at home by myself, I could whip up a very tasty tuna salad by opening a can of Bumble Bee and adding a dollop of mayo. But I lived on a block surrounded by great take-out stores and delivery places: Steve's for superb pizza, which always arrived hot; P. J. Bernstein's, the best deli in town when I craved a turkey sandwich; Grace's Marketplace for elegant dinners that simply needed a five-minute microwave zap; and David's for a moist roast chicken when I felt like being virtuous.

'What do you like on it, Coop? I can never remember.'

'Extra-thin crust, well done, no anchovies, and any combination you want. I'm just going to change – help yourself to a drink. I'll be out in a minute.'

I went into the bedroom and closed the door behind me.

I walked over to the dressing table next to my bed and stared at the answering machine, flashing its red light in the dark. There was no one I wanted to hear from, not even my friends, because I couldn't deal with calling anyone back right now and explaining the situation. Sitting at the table, I laid my head on my arms and let the tears slip out, debating whether to play the messages now or later.

Later. At least two Dewar's later.

I rested a few minutes then picked my head up, turned on the lights, pulled off my panty hose, and draped my suit over the grip on the treadmill. My leggings and t-shirt felt much more comfortable, and I washed my face in the bathroom sink, spritzing on some Chanel 22, before going out to join my baby-sitter in the den. There was something about my favorite perfumes that always soothed me, and I was sorely overdue for soothing.

Mike muted the television as I walked into the room, handed me my drink, and let me settle into my chair before he asked me whether I still wanted to talk about the case.

'Is there anything else we *have* to talk about tonight?'

'No,' he responded. 'It just bothers me. You know as well as I do that most homicides are completely random. I mean if they're not domestic or drug-related, then the killer and victim have absolutely no connection. The best cop in the world can spend a lifetime on a case and never solve it unless somebody walks into the station house and confesses. An outdoor shooting like this, there's no fingerprints, no DNA, no clue. Maybe it's just a hunter who let off some shots and Isabella was in the wrong place at the wrong time. That's how most victims get it. Bad timing.'

'It isn't hunting season, Mike.'

'You know what I'm talking about. Let's knock it off –

you're right. Dinner will be here in another fifteen minutes. Then I'll get out of your hair till the morning.'

'I'll drink to *that*. Cheers.'

We watched CNN until the pizza arrived – Third World civil wars were generally a diversion from a day at the criminal courthouse – and then moved to the dining-room table to eat, working on our second drinks.

'You know what you said when we came in tonight, about your father thinking you've been at it too long? Were you kidding, Alex?'

'No, but that won't change anything. You know how I feel about my job. It's just that no one in my family – no one in my life – understands that attraction. It's not quite what they envisioned for their kid.'

I had been raised in a comfortable suburban neighborhood north of Manhattan, the third child – only daughter – of parents who were old-fashioned and uncompromising in their devotion to each other and their families. My father's parents were Russian Jews who emigrated to this country in the 1920s with his two older brothers, then he and his sister had been born in New York. My mother's background was entirely different. Her ancestors had come from Finland at the turn of the century and settled on a farm in New England, re-creating the life they had known in Scandinavia, down to the primitive wooden outhouse and sauna on the edge of an icy cold lake.

She and my father met when he was an intern just out of medical school and she was a college student, both caught up one night in the same disaster. Manhattan's most famous nightclub in the fifties – the Montparnasse – was a major attraction because of the combination of its glamorous crowds and its great jazz. My mother was there with a date one November evening, while my father was trying to get in the door with three of his pals who had just finished a tour on duty at the hospital. A raging fire broke out in the kitchen and spread quickly through the crowded club, igniting damask tablecloths and chiffon dresses and silk scarves. The four young doctors turned the Park Avenue sidewalk into a makeshift emergency room, triaging the fleeing patrons and performers, socialites and staff, as people trampled each other in an effort to escape the treacherous inferno.

My father spent the rest of the night riding the ambulances back and forth from nearby hospitals, unable to help the eighteen men and women who had perished inside the club, but saving scores of lives and calming dozens more who had been overcome by the combination of smoke and fear. The untrained volunteer who worked beside him for hours had been among the fortunate few to emerge unharmed from the Montparnasse. He learned only her first name that night – Maude – but was taken as much by her strength of spirit and gentle manner as by her perfect smile, green eyes, and wonderful long legs which she disappeared on when the ambulance delivered its final two patients to New York Hospital. When he told the story of that night he always used to say that the only way he could get the deadly images of the injured out of his mind's eye was to conjure up the vision of my mother, sitting across from him in the ambulance all night, holding the hands of the patients he labored over, and then the nightmares subsided.

Two weeks later, when *Life* magazine printed the story of the fire and the rescue, my mother called to thank the young doctor whose name was printed beneath one of the photographs of the HEROES OF JINXED JAZZ CLUB: Benjamin Cooper. She had tried to find him before that, and knew only that his friends had called out to him as 'Bones' the night of the fire. She assumed that was a med school nickname that had something to do with an orthopedic specialty and so had called that department at several hospitals with no success. When she finally reached him and he invited her to meet for dinner, she laughed to learn that the name had been given to him as a child by his grandmother, in Yiddish, because he was so thin – only skin and bones.

They married a year later and my father went on to do his residency in cardiology. I was twelve years old when he and his partner invented a half-inch piece of plastic tubing called the Cooper-Hoffman Valve, which changed our comfortable suburban lifestyle as much as it changed the face of cardiac bypass surgery. For the next decade, barely an operation of that nature in North America proceeded without the use of a Cooper-Hoffman, and although my father continued to do the lifesaving surgery that he found so rewarding, the income that he amassed from the distribution of the valve – and the trust funds it endowed for my brothers and myself – gave each of us the invaluable freedom to pursue our own dreams and our own careers. For me, that had developed into a devotion to public service, with the luxury of a personal lifestyle not possible for most of my colleagues, but which certainly helped to relieve the relentless intensity of my particular specialty.

Four years ago, my mother had convinced my father to retire from his surgical practice. They sold the house in

Harrison, kept a condo in Aspen to be near their sons and grandchildren in the West, and moved to an exquisite Caribbean island called St. Barth's. When they weren't traveling so my father could lecture at medical schools around the world, they were primarily working on nothing more arduous than improving their French, reading all the books that I never seemed to have time to get to, and worrying about why their daughter was still single and so content to be immersed in a steady diet of sexual violence.

Mike had met my parents many times and knew exactly what I was talking about. 'Maybe they're right, Alex. You can still be a prosecutor and do other things – frauds, organized crime, drug cartels.'

'Not for me. You know what I love about this? Most women who survive a sexual assault come to the criminal justice system not expecting that any kind of justice will be done. They doubt that the rapist will be caught, and both fiction and made-for-TV movies have taught them that even if he is, he'll never be convicted. It's great to be part of changing that, of making the system work in these cases, of putting these bastards away. And it's so new. Twenty years ago we had laws in this country that literally said that the testimony of a woman in a rape case was not enough evidence to convict her attacker. It was the only crime on the books like that. Imagine, *your* guys could be found guilty just on circumstantial evidence, but a woman was not competent to be an eyewitness to her own rape. It's very exhilarating to be a part of these victories.'

'Well, it's obvious there's something about it you love. But if you're not serving dessert tonight, I'm outta here.'

I carried the dishes to the sink and walked Mike to the door. He'd be back at six-thirty to pick me up so we could make an early shuttle to Boston in the morning. 'Lock up after I go, kid. The Nineteenth Precinct has a uniformed cop in the lobby all night – he was supposed to arrive at eight tonight and be on till I get here in the morning. I'll check on the way out.'

'That's ridiculous,' I murmured, although I was actually glad to think someone would be backing Victor up at the door.

'Don't invite him up and distract him, blondie. If you get lonely, call for the doc next door. The cop they send for a job like this is likely to be too young for you, don't you think?'

'Too tired to think, Mike. Good night.'

I took the copy of *W* that arrived in today's mail into the bathroom, ran the water as hot as I could stand it, poured a few more drops of Chanel into the tub, and climbed in to decompress.

As hard as I tried to lose myself in the smashing outfits for spring and the gaunt models who obviously didn't indulge in a lot of Steve's pizza, my mind kept making its own connections. I thought back to what I had told the serial rape victim – Katherine Fryer – in my office earlier this morning: like it or not, try or not, you *will* have flashbacks; things you see and hear *will* trigger memories of events or conversations, and some of them *will* be significant to the investigation.

Now things were forcing themselves through my own head. Mike's parting joke about calling the doc next door and the earlier coincidence of running into David Mitchell and the fact that David is a shrink and my skepticism about my own need for a shrink. It all connected back to where I did not want to go at that precise point in time: Isabella.

Why had I blown her off so abruptly when she talked about a second stalker? I knew I was feeling guilty for having done it, since he might have been her killer. Now my mind was racing as the chain of thoughts kept triggering portions of her phone calls to me. What had she said about a shrink? I know she had used that expression in one of our talks, but I couldn't remember whether she said she was seeing one *because* of the stalker or that she was imagining that the stalker *was* a psychiatrist.

There would be more flashbacks to conversation, I knew, especially if I tried to ignore them. Tomorrow I could call Nina in L.A. and she would undoubtedly know more about it. She probably listened to Isabella more seriously than I did and would know the significance of the reference to the shrink. I took my own advice and got out of the bathtub, wrapped myself in a towel, and walked to the desk to write down my chain of thoughts, just as I told my victims to do. Then I started to dry myself off and set the alarm for 6 A.M. Before I could settle comfortably onto the bed, the telephone rang. I picked it up and said, 'Hello,' only to be met by dead silence. I repeated my greeting and again got no response. I reached over to replace the receiver in its cradle, shivering from head to toe as I did so, and convincing myself that the chills were caused by my emergence from the late-night bath, and not by the eerie stillness on the phone line. I pulled up the covers and concentrated on the hopeless task of falling asleep for a few hours, before setting off to see how my beloved Vineyard road had been turned into the scene of a murder.

7

Mike was in front of the building exactly on time, with a cup of black coffee for each of us. Neither he nor I functions well in the early morning, so we were quiet on the short ride to La Guardia. He parked his car at the Port Authority Police Building and the cops dropped us off at the old deco Marine Air Terminal that services the Delta Shuttle.

My bodyguard happened to be terrified of flying so he was also a bit subdued for that reason. It always amazed me that a guy who was so fearless in the face of homicidal maniacs and bloodthirsty drug lords was frightened of airplane travel, but we had been to Chicago and Miami together for extradition hearings so I knew that Mike would be saying novenas until we were up and down safely on each leg of the trip. The odds of an NYPD detective being killed by crossfire on a street in Washington Heights were far greater than his dying in a plane crash, but we each have our own demons and I wasn't about to mess with his.

The jet lifted quickly off runway three-three on the cloudless morning, and as the copilot suggested that the passengers on the right-hand side of the plane enjoy the sweeping view of the Manhattan skyline on a clear day, Mike's gaze was fixed out the window on the sight of something below us to the left.

'There's only one thing that takes the edge off a flight out of La Guardia for me,' he remarked. 'If we go down around here, there's a good shot that we wind up plastered all over Riker's Island, and I get to take a few of those scumbags with me to their final resting place.'

'A generous thought.' Riker's Island, four hundred acres of sanitary landfill sitting in the East River just opposite the extended airport runways, houses the main inmate population for the City of New York. It's not quite Alcatraz, but the strong currents curtailed efforts at water escapes, and unlike the Tombs, it also holds sentenced prisoners.

As we headed out over Long Island Sound, I tried to distract Mike by telling him more about Martha's Vineyard. 'It's not just the beauty of its beaches and the fact that it's such a popular summer resort, but it's a truly unusual place with a fascinating history.'

I had been going to the island for so many years that I had to think back about things that it had surprised me to learn on those first trips. 'The Vineyard's a bit longer than twenty-two miles and about ten miles wide at the deepest point – the largest island in New England – but the topography is incredibly varied, quite unlike Long Island or Nantucket. There are six separate towns, and each one is entirely different in character and appearance.'

'People live there all year?'

'Yeah, probably not more than fifteen thousand permanent residents. Then the population swells to close to eighty thousand when the "summer people" and vacationers swarm on.'

I explained to Mike that it was settled by the English in 1642 and governed by the Duke of York, hence the fact that it is located in Dukes County. It was actually a part of the state of New York for its first half-century – like Kings, Queens, and Dutchess counties – then annexed to Massachusetts, which is only seven miles across the Vineyard Sound.

'How can each of the towns be so different, all on the same island?'

'Two ways, actually,' I answered. 'One is simply the variety of the land. There are great harbors that launched the whaling industry in America centuries ago, thousands of acres of protected forest in the middle of the island, rolling hills that supported sheep farming and an agricultural base further west, and miles of the most glorious beaches you'd ever want to see that stretch from one tip of the island to the other.

'And the other is the way each of the towns has grown up around one way of life or another, as a result of the varied geography. Start with Edgartown at the eastern end of the Vineyard. It's a classic New England village with rows of elegant white houses and churches and shops, quite formal in the Federal style, trimmed with fences and fabulous gardens which spill onto the brick sidewalks in summer. The large old homes are the legacy of the whaling captains who built them in the early nineteenth century, when the island was the center of that industry.'

I went on to describe each of the others. Oak Bluffs has an entirely different architecture and feel. Huge Victorian houses line the seaside area, adjacent to the Camp Meeting Grounds property which grew up around the enormous wrought-iron Tabernacle built by an evangelical association of followers of John Wesley in the late 1800s. In winter, Oak Bluffs is home to a lot of the workmen who are permanent islanders, while in summer its main street comes alive with almost a honky-tonk resort feel. It's also got a summer population of black professionals from all over the Northeast – New York, Cambridge, Chicago, Washington – women and men who have vacationed on the Vineyard for generations.

Then there's Vineyard Haven, the commercial center of the island and site of the main ferry terminal, which combine to make it the center of day-to-day island activities year round, and home to almost one third of the island residents. Once you move away from those three towns, you get to the spectacular scenery of the middle and western parts of the Vineyard, where the open spaces are guarded zealously against development. West Tisbury has always been the agricultural capital, with a geographic range that includes working farms, acres of state forest, a wildlife sanctuary, and stunning homesites on rocky perches that look over Vineyard Sound to the Elizabeth Islands. There's not much more in the way of commerce than a general store and some farm stands, a far cry from the three bustling 'down-island' towns.

'Then we come to paradise,' I went on. 'Chilmark.' The place on earth where I was most at peace, the place that I thought had more physical beauty than any place in the world I had ever visited. Its rolling hills and countryside are very evocative of the English countryside. The landscape is dotted with gray-shingled farmhouses, simple and functional in their beauty; and rambling throughout the houses and fields of sheep and horses are miles of ancient stone walls, built by the early settlers and farmers to mark the boundaries of their property. I like those walls best in winter and early spring when you can see the amazing combinations of rocks that have been fitted together to form their spines, before the wild roses and bittersweet of summer climb out and over to dress them in green and pink and scarlet.

And most of all what I love about Chilmark is that wherever you are in the midst of this glorious countryside, you are never very far from the sight and the sound of the water. Miles of perfectly white sand beaches on the south shore, rocky beaches both south and north, enormous ponds with clams and oysters you can dig out and take home for dinner, and ever-changing vistas of ocean currents from hilltops at every turn, of waves that could carry you anywhere you wanted to go – in a real or imaginary world.

Last town beyond that is Gay Head, the westernmost tip of the island. Much smaller in territory than Chilmark, it is also flatter and rimmed with dunes around its shorelines. But it builds to a spectacular sight at its furthest point: dramatic cliffs of multicolored clay which plunge to the sea at the junction of the Vineyard Sound and the Atlantic Ocean.

By the time we began our descent into the Boston area, Mike was up-to-speed on the island history and description, most intrigued by the fact that only two of the towns –

Edgartown and Oak Bluffs – were wet, and that you couldn't buy liquor in any of the stores or restaurants up-island.

'Sounds fuckin' weird to me – can't even have a beer with lunch.'

'Don't worry, there's a full supply at the house. You'll make it.'

From the shuttle terminal we walked across the drop-off area to a small counter at the end of a row of commuter airline desks, none of which looked as if it had been in business for more than a week and each of which served two or three places you'd never heard of in New Hampshire and Maine.

'Good morning,' I said to the girl – she looked about eighteen – who was standing below the Cape Air logo. 'We've got reservations on the nine forty-five to the Vineyard. Names are Cooper and Chapman.' I handed her my credit card and she pulled up the computer list for the flight.

'Okay. Got 'em – Alexandra and Michael, right? What are your weights, please?'

'Excuse me?' Michael asked.

'I'm one twenty-two and he's . . . what are you these days? And please tell the truth, Mike, my life may depend on it.'

'What do you need my weight for?'

'Like it's a Cessna 402. We've got a weight limit, so we have to know like what the passengers weigh, and the baggage, so we can like distribute it and stuff.'

'What are we flying in, Coop, a rowboat? I can't do this.'

'You'll be fine. It's only half an hour – you'll be up and down before you have time to think about it.'

'Two-ten,' he murmured, clearly miserable as he looked out the window and noticed the tiny nine-seater parked near the exit door.

Picking up on his discomfort, the counter girl chimed in, 'Like you can sit up front next to me, in the copilot's seat. I brought her in from Nantucket an hour ago and it's a perfect day for flying. There's no fog and like very little wind – it's really awesome.'

The kid was playing with Mike and he didn't get it yet. I watched the exchange, and could see she was attracted to him, which got me to thinking about him in a way I hadn't done for years: as a guy, and not just a working partner. Today, even at moments like this when his wonderful smile wasn't working for him, he was handsome and lean, and a standout in most crowds. Dressed in his navy blazer, striped shirt with white collar and cuffs, jeans and loafers, he looked like any other yuppie headed for a fall weekend at a country inn.

'Thanks, but the pilot might get jealous,' Mike responded to her.

'I know you're a very good investigator, Chapman,' I said as I nudged him with my elbow, 'but she *is* the pilot.'

'What? You gotta be kidding me. She's an infant, she's gotta be in junior high school, she's . . .'

'Trust me. She's "like" the pilot, Mike.'

As soon as the three other reservations arrived, the counter girl announced the flight, helped an older man in overalls carry the luggage of the other passengers out to the tarmac, and then gave her clipboard to him and climbed up onto the wing of the plane and into the window-door of the pilot's seat.

We started to board the Cessna, with Mike doing a

soliloquy under his breath. 'Women are terrific . . . they can do anything . . . I believe in feminism . . . equal work for equal pay. But this is bullshit . . . this is a little girl flying an airplane . . . They ought to call this thing Cape Fear, not Cape Air.'

'Calm down, buddy. Women fly combat missions now. Think of them, think of Meryl Streep – you know, Karen Blixen – in *Out of Africa*, think of Sally Ride, the astronaut, think . . .'

'The only one *I* can think of is Amelia Earhart, and the last I heard, blondie, she still hasn't landed.'

I bent down to walk the short aisle of the plane and sit in the empty copilot's seat, knowing how great the view would be as we soared over the island on a clear morning.

Mike was coming in next as the pilot reminded him that she needed his weight near the front, and he seated himself directly behind me.

We taxied out and took off, the light craft shaking mildly as she was steered to a smoother flying altitude of four thousand feet, above the low-lying winds. I could feel Mike's hands clutched on my seat back, but there was too much noise from the busy propellers to say much along the way. About fifteen minutes out of Logan, the Massachusetts shoreline came into view, and the distinctive outline of Cape Cod spread out below. If you were familiar with the landscape, it was easy to pick out everything along the way, from New Bedford and Woods Hole, to Hyannis and Provincetown.

And then Martha's Vineyard rose across the sound, still green in late fall, as we crossed over the whitecaps and watched the ferries plying their regular routes to and from the mainland. I tried to turn my head and point out some of the landmarks to Mike – I always became so animated when we got close enough for me to recognize the places that were such an indelible part of my emotional life. The pilot banked and began her approach from the east, instead of from 'my' end of the island, but she came in low over the shore with its exquisite stretch of white beaches and a seemingly endless array of ponds, which looked like fingers reaching out to the ocean to hold it in place and keep it lapping onto the sand.

Mike didn't relax his grip until the plane had come to a complete stop next to the small wooden terminal and the propellers were shut down.

The pilot unlatched her window and started to climb back out onto the wing. 'Thanks for flying with us . . . not that you have many choices,' she chuckled. 'Going back with us tonight?'

'Yes, thanks. See you later.'

'You, too, Mr. Chapman. Wasn't it like awesome?'

'Yeah, awesome,' Mike responded.

'Looks like we've got a greeting committee – the Homicide Welcome Wagon,' I noted as I looked out my window, waiting for the other passengers to deplane down the narrow steps. 'That's Wally Flanders and one of his guys on the right, looks like a state trooper in the uniform next to them but I don't know him and—'

'Who's the one in the three-piece suit and the shades, thinks he's going formal?'

'Don't know him either, but I assume he's FBI, wouldn't you?'

'Oh no, *federal* sissies? I forgot we'd have to deal with

them, too. Only for you, blondie, a Cessna and a feebie in the same day. No wonder I feel so nauseous.'

'Hey, Alexandra, awful nice of you to come on up here,' Wally greeted me as Mike and I rounded the side of the terminal building. 'This here's Eb Mayhew – I think you know him – works with me in the office.'

'Hi, Eb. I'm Alex Cooper, this is Mike Chapman. I've known your sister for years, Eb – used to baby-sit for my brothers' kids when they vacationed here every summer. Detective Chapman's with the Homicide Squad in New York – the D.A. has him with me on the case.'

'Finest kind,' said Wally, with a cheeriness in his voice at this reunion which made it hard to focus on the fact that we were all together because of a murder. 'And this fella is Trooper Lumbert, he's with the state police. Been real helpful up at your place. Keeps all them tourists away from Daggett's Pond, all looking for souvenirs of Miss Lascar. Finest kind. Then we got Special Agent Luther Waldron, sent up here by the Federal Bureau. Real lucky to get *him*, never had a special agent on one of my cases before.'

I was too far away to kick Mike in the shins, but he was humming the theme song from that old TV show and being fairly obnoxious: 'Secret a-gent man, secret a-gent man, they've given you a number and taken 'way your name.' Typical meeting between fed and NYPD cop, which was likely to take a bit of the joy out of Wally's day.

We all shook hands and exchanged greetings while I asked Wally what he had planned for the day.

'Actually, ma'am,' interrupted Agent Waldron, 'I'm in charge at this point, so we'll be talking about *my* plans for the day, if you don't mind. I thought we'd all go up to your place. Show you the crime scene, then have you take us through the house, tell us how you left it and whether there are any changes, anything you might notice about the deceased's habits or belongings. Will that be all right with you?'

Mike had been trying to hold back but wasn't good for much longer. 'When are you going to bring us up to date on what you've got so far? Leads, clues, evidence, theories?'

'Well, Mr. Chapman, my understanding is that you're here in an unofficial capacity, sort of a shall-we-say "hand-holding" function, for Ms. Cooper. I don't think there's much I can tell you in the way of evidentiary information.'

'Hey, Luther, let me tell *you* something. I'm here as a—'

'Forget it, Mike. Give it a rest. I'll call Battaglia and we'll straighten this out. I'm sure Agent Waldron has his orders, just like we do.'

Waldron turned to the three local investigators and suggested they go back into the terminal office with him to call their respective bases and inform the higher-ups of their next destination. I tried to smooth Mike over, but he and the fed were clearly off on the wrong foot. 'Isn't Wally perfect?' I asked. 'You'd expect to see him working with Angela Lansbury in Cabot Cove, wouldn't you?'

'How come he says "finest kind" after everything?'

'I don't know – it's some kind of old New England expression – Wally uses it all the time.'

'What do you guess Eb is short for?'

'Old Mayhew name, Mike. It's Ebenezer.'

'Jeez, I feel like I'm in a time warp – expect to see the *Mayflower* pull up any minute.'

'The Mayhews were the original island settlers. My house is part of one of the old Mayhew farms, built almost two hundred years ago. They've got classic names, wonderful old names: Zachariah, Zephaniah, Experience, Caleb, Patience, Ransford . . .'

'What's the matter? Didn't they ever hear of John and Mary . . .?'

'And Michael and Kathleen and Joseph? They got a little farther than *your* people on the names, Mikey. Much more interesting.'

Over Mike's shoulder I could see Special Agent Waldron emerging to rejoin us. I was determined to make the day as pleasant as it could be under the circumstances, and so I smiled and asked how long he had been on the island.

'Just twenty-four hours this trip, ma'am. But I was here a few years ago doing advance for the President on one of his vacations. Beautiful spot. First time for you, Chapman?'

I wasn't at all surprised to hear Mike respond the way he often did when he felt insulted and wanted to get back into the game. 'No, Luther, actually not. It's been a while, but I used to sail up here a lot – Edgartown regatta – spent some weekends with a girl whose old man kept a boat here. Think he used to be in the Bureau. Found out the whole squad had been doing her – decided to call it quits.' He could bullshit with the best.

Luther ignored Mike and went right on talking to me. 'I understand sex crimes is your specialty, Alex. At least that's what Wally tells me. Why would a girl like you want to spend all her time thinking about things like that? Beats me.'

It looked like I might have to admit Mike was right. The guy was on his way to proving what a schmuck he was.

'Did you hear the one about the woman who was raped by a man with a very little penis?' Luther went on, clearly thinking he was on a roll and would win me over with this one.

Before I could decide whether to say 'no' or a more strongly worded 'I'm not interested,' Luther announced that the woman said to her assailant, '"Did anyone ever tell you what a small organ you have?" And the rapist looked back at her and answered, "Lady, I never knew I'd have to play it in such a large cathedral."'

I was silent. I had heard lousy, tasteless attempts at humor about rape before, but this was at a time and place to hit a new low. 'Mike, want to go over with me to the Hertz office?'

'We've checked that out already,' Luther broke in. 'It's not the one Isabella used. She picked up the Mustang at the rental office in town, near the ferry terminal.'

'Thanks. But it's not that. We're clearly going to need our own car today, okay?'

'We'll take you anywhere you need to go, Ms. Cooper. I've got a government car . . . you can ride with me.'

'Not possible, Luther,' Mike said as he steered my elbow across the grass to the rental car area. 'She's allergic to polyester. Five minutes in the car with you and she's likely to lose it all over your best suit. Trust me, she's hell on synthetics.'

We were fortunate to get one of the rental cars, since the annual Bluefish Derby, which attracted devotees from all over the Northeast, was in its last days and fishermen were everywhere. I pulled out of the parking lot and yelled to Wally that we would meet them all up on

Daggett's Pond Way. The airport is in the middle of the island, so we turned west and began the ride to my house, twenty minutes up-island, taking the South Road so I could point out my favorite sights along the way.

'We've got to get some information about Isabella and the investigation. You think Wally will give it to *you*?' Mike queried.

'That's our best shot. We should be able to pick up a bit when they walk the crime scene with us. But at some point, back at the house, let's make sure that one of us has a few moments alone with Wally. I don't have to invite the trooper and Luther in for tea once they're through with me as a witness. But we'll ask Wally to stay, and you can suggest to Eb that he take you around the property and catch you up on some Mayhew history. Wally's a softie – I'm sure he'll give us some direction, once we get Luther out of the picture.'

'Luther – is he sent from central casting, or what? He's probably dynamite on a forged check case but your mother could solve a murder faster than he could.'

'I can't wait to tell Sarah Brenner about him. She's working on a "Top Ten" list for sex crimes prosecutors, you know, like Letterman does every night? The Top Ten assumptions people make about district attorneys who handle sex crimes . . . Number 3 – People assume that you want to hear every joke that has the words penis or vagina in it, or has remotely to do with any kind of sexual act between humans, animals, or extraterrestrials . . . Number 2 – People assume that you are interested in any social or sexual problem that they or anyone they have ever talked to has mentioned to them . . . and Number 1 – People always assume that you must be incapable of a "normal" social life – whatever that is – after listening to daily tales of deviancy and dysfunction. She'd just love Luther and his little organ.'

We were well into Chilmark now, beginning the gradual climb up the road at Abel's Hill. Off to the right was the quiet local cemetery, scene of many stoned pilgrimages to Belushi's grave, and then further down around the curve was Clarissa Allen's farm, with its stunning view of the Atlantic beyond the grazing herd of black and white sheep. At the intersection of Beetlebung Corner and the Menemsha Crossroad, I turned left. 'This is the center of Chilmark, Mike,' with its town hall, library, post office, schoolhouse, and the general store run by my friends Primo and Mary. 'We're almost there.'

I envisioned Isabella getting her coffee and supplies from Primo every day, as I had suggested, or maybe going next door to The Feast for dinner. Had Wally checked those places, to see who was with her or whether she had signaled a sense of danger to anyone? If he hadn't, Mike and I could do it this afternoon.

'If she didn't hang out here, she might have gone up to Gay Head. We can check that out, too.'

'What's there?'

'Indians.'

'Dot-and-a-knot?' asked Mike.

I bit my lip, trying not to give him the satisfaction of a smile. One of the truly refreshing things about the Homicide Squad was that political correctness had never had an impact there – it simply didn't make a difference. 'Dot-and-a-knot' was squad jargon for East Indians – the twisted headgear and the red forehead dot of the Hindu religion.

'No, stupid. Feathers. This island was inhabited by Indians – Wampanoags – until the English came. The history was like everyplace else in America – and the Indians were pushed off their land, up to the very tip of the island. Now the tribal lands are protected and the tribe has won official recognition from the government.'

I slowed down as the road dipped at the Gosnold bridge and nodded off to the right, telling Mike to look. Beyond the town boat landing and across the wide expanse of Menemsha Pond was my cherished hilltop. As soon as I hit this point in the drive my pulse always quickened and my spirits elevated: I was home. I hit the accelerator and raced up the winding hill toward the granite markers and row of six mailboxes which stood at the mouth of Daggett Pond Way. But as I made the last turn onto the unpaved path and saw the access interrupted by the neon yellow color of the crime-scene tape, I braked to a halt and pulled the rented car into a clearing beside a faded bush of lacy blue hydrangeas, as I wondered what Isabella Lascar's last moments had been like.

We sat quietly in our car for five or six minutes until Wally's cruiser and Luther's black sedan pulled in behind us. When they motioned to us to get out, Mike and I opened our doors and joined them on the strip of tall grass next to the roadway. It was only thirty yards back to State Road, but that was entirely out of view because of the sharp bend in the old path. And although my house and the homes of my neighbors were straight ahead, they were shielded from sight by the dense growth of pines and cedars that crowded both sides of the hilltop that crested before us.

'Not a bad place for a murder,' I remarked to Mike. 'This one piece of the drive is completely secluded. It never seemed sinister to me until this moment, but it obviously presented a great opportunity for a killer to go unnoticed.'

'Now, Alex,' Luther said as he approached us, 'there's not much left here to point out to you, but I just want you to get an idea of what we think happened.'

The neon tape stretched from one of the evergreens on the east side of the path across to the old stone wall that bordered the property on the west. It ran north on the top of the wall for about five car lengths, then squared off by wrapping around a sturdy scrub oak that stood like a sentinel at the crown of the ridge.

'We figure Miss Lascar was driving back in toward the house sometime in the late afternoon. Still have no idea where she was coming from or exactly what time it was. The rental car was a white Mustang convertible, top down when she was hit. She couldn't have been going more than ten or fifteen miles an hour on this part of the roadway.'

He was right about that. The dirt path was so deeply rutted and uneven that most cars bottomed out on it and you had to slow down to a crawl to maneuver the craters.

'We had a field team down from Boston yesterday,' Agent Waldron droned on, 'but they didn't come up with very much out here.'

'Outdoor crime scenes are the worst,' Mike commiserated. 'Very hard to define.'

We had worked a few together in Central Park and in Morningside Park so I knew exactly what he meant. Without an eyewitness and with no clear boundaries – like the four walls of a room in an apartment or the limited confines of a rooftop – it was a tough job for cops to know how far to extend the search for clues. Close it off five feet too soon and you're likely to overlook an essential piece of evidence, but fail to limit it reasonably at some point and you're pulling in all kinds of extraneous crap that leads your investigators off course.

'Our best guess at this point is that the killer was concealed on the far side of the stone wall. It provides a natural cover, better than a duck blind, as well as a perfect brace to steady the gun. The target drove in, moving, but nice and slow. Whoever did this was a good shot. Probably wasn't much more than ten or twelve feet from Miss Lascar. She took two, maybe three shots to the head and neck. Not much left to help us there.'

'What kind of gun are we talking about?' Mike asked.

Waldron hesitated. I knew he wanted to be a hard-ass and not tell us anything, but his instincts seemed to be fighting that. It looked as if he actually knew he might get more feedback from a genuine Homicide detective like Mike than from Wally.

'We don't have a coroner's report yet. My guess is a high-powered rifle. Lots of internal destruction is what I heard from the guys at the scene. Skull was shattered.'

I winced at that description, although I had seen its image flashing in my mind's eye thousands of times in the past thirty-six hours.

Waldron continued. 'She must have been killed instantly. When her body was jolted by the shots we figure the car lurched and went smack into that big tree. That's just where it was when she was found.'

Wally took over the narrative now, eager to give his men the credit for discovering Isabella's body.

'Yeah, I went home to dinner 'bout six. Call came in from your neighbor, Mr. Patterson. He said his dog – you know that collie he's got, Alex? – well, he said his dog came home, feet all covered with blood. Wasn't cut nowhere, much as he whimpered, but he was bloodier than hell. Mr. Patterson said there must have been a big animal killed up there, makin' so much blood. He was mad – can't stand it when hunters start up your way before the season – and asked my boys to go on up to look.'

The secondhand description of the car, and of what remained of Isabella, was gruesome.

'Damn dog was too nosy. Got his front paw prints all over the side of the passenger door where the blood was drippin' down, that's how he got so full of it. The poor young lady's head – or whatever you can call it – was resting on the top of that door. She was blown clear out of her seat – lucky there wasn't no roof on that car or she would've split that in half. The blood was everywhere.'

Waldron interrupted to tell us that Wally's crew had done a good job. 'They didn't touch anything. Just cordoned it off and called for the state police. The troopers brought us in on it because they had assumed you were the victim, Alex. Thought if you were in Massachusetts for business on any part of your trip, it might be federal jurisdiction. Someone in Wally's office knew you'd been cross-designated a few months back to work on some interstate child pornography case. Anyway, Wally says you've always got work with you when you're up here – can't leave what you do behind you at the end of the week.'

I nodded my understanding.

'Are there photographs of the body in the car?' Mike asked.

'Of course. The scene was thoroughly processed by the team of agents.'

'Anybody hear shots?'

We were still in Wally's territory. 'Not so's we know, Mike. This is a pretty lonely hilltop, and nobody's let us know they heard anything at all. You got some summer people like Alex whose houses are sittin' empty this time of year, and some old-timers like Patterson who's so deaf I could blast my siren in the middle of his living room and he wouldn't look up from his jigsaw puzzle. Finest kind.'

Mike had already walked over to the wall and was examining the large rocks carefully for traces of the gun or its residue. It was obvious that he would have loved to come up with a significant piece of evidence that the feds had overlooked, and equally obvious that Luther Waldron, who eyed him closely, wouldn't give him that chance.

'Let's go on up to your house, Alex. That's where we hope you can be helpful. You'll know what belongs to Miss Lascar and whether anything is seriously out of place or missing.'

'Sure.' My eyes swept the area once more as we headed for our cars. No body, no blood, no Mustang, no gun, no killer – just yellow tape strung out in an enormous square to bring home the reality that a murder had been committed on that isolated piece of road, less than five hundred yards from my house.

I led the way as I steered our rental car around the taped area through the tall weeds, behind the tree into which Isabella's car had crashed, and back onto the uneven dirt path that climbed to its peak and then rolled over and started downhill toward the clearing beyond the thick cluster of evergreens. In less than a quarter of a mile we emerged from the shadows of the trees and Mike was able to see, for the first time, the incredible vista at the end of Daggett's Pond Way.

'Spectacular!' he gasped, as I paused at the divide in the roadway where my drive split off from the others and the granite gatepost to my house defined the beginning of my paradise.

'There are lots of great views on this island, Mike, but not one of them is any better than this.'

The old farmhouse is a very simple building, gray-shingled and unpretentious, sitting on a green rise that flows down to the water, at the point where Daggett and Nashaquitsa ponds meet. Over the years I had added border gardens along the stone walls, filled with daylilies and nicotiana, astilbe and asters, and had replaced an acre of untamed weed with a wildflower field that threw up a colorful sea of poppies, loosestrife, and cosmos. Indestructible lilacs rooted beside my front door as they had for more than a century, and impatiens – a flower perfectly suited to my temperament – lined the sides of the original foundation and bloomed till the first fall frost.

But it was the view beyond that took my breath away every time I came back to it, so I watched with delight as Mike tried to take it all in. 'What direction are we facing? What body of water is that?'

'You're looking north over the pond. There's a tiny fishing village there called Menemsha, then beyond that is Vineyard Sound. Another strip of land – the Elizabeth Islands – and off in the distance is America. Cape Cod.' The combination of dozens of subtle shadings of blue and green was endless today, as the sun danced on the water and the sweeping scope of almost three hundred degrees gave us the illusion of being, literally, on top of the world.

Wally and Luther pulled in behind us and drew me back to the real purpose of our visit. It was a strange and uncomfortable feeling to see Luther walk to the front door of the house and hold it open for me. I had never met him until one hour ago and yet he had already been inside and knew his way around my home, without ever having had an invitation.

'Why don't you walk us through, Alex, from room to room. Perhaps your eye will catch some detail we've overlooked. And if you recognize any objects that belong to Miss Lascar, or that don't belong to you, point them out for us, will you?'

'Of course.' I hadn't been to the house since Labor Day, not quite a month earlier, but no one else had been there since, except my caretaker, and then Isabella. 'Does it matter if we touch things now, Luther?'

'Well, I'm afraid you're going to see that my team has, uh, dusted quite a few items for prints already. Obvious things. Drinking glasses in the kitchen and bathroom, mirrors and metal surfaces . . .'

My stomach churned. Another thing I hadn't focused on, despite all my professional experience. The police and agents would have been looking for clues inside the house, especially if they thought Isabella had been killed or set up by her traveling companion. Hundreds of victims in cases I'd worked on had described to me the painful intrusion caused by their well-intentioned investigators, rifling through drawers and brushing black powder on possessions to see whether the oils from someone's fingers had left latent prints – prints not visible to the naked eye – that could link an assailant to a crime scene.

Waldron continued, 'We got some lifts, Alex, so we'll

have to do a set of eliminations before you leave. I directed the coroner to get Miss Lascar's prints, too. Sorry about the mess – that black powder is terrible. You'll need someone to clean it up after we're out of here.'

It was routine for the cops to take prints of anyone who had legitimate access to the location, to eliminate them from the latent prints found. It would be expected to encounter my fingerprints as well as Isabella's on some of the surfaces. And once we were eliminated, the inquiry would tighten to find the source of the unidentified whorls and ridges that might be hiding on glassware, porcelain fixtures, and cabinet doors throughout the rooms.

I stepped through the front door into the tiny hallway central to most colonial farmhouses, with its staircase leading up to the guest bedrooms. I led the solemn troupe past that to the left, into the living room, its crisp Pierre Deux upholstery and clean lace curtains looking just as I had left them.

'She must have used the fireplace,' I observed aloud, assuming that was the kind of detail Luther might want to know. 'Those cinders weren't there after my trip. It wasn't cold enough to want a fire.' And I had been alone Labor Day weekend, conscious of how romantic the setting becomes with a fire lighting that cozy room.

'That candle is Isabella's, too,' I added. 'I'm sure there's one in the bedroom just like it.'

'You're right about that,' Luther said.

'She always travels with them. Rigaud. Takes her own scent wherever she goes to create the feeling of being at home.' I had seen those tiny green votives – cypres was the one she favored – in every hotel suite or guest room Isabella had ever planned to stay in for more than an hour.

93

Mike rolled his eyes in mock disbelief. The habits of the rich – whether movie stars, yupsters, or cocaine addicts – they were all grist for his mental mill, to be worked into the routines he schemed up to delight the guys back at the Homicide Squad as they waited out the nightwatch for news of another corpse.

I doubled back, seeing nothing else out of the ordinary in that room and passed my three escorts as I crossed the hallway and peered into the dining room. The table was empty, eight chairs drawn close around it, and as I leaned to look at its surface I could see the thin film of dust that usually collected within a week's time of non-use.

'It doesn't look like she ate in here,' I said, which did not surprise me, since the kitchen was twice the size of the dining room and had a sturdy oak table where I usually ate, except when I was entertaining, with the help of a local catering service.

We walked single file into the kitchen, and my jaw dropped at the sight of the black fingerprint powder coating the cupboard handles, refrigerator door, coffee mugs in the sink, the wineglasses still in the Rubbermaid drain, and the receiver of the telephone.

'Sorry, Alex, but we—'

I interrupted Luther briskly. 'I understand what you had to do. It's just unpleasant to see it in my own home.'

'Would you check the food supply, please? Anything different or unusual?'

Luther held his handkerchief around the handle of the refrigerator as he pulled open the door. 'There was nothing in it when I left except diet Coke and beer, so all of this is Isabella's,' I told him.

There was milk and juice, English muffins and butter, yogurt and half a packet of hot dogs.

'Was she a vegetarian?' Wally asked.

'Yes, Wally. But I guess her boyfriend went both ways.'

I looked in the pantry and cupboards, which were pretty bare. Just as I left them.

'Must have cleaned out your shelves so the mice don't get nothing over the winter, Alex,' noted Wally.

'Wally, she's got the skinniest roaches in all of New York City. If they wait around for Alex to serve 'em food, they'll die of starvation,' joked Mike, knowing that my dislike of cooking meant that the cabinets were usually empty.

Luther moved to the old Welsh cupboard which held my collection of antique pitchers and opened the doors below, where the liquor was stored.

'Anything missing?'

'I don't measure the bottles, Luther. I wouldn't have a clue what was here last month or whether something's an inch lower than it was before. I told Isabella to help herself to whatever she wanted, of course.' I thought of my Aunt Gert, who used to swear that her housekeeper sipped gin every Wednesday morning when she came in to clean her apartment. Gert took to using the tape measure from her sewing kit to check the level in the bottle, but could never remember where she hid the slip of paper with the number on it from week to week. The housekeeper long outlasted Aunt Gert, but the old girl would have been right up Luther's alley.

He was about to close the door when Mike asked if the cops had dusted the bottles.

'Obviously not. There's no powder on them, is there?'

'Well, take those three in. The front ones. I'd be willing

to bet you'll find prints – maybe Isabella's, maybe someone else's – but they've been moved since Labor Day.'

Even I looked puzzled.

Mike went on. 'See how the Stoli and Jack Daniel's are in front? If Alex was the last to use them, the Dewar's would be the closest to the door. But the Scotch is a step back and the other two are in front.'

Luther was frowning as he looked from Mike's triumphant expression to my grin. I guessed that he was more upset by the suggested intimacy of our friendship than the thought he had missed a point he had no reason to know about, but I had missed it, too.

'He's right, Luther. And Isabella usually drank vodka, so . . .'

'I thought she was a vegetarian,' mused Wally, puzzled by the significance of any of this. 'Do they drink?'

'She was a man-eating vegetarian, Wally,' Mike said, deadpan, 'and a heavy-drinking one at that. Alex used to tell us she liked vodka, wine, and lighter fluid best, didn't you? That's what kept her so arrogant and frisky.'

Luther had his notepad out and was starting his list of additional things to do. There was nothing else of significance in the kitchen and we paraded out the far door ahead of him, through the room I had converted into a small office – which seemed untouched – and into the master bedroom.

While I stopped to take in the tableau of Isabella's interrupted retreat, Mike walked across the large room to stare out the glass doors, which made up the entire wall, at the stunning view down the grassy slope to the blue tints of the pond and sound. This room was my favorite, sunny and cheerful all day, and so private that not a curtain or shade covered an inch of the opening. My only encroachers were the deer who ventured out at night and the osprey I had built a nest for at the edge of the property. Over my bed was a whimsical trompe l'oeil painting of my wildflower field done by a local artist who liked to come to my hilltop to paint, and who gifted me with it years ago.

Now there was the clutter of Isabella's belongings. I recognized the monogrammed luggage from T. Anthony: two duffels and a train case. A few of the silk lounging outfits she collected had been hung in the closet – much too formal for the Vineyard – but most of the sweaters and leggings were still sitting in the open cases, and underwear – all La Perla – was draped on my chaise and lying twisted on top of the coverlet on the unmade bed.

Luther caught up with us and the three men watched as I circled the room to distinguish between my possessions and those that would be neatly repacked and sent out to Isabella's cousin, her only living relative. Next to my clock radio was the other Rigaud candle and a script of a screenplay for a movie entitled *A Dangerous Duchess – the Story of Lucrezia Borgia*. Isabella had longed to do a period piece about a complicated character, but despite the eagerness she had expressed, it appeared from the placemark – still near the front of the manuscript – that her plans to slip away to read were put on hold by the pleasurable companionship of a playmate.

My eyes moved to the table on the other side of the queen-sized bed. The books and tea caddy that sat there had been in the same positions all summer and seemed unmoved. I tossed through her bags and folded up some of the items I knew were Isabella's, and explained to Luther that nothing I could see gave me any leads. The bathroom was full of her lotions and potions, all from Kiehl's, and more makeup than most women would use in a lifetime.

'We, uh, recovered some used condoms from the bathroom wastebasket and sent them down to the lab,' Luther said.

'No, Luther, they weren't here from my last trip,' I offered, since he seemed uncomfortable about suggesting that. 'I'm afraid there's not much more I can show you here. Are you thinking that the guy who was here with her killed her, or that the shooter came in after the killing and took anything?'

'I wish we could answer that one, Alex. Right now we just don't know. Miss Lascar's purse was right there in the car with her, with plenty of cash and traveler's checks in it. So if you're not missing anything from the house, it doesn't seem like anything of hers is gone either.'

'Luther, was her Filofax in the pocketbook?'

'Her what?'

'Her datebook. It's a red leather booklet, about this size,' I said, outlining its dimensions with my hands. 'That's her bible, she never let go of it. It has every name and phone number she's ever known in it, every appointment, every assignation, every lover. Did you find anything like that?'

Wally answered first. 'Was *my* boys that found the stuff, Alex, and there wasn't any "finderfacts" that I know of. Not in the house either. We went through everything pretty good.'

'There's two things that Isabella wouldn't part with very easily. One was her ring.' She and I shared a passion for Schlumberger jewelry – I coveted it, she bought it. She had a fabulous sapphire mounted in a setting called Two Bees – the most exquisitely delicate gossamer wings supporting the deep blue stone. 'And her book. That book was the key to her entire life, professional and social. Find the book – you'll find the phone number and other vitals for Mr. Safe Sex and most of the other people you'll want to interview.'

'Well, I can account for the ring all right. They had to saw it in half down at the morgue to get it off her hand Wednesday night.'

Mike saw me grimace. 'That's okay, blondie. Keep this up and I'll have enough overtime next year to get you one of your own.' He only said it to rattle Luther a bit more, but it didn't help me either, underscoring the additional brutality of an autopsy to the already ugly fact of Isabella's murder.

'No book, though,' Wally added.

Luther's pad was out again as he wrote my description of Isabella's book.

'It was always in her pocketbook or tote. If that's gone, I'd suggest that your killer had enough fortitude to reach into the bloody car and remove it. That's my guess.'

When he finished writing, Luther asked me to join him in the kitchen to answer a few questions about Isabella.

'Wally, why don't you take Mike out and show him around while we're talking here,' I suggested.

'Finest kind, Alex. Love to do it. Let's go, Kojak,' Wally chuckled, as he led Mike out the side door and Luther and I sat down at the kitchen table to dissect what I knew of Isabella's life.

9

Special Agent Luther Waldron was out to show me just how thorough a federal investigation could be, even though it was pretty clear to the rest of us that he didn't actually have jurisdiction over the murder of Isabella Lascar. He wanted to know the entire history of our relationship and all of the details of our recent conversations, despite the fact that I had gone over that with Mike Chapman the day before. Had I been anything less than cooperative, Waldron's boss would have been on the phone to the District Attorney and I would be forced to waste the rest of my weekend doing this again.

'I don't mean to suggest anything negative by my question, Alex, but why do *you* supervise the stalking cases that come into the office? They're not really sex offenses.'

'No, Luther, they're not. Back when Battaglia asked me to take over the Sex Crimes Unit, he used to joke that my professional territory was everything between the knees and the neck. That covered most of what I did. But with the increase in stalking cases and harassment that all of us in law enforcement began to see in the late eighties – by phone, by mail, by computer, and by physical menacing – we didn't know what to do with them. Once the psychiatric experts started to work with us it was obvious that a lot of the cases involved domestic relationships that had broken up and lovers who had been jilted, so the D.A. thought our unit was a natural home for many of them. They're usually crimes with complex motivations and victims who need especially sensitive treatment. In that sense, they're very much like sex offenses.'

Stalking cases are really an odd variety of criminal behavior, which Waldron knew every bit as well as I did. Most states, like New York, don't even have a law that proscribes the conduct – there is no penal code provision that specifically outlaws what most of us think of as stalking, no crime on the books with that name. We struggle to prosecute under a broad range of petty violations when the bad guy makes harassing phone calls or mails threatening letters. But the risks are enormous between that sort of action – when not punished – and the enraged lover who tires of his calls and entreaties being ignored by his subject, and waits outside her office building with a gun in his hand. Not a week goes by when I don't have several of these pending, with women desperately fearful as they tell me about their estranged husbands standing outside their offices or apartments every day, watching their movements. They plead with me, each of them wanting to know the same thing: if that conduct is a violation of their orders of protection. Can't he be rearrested?

No, I respond, it rarely is legal cause for rearrest, no matter how sympathetic the prosecutor or cop. Lurking and watching and following seem to have no sanction in the courts, and yet the stalker's next move often escalates to a deadly one. You can keep the harasser a certain number of feet away from the victim's front door, order him not to enter her workplace, and demand that his calls and letters cease, but once she's an open target walking in a public space or street or subway, the thin sheet of paper handed to her by a judge as an order of the court is as worthless as Confederate currency. The criminal justice system is far more capable of dealing with murder than with harassment, though the line that divides them is often deceptively slim.

'Tell me what you know about Miss Lascar's latest threats.'

'Well, that's just it, Luther,' I said sheepishly. 'I'm afraid I didn't ask her much about them – I thought they were mostly an excuse to ask me to use the house and to come up here for some privacy.'

He frowned and I knew he was telling himself how unprofessional of me that had been. He was right.

'She told me that she had gotten some messages at the hotel and even some callers who got through the operator, but then hung up on her. She didn't save any of the slips of paper. Isabella attracted attention wherever she went, Luther, and she was used to dealing with it. She did tell me she was annoyed about a shrink – her words – and some letters she had gotten. I don't know if it was *her* psychiatrist or just someone she met who happened to be a shrink.'

'Yeah, we had that information yesterday. Her agent's getting the information on all her doctors for us. She's been through six or seven therapists in the last few years. And we've got the agent and the cousin taking the LAPD through her house on Sunday – the funeral's tomorrow . . .'

'Yes, I know.'

'They'll be looking for that correspondence – plus notes, love letters, business deals. Perhaps we'll fax you copies of any papers that might be connected to things she talked to you about – you can tell us if they relate to the problems she discussed with you.'

'Of course, anything I can do.'

'Have you ever met her ex-husband, Richard Burrell?'

'No, no I never met him. She had told me a lot about him, and Nina Baum – our mutual friend – knew him quite well.' I waited to see where Luther was going with this before I offered the information that Isabella and Nina had gossiped about so freely when we first met.

'They'd been divorced for some time, I understand.'

'Yeah.'

'Well, we're giving him a close look, Alex. The reason she went to Boston was to meet with him last Saturday.'

'What?' That information really came as a surprise to me. Richard Burrell had produced a few of Isabella's first movie projects and she had eloped with him one weekend when she was still an unknown. He had been a big deal in the business once, but just as she started to emerge, his cocaine problem engulfed him and cost him most of his money as well as his short-lived marriage. She dropped him instantly, accepting the advice that she would be poison in

Hollywood if anyone suspected that she was as deeply into the white powder as Burrell was.

'I'd keep it under your hat, Alex, but it's a fact. They were both at the Ritz-Carlton last weekend. Separate rooms, arrived and departed at different times – but it was a planned meeting. Her agent thinks he's been trying to reconcile – wanted to meet with her to show her he's off the coke, clean. He's been living on one of those small islands off the coast of Maine for the past year, trying to write.'

'You ought to talk to my friend Nina about Richard Burrell. I'll give you her number. I think Isabella always had a soft spot for him, but reconciliation was out of the question.'

'Did she ever tell you he was violent to her, or abusive? You know, confide in you because of what you do, what your job is?'

'With a couple of drinks she'd have confided in anyone, Luther. Isabella was quite open about her personal life. Much too open. No, she had a lot of complaints about Richard, and how much it cost her to keep him out of trouble, but he never hurt or threatened her. He was wild when he was coked up – vulgar and coarse and unfaithful – but he didn't direct it at her.'

'How about guns? Did she ever mention he had guns?'

'No, not specifically. But when I listened to Isabella and Nina, I used to think that everybody in L.A. had guns. It always seemed so different than New York. Everyone in the Hollywood Hills, in the Valley, in town – they all seem to have guns. Not necessarily to carry, but at home or to keep in their cars. Weird. The more upscale they are, the more guns, the more automatics. You know, Luther, when the revolution comes . . . they'll be ready.' I don't think Luther followed me, but he was probably a gun freak, too.

'Do you have a gun? I mean, a handgun, for protection?'

'Luther, with my temper that would be a real mistake. No, I hate guns.'

'Oh. Well, that's about all I can think of for now. We'll be able to pick up some speed on this investigation next week. A lot of the West Coast friends and business associates will be more available to us once the funeral is over.'

We got up from the table and I glanced at the clock on the wall to see that it was almost two in the afternoon. Mike and Wally were sitting in the sunshine on the deck off the kitchen, feet up on the railing, keeping themselves out of our way. Wally probably hadn't had a fresh, captive audience like Mike in years and was undoubtedly telling him all the local news and island crime stories.

Luther and Wally thanked us for our help and we made arrangements to be in contact during the week. I saw them to the front door and waved good-bye as each car headed out the gate.

'Don't tell me you're leaving me for Luther,' Mike said as I headed back out onto the deck. 'That is one huge blast of hot air.'

'How come you didn't ask me if I did him? You left me alone in there with him for almost two hours.'

'Nah. I figure Wally's more your type. You got a real thing for those sweet old guys. I can see you living up here, married to Wally, running the local jailhouse, or maybe a saloon – like Miss Kitty – while he rids the island of all the vermin who sail in from the mainland.'

'You guessed it, Chapman. C'mon, I've got to call

the office and check my messages. I'm sure you do, too.'

'Then you have to buy me some lunch – I'm starving. I'm dying to hear what you got from J. Edgar Waldron – Wally was easy as pie.'

Laura answered my phone on the first ring. She expressed her usual concern for me and told me that it had been a relatively quiet Friday. All calls from police officers and witnesses had been transferred to Sarah Brenner. My mother had phoned to get Laura's opinion about how I was holding up – (just fine) – and whether I was really in any danger – (of course not). Nina wanted me to call her when I got back to the city. Dinner invitations from Joan Stafford and another friend, Ann Moore (Tell them thanks but I'll be exhausted. Rain checks). And Jed called from Paris – see you tomorrow.

Mike checked in with his office and then turned back to me.

'Okay, Coop, I'm ready. Who's got the best fried clams on the island? I've got a craving.'

'That's simple – the Bite. Grab a couple of cold beers and let's go.'

A seven-minute car ride from my door was the best joint for fried clams in the world. It's a tiny wooden shack on the side of the road in Menemsha – a stone's throw from the commercial fishing dock – with only two picnic tables next to it. But Karen and Jackie Quinn turned out thousands of the most lightly fried clams from late morning through late night in season, which was only from the Memorial Day weekend through Columbus Day.

I turned the ignition key on in our rented car as Mike asked, 'Who's Luther wound up about?'

'He's so rigid, he didn't give a lot away. He's got Richard Burrell, the ex-husband, in his sights.'

'Sound right to you?'

'Not really, especially if he's off the coke. But there's no question she was with him in Boston last weekend, so who knows if he followed her here. And Wally?'

'Wally says they're trying to find an old boyfriend who was sort of a loose cannon. An actor or stunt guy named Johnny Garelli. Ever hear of him?'

'Shit, I should have thought of him, too. Isabella used to call him Johnny Gorilla. Remember when she did one of those Tom Clancy movies, about gun runners and dope dealers in some Central American country? Johnny was a great-looking, brain-dead ex-Marine who had a bit part in the movie, and they had an affair during the filming. Hit all the tabloids and supermarket magazines.'

'I must have missed it.'

'It worked fine for three weeks in the jungles of Guatemala, but once she got him back to Bel Air, he had trouble holding up his end of the conversation.

'Anyway, she came to New York for a shopping trip – without the gorilla – and we met for brunch at Mortimer's on Sunday morning. The place was packed, everyone there knew who she was, and in the door comes this wild-eyed, oversized madman – who'd gone straight from the red-eye to her hotel, where the concierge who had put Isabella in a cab directed him to the restaurant.'

'What did he want?' Mike asked.

'He just raged at her for leaving him behind. The usual stuff of a B-movie – she thought she was too good for him, she thought she could buy him off, comments about her sexual interests. I was halfway under the table and he wasn't talking about me – but she just took it in great style, put down her bloody mary, rose to her full height, told me she'd be right back, and walked him out to the sidewalk. The people in the front half of the restaurant – the ones who count – watched as she hailed a yellow cab and put him inside, then left the taxi door open as she came back in to whisper an apology to me. As she started for the door again, she turned and smiled at ten or twelve of us within hearing range and announced, "Let this be a lesson to you, girls – always fuck your own rank." I sat there dumbfounded until my friends Joan and Louise, who were at the next table, stopped laughing long enough to invite me to finish my salad with them.'

'And the gorilla?' Mike asked.

'He hung on for a while. Could still be an occasional one-nighter for all I know. I don't think she'd brag it about to *me* after the episode *I* witnessed. She's made a lot of mistakes like that with her personal life. While they're looking for Johnny they'll find ten more just like him. Isabella desperately wanted respectability – a man who was solid, not show biz, not drug-involved – there just weren't a lot of them in her orbit. She never stopped searching for one, though.'

I nosed the car onto the dirt shoulder of the road just before we reached the Bite. Karen saw me first and practically squealed with excitement.

'Alex, what are you doing here? You told us you wouldn't be back till the weekend we close.' She realized as soon as the words were out that she knew the connection. 'Oh,

I'm sorry. Isabella Lascar was staying at your place. I'm so sorry.'

'Thanks, Karen. We're up here trying to help Wally. This is my friend Mike Chapman.'

'She was here, Alex. She was here on Wednesday.'

'Isabella?' I should have known I could get a pretty good scouting report from the Quinn sisters. They were enthusiastic, hardworking young women who loved celebrities, and if they trusted you with the information, they could tell you when Vernon Jordan or Billy Joel or Mike Wallace or Princess Di had his or her last order of clams and oysters.

'Yeah, did you send her to us?'

'Well, of course, you're on the top of my list, Karen, and I would have sent her here, but I actually never got to speak with her on Wednesday.'

Mike casually began to ask for more details. 'Do you remember what time she was here?' was how he started, and when he found out it was between two and three in the afternoon, he moved on to whether or not she was alone.

Jackie had joined in the conversation, too, and both were quick to respond that Isabella had been with a man. No, he didn't seem at all familiar to them, and yes, they had both checked him out, simply because they assumed he might also be a movie star.

'He was a looker,' Jackie offered. Taller than Mike, also with dark hair, and probably in his forties. 'They had a medium order of clams with some fries, and both of them had bottled water.'

'Did you happen to hear anything about where they were coming from or what they were up to?' I knew from lots of experience here that the deep-fryers were against the windows, right over the picnic table. My father once came close to bringing the girls to tears, unintentionally, by sitting below that window and grousing that there were too many potatoes and too few clams in the chowder. So I tried to make it easier for them to admit an overheard by urging, 'It's really important, girls. It could really help us a lot.'

Karen was eager to be useful. 'It sounded to me like they were on their way to the ferry. He had to be somewhere else and she was going to stay on the island. I'm telling you, she was all over him. I'm pretty sure she was driving him to the ferry, or maybe it was the airport. But they were in a hurry and they ate pretty fast.'

'Thanks, Karen. I'm going to ask Wally to come up and take some more details from you, okay?'

'Sure.'

'Meanwhile,' Mike smiled at the sisters, 'let's have a large order of clams, some Bite fries, and two cups of chowder.'

While the order was cooking I walked Mike around the bend to show him the fishing dock and the remains of the ever-shrinking fleet of commercial boats that worked off the coastline. The *Quitsa Strider* and the *Unicorn* were both moored in the picturesque harbor, but no sign of their two island captains, brothers who are descendants of original Vineyard settlers, who still caught their swordfish by harpooning them rather than dragging a gill net at sea for days.

We came back, picked up our food, and sat at one of the tables, barely talking as we devoured our late lunch. Mike inhaled the soup and ate two-thirds of the clams before he came up for air.

'You're right, Coop, this is great stuff.'

'We may have stumbled on an important bit of evidence.

Was Isabella killed *before* her lover left the island . . . or just after? Thank goodness you wanted fried clams.'

'As Mae West would say, "Goodness had nothing to do with it,"' Mike responded.

I reached for another clam belly as I asked Mike what he meant.

'I was all set to eat your friend Primo's pizza for lunch. Then Wally told me about the autopsy report. Looks like Isabella got knocked off within an hour or so of her last meal . . .'

I gagged on the delicious morsel as Mike finished his sentence. 'Fried clams – undigested, sitting in her stomach – big, juicy ones, with a little batter on them. I knew I could count on *you* to tell me who served the best ones on the island.'

He grinned as he raised his soda can to click mine: 'Here's looking at *you*, Coop. Hope you're not still hungry – that fried food is lousy for your diet.'

I had promised Wally that I would pack and ship Isabella's belongings to Los Angeles to save his deputies the trouble of going back to the house another day, so Mike and I returned there after lunch to finish that chore. He turned on the CD player, slipped one of my Smokey Robinson discs in place, and sat in the rocking chair next to the bed as I began to fold the clothes that were so casually strewn about.

'I'm tossing these half-used candles,' I said as I walked behind Mike to reach for the one next to the bed.

He picked up the movie script and thumbed through it as I worked. 'Why don't you keep one of those silk pajama things for yourself, kid? Nobody would begrudge you that.'

'Thanks for the thought. Isabella sent me an identical

set for my birthday this spring. The tags are still on it –
somehow it just doesn't have "me" written all over it.' I
stroked the silky fabric of the champagne-colored lingerie
as I fitted it into the already crammed duffel bag, guessing
from Isabella's descriptions of her pudgy cousin that these
gorgeous indulgences of La Lascar would find their next
life in some charity's thrift shop in Sherman Oaks.

When the three bags were zipped and locked, I called
my caretaker's answering machine, leaving a message for
him to get a house cleaner in to get rid of the dust left by
the investigators.

'C'mon, Mike. Let's lock up and get on the road.'

'This would have been a pretty good movie,' he said, still
carrying the screenplay, which he had obviously decided to
take with him as his keepsake of the deceased. 'Lucrezia
Borgia was an interesting broad for the fifteenth century.
Politics, war, intrigue, religion, sex, poison – some things
never change. Izzy was hot for this one – she's got stars and
exclamation points in red ink drawn all around her entrance
and opening salvo. She's even written in her own poetry in
the margin – or maybe one of her friends wrote it. You know
a Dr. C.? It's got a few lines of poetry, then it says "Dr. C."'

I turned off the CD and the lights and set the alarm
system.

In his most dramatic drag imitation, Mike swept out the
door reading Isabella's poem to me:

'What beckoning ghost, along the moonlight shade
Invites my steps . . . tell,
Is it, in Heaven, a crime to love too well?'

'Whoa, Chapman, maybe they didn't teach you this stuff

113

at Fordham and certainly not at the Police Academy, but any self-respecting English literature major from a woman's college could tell you that Isabella didn't write that. It's a very famous poem by Alexander Pope,' and I shuddered to think how sadly appropriate the title was as I said it to Mike, '"Elegy to the Memory of an Unfortunate Lady."'

'Well, she must have liked it a lot to write it in here herself. Maybe Dr. C. is the shrink she was complaining to you about – you know, maybe C is one of his initials.'

'Sounds more like Dr. C. is from the Psychic Friends Network. A *"crime"* to love too well? Is some guy – one of her exes – so jealous that he killed her because she was with another man? Or did *she* love someone too much? Was this psychiatric advice or just the coincidence of someone's taste for classic English poetry? If poor Isabella had only known the rest of this verse, she might not have liked it quite so much.'

'Why?'

''Cause it's about the untimely death of a beautiful young woman, who once had wealth and fame, and now all that remains is "a heap of dust." That's why. You better read through the rest of the script and see if anything else has been added to the margins.'

'And we'd better get a handle on Dr. C. Let me tell you – British poetry, Motown lyrics, movie trivia – with all the stuff you're good at, I don't know why Battaglia thinks you're so useless. Let's get going.'

I took a last look around at the house and then started the car out the driveway. As we headed down-island, I continued to point out all the sights to Mike – friends' houses, working farms, and beach roads.

114

'How did you find this place, Alex? I mean, why did you start to come to the island?'

'Can you stand a love story? A short one. Sad ending.'

I think Mike was sorry the moment he asked. Most of my office friends had some idea of what had happened to me in law school, but I had never talked much about it. I doubt he had connected it to the Vineyard or he would not have raised it at that moment.

'I'm taking one last detour on the way to the airport,' I said, turning off State Road onto a dirt path that led through two miles of thick brush before reaching an area of wetlands and saltwater ponds. Beyond the dunes, guarded only by gulls and shorebirds, stretched miles of sandy white beach covering practically the entire south coast of the island. I knew when we reached it there would not be a soul anywhere in sight on Black Point Beach, just the great surf of the Atlantic Ocean, constantly throwing up waves to meet the shore.

I started to talk as we drove down the winding road. 'You know that I went to law school in Charlottesville, at the University of Virginia, right? I loved it there and I loved everything about the law school experience, which is quite unusual, as you've heard. It's a great school and it's also one of the most beautiful places in the country. From my first semester I knew that I wanted to go into public service, and I knew that I wanted to be a prosecutor – they were a natural overlap – and Paul Battaglia had the reputation for running the best District Attorney's office anywhere.

'So I was off on the right foot academically, from the start. School was interesting, the friends I made there were fantastic – it was a long time since I'd been in classes with men – and I was playing as hard as I was working.

115

'One Saturday afternoon my friends Jordan and Susan' – whom Mike knew well— 'invited me out to the house they rented to go horseback riding . . . a big mistake for a Jewish girl from Westchester whose only experience on a horse had been at the Bronx Zoo. We were only doing a trail ride, but my horse got spooked by a snake and threw me. I went straight to the University Hospital Emergency Room with my left hand kind of dangling – three fingers badly fractured.'

We had reached the end of the dirt path and I parked the car so Mike and I could get out and walk over the dunes. He followed my lead as I kicked off my shoes and left them in the car.

'Enter Adam Nyman – the resident on duty in the Emergency Room. He splinted my fingers, convinced me that law students – male variety – were pedantic and boring, and took me to dinner. I fell madly in love and we spent every free moment together from that weekend on. Fill in the details – I'm sure you can.'

'Was he a Vineyarder?' Mike asked.

'No, but he'd been coming here with his family all his life.' We stood at the top of the sandy walkway up to our knees in the tall, reedy grass and stopped to look at the incredible sweep of ocean and sky, with not a human in sight.

'This is what Adam lived for – to sail on that water from the first light of day till the sun set beyond the Gay-head Cliffs. Every vacation, every long weekend, every space in our lives we scrambled to get here.

'We became engaged and set a date to get married, right after the bar exam the summer I graduated from law school. We bought the house together and started to fix it up. Adam had known the old lady who lived in it – widow of a fisherman from an old island family – and had promised her he'd never tear it down or modernize it the way so many people have done to the original farmhouses.' We were walking westward, as sand crabs scurried to get out of our way and birds hovered behind us to see if we had scraps of food to drop for their dinner.

'Most of my family and friends had come up to the island the week before the wedding. There were beach picnics and cocktail parties and Sunfish races and clambakes and I never thought there could be an end to my happiness.

'Adam was the one with the inflexible schedule so he was the only person we were waiting for those last days. His final shift was over at midnight on Thursday – he was working in New York City by then – and he got in his car to make the drive up to the ferry so he could be here at daybreak on Friday.'

I was doing fine. I was telling the story so flatly that I knew I could get through it okay – there wasn't enough emotion left in me this week to squeeze out much for these memories, mixed as they were with such swings of joy and agony.

'I never saw Adam again, never heard his gentle voice or felt the warmth of those wonderful hands on my body. Everyone who loved him as I did stayed on the island for his funeral. There was no wedding, and I never got to be his bride.'

My voice was still strong and I wasn't even conscious of the tears streaking down my cheeks, till Mike grabbed me by the shoulders. 'C'mon, Alex, sit down for a minute. I didn't mean to get into this. Sit down and catch your breath . . .'

'Whew. I haven't said it out loud in so long – I just can't be here without thinking of Adam,' I said, crossing my knees to sit in the sand. Mike joined me and watched as I picked up a stick and mindlessly drew a heart and arrow with Adam's initials in it, as I used to do so many years ago. He was too polite to ask me what happened and I was too self-absorbed in the story not to go on.

'It was an accident, Mike, a terrible one. Someone on the highway sideswiped Adam's car. They were crossing one of those bridges in Connecticut, the ones that go over the rivers, and Adam's car crashed through the guardrail and went over the side of the bridge. It was demolished – completely crushed by the impact.'

'Did they get the guy who did it?' asked Mike, as only someone in our business would, I think, since it mattered so little to everyone else once Adam was gone.

'No. It was the middle of the night. No one was around to see what happened. The police didn't find the car till hours later. But you're like Adam's mother. She was sure it had been done on purpose, convinced that he had been working on some secret medical research for the government. She couldn't let go and accept that it was accidental.'

'But you could?'

'The police gave it a hard look – it didn't make sense that anyone needed to kill Adam for anything, for any reason at all. You know me. I just assumed that the gods don't like to see me *too* happy. Adam had given me the future – he was smart and funny and warm and loving, and the happiest person I ever met. As my mother would say, "It just wasn't meant to be."

'So instead of dancing in a white tent on our hilltop, we all came to this beach – Adam's favorite. His father and sister went out on his sailboat, brought it around from Menemsha to this point, and scattered his ashes where they thought he'd want them to be. And this is where I come to talk to him, Mike, like some madwoman in a bad novel, you're probably thinking. But I'll never let go of him. It's where I always come to find him and love him, and know that he loved me better than anything on earth. That's the thing that killed him – driving all night to get here to marry me.'

Mike let me sit there alone for five or ten minutes while he walked further down the beach, before returning with an outstretched arm to pull me up from the sand.

'Give me the keys, kid, and let's get to the plane. It would be *my* luck to get marooned here overnight at a time when you're this maudlin, and stuck on another guy.'

We walked back to the car and Mike drove the short distance to the airport, where we turned in the rental car and waited in the terminal for the perky pilot to come back for the six o'clock Cape Air flight to Logan. There was no wind to speak of so even Mike stayed calm on the short hop into Boston.

I was leading him from the exit gate of the commuter plane to the corridor for the connecting shuttle flight, when I heard Mike call out for me to stop. He was standing still, staring at the television screen that was facing out at him from the airport bar, and gesturing excitedly for me to walk back to him.

'Hey, Coop, can you believe it? "Jeopardy" must be on earlier up here than in New York. C'mon, they're about to do the Final Jeopardy question.'

I reminded myself of a mother talking to a five-year-old kid as I shook my head in annoyance and called out to him, 'No, Mike. Move it – let's not miss the seven o'clock shuttle.'

'Wait a minute. What's your hurry? There's another plane in half an hour. The category's the Oscars. What do you say, blondie? I'll bet you twenty-five dollars.'

Mike and I were both addicted to 'Jeopardy,' although I rarely got home in time from the office to see the seven o'clock show. There were some subjects I wouldn't bet him on – like the Bible – because he beat me every time. And I had a few topics that he wouldn't touch. But we usually passed our ten dollars back and forth from week to week, challenging each other on our known weaknesses, when the ante could rise considerably. Mercer Wallace swears the worst time to get killed in Manhattan is between six fifty-five and seven-thirty in the evening. He has known Chapman to stand in an airless tenement in the middle of July with three bodies strewn around a homicide scene, listening to Alex Trebek recite the answers to the Jeopardy and Double Jeopardy rounds while calling out the questions in response, as the medical examiner silently probes the corpses for clues.

I turned around and reached for my wallet, since we both knew the movies pretty well. 'It'll cost you fifty if you make me stay.' I could see he wasn't leaving in the next three minutes, in time to make the flight, so I put my money on the bar and told Chapman to do the same.

He pulled out a twenty-dollar bill, ordered us each a drink, and turned to me with a sheepish grin on his face. 'I've only got twenty bucks – I have to pick up my paycheck at the office when we get in. Trust me?'

I nodded as Trebek announced that the Final Jeopardy

answer was: the only two actors who have ever won Oscars back-to-back, in consecutive years.

Mike and I both slammed our hands on the edge of the wooden bar counter at the same time, as though pressing the buzzer as the contestants on the program do.

'Tom Hanks and Gary Cooper.'

'Wrong. You better cash your check tonight, Chapman.'

'Whaddaya mean wrong? Who do you say?'

'Tom Hanks and Spencer Tracy. *Philadelphia* and *Forrest Gump, Captains Courageous* and *Boys Town.*'

'What about Gary Cooper? *High Noon* and *Pride of the Yankees*?'

'You're really slipping. Those movies came out about ten years apart. Besides he never got the Oscar for *Pride of the Yankees.*'

'Are you kidding me? I don't believe it. He was amazing in that flick. He was incred—'

'Enjoy your cocktail, Mikey, 'cause you're buying.' Alex Trebek gave him the bad news, we finished our drinks, and made it onto the seven-thirty shuttle for the last leg home.

By the time we landed, picked up the car, and drove to my apartment it was after nine o'clock Friday night, and I offered Mike the chance for another fast-food dinner at home. He declined, explaining that he had a date that evening, although I wasn't able to pry any more details about her out of him.

As I glared at the blue-and-white patrol car at the edge of the circular drive in front of my building, I turned back to Mike. 'Will you help me with one more thing?'

'Sure, what?'

'When I see Battaglia on Monday, I intend to ask him to

call off the baby-sitters for me. I wasn't the target for this, Mike, don't you agree? Whoever did this was there to kill Isabella Lascar, isn't that pretty clear at this point?'

'Yeah, I'm sure you're right. It was the middle of the week and like you said, anyone could have checked that you were at work. The shooting was too methodical and accurate to have been accidental. And there are at least a few characters we're aware of with reasons to hate her. We've probably only scratched the surface on that front yet. Cute as you are, blondie, I don't think anyone who got a good look at that head before he fired could have confused it with yours. Somebody wanted Isabella dead.'

'Well, will you tell *your* boss to tell my boss to call off the dogs? Battaglia will want to speak with you, too, on Monday. You know he'll want an independent opinion – not just what *I* think.'

'I'll be there. Now go get some rest, you got a big day tomorrow. Get plenty of beauty sleep.'

I reached over and kissed Mike on his forehead. 'Thanks.'

As he drove out I waved good night to my bodyguards, greeted the doormen who handed me my dry cleaning and mail, and rode up on the elevator with my keys in my hand. I put down my things, made sure I had a Lean Cuisine Lasagna in the freezer, and went into my bedroom to undress and shower.

Six messages. Two girlfriends – Nina and Joan; two hang-ups; the reporter Ellen Goldman to confirm Monday's interview; and Rod Squires, my supervisor, just to reassure me that it had been a quiet day.

Nina Baum was right about me. It was a good thing I had no children and no pets to take care of. Most days it was a struggle for me to keep green plants alive, and tonight I didn't even have the strength to water *them*. Zap that lasagna, chat with the girls, early to bed, and, if I could force the day's events out of my brain, maybe even sweet dreams about tomorrow.

I fell into a sound sleep, and was startled bolt upright by the abrupt ring of the telephone. It was after midnight, as I could tell by the iridescent dial on the alarm. My heart pounded as I grabbed the receiver, praying I would hear Jed's voice on the line, excusing himself for calling at that hour and blaming his timing on the six hours' difference between New York and Paris.

'Hello? Hello?'

No voice, no heavy breathing, no background noise.

'Who are you, dammit?' I tried not to sound frantic, and assumed I would remember on Monday to order the caller ID service the telephone company had been advertising lately.

I slammed the phone back into place and stepped out of bed, walking in the darkened room to the window and looking out at the clear night. Usually, when I sat at my office desk or the courtroom counsel table, I had the false but comforting sensation that I could control – or at least pay back – the evil spirits that crept around this city after dusk. But now, as I stared down at the empty sidewalks and quiet streets, I had no idea where I could turn for safe haven.

11

By morning – long after I finally put myself back into bed and thought of more pleasant things than my hang-up calls – I convinced myself that for the first time all week, I had a bad night's sleep for a good reason. Jed would be home with me by the end of the day and I was excited about the thought of being with him.

I tossed and turned until nine o'clock, distracting myself with visions of how Jed would caress me and baby me when he arrived from the airport later in the day. When I had played out several varieties of that theme, I went to the door and brought in the *Times* to work on the puzzle while I had my first two cups of coffee at the dining-room table. The Saturday crossword was the only one I bothered with all week – it was the toughest, and for years I used to race against my father to see who could complete it the fastest. When I got stuck in the bottom corner on 57 Across, descendant of Old Norse, I was too restless to struggle over the missing letters so I gave up and headed back to the bedroom to get dressed.

There are almost no forms of exercise that interest me, except that I have had a lifelong passion for ballet. I had started to take lessons when I was four years old, and didn't abandon my dreams to be Natalia Makarova's successor until about the time I entered college. But throughout my days in law school and whenever my erratic trial schedule permitted, I still took ballet classes to stay in shape and to relieve some of the enormous tension of the job.

The patrol car with two officers from the day shift at the Nineteenth Precinct was in the driveway of the building as I walked out the door with my ballet slippers in hand and a raincoat covering the black leotard and tights. Both cops – two rookie women – sat up in their seats as they saw me coming toward them.

'Hi, I'm Alexandra Cooper,' I said, although it was obvious they knew that when they spotted me. 'Sorry you're stuck with this duty, but I think it'll be over in a couple of days. In the meantime, do you mind running me over to West Sixty-fourth Street for an hour?'

'No problem.'

I got in and we drove to the studio on the West Side. It was near Lincoln Center, where one of the retired dancers from American Ballet Theatre gave lessons which I tried to attend on Saturday mornings and occasional weekday evenings, whenever my unpredictable schedule allowed it. William and his six other students were surprised to see me when I arrived a few minutes into the barre exercises for the ten-thirty class, but the necessary silence of the participants during the workout was one of the extra benefits of ballet. I never needed to explain my personal circumstances or my trial results or the day's dealings with the cases they had read about in the daily tabloids.

For close to an hour, as I stretched and pliéd and glissaded across the smooth wooden floor to the familiar music of Prokofiev's *Romeo and Juliet*, the demands of concentration needed to perform the required steps pushed all other business from my mind. I sweated and ached like the other women who surrounded me in the class, and was unhappy only when the recording stopped and William bowed to the group with his customary 'Thank you, ladies.'

I exchanged greetings with the other exhausted dancers and cooled down before going out to the radio car for my escorts to get me back home. They let me out in front of Grace's Marketplace, a fabulous emporium of gourmet foods, so that I could buy dinner for Jed and me. There is a section of elegantly prepared dishes which I relied on regularly – complete meals that need only to be reheated and served – and I knew that he would be too exhausted from the long day's travel to want to go out again that evening. Veal francese, roasted new potatoes, string beans, and a salad, and I was on the express checkout, back in the car, and dropped off at my front door minutes later.

'That's it for the day, ladies. I'm not going out again. My boyfriend will be here later – that's all the action you're going to get today. Thanks.' I left the pair at their steady post in the driveway and went upstairs to put away my packages and get into the shower.

The only message on my machine was from Nina,

phoning from her car on one of the freeways on her way to Isabella's funeral. 'I'll call back, after the show. Don't forget to watch – C-SPAN is carrying the service. Word in the biz is that there'll be a lot of crocodile tears – Sharon, Demi, Nicole – all the girls who want to scoop up her scripts and incomplete projects will be front and center, in their deepest black, feigning grief. Later.'

It was almost one o'clock, so I settled into my sofa in the den to watch Isabella's memorial service, broadcast from Forest Lawn. The commentator came on first, describing the arrival of the movie stars as if it were Oscar night at the Chandler Pavilion. Among the hundreds of celebrity mourners I was able to spot Nina and her husband, Jerry Baum – a literary critic and screenwriter, whom she had met and married when we were still at Wellesley.

The service consisted of a series of speakers who gave their favorite memories of Isabella. There was lots of talk about her great beauty and her screen talent, but very little was said that made one think she had ever done a kind thing or had a generous thought about another human being. I sat forward, scouring the crowd as I imagined Luther Waldron would have done at a Mafia don's funeral – looking for the furtive glance of a killer or the inappropriate smirk on the face of an ex-lover.

Some of the speakers had familiar names. Most had worked with Isabella on one project or another – producers, directors, her agent, a couple of co-stars. Then Richard Burrell introduced himself and began to talk about the private Lascar. I tried to make something of the fact that he wasn't emotional enough about the death of a woman he loved, but it was clear that she hadn't been easy to love, and emotion was visibly lacking from the entire ceremony.

The last salute was what the crowd had been waiting for. I couldn't stop myself from breaking into a huge grin as Kirk Douglas moved up to the podium. I was tempted to pick up the phone and call Mike at home, but figured he must have been watching, too. As a serious movie buff, Douglas was one of his favorites. Mike could imitate him in almost any role, from *The Vikings to Spartacus* to last year's remake of *Blue Lotus*, in which Douglas played Isabella's father and won another Oscar nomination for supporting actor.

If there wasn't any warmth to add to the portrait of the deceased, at least Kirk Douglas closed with the histrionic conviction that the fans wanted to hear. He conjured up every celluloid image of the young star in each of the roles she had played, and invested her professional life with the dignity of his unique voice. '. . . And the final irony, the fatal one, is that Isabella – a name which means "beautiful little island" – met her death in just such a place, a beautiful little island, where she went for solitude, for safe haven . . .'

Yeah, Kirk, that's the bullshit she gave me, too.

A final prayer and the recessional, with six Johnny Gorilla look-alikes carrying out the coffin – and probably having good cause to be sadder than anyone else in the chapel – and I clicked off the television.

Joan Stafford called a minute later, still stunned by the spectacle. 'It's hard to believe Isabella's dead, isn't it? She was so vibrant, so magnificent. It's – oh well, what do you think, Alexandra? Who did it? Could have been anyone in the first two rows, from the looks on their faces.'

I caught her up on yesterday's trip to the Vineyard, told her about my plans for the evening with Jed, made a dinner date with her for later in the week and, hung up the phone.

Then I called Air France and learned that the flight from Paris had been delayed two hours at takeoff because of weather en route. Jed would arrive closer to six o'clock.

I tried to escape into the new Le Carré novel that I had just bought a week ago but my thoughts raced back and forth between trying to solve the real murder that had presented itself in my life and fantasizing about making love to Jed. I didn't get very far on either course.

I picked up the receiver again and dialed the number for Special Victims at the Twentieth Precinct.

'Squad.'

'This is Alexandra Cooper. Who's this?'

'Hey, Alex. It's Frank Barber. Whaddya need?'

'I was just looking for Mercer, to see if there's anything new on the pattern – the Con Ed rapist.'

'Mercer swung out yesterday at four. Doesn't come back until Monday afternoon. But I got the sheet in front of me. All quiet on that case – no developments, no new hits.'

'Anything I should know about, Frank?' Strange business, I acknowledged to myself. I'm looking for news of a good rape case to serve as a distraction from a murder investigation and my own love life.

'Two things, but nothing we were gonna bother you about at home. I got bad news and I got good news. Give you the bad first, okay?'

'Ready.'

'Got a 61 last night . . .' Frank started, referring to the police complaint report made in every case, which gets its name from the designated number of the police document, a Uniformed Force Number 61. 'Twenty-third Precinct.

129

Victim is sixty-eight years old. Lives in an old railroad flat with four bedrooms. She's a widow, rents out rooms to boarders. Guy she's been renting to for a couple of months comes home loaded last night. Mrs. Zalina goes down the hall to the bathroom and this scumbag drags her into his room and tells her to suck his dick.

'She says no, so he punches her in the mouth. She still says no, so he hits her again. He's got her on her knees, trying to make her do it when another renter hears the commotion and tries to help old Mrs. Zalina. The perp has the good sense to run out and never come back.'

'How's Mrs. Zalina, Frank?'

'Patrol responded. Took her to Mount Sinai. Say she's fine. We logged it as an attempted sodomy and an assault. Shook her up pretty good but she was tough as nails. Doctors gave her a head-to-toe exam, and the rape crisis counselors spent time with her and took her home. She told them she didn't need counseling about nothing – if the late Anthony Zalina didn't ever make her do "that disgusting thing" in forty-two years of marriage, she wasn't about to do it for some drunken garage mechanic.'

'Good for her. I take it we know who the guy is, right?'

'Yeah. We found a lot of papers in his room with his name on it. Worked in a body shop in the Bronx, only he didn't show up this morning. It's just a matter of time, Alex – we'll drop him.'

'Okay. I'll assign it to someone in the unit on Monday, so we'll be ready when you pick him up.'

'You'll like Mrs. Zalina. She wants to go all the way with this. Says she could recognize his penis anywhere – "looks just like a teeny-weeny, crooked little sausage."

Cops put that right in the original report with the rest of the description.'

'Ought to be an interesting line-up, Frank. Maybe we should hold it in a butcher shop instead of the precinct. If that's it on the bad news, what's the good news?'

'This could be a new one for you, Alex. I had a call today from a young lady who wants to remain anonymous for now. She was raped a week ago by her ex-boyfriend. They both work at Merrill Lynch, went out for drinks, reminisced, and then she brought him home with her. Wants to know how long she can wait before she reports it and still has a case. But her big question was about the evidence. Seems she kept a washcloth that he wiped himself off with, put it in a baggie, and then stuck it in her freezer so she'll have his semen to prove he did it. Wants to know how long she can keep it and still have the police lab be able to use it.'

'Are you serious? What did you tell her?'

'I told her it depended on whether she had it stored with the frozen peas or with the ice cream . . .'

'Frank, that's revolting.'

'And I told her that I absolutely refused to go to her house for dinner until she got that stuff to the lab. Anyway, what I really told her was to call your office next week and one of the lawyers could answer all her questions about prosecuting.'

'That's it?' I asked.

'For the moment, that's all we've got, Alex. You'll be the first to know if we need you.'

I hung up and decided to busy myself in getting ready for Jed's arrival: setting the table, straightening up the apartment, and removing the tags from Isabella's slinky birthday present to dress up for the occasion. The Four Tops were singing to me as I tried to lighten my mood for the night ahead, urging me to reach out for them if my life was filled with confusion. I put the list of people with motives to kill Isabella, which I had started to scratch out during the funeral, in a drawer, closed the file which contained the motion and bill of particulars that I had to respond to by Thursday for the Vargas case, and finally settled down – unable to concentrate on anything else – with a two-month-old copy of *Architectural Digest*.

'Mr. Segal on the way up, ma'am,' the doorman announced on the house phone when Jed finally arrived from the airport.

I checked myself again in the bathroom mirror and got to the front door just as I heard the elevator opening. Jed stepped out, carrying his suitcase, and did a double-take when he saw me in the doorway of my apartment at the end of the hallway wearing my sexy silk outfit. It was a radical departure from my usual lounging uniform: an oversized man-tailored shirt and a pair of leggings.

'You're in the right place, darling. Welcome home.'

'You may have found the perfect antidote for my jet lag, Alexandra,' he said with a smile as he pinned me against the wall and reached down to find my mouth.

We kissed for several minutes, hard and deep, our tongues exploring each other's mouths. Jed ran his hand down the smooth surface of the pajama top and found my nipple waiting at attention for him. 'Are you okay?' he whispered to me as he started to work at the buttons of my shirt.

My eyes were closed now and I nodded my head in answer to his question.

'Tell me what happened, Alex. Tell me how you've been involved and what they've put you through all week.'

I pushed away from the wall, looked at Jed, and pressed my finger to his lips to silence him as I led him by the hand into the bedroom. 'I'll tell you everything you want to know later, but for now, I have other plans.'

'But did they actually think the killer was after you and not Isabella? Do they think they know who did it?'

'Really, Jed, you're the one who's always telling *me* not to talk about my cases all the time, and when I finally want to leave it behind me, you become the Grand Inquisitor.'

'I'm sorry, darling. I've just felt so useless being in Paris while all this was going on, worried about your safety, and . . .'

'If you want me to prove to you that I'm absolutely fine, you're going to have to take off all your clothes right now and save the conversation for dinner.'

'Sounds fair to me,' Jed responded, starting to undress. 'I've been traveling for hours – you'll be much happier with your suggestion if you give me a few minutes for a shower.'

I watched him undress and smiled at the familiar sight of his lean body. It had only been three months since we'd met in June, but the attraction had been immediate and intense, and I was relieved to know he would hold me and tether me to reality as the circumstances of Isabella's death continued to unravel.

'I didn't have any time for shopping, but I just want you to know that I thought of you wherever I was,' Jed said, smiling as he tossed bottles of Chanel 22 perfume and body lotion onto the bed and headed for the bathroom.

'Thank God for airport duty-free shops,' I laughed and unwrapped the cellophane from the sharp black-and-white packages. Nothing could distract Jed from his deal-making when the numbers were on the table and the stakes were climbing – so I was delighted that he had thought of me at an odd moment during his trip. As he knew, shopping was a passion of mine, and there weren't many things other than crime scenes that could dull my interest in a good sale. I was pleased that he had remembered my brand and that he had tried to cheer me up with these luxurious tokens.

I heard the shower water running, so I slipped out of Isabella's satiny garment, dropping the pajamas onto the floor, and opened the bathroom door. Steam had filled the tiny room and clouded the mirror completely. I held apart the white eyelet curtain and stepped in with Jed, whose head was arched back so that the hot water was spraying in his face and running down the length of his frame. I took the bar of soap from its niche in the tile wall and began to lather his shoulders and back. He sighed approval and shifted his body, so that his hands leaned against the front of the shower and his head dropped forward between his arms. My hands gently rubbed every inch of his torso, then down each leg and back up to the top of his thighs, like a slow wet massage on a very compliant subject.

I stood as Jed let go of the wall against which he had braced himself and turned to face me, his penis fully erect, but his eyes barely able to see through their water-soaked lids. I reached up to kiss him and again we embraced, tasting each other and letting the shower rinse me free of any thoughts except the man and the moment. He entered me and all my fantasies of a slow and languorous reunion on my comfortable bed yielded to the reality of our eager bodies finding each other and mating against the slick tile wall.

When we released each other a minute later, I turned off the water and we stepped out to wrap ourselves in heavy bath sheets. I left Jed to shave and change and went back to my bedroom to put on my more familiar costume of leggings and a shirt.

Jed followed me in after he had dressed. I hugged him to me and told him how much I had missed him during the week. We rolled back onto my bed together, and I let him kiss the dark circles under my eyes, which I teased him that he had caused by making me sleep alone. I rested in his arms, delighted at not having to talk or explain or resolve any of the problems which had plagued me since he had last been with me in this room so many days ago.

'Can I fix you a drink?' he asked, as I finally untangled myself and started for the kitchen, prepared to nuke our dinner in my microwave.

'Sure, if you'll join me.'

'I think I'll just have a glass of wine with dinner. Between the jet lag and your magic-fingers-welcome-home treatment, I'm not going to last too long this evening. Is that very rude?'

'I'm so glad you're here, Jed, of course not. I haven't slept in three days, so we'll just eat and go to bed early.'

'When I got off the plane I almost changed my mind and went directly to my own apartment. I never thought I'd have the strength to, well, to . . .'

'I'd have been so hurt if you hadn't come here.'

'But, Alex, I want you to understand that I had to come

here, too, for my own sake. Not just because you needed me. Because of everything that's happened. Now it's clear to me that I really love you and that I had to be with you – and that once I held you in my arms there wasn't any way I couldn't make love to you.'

My mind scrambled for a diversion from the direction this conversation had started to take. Our romance had progressed with great speed, and for weeks it seemed that I had been more anxious to engage Jed's sentiments than he had wanted. The physical attraction had been a perfect fit, and I knew he would be slow to involve and yield his reserve. He had left Santa Barbara earlier this year when his marriage split up, and he was plagued by thoughts about the effects of the divorce on his two kids. By late-summer, I knew I was falling in love with him, once he had opened himself up with a warmth and playfulness that I found irresistible.

Still, I reminded myself that at the height of my crisis he had been an ocean away and unwilling to cancel the deal he was negotiating to wing his way to my side. It excited me physically and calmed me mentally to have him with me tonight, but I wasn't ready to confuse it with loving him.

'Darling, I wish I could have dropped my clients or called in one of my assistants, but you know—'

'Sssssh. Stop apologizing. Do you think I'm going to say I'm sorry for pouncing on you in the shower?'

'Nothing to apologize for. I didn't seem to mind very much, did I? Kind of reminds me of that story you told me about your first rape trial – I think you were just showing off.'

The first sex crimes case I had ever taken to trial was a ground ball – so easy the jury should have reached a verdict without ever leaving the box. The victim was a twenty-one-year-old college graduate on her way to her first job interview in a towering office building on Lower Broadway in the middle of the afternoon. As she entered the elevator to go upstairs a man got on with her and – as the elevator started to move – pressed the button to stop it between floors. Before the startled young woman could react, the defendant grabbed her by the neck and slammed her head against the wall to daze her and render her semi-conscious. Then, as he held her pinned in place with one arm, he lifted her dress, ripped down her panty hose, unzipped his pants, and penetrated her while she stood up – slumped in the corner of the elevator.

Impatient workers on the ground floor kept ringing for the stuck car, which finally returned to the first floor. When the doors opened, the girl screamed and the defendant bolted for the street. An off-duty cop – the building coincidentally housed the Patrolmen's Benevolent Association offices – chased the rapist for two blocks and dragged him back to the scene where other officers arrested him.

No wonder the bureau chief had given it to me as a first trial. The defendant's attorney made a very weak argument for mistaken identification, and there didn't seem to be any reason to worry about the outcome of the case. The jury got the charge at noon, and should have been back before lunch. By ten that night, we all knew some issue was giving them trouble. When the twelve very angry men and women returned with a guilty verdict close to midnight, several of them asked to talk with me.

The hang-up? An elderly man – married and the father of four children – simply didn't believe the victim's story, even though the defense had conceded that the rape had occurred exactly as she described it. Number eight told the others that she had to be lying: no one could have intercourse in a standing position – it just wasn't possible! Eleven jurors had spent the rest of the day arguing with this old-fashioned gent, whose four offspring had been conceived in the missionary position. He was convinced that was the only manner in which sexual coupling could be accomplished . . . until jurors three (a thirty-six-year-old masseuse) and eleven (a forty-three-year-old mailman) volunteered to demonstrate to him, in the interest of justice, exactly what the victim had described.

From that experience I learned that a prosecutor could never assume any aspect of a case, especially when it comes to the complicated world of sexual assault. Jurors bring to the courtroom with them their own biases, prejudices, and personal knowledge, which was frequently quite limited. And the biggest problem is their natural impulse to confuse consensual sexual events, familiar within their own lives, with the very different phenomenon of forced, assaultive acts. Never again have I presented an event to a jury without using my closing argument to explore the distinctions between what I could suppose were their own private habits and the criminal elements of the acts charged.

Jed poured me a drink while I opened a bottle of wine for him. I set out the meal, lit the candles, and tried to bring the conversation around to what he had seen and done in Paris and at which restaurants he had eaten.

But I had put off the obvious topic of conversation for as long as I could and he was determined to be brought up to speed.

'Alexandra, don't you want to tell me what happened? Do they know who killed Isabella?'

Like anything else, I had answered this question so many times since Wednesday evening that I could respond quite easily at this point. I summarized the details of her death and the investigation. 'No suspects right now. At least none that they're telling me about. Ex-husband, psycho co-stars, pen-pal psychiatrist, obsessed fan – maybe even a secret lover. What's your guess? I think I'm too close to it to see it clearly.'

'I didn't know she'd ever been married. And what lover? Had she told you about him?'

'No. Talk about using me. You know the crap she gave me about being stalked and needing to get away? Well, she neglected to tell me that she was taking someone with her. A guy.'

'Maybe it was platonic, a friend—'

'Well he left some very unplatonic condoms in my garbage. I suppose if I look at it scientifically instead of with my gut, at least when they get a suspect they can always test what's in the condoms for DNA.'

'Don't the police know who he is? Didn't anybody see them together?'

'Not many people. That's the beauty of the Vineyard.' Jed had not been to the island with me yet because he had spent most of his free weekends commuting back to the West Coast to spend time with his kids. 'Anyway, they're talking to everyone who Isabella ever crossed in her inimitable fashion, so I think this is going to be a long haul.'

'But are they sure the killer was after Isabella and not you? That's what had me tortured when I couldn't get here.'

'Now it seems quite obvious, but it was truly frightening

before we could reconstruct the timetable. I was pretty distraught when I called you that first time.'

I knew Jed had been harassed by a stalker during his brief foray into politics last year, when he lived in California. 'I remember those stories you told me about that woman who had followed you all around during the primary.' He had been a candidate in the Senate race, and like most people in prominent positions had attracted a few nuts in his search for legitimate support. 'You know what sitting ducks men and women become when they achieve some kind of celebrity status. Most of the time it's just a nuisance, but quite harmless. Then one of those psychos loses all connection to reality and the result is suddenly lethal.'

'I tell you, when you're in the middle of it, there's nothing worse. Every time I was giving a speech or standing on a reception line, I'd look up and she'd be there. Nothing threatening, mind you. Just the opposite. She attended a single campaign rally in Century City – probably because there were supposed to be a lot of movie stars there – shook my hand once, and was smitten.'

'Hey, she's only human,' I teased.

'Yeah, well that's half the problem. Nobody took it seriously because she told everyone we were lovers.'

'And?'

'Of course not. She was completely delusional. But nobody – my staff, the police, private security – nobody thought it was worth worrying about because she was a woman, and because I think most of them really believed we had been having some kind of affair. She was smart, reasonably attractive, knew my travel schedule better than my staffers did. She was everywhere I was supposed to be. They all knew my marriage was hanging by a string and they just winked at each other whenever I tried to deny that something was going on.'

'What did you do about it?'

'Got an order of protection, finally. I sure as hell didn't want to do that in the middle of a campaign – prosecute someone for being at my events. Hell, some days she was the *only* one who showed up. And paid to do it.'

We both laughed. 'One of the reasons I was thrilled to move to New York for CommPlex was to put all that behind me. I assume she's still in graduate school in L.A., and that she's attached herself to some other unsuspecting soul. Anyway, I know how distracting and unsettling that kind of harassment is, even if I didn't know it was so dangerous. Now I've got you to protect me – I went right to the top.'

Jed got up from the table and came around to my side. 'Alex, I'll never let you down again, I promise,' he said, as he leaned over behind me, brushed the damp strands of hair away from my neck, and kissed me softly below my ear until I turned and offered him my mouth. We left our uneaten dinner on the table, carried the wine bottle and glasses into my bedroom, and stripped down a second time to get under the covers.

'Forgive me, darling, but I don't think I'll be much good to you now,' he whispered as he let me cradle his head on my breast. 'I'm really exhausted.' He was asleep almost as soon as his eyes closed, and I looked at the clock, noting that it was barely ten as we settled in for the night.

I stared at the dark, silent figure lying beside me, and thought about how my life had changed in the three months since we had started to date. I met Jed through my closest friend from law school, Jordan Goodrich. Jordan had left

Skadden, Arps to go into the investment banking business and worked a few deals with Jed on the other side. When Jed's twelve-year marriage broke up and he moved to New York, Susan Goodrich began to invite him to some of her dinner parties. She obeyed my rule about no blind dates, but Susan had grown to like Jed and was convinced that I would, too, so she was intent on coming up with an easy introduction.

In mid-June, Susan rented a movie theater on East Sixty-fourth Street to surprise Jordan for his thirty-fifth birthday. The party was a screening of his favorite movie, *Thunder Road*, with a fifties theme and everyone in fifties dress, playing pinball and dancing to Coasters music for hours after the film. I saw Jed dancing with Susan, and he was better than anybody on the floor. With my ponytail swinging, my turquoise poodle skirt and matching twin-set ready to move, I asked him to rock 'n' roll when the record changed and we danced about ten cuts before we stopped to exchange introductions.

When the party was over, the four of us hopped in a cab – despite our ridiculous clothes – and went downtown to the Gotham, where we sat for hours telling stories and trying to catch up on each other's lives. The Gotham then became 'our place' for dinners together or entertaining friends as the romance flourished despite our mutual reluctance – my fear of losing someone forever if I dared to love him too much, and Jed's fear of involvement so soon after a disastrous divorce.

I thought, as I studied him in sleep, that perhaps this crisis would be the path for each of us to become more open to the other. I needed him to come to the Vineyard with me – I had struggled for too long to keep my lovers away from where I had been happiest with Adam, and with the passage of so many years that division had become too artificial and unnatural. I also wanted Jed to let me understand what had happened to end his marriage, and to let me meet the children who meant so much to him.

Now that Jed had expressed his love for me tonight – something I hadn't felt ready to do yet – I was confident we were on our way to a more secure relationship, and I eased myself onto my side next to his body. I hugged him tightly against me and finally gave myself to pleasant dreams, unpeopled by the stalkers and rapists and murderers who loomed before me every day.

12

'Was it good for you?'

'Mike, there aren't words to describe how good it was,' I responded when Chapman called the apartment in the middle of Sunday afternoon. 'If you stop playing with yourself and give some girl a chance, maybe you'll find out.'

'Am I interrupting something warm and wonderful right now?'

'No, Mike, he's gone. This is fine.'

'Gone? Already? Jeez, I figured you two would still be making up for lost time. The guy doesn't have a problem, does he, blondie? Not a long-ball hitter?'

'No problem, Mikey. Now why don't you pretend to be mature and tell me what's on your mind.'

Jed and I had awakened at daybreak. I was happy and

excited, and we made love again, unmindful of what the rest of the world was worrying about. We had coffee together and read the Sunday paper, but he left early to catch up on the mail and messages that had accumulated in his office while he was out of town, before going to his apartment to unpack and settle in for the work week ahead.

'Did you catch the funeral service yesterday?'

'Of course. What did you think?'

'I'm throwing Kirk Douglas on the list of possible perps – that was the worst acting job I've ever seen that man do. He's practically my hero – you know that – but this was a lousy performance, pretending that broad was a saint.'

'He made Isabella furious, Mike,' I chuckled as I recalled her outrage. She had thrown herself at him during the filming of *Blue Lotus*, tried every one of her teddy-bear tricks to seduce him, but he reminded her that he was very much in love with his wife and wasn't the least bit interested in a dalliance with her.

'She really thought she was irresistible. Thought a man had to be dead or insane if he didn't react to her charms.'

'What are you doing today?'

I looked out the window as the rain streaked against it, the gray clouds mirroring my mood. 'Nothing, really. I've got some motions to answer for my next trial, so I'm just going to hang around and do my homework, return some of my phone calls.'

'Good. Lieutenant Dane just reached me. He had a notification from the Chief of Detectives. Thought you'd be pleased to know that they're lifting your bodyguard tomorrow. Uniform team will drive you to work in the morning and then you're on your own. Battaglia approved. And I'm back on nightwatch as of midnight tomorrow.'

'Oh, Mike, that's great news. Living with these watch-dogs could really drive me nuts, I'm so used to just picking up and moving when and where I want to.'

'Here's the case update. LAPD is going through Isabella's house right now – they'll let us know if they find anything of interest. Wally Flanders is letting us work this with him, so we'll get copies of any reports he gets. And best of all is that he wants us to do some of the interviews. Richard Burrell and Johnny Garelli for starters – both'll be coming into New York this week.'

'As suspects or witnesses?'

'Hey, everybody's a "possible" in my book until they convince me otherwise. Now, for whatever it's worth, Wally FedEx'd some of the photos that have been developed and turned in. Should be in the squad office tomorrow. He thought Isabella was in a couple of frames but didn't see anything else of interest. I left orders to get them to the lab immediately for enlargement, so by the time I get in at eleven-thirty to start a midnight tour, they should be available.'

'Great. Let's not waste any time. I have to go to a black-tie dinner with Jed tomorrow evening, but I'll be home by eleven. I'll make a pot of coffee for you. Bring the pictures by when you swing out and we'll look through them together, okay?'

'Long as nobody gets chopped up in little pieces or dumped in the East River before midnight, I'll be there, Coop. Lighten up – we're going to break this thing open ASAP and get your life back to normal . . . if that's what anybody calls normal. It's really nasty outside – just

146

stay in and relax, you're not missing a thing. See you tomorrow.'

I hung up the phone and went back to the dining-room table to work on the Vargas case. Not a complicated matter, a typical 'push-in' burglary that escalated into a rape, and my white legal pad filled up quickly with the draft of my answers to the demands for information made by the defendant's attorney in the pretrial stage. I flipped through the complaint to find the exact time of occurrence, then backed up to get the precinct arrest number from the rap sheet. Like most stranger rapists, thirty-four-year-old Ervilio Vargas had a record that stretched back to his early teens. From fare beats and car boosts he moved to break-ins, then began to commit felonies with weapons, then threw in sexual assaults when he encountered women during his burglaries. He had done city time and state time, released to early parole on his last sentence, but never able to stay out of trouble very long. I planned to try him as a 'persistent felony offender' – with more than five felony convictions to his credit. I was looking for a life sentence and no shot at parole. He had ruined far too many lives and been given more chances than any human being deserved. The victim was very cooperative and anxious to put Vargas out of business, too. If all the paperwork was done expeditiously, we'd be ready for trial before the Christmas recess. Happy New Year, Ervilio.

I had worked for more than an hour when the phone rang again, and I was delighted to hear my best friend's voice on the line. Talking to Nina was the easiest thing in the world. We had been close since the first day at Wellesley and had guided each other through every significant event and every trivial detail of our lives. There were very few secrets we kept from each other, and she was unique in that her friendship had always been completely unconditional. Nina didn't pronounce judgments or exact demands or hold grudges – she was simply a loyal and loving friend.

'I know your life is upside down at the moment, Alex, but you've got to stay in touch with me. No calls, no messages, no cards . . . what's going on?'

'I'm fine, Nina, really, I promise.' She was referring to the fact that we had a regular routine of staying in touch with each other, and it was always pretty easy to guess when our lives were disturbed, because the flow of communication was interrupted as well. Despite the three-hour time difference between us, we called each other several times every week. We didn't always speak directly because of our work schedules, but we left messages on our home machines, so that no matter what hour I got in after a long day, the sound of Nina's familiar voice would frequently help me unwind and put my day in perspective. Her joys, her heartaches, her professional triumphs – all strung out on an endless strip of rewound tape, as mine were on her machine in L.A. And we both collected art postcards from museums all over the world, writing each other a note on one of them almost every evening to track our lives through almost fifteen years of graduate school, legal jobs, romances, motherhood, and now, mystery.

'Can you talk? Are you in the middle of anything?'

'Are you kidding? It's been pouring all day. It's the first chance I've had to stay in and relax – I'm just catching up on everything. How about you? How're Jerry and Gabe?' Gabriel was their two-year-old son, my godchild.

'They're great. They're out in Malibu at the beach today. So what did you think of the service?'

'Compared to what, Nina? It didn't sound like they were eulogizing the woman *we* knew.'

'Let me tell you what nonsense was going on at this end. Did you ever dress for a funeral – I mean, worry about what designer you were going to wear? The girls in the front row were tripping over each other for the photo-ops, black Armani versus black Ungaro versus black Bob Mackie . . . for those who like sequins graveside. I doubt any of them even listened to what was being said. What do the cops think – have they got a killer?'

'All the usual suspects. I understand the LAPD is at the house this afternoon, looking for clues, papers, diaries, whatever. I'll know more tomorrow. Did you find anything else out about her shrink?'

'Just that she's had about four different ones the past few years. I don't know names, but the police will find them on the pill bottles in her bathroom. The rest of the world had problems, according to Iz. She was fine – but used these guys for pills. Ups, downs, whatever the latest fad. As soon as one of the psychiatrists got wise to her, she'd switch to a new one and start the prescriptions over.'

'Did I tell you that she wasn't alone for the last couple of nights she stayed at my place on the Vineyard?'

'You're kidding! Don't hold out on me – who's the masochist?'

'We have no idea. I was hoping maybe she told you.'

'Nope. She talked about some guy she ran into on a plane about a month ago. She had taken the Concorde back from London – said he referred to it as "the rocket."'

'Yeah. That's investment banker lingo.'

'Said the guy was fascinating because he wasn't in show biz and was still powerful and important – her words, darling. You know how it always impressed her that people who weren't in *People* could still be worth talking to occasionally, and could even get a table at Le Cirque.'

'Well, did she date him or come on to him? I'm dying to know who he is so I can ask whether he enjoyed my hospitality.'

'I'll check around. To me it just sounded like her perpetual search for Mr. Right.'

We chatted for another ten minutes before hanging up. The talk of psychiatrists reminded me of my neighbor.

I dialed David Mitchell's number as soon as I hung up with Nina. It was our Sunday evening tradition to watch '60 Minutes' together at seven o'clock, and if neither of us had a date, to order dinner in while we watched. 'Are we on?' I asked when David picked up the phone.

'Sure. Zac and I will be over a few minutes before seven. Any other company?'

'No, Jed had to leave this morning.'

'Why don't I order in from Pig Heaven?'

'Ummm. Chinese – great idea. I'm just warning you, I'm switching channels if one of the segments is about some other guy on death row who admits killing twenty-seven people but didn't do the one he's been convicted of. I'm only watching if they profile a scientist who discovered that red meat, french fries, ice cream, and Doritos are good for your health, or some other upbeat story. See you later.'

David and Zac appeared just as the local news signed off. I liked David a great deal, but I never felt that I knew him well at all. He had that wonderful trait of a good counselor that encouraged you to tell him everything you thought and believed, but revealed nothing of his personal feelings in the process. Like my own, his professional life was all-consuming, and while I had seen him with a number of his dates from time to time, I had no idea who they were or what his social life revolved around.

Prozac, on the other hand, was the ideal neighbor. A sleek taupe dog, nicknamed Zac, she was always eager to greet me when I came home after a difficult day in the office. When our paths crossed, she would bound down the hallway and cover me with friendly licks, anxious to be petted and stroked. Occasionally, when David had out-of-town meetings to attend, I'd keep Zac with me for the weekend, taking her for long walks in the park and jogging with her at my side.

Davis did a gentle cross-examination to make sure I was really okay, while Zac assumed her usual position at my feet and rolled over on her back so I could scratch her belly till she almost purred like a feline. The food delivery arrived before the end of the hour, and we devoured our ribs, scallion pancakes, and hot, spicy chicken while I enlisted David's help for later in the week, when I was promised more information about Isabella's psychiatric history and correspondence.

When they left, I put on my *Private Dancer* disc and luxuriated in the bathtub for almost an hour. I worried about whether David was too interested in Isabella's case or simply being a good friend. He denied having met her, but I was certain I had introduced them to each other when she picked me up in our lobby one evening, more than a year ago. I told myself to stop being so paranoid and went back to planning the week ahead, actually looking forward to getting back to my desk and the office routine tomorrow.

*　　*　　*

I was so glad to see the sunshine again Monday morning that I was out of bed early, dressed and ready to go before eight, with my evening clothes packed so that I could shower and change in the ladies' room and be at the Plaza to meet Jed in time for the dinner honoring his boss, the CEO of CommPlex.

The same two policewomen were waiting in the radio car in my driveway. I greeted and thanked them, knowing they were as relieved as I was that this boring assignment would be over after the twenty-minute ride downtown. They dropped me in front of the entrance to the District Attorney's Office and I swiped my photo ID over the security scanner to let myself in and get up to my office to check Friday's mail and memos.

I turned on the computer and entered my password and user code. Once I got into the e-mail system I got caught in the unwanted personal messages that the administrative assistant had been directing the legal staff to cut out – apparently in vain. An assistant in Bureau 30 had four tickets to *Phantom* that her Aunt Lucy couldn't use for Wednesday's matinee; a colleague in Frauds had a Himalayan long-hair that was expecting kittens and she was looking for a good parent ('J.D. Degree preferred'); and a paralegal in Special Projects was desperately seeking tickets for Knicks games, not located in the end zones and no higher than twenty rows off the court.

Once those were erased, I skimmed through the in-house equivalent of help-wanted ads. Has anyone ever used a ballistics expert who can tell the effect of weather conditions on the sound of gunshots? Has anyone seen the case jacket that was inadvertently left in the courthouse coffee shop (and which, by the way, contains all of the witness interview notes that the defense shouldn't get to see till the middle of the trial)? Does anyone want to piggyback on a telephone dump that we're preparing for a rackets investigation? Has anyone ever qualified an Albanian interpreter (Gheg dialect, not Tosk) in the Grand Jury and can he or she get here on short notice? It's faster to send an urgent message through to a co-worker by Pony Express than by an e-mail system overclogged with the individual requests of six hundred lawyers and thousands of support staff users.

I moved on to messages addressed only to me. Lots of notes from friends in various bureaus offering consolation, advice, support, and free drinks (that last being a typical law enforcement solution for most traumatic events) because of Isabella's death and my connection to it. A notice that Rod was calling a bureau chiefs' meeting for Tuesday afternoon at four, so I put that in my book. Updates from Sarah on the new matters that had come in over the past few days and suggestions about witnesses who needed to be interviewed. Reminders from Laura about appointments she had scheduled for me and penciled in my calendar for the week. A note from Battaglia's assistant, Rose Malone, suggesting that I stick my head in later today to see the boss.

I got to work knocking out some correspondence on the word processor that Laura could clean up and print out for my signature when she got in. Two were disposition letters, informing victims of the pleas I had taken in both cases, resulting in lengthy prison terms and sparing the women the need to confront their rapists at trial. One was a letter confirming a request to present a lecture about date rape to the freshman class at Yale at the beginning of the next semester, and another accepted a meeting to bring Sarah with me to Mount Sinai Hospital to lecture to the ob-gyn staff on the protocol for the examination of sexual assault victims at Grand Rounds in early January. I did as much as I could before the doors opened to the general public around 9 A.M. and all of my colleagues went into high gear.

Laura was the first one to check in with me when she arrived. We caught up on what I had missed the previous Friday and she went over the day's appointments with me. I usually liked to leave some open time on Monday morning because weekends often generated a dispropor-tionate number of cases that needed emergency triage at the beginning of the week.

'I had you set for a ten o'clock with a woman whose ex-boyfriend came back to the apartment to pick up some clothes, then smacked her around and raped her,' Laura began. 'But she left a message canceling on my voice mail. Her name's Shaniqua Simmons – here's the number. Call it yourself – you'll see why she's not coming.'

'Anybody need that space?'

'Yeah. Jackie Manzi called from Special Victims. She'd like you to see a Hunter College student – case came in yesterday morning and she doesn't know whether to make an arrest. Wants you to decide and let her know.'

'Fine. Call and tell her to get her witness down as soon as possible – she can have Shaniqua's spot.'

'Rose Malone said to ignore her e-mail. Battaglia wants to take you, Rod, and Pat McKinney to lunch to brainstorm for some ideas on bringing down the arrest to arraignment time. She warned me that he also wants to see how you're functioning under all this stress.'

'Thank her for the warning.'

'Then at two you have that interview with Ellen Gold-man, the woman who's doing the profile for *USA Lawyer's Digest*.'

'I really don't have the patience to sit for that kind of thing today. I have too much to make up here.'

'Well, I doubt you'll be able to put her off much longer – she's very persistent. Plus the District Attorney thinks it's good P.R. for the office, so don't fight it.'

'Yes, ma'am.' I smiled and bowed my head in deference to Laura's sound advice. 'Anything else?'

'An avalanche of calls – some media, some friends – you can go through them yourself. And one guy kept calling all day Friday. Wouldn't leave his name or a message – says he must talk with you about Isabella and will try you again today. You want to take it?'

'Sure.'

'And Alan Glanton called already. He's opening in the Bodega rape case this morning. Judge Callahan told him he's much more likely to rule favorably on the prosecution's objections during the trial if you give Alan the same "equipment" you used so successfully in the Boynton trial. Can he stop by and pick them up before he goes to court?'

I laughed and walked over to the last filing cabinet along the wall, which held all of my personal belongings. Shoes with varying size heel heights, pantyhose in a wide variety of shades to guard against daily snags and runs, makeup and perfume for unanticipated evening invitations. And my way to Judge Callahan's heart: packages of Stick-Ups, the air freshener, deodorizers in different scents, which adhere to wood surfaces. Philip Boynton, a serial rapist I tried last spring, refused to shower from the day he was arrested till the trial. His stench was so overwhelming that none of the court officers wanted to work Callahan's part. I brought the Stick-Ups to court every day and we covered the underside of the defendant's chair and counsel table with spearmint, peppermint, and evergreen to make life bearable for the personnel. Bodegaman was in the same category so I gave Laura my secret stash to pass along to Alan.

When Laura left I sat down to return calls, and started with the message from Shaniqua Simmons. It was common for domestic abuse victims to cancel appointments after making an initial police report, but it always concerned me in case they had been threatened or revictimized because of the meeting with a prosecutor. Her phone rang twice, then kicked into an answering machine which played a recording. 'Hi, this is Shaniqua,' in her sultriest voice. 'Me and Nelson can't come to the phone right now, 'cause we got some makin' up to do.' The background music, quite appropriately, was written by the immortal Marvin Gaye, advising Shaniqua that this was the time for sex-u-al healing.

I tried to look at the bright side. It did give me an extra hour to get Manzi's victim an interview without any delay.

There was plenty of work to busy myself with until the Hunter student arrived shortly after eleven o'clock. Laura buzzed me on the intercom: 'Beverly Vaughan is here – she's the witness in Jackie Manzi's case.'

'Fine. Please start me a screening sheet and I'll be out to get her in a minute.'

Laura handed me a screening sheet, which was the printed form we used to record all the data about each case interview, including the pedigree information about the victim, which was how I usually began the conversation. I introduced myself to Ms. Vaughan and explained the process we would be going through.

'I've got a lot of questions I need to ask you, but before I begin, is there anything you want to ask me?'

'Yes, Ms. Cooper. I want to know why Steven wasn't arrested last night. The police know exactly who he is – they even talked to him last night. I want to know why he isn't in jail.'

'As I understand it, Beverly, there are some questions you weren't able to answer for Detective Manzi, some things you didn't remember about Saturday evening. You told them you "thought" you had been raped, but you weren't sure . . .'

'Well, I don't exactly remember everything that happened, but I know I was violated.'

'Steven tells a very different story than you do. And before we lock somebody up for first-degree rape you can be damn sure we're going to explore every detail of the events and try to reconstruct them. If it's clear he committed a crime, Steven will be arrested and charged.

'The best thing you can do is relax, try and answer all my questions as candidly as possible, and understand that *I* need to know every bit as much about you as Steven knows – everything that *he* will tell his lawyer about your encounter on Saturday.'

'What do you mean?'

'I mean, Beverly, that your case is different than a case where a man climbs through a window or stalks a woman from a subway station and attacks someone he's never seen before. It may be every bit as serious, but it's different.

In those situations, they're only together for as long as it takes to accomplish the rape – but the attacker doesn't know anything about his victim, she hasn't confided in him, she hasn't trusted him like someone on a date with a friend does. Understand?'

'Sure. But that doesn't mean I wasn't raped.'

'No. But it means that Steven knows a lot more about you than I know, information he can try to use against you. I can't just limit my questions to the point in the evening that you went to his room, I've got to start with what brought you together in the first place, what you told him about yourself, whether there was any foreplay during the evening, whether there was any conversation about sex. And first of all I need to know why your memory of the events is so unclear – is it because of the trauma, or is it the amount of alcohol?'

'Oh God. This isn't going to be easy, is it?'

'No, Beverly, it's not going to be easy. There's too much at stake for both you and Steven, and now is the time to get the answers – not six months from now, at a trial. I'll just begin with the background information I need – try and relax.'

I walked the young woman through the personal material the sheet called for: date of birth, permanent address, roommates, status at school, medical history, means of support. Like most of the witnesses who had preceded her in that seat, this overweight nineteen-year-old was nervous and uncomfortable, barely able to meet my eye when she responded to questions. She was a sophomore at Hunter College this fall and living in an apartment with two other students, the first time she was away from her parents' home. She explained that she didn't want them to know what happened because she was sure they would make her move back to Queens or drop out of school. I assured her that our meeting was confidential.

'Why don't you tell me how and when you first met Steven.'

'Who, me?'

'Yes, Beverly.'

She explained how she saw him at a school mixer a couple of weeks earlier, talking with a guy she knew from her sociology class, and she had gone out drinking with them after the mixer.

'What did you have to drink that first night?'

'Who, me?'

'Yeah.'

Beverly struggled to remember what combination of rum and sodas she had the first time she and Steven sat at a bar for four hours, drinking and talking about their classes, their interests, and their mutual friends. She had called him several times during the last few weeks but he had never returned the messages. He seemed to be interested in one of her roommates, and yes, Beverly admitted that she had a bit of a crush on Steven.

We finally got the events up to last Saturday night, when she ran into Steven at Zoo Bar on the Upper West Side.

'What were you drinking, Beverly?'

'Who, me?'

Three 'who, me?s' were my limit. 'We're sitting in a small room with the door closed. We're sitting face to face with each other, in two armchairs, barely a foot apart. I'm staring directly at you, and there's nobody else around. Of course I mean you.' I was beginning to lose patience with Beverly, whose resort to 'who, me?' was an effort to stall and think of whether or not to give a candid or complete answer to the particular question I was asking.

I got tough with her and she stopped wasting my time. Out poured the rest of the story in a far more direct manner. She told me that Zoo Bar is famous for serving drinks in fishbowls. One fishbowl containing an unidentifiable mixture of alcoholic beverages is served with eight straws, to be shared by a group of drinking friends. Beverly remembered splitting the first one with just her two roommates and ordering a second one, which she consumed most of by herself. She remembered flirting with Steven, while he was unsuccessfully flirting with her roommate. She remembered little else: when she left Zoo Bar, how she traveled to Steven's apartment, who else was with them, how she wound up in his bed, and how her clothes came to be on the couch in his living room. But she could assure me that she would never have slept with him – if indeed she had slept with him – had she been sober. Somewhere in that story I was supposed to find the crime.

A buzz on the intercom interrupted the meeting. 'Sorry to break in, Alex, but Chapman's on the phone.'

'I'm almost done, Laura. See where he is and tell him I'll call him right back.'

I had been working with Beverly for more than an hour and she seemed ready for a break. Her mouth was drawn taut with anxiety and her fingers tensely folded and unfolded the edges of the newspaper she had held on her lap since she walked into the room. 'This is a good start, Beverly, but it's only the first step. I'm going to have to interview everyone else who was with you at the bar, anyone who observed what you said and did, when you left, how you left. I'm going to have to talk to your roommates and to Steven's. I'll need to speak with the doctor you saw last night. I'm trying to find out why you said you "think" you were raped – after all, if *you're* not even sure, I don't know how we can be.'

'Well, I didn't plan to report this to the police, Ms. Cooper. I just went to the doctor at Student Health Services to make sure I didn't have any risk of infections or pregnancy, in case Steven had penetrated me, and she said maybe I had been raped. She's the one who called the detectives.'

Maybe? We're going to start to prosecute people for felonies on the basis of drunken conjecture and the suggestion of roommates and doctors and significant others who weren't anywhere near the scene of the 'crime'? Neither Beverly nor her doctor knew whether or not a sexual act had been consummated.

'One step at a time, Beverly. We'll look into every aspect of this very carefully. In the meantime, just keep in touch with me and if you have any questions, leave a message with Laura and I'll get back to you as soon as I can.' And I bit down on my lip to stop myself from giving politically incorrect advice about how foolish I thought she was to drink unknown quantities of unidentified substances in uncontrolled situations the way she did. Save that for another visit.

I ushered her out and picked up the slip of paper with Mike's home number on it.

'Just thought you'd like to know that Wally Flanders called. He's coming into town tomorrow 'cause he wants our help. Nice enough to admit he has no experience with homicide. He's got Burrell and Garelli agreeing to fly in

161

here to be interviewed so we can do it together. Only downside is that it keeps the FBI in this, so Luther will be here, too – we're letting Wally declare it an interstate investigation, so the feds keep a piece of the pie. Anyway, we'll do the work up at the squad. Also, LAPD got some shrinks' names from Isabella's house, so they're trying to round them up, too. See if any of them look like whackos.'

'Hey, they're shrinks, aren't they? Any of them fit our poetic "Dr. C.," the initial on the manuscript you found?'

'Nah. I asked the same thing. Usual bunch of Schwartzes, Greenbergs, Bernsteins . . . You know, Cooper, beanies – like you.'

Beanies was Mike's euphemism for yarmulkes, his slang for Jews. He was trying to get a rise out of me but it wouldn't work today. 'Any chance you can slip me in on any of the interviews?'

'Not a prayer. Battaglia made it clear to the chief, just like he did to you, that you are *not* to play Dickless Tracy – you are not an investigator on this case, you're just a witness. Don't worry, I'll tell you everything you need to know.'

Rod was waiting at Laura's desk when I got off the phone. He had waved Pat McKinney ahead to Battaglia's office, and waited to escort me there on our way to lunch. Good friend that he is, he filled me in on the District Attorney's latest plan to cut down the prearraignment time of prisoners so that I could perform adequately at the meeting. He explained the setup of the new video systems that had been installed in the precincts so that prosecutors could do the preliminary case interviews with cops by remote, saving the time of the long ride down to the Criminal Courts Building and Central Booking.

The four of us walked out of the office and around the back street to Forlini's, where we had Battaglia's regular booth. The place was packed with its regular assortment of assistant D.A.s, defense attorneys, judges, and neighborhood wise guys. If anyone was stupid enough to come in and hold the place up during any weekday lunch hour, we could organize all the personnel for a trial and jury and have a verdict without any of us leaving the dining room.

We completed our conversation about the video link by the time we had finished our meals, then Battaglia engaged me in some chatter about new cases, just checking to see if my head was on straight. We strolled out after drinking our coffee and Paul made a point of lagging behind to walk with me.

'Glad to see you're okay, Alex. Is it for real?'

'I think I'm fine, Paul. Isabella's murder doesn't seem to involve me at all, the police are in charge – as you know – and I'm back doing what I love to do. Thanks for your help—'

He cut me off – he hated to be brown-nosed and sucked up to – and went on with talk about his plan to create a new welfare fraud unit. We took his private elevator back up to the eighth floor where Rod, Pat, and I left Battaglia and returned across the corridor to the Trial Division Executive Offices.

There had been six calls while I was out to lunch. Jed rang twice, to confirm arrangements for the evening; two of my colleagues had asked for time to review new cases; Joan Stafford had called to make a dinner date for me to meet her new beau; and Friday's male caller had tried to get through twice. I should have told Chapman about the caller and about my hang-ups at home when I returned his call. Dammit. Oh well, I can tell him tonight.

13

Ellen Goldman presented herself at Laura's desk at precisely two-fifteen. I stepped out to greet her and we both started the less-than-subtle process of looking each other over to form our first impressions. I would read about hers in a very widely distributed legal journal, so I approached her with caution and some trepidation, knowing that her profile would be based on the interview, some observations in court during the week, and comments from colleagues and adversaries.

She would be hoping for my trust and openness, and perhaps some anecdote or item of personal information to scoop her competition, so I was aware that she would lay on the charm and flattery in our first encounter. I assumed she was salivating to have this chance to talk with me, set up prior to Isabella's death, in the midst of the turmoil in which I was embroiled.

I guessed that Goldman was roughly my age, perhaps a year or two younger. She was much shorter than I, with dark, curly hair and an athletic build. Her khaki suit was serviceable for a business meeting but completely lacking in style. When she introduced herself there was the vague trace of an accent which I could not place but knew I would learn about in the hours we were to spend together. We shook hands and I brought her into my office, thanking her for the flowers she had left with my doorman the preceding week when I had canceled our first appointment because of the murder.

'Let me start by describing my project, Miss Coop . . . may I call you Alex?'

'Certainly.'

'Good. Well, I'm Ellen. I'm a freelance writer, doing this piece, as you know, for *USA Lawyer's Digest*. I'm very familiar with your work – read all the pieces about you and your unit in the *Times* and all the women's magazines. I've covered a variety of issues, but I concentrate mostly on law, lawyers, business – that sort of thing. If it would help you to see the kind of stories I've done I can bring a few back tomorrow. I'm sure you've read some of them without knowing it's my byline.'

'That's not necessary. I'm sure I have seen some of them.'

It would have made more sense for me to have learned if she had an ax to grind or a point of view, but it was too late for that now and I supposed that the Public Relations Office had vetted her before granting the interview. I didn't have time this week to read puff pieces about corporate

rainmakers and their golden parachutes or women at mid-
town law firms making six times my salary but whining
about breaking the glass ceiling.

'I won't waste your time,' she went on. 'If the details
on your curriculum vitae are accurate and the articles
Laura faxed me have correct background, we won't have
to rehash that.'

I smiled in approval. She was obviously a pro, and an
intelligent one at that. It was always aggravating to sit for
a profile when the questioner spent the first hour asking
what schools I had attended, how long I had worked in
Battaglia's office, and whether I liked my job.

'Is it all right with you if we start with some information
about the Sex Crimes Prosecution Unit?'

'I'd like that,' I replied.

'Do you mind if I use a tape recorder? It's so much easier
than taking notes.'

'Not at all.' I launched into a narrative about how the
unit was set up in the mid-seventies, as our archaic laws
– based on medieval English concepts – began to change
and modernize. Although I had not even been to law
school at the time it was founded, my name was now
the one most closely associated with the work because
Battaglia had given me the scope and support to undertake
aggressive investigations into these previously unprovable
crimes. A few innovative probes which led to convictions
in high-profile cases, a gradually emerging view in the
victim-advocate community that law enforcement response
to these issues was improving, and the unit had become the
darling of the criminal justice system. We now had more
than twenty senior prosecutors handling the bizarre range
of matters that came over the transom daily, and Battaglia

had even spun off related models to handle the connected specialties of family violence and child abuse.

'It's not hard to get you talking about this work, is it, Alex? I assume that you've stayed in the office because you love what you do, not because you couldn't get a job in the private sector. I know you've had lots of offers.'

'I know that most people think this is a very grim job, Ellen, but it really isn't. My work is on the side of the angels, if you will, with the good guys. The uniformed cops who respond to all calls, the Emergency Room workers, they're the ones that have a much harder job than we do. They see the victims in much greater distress, even closer to the time of the crime than an assistant district attorney. By the time we're in the picture, even if it's the next day, the process of recovering is underway. I spend my days with the victims – I don't have to deal with the rapists much at all, and that's the way I like it. The emotional rewards of this work are enormous. Victims still don't expect it to work for them, and when it does – with more and more frequency – they're surprised and gratified. It can be very cathartic for them to confront their attackers in a courtroom, and to win. It's a great part of the recovery process.'

Maybe Goldman was just humoring me – it was too soon to tell – but she seemed genuinely interested in our unit's work. We had talked about legislative reform and the history of the movement that led to the police and prosecutorial strategies of the seventies. By four-thirty I told her that I needed to stop for the day. I was tired of talking and wanted to see a couple of the lawyers who were on trial to help them prepare for tomorrow.

She turned off her tape machine and we both stood to stretch. 'What are you changing into for tonight?' she asked, and I immediately bristled at the crossover of the questioning into my personal life. How did she know I was going out tonight? I must have glared as I turned to look back at her, but Ellen was quick to spot my reaction and put me at ease. 'I mean, I see you have a garment bag hanging on your coat rack, so I just figured you were going somewhere festive after work.'

Never snap at the interviewer, I reminded myself. I was too sensitive after the events of the last week, and it took me a second to realize that Ellen hadn't been spying on me – she'd simply made a logical assumption from a glance around the room. 'Sorry, Ellen. Yeah, I'm going to a formal dinner tonight.'

'I was just curious about what you've got in the bag – for me, not for the article. I know you've been described as a clotheshorse in some of the other interviews.'

I laughed at the description. 'I do love beautiful clothes.' I had no problem discussing designer labels that anyone with a good eye could recognize by looking at me if it diverted Ellen from details of my social life that I really didn't want to see in print.

'If I remember correctly, *Glamour* said you favored Calvin Klein, Dana Buchman, and Escada for your business wardrobe.'

She had done her homework.

'Not exactly the kind of things a girl can shop for on a public servant's salary, but then I've also read about your family background, too.'

Time to turn the tables for a minute and see how she liked getting personal. 'Well, since you know so much about me, Ellen, when do you start to tell me a bit about yourself?'

'What is it you'd like to know? I'm a sabra, Alex.

Israeli-born, to an Israeli mother and an American father. My father was West Point – a missile expert. He met my mother when he was working on a United Nations project in the Middle East. I grew up like an Army brat, on bases around the world, but did my high school and college, as well as my military service, in Israel. But I've always been fascinated by the States, so I spend a lot of time here, even though my family is all abroad.'

'That's an interesting background.'

'People's lives always seem more interesting to those who didn't live them. It wasn't a very stable upbringing, Alex. The constant moves throughout my childhood, never staying in one place long enough to develop relationships that outlasted the posting. In and out of new schools, having to prove each time that you were capable of doing well. And a father in the service. Let me tell you, no matter how brilliant I knew he was, it's not a profession that enjoys great respect in this country. I suppose some of that is why I spend so much time examining the lives of successful people, to see what makes them achievers – and to see whether that brings happiness.'

I had no glib response. I thought to myself that my only comment had been, 'That's interesting.' I didn't intend to unleash Ellen Goldman's inner torment, but now I knew more than I needed to know. Maybe it was just easier to go back to the benign inquiry she had made.

'Well, to answer your original question, Ellen, the dress in the bag is a very elegant navy blue Calvin Klein sheath. It should do just fine at what I imagine will be a boring testimonial dinner to a boring gentleman I barely know.'

'Someone in your business?'

'No, actually, the boss of a friend of mine. Anyway, if

we're going to continue this interview tomorrow, why don't you just meet me across the street in Part 53, Judge Hadleigh's courtroom. I have a sentence there in the morning which you might want to see. Then we can come back here and go on with what you need, okay?'

'That's fine. Alex, before I leave, I wouldn't be a good journalist if I didn't ask about Isabella Lascar and her murder. Are there any leads yet, anything you can tell me about?'

I caught myself again. Goldman had resisted asking the question for more than two hours – better than I would have guessed – and I almost had her out the door. 'Nothing at all, Ellen. Keep in mind, I'm not working on the case.' And you must really think I'm an idiot, I thought to myself, if you think I would tell some stranger I just met about suspects in a murder investigation. Well, these are the professionals who hold a camera in front of a hysterical woman's face and ask how it felt to have watched a grizzly bear eat her three children while camping in Yosemite. It's a job.

Ellen left and I dialed Jed's number.

'Shall I have a car pick you up at the apartment?'

'No. I knew I couldn't get out early. I've got all my things here, so I'll shower and change and meet you at the Plaza.'

'Well, please try and get there in time for some of the cocktail hour. Anderson's anxious to see you, and we'll never get a chance to talk to him once we're all seated and the banquet begins.'

Anderson Warmack was Jed's boss and the dinner tonight was in his honor. 'This must be something new. He blew me off at the summer picnic – didn't seem too anxious to meet anyone except the bartender and the twenty-year-old bimbo who was with his son that afternoon at the club.'

'Sweetheart, he didn't know who you were then. Now he's heard all about you. He was a huge fan of Isabella's, and once he found out you were her friend and that we had actually taken her to dinner one night, he's got a million things to ask you.'

'You're not serious, Jed. How could you?'

'What?'

'How could you trade on the gossip of that girl's death?' I was aggravated and angry. It seemed so unlike Jed to use Isabella to get to Warmack.

'Oh, c'mon, Alex. You must be aware that everyone is talking about it. Things like this don't happen every day and people are interested in it, especially when it intersects with the lives of people they actually know.'

I was silent at the end of the telephone line. Thanks a lot for your concern for the deceased, Mr. Warmack, it's heartwarming.

'I mean, there are fascinating things, like the DNA you were talking about. Do they have results on that yet?'

'Jed, I hope to God you haven't been talking about evidence to anyone!' I was livid. 'I told you about things because they happened in *my* house, behind *my* back, and I thought you'd care about that. I never expected that you'd tell other people – I don't intend to lose my job because you use—'

Jed interrupted me. 'Calm down, Alex, calm down. I haven't told Anderson or anyone else what you've told me. I just meant that as an example of an interesting fact people don't know much about.'

'Well, let's keep it that way. DNA takes six weeks, eight weeks, sometimes longer to develop,' I said, trying to mollify Jed with technical data. 'If the case isn't solved by then, I'll really be out of my mind.'

'I didn't mean to upset you, Alex. I'm trying to keep Anderson happy.' The rumors had been circulating for weeks that Warmack would step down by the end of the year, and that Jed had a great shot at being picked to succeed him. 'Sorry I was so casual about Isabella – I didn't know the old guy was such a fan, and I guess I'm trying too hard to please him these days. I never should have mentioned I had met her with you.'

'And I'll never get out of here if we don't get off the phone so I can finish up at my desk. Kisses.' Truce. I pursed my lips and smooched into the phone line.

I buzzed Laura and asked her to tell the two assistants who wanted to see me to bring up their case files so we could go over their problems. She gave me all the messages she had been holding during the Goldman interview, and told me she'd be gone by the time I got underway with the next meeting.

'Mercer Wallace called, too. No need to call him back. Just said to tell you they're overdue for some noise from the Con Ed rapist – there's a full moon this week so maybe the squad'll get lucky – you'd know what he means.'

I knew exactly what he meant. As folk literature and old wives' tales had reported for centuries, the full moon seemed to bring out with it all forms of madness and lunacy. There's not a cop in the city who didn't believe that unusual happenings and strange phenomena accompanied the glorious sight of an iridescent full moon. Wallace was hoping the inexorable draw of the tide would bring out his serial rapist and lead to the demon's capture.

Thinking of Isabella's stalker, with any luck, I hoped for twofers.

It was almost six-thirty when I said good night to my two young colleagues and took my dress bag and makeup kit into the ladies' room. The ugly taupe tile and institutional decor was even more depressing than the rest of the drab office space. I undressed, stepped into the shower stall, and washed quickly, always amused by the irony that there were no locks on the bathroom doors and that the building cleaning crews who serviced the rooms at night were all ex-cons prosecuted by my colleagues, out on work release and employed by Wildcat – the company which attempted to rehabilitate serious offenders.

I toweled off, twisted my hair into a French braid, slipped into the slim sheath and traded my mid-heel work shoes for a spiky silk pump. There was room in my tiny Judith Leiber minaudière for my blue and gold shield – always a hit with corporate types – my beeper, a lipstick case, and a linen handkerchief, but not for much else. My Schlumberger wing earrings were the only jewelry I put on. A few spritzes of Chanel and I was ready to walk back to my office and call for a car service.

The long corridors on the eighth floor were quiet and empty at this hour, with most of the worker bees toiling through the evening on the flights below the executive wing. I was conscious of the clicking noise my high heels made as they echoed in the hallway while I strode toward my office, thinking about the position I planned to take at the sentence hearing before Hadleigh the next morning.

I turned the corner and continued past Laura's desk into my office, where I stopped short in the doorway at the sight of a stranger, a man I had never seen before, standing in front of the bookcase against the far wall.

14

My heartbeat was racing as we spoke over each other's voices. I demanded to know who he was and how he had gotten in past the security desk while he blurted out his apology for appearing unannounced and explained that his name was Richard Burrell and he needed to talk to me about Isabella Lascar.

'I called all day Friday and several times today and was never able to get through to—'

'Well, if you thought just breaking into the District Attorney's Office was the answer,' I started to say as I backed out to Laura's phone to call the lobby security guard, 'you've made an enormous mistake.'

'No, please, Miss Cooper. I'm – I'm Isabella's ex-husband. I really need your help on this and I just didn't know

176

where else to find you or whether your calls were being taped.'

Burrell – if he really was Richard Burrell – looked harmless enough in this setting. My mind tried to quickly filter all the stories I had heard from Iz about him, and as I had told Luther last Friday, none of them suggested violence or danger. Yet here I was alone in my office after hours in a practically deserted building with a man who was certainly on the short list of murder suspects. Not very smart.

'How did you get in here?'

'To be honest with you, Miss Cooper, I lied to the guard. I told him we had a dinner appointment together and he let me right up. Sorry to do that.'

Did he realize how stupid I thought that was? Here he was coming to me for help about some aspect of this case, and the first thing he did was lie to get in to see me. At least I was on notice about his credibility.

'May we close the door and talk?'

'No. Absolutely not. The door stays open and you have five minutes to tell me what this is all about.'

'Look, Miss Cooper, I'm scared, terrified. I've come into Manhattan voluntarily because the police want to talk to me. They obviously think I had something to do with Isabella's death, but I swear it isn't true. They know that I saw her in Boston the weekend before she was killed, that I wanted to reconcile with her. They think I might have killed her because she rejected me again, but that's absurd. Iz trusted you completely – I need you to help convince the police I had nothing to do with the murder, please.'

'Mr. Burrell, this is very inappropriate. Just because I had a relationship with Isabella doesn't mean I can vouch for you or anyone else she knew. It's quite the opposite. Either you tell your version to the detectives and rely on their ability to check out your story, or you get yourself the best damn defense attorney in town and get some professional advice. That's already more help than a prosecutor should give you.'

'But there are things the police probably don't know yet that won't help me, and I'm sure they'll find out.'

'Like your cocaine problem? They're well aware of it.'

'No, that's not what I mean. I don't have a coke problem anymore. That's why I left Los Angeles, Miss Cooper. That's all behind me. I've just completed a new screenplay and I'm ready to try to re-establish myself in the business. Being implicated in a homicide will kill every opportunity I have.'

Not to mention what it did to every opportunity Isabella had . . . but he neglected to mention that.

Now I was curious about what was a more current dilemma for Burrell. 'What sort of thing are you afraid the police will misinterpret?'

'Guns, for one thing. I've got guns.'

'What for? Like pistols, for protection?'

'No, like high-powered hunting rifles. I never had a gun when I was in Hollywood. I always had gophers to handle my drug transactions. I never carried. But I moved to Maine when I detoxed – it was easier for me to stay dry in a new environment. Now I live on one of those primitive little islands off the coast – no highways, no airports, no police department. Just beautiful vistas and lots of wild animals. The island is crawling with moose and deer and woodchucks and skunks. I started hunting with the guys who live around me – not for sport, but when the animals got destructive or like the time a rabid woodchuck attacked my golden retriever. Anyone up there will tell you that I can draw a bead on a four-legged creature and hit it between the eyes like a trained sharpshooter.'

I shuddered at the tone of pride in his voice as he described the strike, since it jolted me abruptly back to the neon-taped crime scene that marked Isabella's execution.

Chapman, Flanders, and Waldron would certainly be interested in this piece of information. Maybe Burrell would be stupid enough to give me more. Or was he playing *me* for the fool, so he could defuse this kind of fact by getting it on the table – through me – before his police interview later in the week.

'Everyone involved with Isabella seems to know something about guns. That hardly makes you a prime suspect, Mr. Burrell.'

'Miss Cooper. I'm telling you this because I'm sure Iz mentioned to you when she got to your house that she had just seen me in Boston. I realize you must be aware of what went on between us, and I need to know what you've told the police about it, do you understand? I don't plan to hide anything, I'd just like to walk into that interview with an idea of how much they know about me.'

He had made the mistaken assumption that Isabella had called me with confidences about her Boston rendezvous with Burrell when she arrived on the Vineyard. My lie of omission was simply to let him believe that, and my larger deceit was to bluff him about what I had learned in the conversation we never had. From the cast he put on the revelation, it was easy to infer that their encounter had not gone well.

'I do know how much the weekend upset her. She was quite unhappy about it,' I baited him. 'Maybe angry is a better word.'

'You have to understand my frustration, Miss Cooper. I adored Isabella, I worshiped her from the first moment I met her. I helped create the Isabella Lascar the world fell in love with on the screen.'

Here we go, another Pygmalion story. Another man behind the woman, responsible for her success. You're losing me now, Burrell.

'We were fabulous together, before anyone knew who Isabella was capable of becoming. Then I screwed it up, all my own fault. My addiction destroyed everything in my life, personally and professionally. But I've got it all together again, I can assure you. I've written a great property, something that would have been perfect for Isabella. She wanted to meet with me, to read it, to talk about it. For me, it was my foot in the door to ask her to take me back. The movie was secondary – I wanted to be her husband again, I wanted her to let me love her.'

As far as I could tell about Lascar's love life, it would be like standing on line at a bakery the night before Thanksgiving to buy a couple of pies. Take a number.

'Bottom line, Mr. Burrell? She told me it didn't fly.'

'Bottom line, as you say, Miss Cooper. I realize I'm running over the five minutes you gave me, but you see the urgency of all this, I'm sure. Isabella wanted a script but had no use for me, other than as a friendly old shoulder to lean on.'

'So the two of you fought.'

'I don't think either one of us meant to, really. But she got sloppy – the combination of vodka followed by too

180

much red wine – and all the while I was sober. And as you know, she could have a pretty cruel tongue when she was liquored up, and I didn't have the benefit of any alcoholic anesthesia to ease her blows.'

'Yes, I've heard her barbs, Mr. Burrell. They could be very painful, I'm sure. Is that why you put your hands on her? She'd always described you as such a gentle person.'

It worked. 'Iz was getting so loud, Miss Cooper. I had images of people in adjacent rooms calling the front desk and someone generating publicity about her drinking or her temper. I didn't hit her, you know, she didn't tell you that, did she?'

'No, no she didn't.'

'I just grabbed her by the shoulders and tried to shake her a bit. Merely to quiet her down and bring her to her senses. That only made her angrier and raised her volume a pitch or two. Her glass fell to the floor and splintered. She screamed some more insults, called me some names, went into the bathroom, and locked herself in. I waited awhile. When she refused to come out, I eventually went back to my room.

'I was afraid you'd consider that some kind of domestic violence, you know? Especially if housekeeping reported the broken glass and guests complained about the scream-ing. Maybe I'm just being paranoid, Miss Cooper. Anyone who knows the two of us knows that all I ever wanted was to be together with Isabella again. I could never have hurt her.'

Haven't I seen this scene in a thousand B-movies?

'Did you see her again, after that argument?'

'No, no. I wanted to, I really did. But I gave her the night to sober up, and when I called her room in the morning she had already checked out. I knew she was going to your place on the Vineyard. I didn't know where your house was and, quite frankly, I didn't even know your name. Iz talked about you a lot, but just by your first name – I never paid close attention, then I saw your name in all the newspaper articles, of course. It never occurred to me that she was taking someone to the island with her. She let me think she was going to the Vineyard alone.'

Me too, pal. 'Did you hear from her after that?'

'No, that's what I mean. I hung around for most of that day, then just drove myself back up the coast to home. It's not a very helpful alibi, Miss Cooper. Eastport Harbor's a pretty lonely place, and there aren't any neighbors or deliverymen or camera crews to record my comings and goings.'

'Mr. Burrell, those things you've told me aren't much to worry about. There'll be hotel check-out records and garage receipts and a mini-paper trail to back you up, I'm sure.' He seemed much too frantic and concerned for the amount of information he had given me. 'Is that really all?'

'I swear to you, Miss Cooper, I swear on Isabella's life . . .'

That oath had a rather empty ring to it.

'You've got to tell these things to the detectives, and you've got to do it yourself.' I didn't want to be alone with this man a minute longer than I had to. 'There's no use pleading your case to me. I can't help you with more than an introduction to the police, please believe me.'

He looked desperate, not evil, but my instincts had been wrong on more than one occasion and I was not in a good position to figure this one out tonight.

'Where are you staying in town?'

'The Peninsula.'

'Go back to your hotel. You'll get a call from a detective named Chapman in the morning. Just tell him everything you've told me.' Only Mike will be able to play hardball with this guy and maybe we'll be on our way to a confession.

Burrell tried to thank me as he slouched out of the office and I noticed my hand was still trembling as I reached for the telephone to call for a cab.

As the cab crawled up Center Street, which became Fourth Avenue, which became Park Avenue, I tried to think whether there had been anything memorable about the evening Jed and I had taken Isabella to dinner. It had been just before the Labor Day weekend, which Jed was going to spend in California with his kids. We had planned to meet for dinner on Friday evening, and as I was dressing at my apartment, Iz called from her hotel room. She was cheerful and pleasant – the second stalker hadn't started to call or write yet – and she only wanted the name of my hair colorist for a touch-up while she was in town.

'Is this Elsa discreet, darling? The fans like to think I'm all natural,' she laughed into the telephone.

'She's a dream, Isabella. I'm sure she'll do it in your hotel room, if you'd like.'

'Marvelous, I'll ask her. Is the D.A. a little house-mouse, tonight, Alex. No crime? No romance? None of those handsome detectives to drive you all over town?'

'Actually, I'm on my way out to dinner with a man I've been dating. You're very welcome to join us.'

'Ah, this must be the rich one that Nina's told me about. Would I be in the way? I don't eat much.'

183

'We'd love it, Iz. Let's surprise him, okay? I'll pick you up at eight and we'll meet him at the restaurant.' I knew Jed would get a kick out of meeting Isabella – what man wouldn't? – so I called '21' and changed Mr. Segal's reservation from two people to three.

Jed was seated in the middle of the front room when the two of us arrived. The puzzled look on his face changed to delight when he 'made' Isabella vamping toward his table. He was a regular at the club, but his stock soared that night as the captain and waiters watched the glamorous movie star sweep over and embrace him with a loud, 'Jed, darling, it's been far too long.'

It was an easy mix. The good Isabella was performing – funny and charming and eager to be liked. She was the center of attention in the room, and she enjoyed that.

Jed had spent most of his life in California, so the two of them knew some of the same people and all of the same places. The law firm he had started out with in Los Angeles had done a lot of work in the entertainment field. He left it to move to Washington for a special securities commission, then returned to the West Coast to make his unsuccessful run for the Senate from California.

'A Democrat, no doubt? Alex would only get in bed with a Democrat, I'm sure. I'm strictly a Republican, Jed, although I must say if I had noticed your face staring down at me from a campaign billboard, I might have pulled your lever.'

Iz loved to flirt and reveled in making sophomoric comments about sex. I can't say she was all talk and no action – if one believed her stories, then intercourse was to her what aerobics classes were to my working friends.

'What's CommPlex, Jed?' she asked in her most sincere

voice, but zoned out of the conversation and back into her Stoli as Jed proceeded to give a detailed explanation of the giant communications and computer operation that Anderson Warmack had built from his home office into a Fortune 500 corporation over the last fifteen years.

We had almost gotten through the meal without Isabella asking for a favor – a rare stretch of time for me – when something Jed said about money and business ventures seemed to spark her memory. She told us that she thought her business manager had been stealing from her investments, pilfering increasingly substantial sums of money from deals he set up, but she didn't know how to hire someone to look over his shoulder to confirm her suspicions. Jed asked the captain for a piece of paper and gave Isabella the name and number of his accountant in Los Angeles, assuring her that his man would be able to refer her to the right person to check her records for a scam.

'He's a good man, Isabella. And extremely trustworthy – he runs all Anderson Warmack's personal finances.'

'And how many millions might that involve?'

'Three hundred, maybe three-fifty. That's if the market had an average day today, Isabella. Even more if it was strong.'

Isabella was grinning now, licking her chops for effect. 'And is he cute, this Anderson fellow?'

'Well, did you think Charles Laughton was cute?' I asked her. 'Like in the last three or four movies he made? We're talking rich, old, fat, and usually intoxicated.'

'One out of four isn't bad – especially if it's my favorite one. Rich. Now that you two are so happy together, Jed will just have to introduce me to Anderson Warmack. I insist on it.'

Isabella and I left the table to go the ladies' room, like two girls at a high school prom, while Jed signed the tab – '21' had the best steak tartare, the best Dungeness crabs, and the most wonderful ladies' room attendant in New York. She was smart and lively, and instead of sitting sullenly in a corner with a stack of paper towels, Marie was always reading. Current fiction – mostly mysteries – usually with a library dust jacket, and she was always eager to give me her opinion of the writer.

'Hey, dear, how are you? Haven't seen you in weeks. Put anybody away lately?' she giggled.

I introduced her to Isabella, who rudely blew her off and wanted only to gossip about Jed.

'Darling, hang onto this one. Handsome, smart, rich – I'm not kidding, I really want to meet his boss.'

'The old guy does have a wife, Isabella.'

'Really, Alex. I didn't say I wanted to marry the old coot, did I? I might just want to play with him for a while, see where he likes to spend his millions.'

'Good night, Marie,' I said, tripling my usual tip out of guilt and annoyance over Isabella's display of vulgarity.

Jed's car was waiting in front of the restaurant so we dropped Iz at the Carlyle, then went on to my apartment together. We both agreed that once a year might be often enough for an evening like that, and put thoughts of La Lascar behind us as we undressed and made love to each other with great enthusiasm after ten days of separation.

Now, as the cab squared Grand Army Plaza and dropped me at the front steps of the Plaza Hotel, I wondered whether Jed had told Warmack about Isabella's short-lived expression of interest in him . . . and whether I should suggest to Mike Chapman that her business manager be added to the list of suspects.

I realized that I was arriving almost an hour later than I had promised Jed, because of Burrell's unannounced visit and the crush of traffic on the streets uptown. Cocktail hour was long over and I was grateful for my thin build as I wiggled and squeezed my way through the Grand Ballroom between two hundred round tables packed to the gills with CommPlex sycophants and rival business leaders, surrounded by surly waiters trying to serve platters of rubber chicken to the noisy crowd.

The program I had picked up at the entrance listed our names at Table 2. I could spot the top of Jed's head as I plowed halfway through the room, waved to the mayor, who was working the tables near the podium, and stopped for a kiss from one of Jed's partners as I neared my empty seat.

'Sorry, Jed, the usual complications and excuses,' I whispered to him as he rose to introduce me to the rest of the men and women at the table. Anderson Warmack grinned down at me from the dais on the stage, and it seemed that I owed Richard Burrell a small 'thank you' for the timing that had made it possible for me to avoid any discussion of the late Lascar with the fat tycoon.

Jed was in a good mood, despite my failure to show up for the reception. 'Warmack came into my office at the end of the day,' he explained, *sotto voce*. 'He's not ready to make any public announcement tonight, but he's going to issue a press release right after the Christmas holidays, and I'll probably be named to the presidency of the company by February. I'm going to plan a wonderful trip for us over

New Year's, to celebrate – it may be my last vacation for a year.'

I was thrilled for Jed, knowing how much he had wanted all this to fall into place and how hard he had been working for Warmack's approval. I squeezed his thigh under the table as he tried to run his hand under my tight sheath and pinch me, winking at me with an enormous grin on his face.

'You're not going to make me wait till New Year's to celebrate, are you?' I teased. 'Can't we start sooner?'

'Of course, darling. We can get a room here tonight and go right upstairs after the speeches and . . .'

'Whoops, maybe tomorrow. That's a wonderful offer, but I've got to leave after the testimonials, Jed. Chapman's meeting me with some evidence that just came in from Massachusetts so I can look at it tonight.'

'Evidence? What kind of evidence? I thought there was no other evidence.'

I laughed at Jed's concern. 'I'm not making that mistake again. My lips are sealed. It's just a long shot, some things I want to look at, in case they contain any leads.'

'Will you come back and meet me later for a nightcap? Larry, Stan, and I are taking Anderson over to the Tap Room at the University Club for a more intimate toast when this is over.'

'Are you crazy? I've got a sentence first thing tomorrow morning. You take care of what you've got to do – you should be very happy with the news you got today. And don't make any plans for the weekend – the celebration will be *my* surprise, okay?'

The speeches went on interminably, and I was relieved that Warmack had finished his remarks before I checked my watch, rose, and said my good nights, and kissed Jed good-bye. It was a little after ten-thirty when I went out of the hotel through the revolving doors and let the doorman help me into a yellow cab for the short ride home.

15

Mike's car was parked at the end of the circular driveway when my cab pulled in and dropped me at the apartment. He was standing in the lobby with the two doormen, critiquing whatever sports event had been on the tube that evening.

'Whoa, blondie, bet you ten on the Final Jeopardy question tonight – you didn't catch it, didya?'

'Hardly.'

'Category was African history. Wanna bet?'

Damn. Not one of my strengths. 'Did you get it right?'

'Yeah. You chicken?'

'All right, ten dollars.'

We were in the elevator on the way up to my floor. 'The Final Jeopardy answer is: Napoleon defeated them at the Battle of the Pyramids in 1798.'

I shook my head. 'Just deduct the ten from whatever you owe me.' I didn't have the faintest idea.

Mike gloated: 'Who are the Mamelukes? I knew you wouldn't know that. I should have doubled my bet.' He proceeded to give me a thumbnail version of the battle, which was apparently fought nowhere near the great pyramids, and explain who the Mamelukes were and where they came from. He was a whiz at both world history and military battles, and delighted in showing it off.

'I hope I do better with Wally's photos,' I said, as I turned my keys in the locks.

'Not much to see.'

'Do me a favor and put up the coffee. I'm just going to get out of this dress, okay?'

It only took me a minute to change from the silk dress into my long shirt and leggings. I hurried back to the kitchen to get out mugs for the coffee that Mike had already scooped into the coffeemaker, then we both went into the living room to look at the blowups he had picked up from the lab when he came on duty half an hour earlier.

'Who took the photos?' I asked as Mike untied the brown Homicide folder in which he carried his case file.

'Wally says tourists are calling in from all over. But most of these first shots are from islanders. You'll see in a minute when you start to look at them – almost all of the ones I have with me tonight were taken on the ferry on different trips throughout the week. The story and appeal for the film was on the radio as well as in Friday's *Vineyard Gazette*, and locals started showing up at Wally's office on Saturday morning with rolls of film, claiming they thought they saw Isabella on the boat ride. He thinks some high school kid with a serious case of acne and a hard-on for Isabella actually made her on the ferry and was trying to get pictures of her along the way. Wally figures that's why most of the time she's got her back to the camera and she's looking out at the water.'

Mike stacked the pile of photographs on the table, and I sat next to him on the sofa as we scrutinized them one by one.

There were a few false starts – photos of the vista with a blonde on the edge of the pack, but if you looked closely at the eleven-by-fourteen enlargements, you could tell that the bad legs or the wide beams were not those of Isabella Lascar.

When we got to the fifth picture, Mike looked down to remind himself, 'I think this starts the roll taken by the high school kid. Doesn't that look like Isabella in the corner?'

No doubt about it. It was like looking at a roundup of hundreds of horses going to the glue factory and spotting a thoroughbred in the mix. Her long lines and elegant bearing made her a standout in the crowd, even though the camera range was too distant to catch the distinctive features that took your breath away when she was illuminated on a giant movie screen.

'That's Iz in the far left corner. Makes you guess that the photographer hadn't spotted her yet – she's just part of the background at the moment.'

The next three photos were also panoramic views of the sail back to the island, like the kid's soccer coach had told the whole team on their way home from the game in Hyannis that they each had to shoot a roll of film before the boat docked. Mike walked to the kitchen to bring us both a cup of hot coffee.

'Should be coming up on some one-on-ones.'

Sure enough, the next few photos looked like the high school inquiring photographer had figured out who the great-looking woman was, and perhaps had even approached her with the camera. Isabella seemed to be turning away from his lens, shielding her face – already half-hidden behind oversized tortoise-shell sunglasses – with one raised arm and grabbing the railing to her far side with the other.

The cameraman kept a respectable distance, but the next frames were all focused on Isabella, even though she had turned her back to her earnest admirer. I could recognize the outfit she was wearing – a turquoise-and-white-striped Escada sweater with white walking shorts, and those unmistakable racehorse legs extending forever above platform espadrilles that tied at the ankles.

'You get to the guy yet?' Mike stood across from me, sipping his brew while I let mine cool to a drinkable temperature. 'I figure I can do an APB' – all-points bulletin – 'for a reward and information leading to the identification of the man attached to the five fingers you can see in the photo. Right?'

I laughed when I came to the shot he was referring to. The movie star was still showing her back to the camera – mind you, her good side in semi-profile to her pursuer, as though she was saying. 'If you insist on doing this, you might as well have the angle I prefer.' But now, for the first time, a man's arm was stretched out across Isabella's back and appeared to be waving at the photographer to stop shooting.

'See what I mean?' Mike joked. 'Do a sketch of a giant hand and hang it in post offices all over the country. You'll have nuts calling in from Alaska to Mississippi before the ink is dry: "Detective Chapman, I'd know that hand anywhere." "Chief Flanders, my dog once bit a hand that looked a lot like that hand." "Agent Waldron, I've shaken a hand that reminds me very much of that hand." We'll break this wide open in no time.'

Mike babbled on but I was fixated on the photo that stared up at me from the coffee table. My focus was not Isabella, nor was it the man's hand that showed itself for the first time. My thoughts were tripping over each other as they competed for my full attention.

'Oh my God.'

Mike ignored me the first time, or perhaps my mutterings started under my breath and were inaudible to anyone except me. In my brain they were pounding louder than thunder.

'Oh my God. It's not possible.'

'What?'

'Paul Stuart,' I managed to say out loud.

'Who's that? Are you telling me you know—'

'It's not a who,' I interrupted him, 'it's a what.' My stomach rolled with nausea as my thought processes reached my gut before I could even articulate what I was thinking. 'Paul Stuart is one of the best men's stores in New York, Mike. Madison Avenue and Forty-fifth Street,' I rambled on. The pale blue-and-green plaid of the shirt that covered the man's arm in the photograph – Isabella's protector – screamed at me from the detail of the photograph which sat before me. 'I bought that fucking shirt at Paul Stuart the week before Labor Day. Sea Island cotton, a hundred and forty-seven fucking dollars. Call off your APB, Detective Chapman, that rotten, lowlife piece of human excrement standing next to the screen goddess on her way to my home is Jed Segal.'

I picked up the photograph and winged it at full force across the room like a Frisbee, so that it ricocheted off my huge armoire and came to rest under the sideboard that held my favorite assortment of silver-framed snapshots of family and friends. Then I sank back into the deep pillows of my oversized sofa to wallow in the revelation that Jed and Isabella had betrayed me in the most profound way two humans could torment a third.

'Jesus, Alex, calm down a minute. You can't tell from one of these pictures who this guy is,' Mike said as he went to retrieve the telltale photograph and study it again. 'That store must have sold dozens of shirts like that one, and stores all over the country sold hundreds more. There's no way you can say who that arm belongs to on the basis of an inch of plaid material in a blown-up photograph. Don't start with the self-pitying martyr bullshit – you can't jump to any con—'

'Maybe you're too fucking stupid to make conclusions at this point, Mikey, but don't bet the farm against me on pieces of fabric and clothing. That's like you and the Mamelukes. I have been stabbed in the back – no, in the heart – by that miserable bastard. It's not just the shirt, it's everything else that's falling into place.'

'Please don't start crying on me again tonight, Cooper. Let's look at this very care—'

I interrupted him again, amazed he couldn't see that there should have been smoke coming out of my ears by this point. 'Cry? Cry?' I was practically shrieking at him now. 'Do you actually think I'm going to waste any more of my very short supply of emotion on that man? You must really have a very low opinion of me after all this time. Don't worry, no more tears.' I stood up and reached across the table to grab the picture out of Mike's hand.

The section of the photo containing the man's hand and sleeved-arm represented about three inches of surface in the enlargement. I looked at it again, hoping that the distinctive fabric I had found so attractive the day I had gone shopping had changed to stripes or polka dots or pink elephants. Instead, the second glance confirmed all my fears. I lowered myself back onto the sofa as I inspected Jed's fingers on the film – fingers that had caressed my breasts, stroked my thighs, and knew exactly how to make me respond excitedly to their pressure and touch.

'It's not just the shirt, Mike.' I didn't have to tell him out loud about Jed's fingers. He would know what I meant just as well as I did. 'Take this away from me before I tear it in shreds,' I said, handing the painful image back to Mike. 'I could kick myself for missing all the little clues. You should have seen the way his mouth dropped open when he got off the elevator on Saturday and saw me standing here wearing those silk pajamas Iz had given me – you know, like the pair we saw in my bedroom when we packed up her stuff? He must have thought he was seeing a ghost.' Of course, the one thing Isabella wanted that I had provided for her: a respectable man. 'I could kill him with my bare hands.'

I was out of control and Mike didn't know how to bring me back. 'Calm down, Alex. You'll wake the neighbors.' A light seemed to go off in his head when he said the word 'neighbors.' 'Hey, you think maybe your shrink friend is still awake at this hour? Maybe he could come in and help—'

'Help what? There's nothing wrong with me. I'm just angry and pissed off and mad and miserable and—'

'And maybe he should like tranquilize you or something. I don't know. I don't want you to hurt yourself over this. I can't leave here with you in this condition.'

'Leave David out of this. There's nothing wrong with me. No wonder I couldn't reach Jed at the Ritz the first time I called there on Thursday. He probably hadn't even gotten to Paris yet – of course he couldn't get back here till Saturday. That whole trip must have been just a sham to cover his rendezvous with Isabella.' I stood up and started pacing around the living room to calm myself down. Mike and most of my other colleagues had seen the Cooper temper in a flare-up, and most tried to avoid it. It finally occurred to me to move toward the bar and fix myself a drink.

'Not a prayer, blondie. No drinking. C'mon, let's deal with this rationally. I should have known, too. Anybody who drank bottled water with fried clams had to be a yuppie – and an asshole. What a fucking phony.'

'Oh, jeez, Mike. Worse thought. Do you think I should phone Battaglia and wake him up at this hour? He hates to be the last to know. Oh, I think I'm going to be sick – no kidding.' I sat in one of the armchairs and doubled over with my head pounding against my hands.

'That's your call, Alex. You have to answer to him, I don't. I suppose if you get to the office at the crack of dawn and tell him then – nobody's gonna find out before that. I mean, I think the chief has to know tonight, but—'

I snapped my head up to protest that idea. 'Why does the chief have to know anything about this? Suddenly my aborted love life is going to be fodder for the department? No way, Mike, no way. No way.'

Chapman squatted down directly in front of me, put his hand on my knee, and tried to force me to look him directly in the eye. 'You don't get it yet, kid, do you? If that sleeve really does belong to Jed Segal – and that's the very first thing we have to find out for sure – then this is not just about someone cheating on you with one of your friends. If you're right about Jed, then we've got to look at him as a suspect in Isabella's murder.'

My head started shaking back and forth slowly in disagreement with what Mike had just announced. I hadn't thought of that at all, as busy as my mind was with its own unhappiness, but I could not accept or absorb that concept when it emerged from his lips.

'That's ridiculous, Mike. That's – that's not possible,' I stammered as I tried to reason why someone who was capable of such deceit and who lied so facilely and convincingly could not have carried out the cold-blooded murder of his consort.

'Better face it. Jed Segal goes to the head of the class. He has some very serious explaining to do before he gets cleared from the list of possibles. If he was the guy sharing the clams with Isabella an hour before she was killed, he's got the access and the opportunity and—'

'But no motive, Mike, he's got absolutely no motive to kill her. She's the goose with the golden egg, for Chrissakes. The guy is making love to a gorgeous, world-famous movie idol – it ain't getting better than that for Jed Segal – what the hell would he kill her for?' I almost gagged on the expression 'making love.' Clearly, those had been Jed's condoms in my wastebasket. No wonder he was so concerned when I said we could do DNA testing to find out who Iz's lover had been.

'No motive? Ha, that's more bullshit. Suppose she threatened to tell you about their tryst? Suppose she told him he wasn't as good in the sack as Johnny Garelli? Suppose she pissed him off like she did almost everyone else I've spoken with who was in her presence for more than ten minutes?'

I rocked back and forth in my chair, my arms crossed over my stomach as though they could quell the sickening waves that rippled underneath their grip.

'I can't handle this, Mike, I really can't handle this.'

'Sure you can, Coop. We'll get you through it. What do you think you're doing now?' Mike asked as I brushed past him and headed for the door to my coat closet. I reached in for my trenchcoat and threw it on over my outfit, grabbing my keys, some cash, and moving toward the apartment door.

'Take those photos out of here with you when you finish your coffee and leave. I'm doing this one face to face. I know exactly where to find this lying piece of shit and I'm going to be the first one to accuse him of murder. It'll be a pleasure.'

'Your old man is right about one thing, blondie – this job really has trashed your vocabulary. Where're we going? It's after midnight.'

'Uh, uh, Mikey, I'm alone. I'll grab a taxi. Point of honor. I can't wait till tomorrow to look this guy in the eye and tell him all the things I want to say.'

Mike had a grip on my arm, holding me inside the apartment. 'I'll handcuff you to this closet door and leave you here unless you tell me where Segal is and let me go with you. At worst, he's a killer and he's dangerous – and at best, *you're* a killer and I gotta protect him. C'mon, be reasonable. You need me there as a witness, if nothing else. Don't do this, Alex, please – don't make a scene.'

My despair of ten minutes ago had turned to an almost manic punchiness at the prospect of confronting my infidel.

'Fine, Chapman, you want to be there with me, that's fine. Wish I could get hold of Court TV – this could be one of my better cross-examinations.'

We were out the door together and I turned to lock it as Mike warned me to remember my job and behave myself.

'Balls, Mikey! You better have balls tonight. I don't care if I lose my job and I'm working at the Chilmark dump next week.'

'Where to?' he asked again as we began our descent in the elevator.

'The University Club. Tap Room. Lights and sirens, please, Detective Chapman.'

Mike pulled out of the driveway and headed west till we reached Fifth Avenue, where he turned left at my direction to go south to the 'U' Club.

'You belong there? I mean, are you a member of this place?'

'No.'

'No broads?'

'Yeah. They admitted women a few years ago, but it's not for me. Jed's a member, though. Likes to breakfast there or have lunch in the Grill, drink at the end of the day, use the pool and squash courts. The old guys – the sixty- and seventy-year-olds – most of them voted to let women in when the first lawsuits started. The thirty- and forty-year-olds – you know, the ones who are a bit threatened by skirts – they tried to keep women out. Male bonding, Mike. Doesn't it move you?'

'What street?'

'Corner of Fifty-fourth and Fifth.'

As we crossed the intersection of Fifty-seventh Street I saw a caravan of *Daily News* trucks lumbering eastbound with their first load of morning papers for the all-night newsstands.

I groaned as I leaned my head onto the seat back. 'Oh no. Don't even let me think that this story's going to be another tabloid headline.'

'You can go to the bank on that one, Coop. You better hope somebody goes through the front door of Cartier's tonight with an atomic blowtorch and walks out with the Hope diamond. Otherwise, if it's a slow news day, you and Jed could be right on the front pages. I can see them in the newsroom now – *Post* goes with single-word header in all caps: "BETRAYED" – *News* uses "SEX PROSECUTOR IN DEADLY LOVE TRIANGLE."'

'I'm not a "sex prosecutor," dammit. That's the same thing they tried to write when Iz was killed. I prosecute crimes of sexual assault, not sex.'

'That's a healthy approach, blondie – the semantics. Don't worry about what the headlines say, it's *how* they say it.'

'I don't know who I feel worse about – Battaglia, my mother, or me.'

'Good thing you got an alibi for the middle of the afternoon when Lascar was killed. You can bet that Pat McKinney will be in there telling Battaglia that *you* had the best motive to knock off your fair-weather friend – for playing with your man behind your back.'

I was silent as I thought of the endless rounds of gossip this case would now generate in the office, where I had always worked to maintain a healthy distance between my personal and professional lives. Chills ran through me as I tried to make a mental list of my friends and my enemies, but I would have a chance to see them all by the end of the next day before I could ever attempt to parse up the groupings in my head.

Mike had gone around the block and come up directly in front of the club building at One West Fifty-fourth Street, defying the 'NO PARKING' sign by sticking his laminated NYPD vehicle identification plate inside the windshield on the dashboard, announcing to the handful of nocturnal passersby that we had come to this bastion of gentility on official business. Sort of.

It was well after midnight as I led Chapman up the front steps and through the glass entrance doors of the University Club. It is one of the handsomest buildings in the City of New York – a McKim, Mead, and White structure, built to house the private retreat established for educated gentlemen in 1865.

Up another few steps to the lobby where, on the left, a uniformed employee stood beside a large wooden board to record the comings and goings of members as they entered and left the building. Most of the time the initiated simply nodded their greetings upon arrival and he recognized them, sliding their small wooden nameplates into the appropriate place to mark their presence at the club.

I trooped past the startled guard, crossed through the formal lobby with its double-height ceiling, massive columns, and enormous marble fireplace, and went beyond the slow-speed elevators to the back staircase which led directly up to the Tap Room, the bar on the second floor.

'Madam,' the unhappy lookout called out several times after me as I continued to ignore him, refusing to look back and hoping that Chapman was still at my heels.

'Who are you, madam? I'm sorry but you're not appropriately dressed for the Tap Room.'

My trenchcoat was wide open, so he could see that the oversized man's shirt, leggings, and Capezio ballet flats marked a blatant departure from the dress code preferred for the public rooms, which gave me added pleasure on my late-night odyssey.

'Madam, I must insist, madam. Whom are you meeting?'

I had practically reached the landing at the top of the stairs when I looked down at the source of the voice calling up to me. All I could see was the top of his uniform cap.

'Oh, I'm terribly sorry. Were you talking to *me*? I'm with an escort service – Mr. Segal called for me half an hour ago – said just to come ahead as I was, what he needed wouldn't take us very long.'

I continued down the short hallway and waited at the entrance to the bar so that Mike could catch up with me before I pushed open the padded leather door and walked in.

There were about five clusters of drinkers scattered about the large room, relaxing around cocktail tables with armchairs and easy chairs, nursing their nightcaps before heading off to rest up for tomorrow's deal-making.

'Alexandra!' Jed spotted me almost immediately and called out to me as I stood in the doorway, scanning the room to find him.

'Come with me, Mike,' I whispered as I moved forward.

Jed rose to his feet, followed in rapid succession by his two bootlickers, Larry and Stan – slightly younger versions of Jed, hoping to grow up just like him, I was sure. Anderson Warmack, the centerpiece of the group, never budged from his chair, but just leaned in and rested his elbows on the table as he winked at me in welcome.

'Jed, I think you remember Mike Chapman. He's with Homicide. Mike and I need to ask you some questions, Jed. We'd like to—'

'Alex, darling, why don't you and Chapman join us for a round. We're celebrating Mr. Warmack's big night and anything you want to tell me can certainly wait till we get home.' Could he really be as cool and unconcerned as he appeared to be, seeing me burst in here – looking like a shrew – with a detective at my side? Was it possible that I had made a ridiculous mistake?

Larry and Stan – or was it Curly and Moe – were scrambling to pull up two extra chairs from nearby tables now.

'Don't bother. We're not sitting. Jed, this is not a joke. We need to go somewhere private and talk. Right now. We can go upstairs to the library on the fourth floor – I'm sure it's empty at this hour.'

Anderson Warmack chose that moment to begin to blow his hot air into our business. 'Alexandria, my dear . . .'

'It's not Alexandria. It's Alexandra.'

Now I had Jed's attention. I could mess with him but I better not cross old moneybags.

'Alexandra – young lady – I've been keeping your sweet-heart from you too long, is that the problem? Called the police in on me, have you? You look mighty perturbed.'

Well, you're a master of understatement, you pompous old fart. I'm not perturbed – I am fucking pissed off and heartbroken and confused and hurt and angry, but I am much too well brought up to say exactly that to a polite fool like you who likes to have his dimpled old ass kissed as frequently as possible.

'Quite the contrary, Mr. Warmack. I only need to see Jed for fifteen or twenty minutes, and if you'll be good enough to wait for him, I won't ever need to take him out of your presence again, for as long as I live.'

Jed was mad now. He was furious that I was bringing his idol and his underlings into some spat they thought I was starting, and he was trying to placate Warmack before he dealt with me.

'I'll just finish up with you, Anderson. Alex and her friend can have a wait—'

Mike was ready to jump in, at last. 'Hey, Mr. Spiegal, we're ready to—'

'It's Segal.'

'Nobody wants to embarrass you. I do have a few questions that need to have answers tonight. Now be a gent and do what the lady would like you to do, understand?'

Larry thought it was time for a little levity. 'Go on, Jed, we'll still be here. Don't make the tough guy take out his gun and shoot you in the foot to make you dance. What is it, Officer Krupke, a parking ticket? Did he expose himself in public? Better go with the nice policeman, Jed, I can't afford to call a lawyer for you.'

Stan thought that was a real knee-slapper. Warmack, on

the other hand, saw Jed's tightened jaw set in place and his two fingers locked onto his expensive Cohiba cigar, creasing its very costly skin.

Warmack glared back at Jed. I knew he was too white-bread to enjoy a public display of anybody's dirty laundry. 'Why don't you go along and clear up this business, whatever it is. I'm in no rush to go anywhere, as long as they see fit to keep some brandy in my glass.'

Jed excused himself and led us out of the room, around the corner to the elevator, and up to the library, without any one of us uttering a word.

The library was a strikingly elegant room. Dark-paneled and comfortably furnished, it featured second-story galleries reached by spiral wooden ladders and housed an eclectic selection of books, both commercial and rare. I used to love the evenings I had to wait for Jed to finish a negotiation downstairs, while I sat and browsed through some first-edition poetry volume from the thirties, interrupted only by staring at a section of the vaulted ceiling, painted with maps and mythological figures that showed me a new aspect every time I settled in a different chair.

This time, there was no looking at the ceiling. I walked to one of the long, narrow reading tables and sat down, pointing to the men to join me. 'Do I have to interrogate you, Jed, or do you think you can be honest with me for a change?'

'I must say I'm rather surprised at this Gestapo-like approach, Alex. I assume you and I can talk out our problems without any interlopers present.' Jed refused even to glance at Mike Chapman, who was sitting on my side of the table, across from him. His dark eyebrows were drawn together and wrinkled over his nose, as he seemed to try to puzzle why my mood had snapped so radically in the brief time since I had kissed him good night at the Plaza.

'I thought so, too, but apparently I was wrong. I didn't even know we had problems. Why don't you tell me what was going on between you and Isabella?'

'What's gotten into you, Alex? I don't understand what's happened to you in the last hour, darling.' This time he nodded in Chapman's direction, suggesting we could talk more intimately if we were alone. 'Why don't you and I—'

'This has gone beyond "you and I." Just start explaining everything to Detective Chapman.'

'Take it easy. I can't figure out what has you in such a rage.'

'It's one thing to take advantage of me, Jed, but don't play me for stupid on top of that. Tell us about your relationship with Isabella Lascar.'

'Ah, this is about jealousy, is it? You're the one who introduced me to her and encouraged me to help her. What suddenly makes you think anything else was going on? It's not like you to be so insecure.'

'Try me. When did you decide to go with Isabella to my house on the Vineyard?'

How could I lie in bed beside you Saturday night and believe the things you whispered to me as well as the responses you evoked from me, is what I really wanted to say out loud.

'Now hold on right there, Alex. That's insane. I never went to your house—'

My hand slammed down hard on the solid table, piercing the silence of the cavernous room. I was almost as mad at myself as I was with Jed. I prided myself on my ability to cross-examine witnesses, and I wasn't even doing an amateur job at it. There was no subtlety to my technique, no clever buildup of incontrovertible facts. I just wanted to crash my way through to the only thing that mattered. Why had he double-crossed me with Isabella Lascar? Our relationship wasn't so entrenched that he couldn't have ended it and moved on to be with her or anyone else he chose. Why did he have to humiliate me so openly?

'Don't play with me anymore. This is not about jealousy or my feelings or anything as trivial as that. This is about m—'

Mike was ready to try a more competent approach. 'What do you drink, Mr. Segal?'

'Oh, are we ready to be civilized now? Shall I order us up something from the bar?' Jed actually turned to look for a house phone before Mike made him realize the question was not a social one.

'We're not interested in drinking with you now. I asked you what you drink.'

I knew the answer to the question. I'd heard Jed order it dozens of times, usually having to explain to the bartender – except in his regular joints – exactly what it was.

'Booker's, Mr. Chapman. I like Booker's.' I mouthed the next phrase along with him, knowing he would feel the need to describe it to Mike. 'It's a single malt Bourbon, from Kentucky. Quite pricey. I've always had a preference for Kentucky Bourbons over Tennessee. I'm sure there's a reason you need to know this.'

'And when the barkeep runs dry on Booker's, what's your second choice?'

'It doesn't much matter then. Something comparable from Kentucky, before I cross over the border into Tennessee.'

Nice start, Mikey, although I had been slow to catch up with you. Mike was thinking back to the arrangement of the bottles in my liquor cabinet on the Vineyard, when he had noticed that the Stoli and the Jack Daniel's were in front of the Dewar's. I never associated the Jack Daniel's with Jed because he had never ordered any in all our time together. But that Tennessee sour mash was the only Bourbon I had in my house, and he had obviously had to settle for it when he and Isabella were drinking together.

'Where'd you buy me that perfume, Jed?' I wanted to get back in the game.

'Paris, Alex. Are we at the point where I have to produce receipts for gifts I brought you?'

In the typical fashion of a guilty defendant, Jed hadn't even asked us what all these questions were about. Someone who was really in the dark would be more outraged and demanding explanations for our conduct. Instead, he seemed to think that we were bluffing and as long as he was smarter than we were – a woman and a blue-collar civil servant – he could simply hold his course and continue to mislead us.

'What store, Jed? You so rarely go shopping I'm sure you remember which store in Paris you nipped into to buy the perfume.'

He took what he assumed was the safest way out of that one. This is a no-brainer, you dumb broad, he was probably thinking as he smiled smugly at me. 'Chanel. Chanel 22 direct from the salon on Avenue Montaigne.'

I had been hoping he might have even tried to say the duty-free shop, as I had joked at my apartment on Saturday evening. But no, he was determined for some reason to make me think I had been in his consciousness in Paris. The irony was that Chanel 22 is the only one of their perfumes that is made in America. It isn't sold in a single place in France, not even in the company's own stores.

'Make a note to check with American Express for his charges, Mike. See where and when he bought it.'

'Look, I agreed to come up here with you two because I wanted to resolve what I assumed were some petty issues that had arisen in your work. I didn't know you were so damn paranoid, Alex, and this is a pretty ugly way to find it out. But if you think you can make these absurd allegations about me because I agreed to help your friend Isabella sort out her financial difficulties, you're both out of your very unprofessional minds. I've never been to Martha's Vineyard, I've never been involved with Isabella in any other way, and I'm not going to let you derail my plans by breaking up this evening for Warmack. Alex, if there's an explanation for any of this, maybe we can talk about it by ourselves tomorrow.'

'You'll have time for that after you finish at my office, tomorrow at four,' Mike said, drawing a business card out of his wallet and handing it to Jed. 'We'll need to do a set of fingerprints for elimination purposes, and we'll have to get the medical examiner in to draw a vial of blood – I guess Alex has explained the potential for DNA evidence here. And bring your airline tickets and boarding passes for the flight to Paris, too. We'll need a copy of them for the file.'

Jed exploded as Mike went from liquor and perfume discussions to submission to evidentiary tests for a murder investigation. 'This is a goddamn insult. You're just trying to embarrass me for whatever it is you think I've done to hurt you. Have you gone mad? Does Battaglia know you're playing these games with real people, not some bum you picked up in a homeless shelter? You want evidence from me you better call my lawyer or get a warrant.'

'You watch too much television, Jed. Why don't you just give it up?'

'Hey, Alex,' Mike said, pushing himself away from the table and standing up, 'I guess this is when I'm supposed to do my Columbo imitation, huh?' He slouched a bit, stuck his left hand in his pocket and faked a cigar in his right, closed one eyelid and sounded more like Peter Falk than Peter Falk ever did. 'Ya know, I'm-just-a-stupid-cop, Mr. Segal, but I gotta ask ya, d'ya know anybody who drinks Bourbon and maybe put his hands all over a bottle of Jack Daniel's when he couldn't come by any Kentucky mash up in Chilmark last week, who wasn't in Paris when he was supposed to be in Paris but went to Paris afterward anyway so he could come home from Paris, who's got a really classy blue-and-green-plaid shirt that ain't sold by the gross at Kmart or Woolworth's like my shirts, and who left a wad of semen in some condoms in a house where a very famous lady he knew was murdered, even though he wasn't a real prince for being there at the time because it woulda made some other nice lady who liked him a lot very unhappy? You know anybody like that? 'Cause, jeez, if you do, a dumb cop like me could sure use your help.'

I didn't think anything could have made me laugh when we had walked into the club half an hour earlier, but Mike's imitation of Columbo was perfect and refreshing, causing Jed to storm out of the library and down the staircase as we pressed for the elevator to take us back to the lobby.

'I dare you, blondie. The only thing you can do to beat the way you got us into the club tonight is if we both take all our clothes off in the elevator right now and just walk out of the building stark naked. Game?'

'Nah, Mikey. It would be my luck to run into Anderson Warmack on his way out of here, and it might just give him too much pleasure to see my bare ass. I'll take a pass.'

We were down and out without incident, through the lobby, which was quiet as a mausoleum, and back in my driveway ten minutes later.

I opened the car door, said good night to Mike, and started to get out.

'Talk about role reversal, we've really come full circle,' he remarked to me. 'Remember those lectures you used to give me during the Quentiss trial? "Go directly home – no gin mills, no drinking all night with the guys, no dropping in on flight attendants who are here on a turn-around. Go home and go to bed 'cause you're gonna get pounded on cross tomorrow." Remember the perky young prosecutor trying her first high-profile case, reading me the riot act whenever I had to be in court the next day? Well, same goes for you, Coop. Get upstairs, go directly to bed, don't drink anything alcoholic, screen your calls in case that weasel tries to worm his way back into your affection, stay clearheaded for the morning. Understood?'

'Yeah, boss.'

'Alex, can I leave you alone, really? I mean, if you want company or you're, well, you know . . .'

'Thanks, Mike. I'm really okay. This whole thing – since the first phone call about Isabella's murder last week – has taken on a life of its own. I just feel like I'm being dragged along in a vicious riptide. I've sort of stopped fighting it now. I think I'll just try to ride it out and see where I land.'

212

'Hang tough, blondie. The most important lesson for tonight is to think Aretha. No Tammy Wynette. No "Stand by Your Man." I'm talking "Respect" – all capital letters. You tell the doormen not to let Jed in if he shows up, and not to take his calls. We know he's a liar – and I know you don't want to admit this to yourself – but he may be more dangerous than that.'

16

The message light was flashing on my phone when I got into my bedroom and started to undress. One solicitation to change phone companies and reach out to friends all over the U.S.A. for pennies less than whichever system I was using, one hang-up – getting to be a bit too commonplace lately – and two terse messages from Jed that had come in during the last ten minutes. The first was short and angry in tone, berating me for creating that ridiculous scene with my 'pet cop'; the second was short and conciliatory in tone, urging me to meet with him alone tomorrow, and to believe in him. The Easter bunny, the tooth fairy, Santa Claus, and Jed Segal – I had believed in each of them and they had proven to be among life's great disappointments. Jed would never get the honor of rising to the level of those others.

I toyed with the idea of ringing David's doorbell and asking his advice, but I was afraid to find out that he, too, would admit some previously unacknowledged connection to Isabella. Instead, I climbed into bed and picked up the phone to call Nina Baum. Not even eleven o'clock in Los Angeles yet, so I knew I wasn't likely to find her at home. 'We can't come to the phone now . . .' the message droned on, so I waited for the beep and left her an update. I vented all my pain about Jed's faithlessness, and concluded with Mike's concern that Jed was actually a suspect in the murder. A best friend was better than a shrink any day, in my book. I knew Nina would call back first thing tomorrow, suggesting ways to put these events in perspective with the rest of my life and loves.

I switched off the light, rolled over onto my stomach, and tried to fall asleep. Whatever pleasant thoughts I attempted to balance in my mind danced there for only brief seconds before being pushed off center stage by the reality of the last few hours. I lay in the dark reliving all of my days and evenings and nights with Jed, wondering whether particular moments together had been artificial or genuine, whether they had occurred before or after his first contact with Iz, whether there had been someone else before her.

Sleep was impossible. I sat up and turned on the light, got out of bed, and slipped into the least sexy, snuggest bathrobe I owned. I had instantly reverted into that end-of-relationship funk in which I knew I would never need sexy robes or underwear for the rest of my life. Never would I expose myself again – in my most fetching lingerie – to any other untrustworthy man who crossed my path. I traipsed from room to room, illuminating all of them as I looked for some diversion to keep me occupied until, as I hoped, drowsiness would overcome me.

I went into the kitchen and made myself a cup of hot chocolate. The October evening was much too mild for that, but I remembered some vague childhood thing about my mother and warm milk as a soporific, so I figured I'd give it a try. On to the dining-room table to do the Monday *Times* crossword, but it was so ridiculously simple that I knocked it off in less than fifteen minutes. It was a bad reminder that the week still had four days to go.

Finally, I moved through the living room and perched in the den where my television and stereo were set up. I reclined in an armchair with my feet on the ottoman and turned on the tube to see what old black-and-white rerun might lull me into a little nap. It was the first stroke of luck I'd had in days, even though that meant I wouldn't close my eyes for a minute. One of the cable channels was playing *Notorious*, which is my favorite movie ever made. It had started at two-thirty so I had missed the first few scenes, but I could practically recite the lines from memory for all the times I had seen it.

There was the splendidly youthful Ingrid Bergman and the dashing Cary Grant. They were already in Rio and she had agreed to the perilous plan to seduce the evil Claude Rains, and ultimately to move into the palatial home he shared with his monstrous mother. Ingrid and Cary were daring to have her debriefings in the most public of places, the park in the middle of the city where they pretended to meet – by chance – on horseback.

I lost myself in the Hitchcockian brilliance of the double-crossings and treacherous dealings, the principled spies and the demonic Nazis. I marveled at Ingrid's willingness to accept Cary's dare and actually marry the enemy, though she ached for Cary to love her. I tensed as I always did at the champagne reception and the riveting scene in the wine cellar with the missing key and the broken bottle. And as the very large, bright moon outside my window threatened to disappear into daylight, I wanted to be saved just as the deceived Ingrid had been: by Cary, sweeping me into his arms and down the grand staircase and out of all danger. Just what I needed – an escape from my troubles into a cinema life of intrigue and romance and lovers not knowing whether they could trust each other. Worked like a tonic.

Now I was wired. It was almost 5 A.M. and I clicked the dial past an endless array of gadgets like Veg-O-Matics and Ginzo knives and tummy-slimmers. Nothing engaged me on any channel and I was resigning myself to the fact that this was going to be an all-nighter – I was much too edgy to sleep.

I leafed through the current *New Yorker*, hoping for a long piece on the most current Washington scandal, but finding instead a dull treatise on ozone levels in the Brazilian rain forest.

The buzz of the intercom in my kitchen, connected to the phone of the building's doormen in the lobby, nearly lifted me out of my chair when it shattered my quiet daze a few minutes later. It would be Jed. Should I let him in when I was alone? The ringing kept up interminably, but I held my resolve not to pick up the phone and acknowledge his presence. I was annoyed that the doormen had ignored my instruction not to admit him if he showed up, and assumed he had greased their ever-open palms with some large bills.

I had stopped counting rings at sixty-five, and was now toying with the idea of calling 911 to have the cops usher him away. That would be a terrible waste of police resources, as I knew better than anyone, so I let it ring on instead.

Then I heard the elevator doors open in the hallway. He was actually upstairs and was going to try to get in to me. What if Mike Chapman was right – that Jed's greatest fault had not been his infidelity, but that he was, indeed, a murderer? Maybe he was coming to kill me, to silence me because I had implicated him in Isabella's death? My mind didn't seem to work. I simply didn't know what to do next but I had clearly waited too long to call the police. There were voices in the hallway now. That meant he had come back with at least one other person and I was terrified that he had found some thug to do his dirty work for him. I stepped over to the bar next to the television set and picked up the wine-bottle opener which lay on top – the 'screw-pull' version with the wickedly sharp-pointed tip that projects into the cork. I had no idea what I would do with it but its mean metal point felt good in the palm of my hand as I tiptoed closer to the front door.

'Coop, Coop? It's Mike. Open up, I got a surprise for you.'

Lucky I didn't have a gun because I probably would have blasted it through the door at Chapman at precisely that point, for freaking me out and heightening my growing sense of paranoia. I looked out the peephole for a confirmatory sighting, threw back the bolt, and turned the lock to open the door.

I was fuming, again. 'Do you have any idea—'

That's when I saw Mercer Wallace standing next to him,

holding three pints of Häagen-Dazs ice cream – the most direct way to my heart – stacked up in a pile as his deep bass hummed the melody of 'What Becomes of the Broken Hearted?' while Mike laughed.

'Great music, Mercer. But I can't dance to it tonight.'

'This shit's gonna melt all over your hall carpet if you don't let us in, Alex. Move it.' Chapman pushed past me and the two of them headed straight for the kitchen to dish up the portions. 'What happened since I left you off, kid?' he asked, eyeing my tattered chenille robe. 'You look like Ma Kettle in that getup. Here you got the two most eligible guys in the city banging at your doorstep and you won't open up. Look at her, Mercer, she's prayin' for somebody to show up at this hour with some vintage Château Lafite. Who ya gonna kill with that bottle opener? Okay, we got Cookie Dough Dynamo, Chocolate Chocolate Chip, or Vanilla Fudge? What'll it be, blondie – let's put a little meat on those bones.'

'Now that we're having this cozy breakfast party, boys, who wants to explain to me what it's all about? Chocolate for me, of course.'

'Not my fault. I was lookin' deep into the most beautiful pair of ebony eyes, in a gentrified townhouse – we used to call 'em tenements – on West Ninety-third near Amsterdam' – Mercer was dropping a hint that was supposed to suggest the identity of the recipient of his enormous charm, undoubtedly one of my colleagues— 'when my beeper went off an hour ago. Seems Brother Chapman's knowledge of Motown is a bit shallow. It started and ended with "Respect." The man wanted help with some lyrics – life-will-go-on-after-your-man-is-gone kind of stuff. When he told me it was you he was gonna serenade, I volunteered to do backup for him.'

'What's the story, Mike?' I asked once more, leading the three of us, each with a bowl of ice cream, back into the den.

He hemmed and hawed and stalled a bit more before coughing up the real answer. Chapman had waited in his car at the parking space at the end of the driveway, thinking he would watch for an hour or so to make sure Jed didn't stop by and try to see me.

'I walked down to the all-night coffee shop to get a cup of brew to keep me awake. Called the office from a phone booth outside the place to explain the situation to the lieutenant – can you believe it, the City of New York is paying me to do this little "power breakfast"? When I looked up at your apartment – I can always pick it out 'cause it's on the corner, and it's got those fancy-drooped drapes your mother had done for you – your lights were all off. While I stood out there drinking my coffee, I looked up again and every few minutes another light went on, till you got comfy in front of the TV.'

'Geez, you put that much deduction into one of your homicides you might close a case now and then.'

'By that time it was almost three o'clock. Figured I might as well sleep in my car instead of dragging home.' Mike didn't live very far from my apartment, actually, in a tiny studio off York Avenue near the East River in the Sixties. He had been in the rent-controlled cubicle – he referred to it as 'the coffin' – for almost fifteen years and paid very low rent, but it was a sixth-floor walk-up, which got harder to go home to the later the hour. 'I napped for a while, checked to make sure your lights were still blazing, then decided if neither of us could sleep we might as well be miserable together. I beeped Mercer for some inspiration – never dreamed the guy would crash my party. But he did have the good sense to find a twenty-four-hour Food Emporium with a great selection of ice cream. Cheers.'

I thought of Nina Baum and how happy it would make her when I told her later that I had not been alone. That two of the most decent guys I had ever known had taken it upon themselves to hang out with me through the last desolate hours of the morning, and tried to entertain me at a time when I was content to wallow in my misery.

We gossiped about prosecutors and cops, we told each other war stories we had told dozens of times before, and we took turns doing impressions of the most outrageous defendants we had encountered.

'Remember the first case I ever brought you?' Mercer asked.

'Of course. The two brothers who assaulted the woman on Lenox Avenue, the rooftop?'

'I was still in uniform, Mike. Got a 911 to the address, civilian holding two in a stairwell. Some guy heard a woman screaming in his building. Started to go toward the noise on the roof and these two teenagers were running down from the top landing, zipping up their pants as they came down. Guy had a licensed gun – stopped 'em in their tracks. Yelled to his wife who called us.'

Mercer went on. 'My partner holds the kids and I go up to the roof to see what happened. Fifty-five-year-old lady, pretty hysterical, tells me these two kids she never saw before followed her onto the elevator, the bigger one pulled out a knife and forced her to the roof. Stripped her and tried to rape her. When the tall one put down

221

the knife to unzip his fly, she began to scream and they ran off.

'I radio for a bus' – police jargon for ambulance – 'to take her to the hospital, and I go back down to cuff the kids. They're jivin' my partner like crazy. "That's our mother, man," they're tellin' him. "That's our mother – she's just mad at us 'cause she says the rent money is missing. Man, we didn't do nothin' to her."

'So I say, "What's her name, your mother?" For the first time, they're both real quiet. They look at each other but that's no help. Finally, the older one looks up at me with one last try, "I don't know – we jus' call her Mom."'

It wasn't his best story but it always made him laugh.

'Not as good as when we almost screwed up that murder trial for Cooper, when you got promoted to the squad,' a case Mike loved to remind both Mercer and me about.

A few years back I had worked on an investigation that involved the discovery of a murder victim who had been sexually assaulted and whose body had been found near the Lower West Side piers, left in an alley in a large packing crate. She hadn't been identified for weeks, and the detectives working on the case observed their usual tradition of giving an identity of their own to the victim. Eventually a truck driver was arrested and charged with the crime. I never heard the casual references to the young woman – which the cops had dared not make in my presence – nor did they appear anywhere in the police reports, so it came as just as much a surprise to me as it did to the jury when the defense attorney drew it out on his cross-examination of Mercer.

Mike played all the parts for us. 'Did you know the name of the deceased when you commenced your investigation on April 10, Detective Wallace?' 'No, sir.' 'And how did the medical examiner refer to the deceased in her report of April 11, Detective Wallace?' 'As Jane Doe, Number 27, 1991.' 'And how did you refer to her in your D.D. 5 of April 12, Detective Wallace?' 'Case number two hundred thirty-four of 1991, Counselor.' Mike finally reached the point at which Detective Wallace had admitted that by the end of the first week, when the late-lamented unknown hooker had ceased to interest the editors of the local tabloids and had dropped off the evening news shows, his team had given her the rather callous nickname of 'The Fox in the Box.'

It had been a very uphill battle to try to restore the jury's faith in the able young detective as the judge threatened – in the presence of the panel – to bring the matter to the attention of the commissioner. But somehow, as usual, justice was done.

That led us to a discussion of the nature of the dark humor that seemed to be the province of law enforcement types all over the world.

And that led Chapman to his next attempt to occupy my wandering attention. 'Ya know, I got an idea for you to make a lot of money, Alex, when you're ready to go private. It came to me last Thursday when I had to go through all the files in your office.'

'Let's hope it's not a step I'm going to have to take today, Mike. I'll bite – what is it?'

'A dating service. Now, you take a look at the women first. You got a twenty-three-year-old receptionist, a Libra. She likes reefer, jazz clubs, and picking up guys in Washington Square Park on weekends. She likes regular intercourse and oral sex, she just doesn't like—'

'You're a pig, Chapman. You are an insensitive, disgusting pig. No wonder you have to work Homicide. You shouldn't ever be allowed to work with a living, breathing human being who has been traumatized,' I looked at my watch and stood up to go inside to dress for the next battle.

Mike barely missed a beat. He didn't need my approval – he was content with his audience of one. 'Then you get a perp, Mercer. Not a real violent one. There's that thirty-five-year-old cook from that restaurant in SoHo who got collared last month. He's a Capricorn. Are they good together, Mercer, Libra and Capricorns? Anyway he likes reefer, too. Prefers Battery Park City to Washington Square Park, but she might be flexible. He's also into oral . . .'

I was out of earshot by then and into the bathroom to shower and wash my hair.

Mike would never understand the cases that Mercer and I liked to handle. He really did prefer working on murder investigations, as he had told me many times. You didn't have to hold the victims' hands, as it were, and deal with the emotional struggle of their recovery. You didn't have to help them manage the pain of reliving the devastating event – the pain and torment were long over by the time Chapman got to a crime scene. And you didn't have to deal with victims who lie on occasion, even when we're trying to help them convict their assailants. Mike was happiest when he could work on the intricate pieces of a puzzle – silent clues, words offered by or cajoled out of occasional bystanders, pathological findings – slowly and carefully unraveling the mystery of a brutal, untimely death.

Death. Which brought me back to Isabella Lascar and then to Jed. I finished toweling myself off and began the tedious process of blow-drying my hair as I re-examined the damage of a sleepless night in the bathroom mirror.

I dressed in a navy blazer, red-and-white wide-striped Charvet shirt and red skirt – businesslike but not somber. I refused to look as if I was in mourning for a lost love.

Mike and Mercer were sitting at the dining-room table with cups of coffee they had made while I primped for the day. It was just after seven when I rejoined them. 'Can I get on the school bus by myself, or do you have to escort me?'

'I'm on this watch for another hour. Mercer's got the day off. I'll drop you at your office then go home and crash. I have to be back at the squad for the four to twelve.'

We all walked out together. Mercer saw the two of us into Mike's car and continued on his way with a wave. 'Do something to make me look good for a change,' I called after him. 'Catch that bastard in the serial rape case, will you?' He nodded his head and gave me a thumbs-up.

I spent most of the car ride fumbling for a way to thank Mike for looking out for me the night before.

'Cut it out, blondie. That's what friends are for. Besides, defenestration is the fuckin' worst. I couldn't bear the sight of your body splashed and splattered all over the sidewalk.'

'What's that supposed to mean?'

'That's what I was really afraid of last night. What if you threw yourself out of a window because of that asshole? I hate jumpers. Give me shootings, stabbings, bludgeonings, but no defenestration. I was gonna stay down there all night – even if the boss didn't offer to pay me to do it – just to make sure you didn't go out on a ledge.'

'You thought I'd leap out a window over Jed Segal? I will

leave you for the morning with the solemn promise that I have no intention of doing anything that would cause Pat McKinney to have such a nice day. You know, Mike, I met Jed less than four months ago. I fell hard and too fast, and never stopped to scrutinize the relationship very deeply. It just felt good and I liked it. But it isn't the end of my world. Really, you got me through the first night and I am sincerely grateful for that. I'll be fine – I've got a very busy day ahead of me.' Maybe if I said it out loud I'd start to believe it.

17

I went into the building and up to my office, pleased that I had arrived early enough to enjoy the solitude of the place to prepare for my court appearance and my next 'save face' with Battaglia.

I had worked at my sentencing remarks for nearly an hour before the phone rang for the first time.

I froze at the sound of Jed's voice.

'Don't, Jed. There's nothing you can say—'

'You've got to listen to me, *please*. I'm not a killer, Alex. I haven't committed any crime. You've got to see me, you've got to let me talk with you before this goes any further.'

'You ran out of "got to's" with me when you started sneaking around behind my back. Don't push me on this, Jed. It's Chapman you have to talk to, not me.'

'I need your help with all this. I never meant to hurt you or do anything to destroy what we were building. I love you too much for that.'

I placed the receiver back in its cradle without saying another word. I swiveled around in my chair and stared out the window at the roof of the building across the narrow street, which was at eye level with my view. The gallery of gargoyles that decorated the edge of the façade seemed sinister today as they gawked back at me, panther-like creatures with their tongues extended and their eyes rolled upward, mocking me in disbelief.

Most mornings I welcomed their company as I sat at my desk alone, before the office swarmed with colleagues. But today they had turned on me and sneered their disapproval, so I braced my foot against the radiator and kicked the chair back around into place at the desk.

I called Battaglia's assistant, Rose Malone, and told her it was critical that I see him as soon as he arrived. He had gone to Washington the night before, she explained, to testify at Senate subcommittee hearings on gun control and would not be back until tomorrow. Damn. It was the rare occasion that I didn't even want to tell Rose the information about Jed, and so I simply asked her to connect me to him as soon as he checked in.

Joan Stafford was my next call, and I was doubly appreciative as I dialed her number that my loyal friend was a novelist and therefore easy to reach at home most of the time.

'You're a grave, right?' I asked as she answered on the first ring. It was one of Joan's expressions, meaning that the questioner was confirming that the information about to be given was sworn to deepest secrecy.

'Of course. You got something good?'

'I wouldn't call it good. I'm in the middle of a dreadful mess. No one else but Nina knows this yet and I'm not supposed to tell anyone, but Mike Chapman thinks Jed had something to do with Isabella's death. Mike thinks he may have killed her.'

'Oh my God.' Her tone changed rapidly from her good-humored response to one of appropriate concern. 'Tell me—'

'I can't tell you anything else right now. Can you meet me for dinner tonight?'

'Sure.'

'Don't you have that fund-raiser for—'

'Don't be ridiculous. They have my check, they don't need me. Tell me where and when.'

'I've got to be in court this morning. Would you call Primola when it opens? Ask Giuliano for that table in the corner near the bar – the one he kind of pulls the palm tree in front of for privacy. I'm going to try to take a ballet class right after work – I'm really in knots. Meet you at the restaurant at eight.'

Laura arrived moments later. I couldn't bring myself to explain the situation to her, so I sheepishly gave her a set of instructions before packing up my Redweld – the rust-colored accordion file that held my case papers – to go to court. 'I've got my beeper on if the D.A. calls in from Washington. And you can also beep me if anyone needs me on the murder investigation. Sarah can cover the new cases that come in. If Jed calls, tell him I'm not interested in any messages. I don't mean to put you in the middle of this, Laura, but my relationship with Jed is over and it's a bit awkward right now. You'd also better call the switchboard and tell them to disconnect my private line for the time being. I want all calls coming through you, okay?'

She was as discreet as always – no questions, no comments, just an understanding nod.

I left my office and began the circuitous route to the other courthouse up the street – originally built for civil cases, but usurped by the criminal justice system when we outgrew our old quarters more than a decade ago. Down and out through the turnstiles of the District Attorney's Office, around the corner and across Center Street; up the block and into the ugly modern building; through the security check again; and on to another line for an even slower series of elevators. Not bad without a trail of witnesses and the shopping carts we push around for major case trials. This was just a scheduled sentence on the last case I had tried, so no witnesses or police officers were present.

I was lost in thought, somewhere in the events of my life in the last four months, smiling in acknowledgment and responding to greetings as I passed other assistants on their way to courtrooms for hearings and trials.

'Did this case keep you up all night?' I snapped out of my reverie at the sound of Ellen Goldman's voice when she approached me at the elevator bank.

'No, no – not this. Sorry, I just didn't see you there. I'm a bit preoccupied.' I tried to force a smile, but I had forgotten that she would be back today and the last thing I needed to deal with was a reporter.

'Forgive me for saying this, but – you look so pale. Do you feel okay?'

'Oh yes, thanks. I'm, well, it's just personal. It hasn't been a very good week.'

I pressed the button for the seventh floor, and the crush

of other litigants filled the car completely, so we were able to ride up in the crowd without my having to make small talk with Ellen.

'Judge Hadleigh's courtroom is around this way to the left,' I said as I led her to the small setting in which the trial of the *People of the State of New York against Ernesto Cerone* had been conducted.

'Was anything reported about this case, anything in the press?'

'No, actually, not a word – fortunately for the victim.'

'Can you tell me something about it, so I know what's going to happen today?'

I took Ellen through the facts of the case as we entered the room and sat on the front bench to await the arrival of both the judge and my adversary. The victim was a twenty-eight-year-old woman who lived in an apartment building in Harlem. She was mentally handicapped and had the developmental level of a seven-year-old child. A carpenter who was doing construction work in a unit in the building lured her into the empty room one afternoon last spring, trapped her in the bathroom, and anally sodomized her and raped her. Her screams were heard by a neighbor who rushed into the apartment and actually pulled the rapist off the body of the terrified woman.

Since the identity of the attacker – Ernesto Cerone – was not an issue, the defense turned the matter around and claimed that there had been no forced assault, but instead, that the victim had consented to the intercourse. Then, she started to scream only when Cerone refused to pay her for the pleasure of her company. The severe mental handicap of the woman made her a scapegoat for a vicious cross-examination at the trial, and the conviction was possible only because of the compelling testimony of the neighbor who had intervened to save her.

'This shouldn't be very complicated. I'm going to ask for the max, the defense attorney'll jump up and down about it, and this judge is likely to end up somewhere in the middle.'

'Doesn't sound like there's much of a middle to me. Oh, by the way, I was talking to my editor last night, Alex, and he'd really like me to flesh out some more detail, if you understand me. He thinks the story will be too dry if we don't get sort of a "behind-the-scenes" view of what makes you do this. He'd like some more personal information about you.'

I let out a very soft groan. 'Like what?'

'Like how do you spend your free time, what do you do on weekends, who do you see when you go out?'

'Look, Ellen, I don't mind talking to you about my work when the press office directs me to, but I've just got to separate my private life from this business.'

'That's just the point. Most people can't understand how you do that. Don't you take this work home with you every night? I don't mean the papers and documents, I mean the emotional baggage. Doesn't this job just make you hate men?'

I laughed at that one. Maybe Goldman wasn't as smart as I had initially thought, to ask such a hackneyed question. 'No, of course not. The people who commit these crimes are deviants, Ellen. This is really extreme, aberrant behavior. Most of the men I've ever met in my life are incapable of this kind of conduct. I am *not* one of the women who believes that all men are potential rapists. That's one of the main reasons I can deal with these cases. And it really doesn't carry over into my relationships with men – not for a moment.' But if you want to know what makes me hate men, I thought to myself, this is the right day to ask me.

'Are you seriously involved with someone now, Alex? This investment banker you were out with last night?'

'Did I tell you who I was going out with yesterday?' I shot back at her. 'I wasn't aware I mentioned—'

'I told you I've done my homework. I've already interviewed a lot of your colleagues.'

'What branch of the Israeli military did you serve in – Intelligence?'

'Not so lucky. I was in a special patrol force on the West Bank. Actually an elite antiterrorist unit. Not a cushy desk job doing background checks.'

I was impressed. 'Listen, Ellen. Can we go off the record for a few minutes?'

'Sure. Off the record.'

'Whatever you heard about the investment banker and whoever's been talking about it, you need to know it's over. I'll give you other stuff – personal stuff if you have to have it – but I beg you to leave the romance angle out of it. He's not a part of my life anymore and I don't want to see anything about us in print. Please.'

'Yeah, sure, I'm really sorry. People had been telling me you were very happy together. Picture-perfect couple and all that kind of thing. Of course I won't write about it if it's not true. Is this all very recent?'

It was a Catch-22. I couldn't get her off the subject without going on to explain why it didn't make sense for her to stay on the subject.

'Recent? Let's just say if you had asked me the same

question before you left me in my office yesterday afternoon, you would have had a different answer. History,
Ellen, it's over.'

I was relieved to see Cerone's court-appointed attorney
come out of the door which led from the holding pen behind
the courtroom. The clerk stepped back and knocked on
the judge's robing room and I couldn't hear what Ellen
murmured to me as the court officer announced 'All rise,'
when Hadleigh mounted the three steps to his seat at
the bench.

The clerk called the case from the calendar, directed
both counsel to state our appearances for the record, and
arraigned the defendant for sentence. He went on to ask,
'Does the assistant district attorney wish to be heard?'

'Yes, Your Honor.' I recalled for the judge the facts of
the case, referring to actual pieces of testimony about the
victim's ordeal which I had pulled from the transcript. In
greater detail, I described her mental condition and the
vulnerability that handicap also endowed her with. Her
legal guardian had called to tell me that, even to this day,
the young woman awakened with nightmares, screaming
the name of the defendant and pleading for help. I closed by
urging the Court to impose the maximum sentence, a range
of eight and one-third to twenty-five years in state prison.

Cerone's lawyer spoke next. He still disputed the verdict
of the jury, arguing that his client would be vindicated by
an appellate review of the facts. He assailed the descriptions
that had been given about the woman's mental capacity,
saying that there really wasn't anything wrong with her at
all: she was just slow. 'There is nothing in the trial record
to indicate that this was a violent, brutal attack, like the
People claim.

'Your Honor,' he continued, 'I must also call your attention to the history of this complaining witness. Ms. Cooper mentioned the victim's guardian, who reports her nightmares to the district attorney. May I remind you that the reason she lives with a guardian is that she had to be removed from her natural home because she had been the victim of years of sexual abuse by her father and her brothers. All of those events, Judge Hadleigh, have had some kind of impact on this witness – and all of those abuses occurred before the events she testified about in this court.

'They don't excuse my client, Your Honor, but surely the impact of Mr. Cerone's actions on her is lessened by her past experience.'

Did I hear this guy right? Is he about to tell the judge that it's okay to victimize someone who has been abused before?

Now Hadleigh was awake, too. 'Well, certainly, the impact of this crime is less severe because of her incest experience. She's not inured to it, I'm sure, but it had to be less serious than the first or second time she'd been through this, I have to agree with you.'

I was on my feet in a flash. 'I'm going to object—'

'Just a minute, Miss Cooper. You've had your chance. Sit down. I'll hear counsel out on this, he's entitled to his position.'

'My client still denies his guilt, Your Honor. And I just want to close by asking you to take all these things into consideration in sentencing my client, who has no prior criminal history, and by—'

'Objection. Judge Hadleigh, Mr. Cerone has no felony convictions but he certainly has a criminal history . . .'

'Miss Cooper, that's all before me, as you know, in the pre-sentence report. Let's keep some order here, please. There's no jury to perform for – I know the record, too.'

'So on my client's behalf, Judge, I'd ask for the minimum in this case – two to six years.'

The Honorable Horace Hadleigh – we all called him Horrid, on the prosecution side, which was either the result of or the causal factor in why, for the more than thirty-eight years he had been on the bench, he generally handed members of the defense bar exactly what they wanted – was about to deliver his view of the Cerone case.

He hadn't bothered to write out any comments about the case in advance – that would have taken both time and intelligence, two factors of which he was in limited supply. So he began by rambling on a bit about the trial and the pathetic young woman who had testified in his courtroom.

By the end of five minutes it was clear that he had bought the defense position lock, stock, and barrel. 'And quite frankly, I don't see what the People gain by describing this rape as brutal and violent.'

There was no point in my sitting down at the table. If I could manage to get a word in edgewise, this was going to be lively. 'Your Honor, the Penal Law of this state defines rape as a "violent felony." Of course this situation was violent – it was a forced physical assault by a man who overpowered an unwilling participant.'

'Miss Cooper, don't stand here and lecture me on the Penal Law. There are rapes and there are rapes. He didn't chop her up in little pieces, did he? He didn't cause any other injuries, did he?'

'Thank God he didn't, Your Honor. The law doesn't

require that either. That's a separate crime, as you know. Rape occurs without any external physical injury in the overwhelming percentage of cases. She didn't have to sustain any injury. She was raped and anally sodomized – that's trauma enough.'

'You're losing your sense of discretion, young lady, as well as your temper. You can't differentiate between one case and another, and that's fatal for a prosecutor.'

I took a deep breath and modulated my tone. 'I'm sorry, Your Honor, but I must disagree with you. I see three, four hundred rape cases a year – supervise several hundred others – that's more than any other prosecutor in the country, Judge Hadleigh. I am very well aware of the factual distinctions, the nuances, the differences in kinds of threats – all of the minuscule features that make each of these cases so distinct to each victim – woman, man, or child – despite the fact that several Penal Law definitions cover the entire spectrum. I think I know, as well as anyone in the world, how to differentiate among every single one of the cases that cross my desk.'

'Well, then, you'll have to agree, Miss Cooper, that this girl is so retarded that she really can't understand what happened to her, isn't that so? It's not like if it happened to you or to my daughter? You'd know what it was all about now, wouldn't you? She can't absorb what happened to her, she can't even explain it to us.'

I was thunderstruck. This was a triple-header: Cerone's attack was forcible but not violent; other people had abused this victim in her past, so she was fair game for Ernesto Cerone this time; and because she was handicapped – the very reason she had been preyed upon, in all likelihood – it didn't matter as much as it would to a fully abled woman.

'Judge Hadleigh,' I began, unable to let his comments stand unaddressed on the record. 'Most respectfully, sir,' you complete fucking moron, 'I must take exception to the views you have expressed here today. I think it's fair to say that not since the case opinions generated by the medieval English courts have I heard observations like these about rape victims.'

'What did you say?'

'The three statements you made about this trial, Judge, they really reflect antiquated attitudes.'

'Did you say something to me about the Dark Ages, Miss Cooper? Are you making fun of me, young lady?'

'Not at all, sir. But surely you remember the legislative history of these statutes when the laws changed, just two decades ago?' Give him a hand; he hasn't cracked a law book since he was in knee-pants. 'Sir Matthew Hale, 1671 – all those archaic writings about women being the property of their husbands and rape not being a crime unless the victim had been virginal before the assault. Those views went out—'

'Miss Cooper. I'm going to do you a favor. I'm going to put off this sentence today and let you walk out of my courtroom without holding you in contempt. I'm going to let you reflect upon this for a bit and come back next week with an apology for me and a more reasonable view of the facts of this case.' Ernesto Cerone was grinning as if he had just been paid a million dollars to do a commercial for Fixodent. He wasn't going to get out of jail free, but every time I opened my mouth, his sentence time came down a notch.

'Thank you for that opportunity, Judge, but I am ready to go ahead with Mr. Cerone's sentence today.' I'd like nothing better than to see this whole thing written up in Ellen Goldman's article and expose this ignorant throwback for what he is.

'You're flirting with contempt, miss.'

What the hell, Judge, I'm giving up flirting with men. And I do so love flirting.

My adversary played right into the judge's hand. 'I'd like the matter adjourned for a week, too.'

'Thank you. At defendant's request, this case will be put over until next Wednesday, 2 P.M., for sentence. I expect you to come back a bit more courteously, Miss Cooper. I don't want to have to report this as a complaint to the Disciplinary Committee. Has that ever happened to you before?'

'No, sir.' But I would wear it as a badge of honor if you did it with this record you've just made today.

Hadleigh strode off the bench and back to his robing room as I gathered my papers and stepped out of the well to join up with Ellen Goldman.

'I can't believe I heard the things the judge said, but I did.'

'Can you just imagine, if those are the views of an edu-cated jurist, what victims encounter all over this country from people who are uninformed about issues like this? It's unthinkable. Hadleigh's the exception around here, I should add – most of our judges in New York are terrific on these cases. He just reminds me that there are still a lot more Neanderthals around than I like to admit to myself.'

'Do you mind if I trail you back to your office and talk a bit more today?'

'Look, Ellen, I'd like to do it, but I'm really pinched for time. Can we push it back a few days?'

'Yeah. I've got a good start from the two hours you gave me yesterday, as well as my research. I'll call you tomorrow. If you see me around, it's just for background and interviewing other people about you.'

'Thanks, Ellen.' Yeah, great. Poke around – let me know if you find out anything I should have known weeks ago. We shook hands on the corner of Center Street and I went back into the building to see what awaited me in the office.

Sarah Brenner was standing at my desk, using the phone. I closed the door and sat until she finished her conversation.

'How did Cerone go?' she asked. 'What did Horrid hit him with?'

'Not as much as he wanted to hit me with, I'll tell you that. Adjourned for a week. Anything come in while I was over there?'

'That was Bruno. He just called from the airport, with Antonio Partigas.' Detective Bruno and his partner had come in from Miami on the first flight. They had gone on a rendition, to bring Partigas back to New York to stand trial here for a series of rapes he had committed before fleeing to Florida two months ago. 'Class act, Partigas, all the way. You know why Bruno called? Just to tell us that while Antonio was sitting on the plane, cuffed and seated between two of New York's Finest and under arrest for six counts of Rape in the First Degree, he exposed himself to the stewardess. Fly the friendly skies. I tell you, it's never dull here.'

'Sarah, be honest with me. How do I look? I mean, I feel like I'm losing it – do I look as crazed as I feel?'

'You look fine. Fishing for compliments today, are we?'

'Listen, Jed and I broke up last night – you need to know

why, although I'd like you to keep it between us for a while. I'm really running on empty, though, and I'm afraid you're the one who'll get stuck with all the overload.'

'Keep it coming, Alex. Whatever I do here is easier than being home with a six-month-old kid. We'll manage. The only other call while you were with Hadleigh was from a uniformed cop in the two-six. He wanted to know if it was sex abuse for a man to fondle the breasts of an eleven-year-old girl, even if she really didn't have developed breasts yet. Can you believe it? Rocket scientist. And if she's a forty-year-old woman who just happens to be flat-chested, I guess we should give him a pass, too.'

'Let me fill you in on what happened last night. I'd rather have you hear it all from me.'

18

Battaglia called in from Washington just after one, as I was eating a salad ordered in from Broadway's Best at my desk. 'Guess you can't even stay out of trouble for twenty-four hours, so I can make an appearance in Washington, hmm?'

'Paul, I don't know where to begin on this, I feel like such a fool.'

'Forget it, Alex, this one's easy.' Great, the Battaglia I adore, understanding my dilemma. 'I'm behind you one hundred percent. Don't worry about his complaint.'

Whoops. It was suddenly obvious that we were talking about two different things. 'Hadleigh? How did you hear about that already? I haven't been back from the courtroom for an hour yet.'

'He got right off the bench and called Pat McKinney to complain about you. Relax. I still owe him a few jabs for dismissing the indictment in that Asian Gang Unit case last winter. He tried to grandstand on that and it nearly cost us half the forfeiture money we collected to re-present it to the Grand Jury.'

'Well, I'm glad that's the way you feel, Paul, but that's not the reason I sent up the alert. I didn't even tell this to Rose, but Chapman and I are pretty sure this guy I've been dating – Jed Segal – well, that he was cheating on me, with Isabella Lascar. Chapman's even put him on the suspect list.'

Silence. Deafening silence.

'How many people know about this?'

'Not many. And not the press, yet. It's not even con-firmed. We should know more this afternoon when we talk to—'

'Dammit. It's not "we" – you're not to have a hand in this. Can you get that through your stubborn skull yet? Have the Chief of Detectives give me a call – Rose can patch him through to me. And you better do exactly what I pay you to do – nothing else. I suppose I have to worry about having you guarded again.'

'Oh no, that's ridiculous.' I had Jed claiming he was des-perate to see me, Richard Burrell showing up unexpectedly in my office, Johnny Garelli due in town any minute now, and I'm arming myself with a bottle opener to answer the door for Mike and Mercer. 'No, I'll be okay.'

I hung up and opened the door, picking up my messages as I headed for the Bureau Chiefs' meeting that Rod had scheduled for the afternoon. Jed had telephoned three times, but Laura had gotten my signal and took no details from him, only the record of the call.

It was going to be more difficult than usual to focus during the meeting, as thirty of the Trial Division administrators sat around a long conference table, arguing over whether too many buy-and-bust cases were being indicted instead of given misdemeanor pleas, or too few defendants were being recommended for alternative sentencing plans. I scripted imaginary conversations with Jed in my head – what I really wanted to hear him say to me, and what I planned to say in response. By the time the meeting ended, none of the major issues we had come together to discuss had been resolved, and the next session was planned for two weeks thereafter.

It was four-fifteen when I returned to my desk with my third diet Coke of the afternoon, hoping the caffeine would kick in and keep me alert.

'Call Chapman at the squad. You just missed him.'

'Thanks, Laura.' I speed-dialed the number.

'Segal's a no-show. Thought you'd like to know that. Jerk got himself a lawyer who isn't bringing him in today.'

Shit. Why would he do that unless he had something to hide? 'Let me guess. Jimmy LaRossa? Marty London? Justin Feldman? He'd only go for one of the top dogs. Which one?' My luck – I'm the one who introduced him to the best lawyers in New York. Now he'll try to use one of them to thwart us.

'Nah. Some guy I never heard of – name's Bergin, from Washington.'

'Of course. Anderson Warmack's lawyer. Great trouble-shooter if you've got a federal securities case. I doubt he could even find the jury box in state court.'

'Yeah, well, he knew enough to tell Romeo to stay away from my office. And he refuses to let Jed submit to a blood test for DNA. Says we don't have probable cause.'

'He's been calling here all day, asking me to see him. I hung up on him once. Laura's not putting him through anymore.'

'Good girl. I spoke to Wally. I had Motor Vehicles FedEx Jed's new photo from his New York driver's license up to Chilmark. Told Wally to put it in an array and take it over to the Quinn sisters at the fried clam place, to see if they can make an ID or not. He should get that tomorrow and have it done. I hate to tell this guy how much probable cause I'm gonna have by the end of the week.'

'Don't gloat about it, Mike.'

'Sorry, Coop. I hate to be stonewalled. If he didn't do it, why doesn't he just come in and tell me?'

'It's more complicated than that for someone in his position, Mike. You know that.'

'Don't defend him, blondie. Look at this objectively, okay? Arm's length.'

'Anything else?'

'Yeah, got a confirmation from Maine. Burrell's got an arsenal all right. Lots of guns. Likes to shoot those little furry things, mostly. Be nice to him and you could probably have yourself a warm coat for the winter. Like the man said, no one can tell us when he got back to the island. But the Vineyard police are canvassing all the inns and guest houses anyway. We might turn up something there.

'Next thing. That story you told me about Isabella asking Jed for help 'cause she thought her accountant was stealing from her? Well, it's true. I spoke to her agent this morning. Seems the accountant, Fred Weintraub – a beanie, of course – was cooking the books. Iz had reported it to the IRS and they were gonna open a case on him. I did a run on the guy and he's got two convictions for fraud – one here in New York and one in Jersey. Freddy the Felon. Basically an East Coast guy, so I guess I gotta dig a little deeper on him, too.'

'Well, you're having a more productive day than I did. I'm ready to call it quits.'

'You okay for the evening?'

'Fine, thanks. I'm going to get some exercise for a while. Then dinner with Joan, and home to sleep, for a change.'

'There'll be an envelope at your door when you get home. I made a copy of a couple of letters the LAPD found in Isabella's house from this person who claims to be a shrink. Sounds crazier than a bedbug to me. Maybe they'll mean something to you. Ask your neighbor to look 'em over. Maybe it's shrink talk and he can figure it out.'

My backup line was flashing as I got off with Mike. It was Nina.

'Can you talk?'

'I can, but the better question is whether I want to. Nina, I've never been so confused or alone in my life.'

'I can be there tomorrow. I can take the red-eye tonight.'

'No, honestly, save it. Believe it or not, things might get worse, and I'll be begging you to come.'

'I called Joan while you were in court this morning and I couldn't reach you. I think I see the picture. She's going to meet you for dinner, right?'

'Eight o'clock.'

'Alex, I've been going over this again and again. Did Jed spend any time in England last month?'

'Well, he's been in Paris a lot. And usually makes a side trip to Zurich or London, if there's business to be done.'

'Remember when we were talking after Isabella's funeral and I told you she mentioned running into some guy on the rocket, the Concorde, coming back from London. That he was "powerful and important," remember? Maybe it *was* Jed. Maybe it was after you had introduced them to each other at "21," and they accidentally ran into each other on the same plane. Kismet. Serendipity. Don't blame yourself for this one – if she thought he was attractive and stable and rich, she'd have her claws out for him.'

'Even if she knew I was crazy about him?'

'All the more likely. That surprises you? C'mon, we all know women like that, Alex. There's Jezebel; there's the Duchess of Windsor, who stole Edward away from her best friend, Thelma Furness; there's Elizabeth Taylor going to the mats with Debbie Reynolds over Eddie Fisher. You think for a minute that Iz would have scruples about stepping on your toes? Give me a break. Anyway, the London airplane encounter was just a thought.'

'Thanks.'

'Look, whenever you're ready, I want you to come out here and get away from everything for a while. I'll take a few days off, leave the baby with Elena, and we'll just go out to the cottage at Malibu and relax for a week. Please?'

'Sure, Nina.'

We exchanged good-byes and I took my tote filled with ballet paraphernalia out of the filing cabinet. 'I'm sneaking out a bit early, Laura. Trying to make a six-thirty class. See you in the morning.'

'Two more from Jed, while you were taking these other calls. Sounds like he was at a phone booth. He's really anxious to see you. I'm just worried he might be waiting here at the corner of Center Street, hoping to catch up with you on the way out.'

Don't do this to me, you bastard. You know what it's like to be followed and harassed and watched and intercepted. You even went to court to get that woman to stop doing it. Don't start it with me.

I decided not to take the chance of running into him, if indeed, he had figured out that the easiest place to find me was outside of my office. I took the stairs down one flight and crossed into the corridor that led through the length of the building, exiting by the doorway two blocks to the north, instead of the executive wing elevators. That dumped me out at the rear of the courthouse, in the middle of Chinatown. I saw no signs of a yellow cab, so I hurried myself to Canal Street, turned west past rows of vendors hawking counterfeit Vuittons and Guccis, and symbolically held my breath as I descended the steps to the subway station and pushed through the turnstile for the uptown N train.

I hate the subway. I hate its filth, its odor, its crowds, and its unreliability. But when it worked, it was without exception the most efficient way to travel around the city. The Canal Street stops were my least favorite, since most of the people arriving in the morning and leaving in the late afternoon were either colleagues of mine who worked in the system, or defendants and their rent-a-baby-so-the-judge-will-be-sympathetic families, on their way to be arraigned for their latest arrests. I dreaded making eye contact with perps I would be squaring off with later in the day, or girlfriends with earrings the size of door knockers who had just left their main men in the Tombs because I had asked the judge for remand without bail.

The platform was practically deserted and my footsteps rang with an eerie echo as I tried to find a position to wait in for the next train. I was unusually jumpy and kept looking over my shoulder in hopes that no one would trap me against the dead end of the tunnel wall toward which I had chosen to move, or be hiding behind the thick steel girders which lined the middle of the station. I walked to the edge to see whether there were headlights to signal the approach of a subway car, but reminded myself of the recent spate of women being pushed onto the tracks by an escaped mental patient. I turned back to stand closer to the graffiti-streaked wall. Two or three times I glimpsed the head of a man coming toward me, weaving in and out of the posts, but I was unable to get a clear shot at his face and was relieved when I heard the rumble of the train as it approached the station.

So I clutched my tote to my side, moved briskly through the doors as they opened in front of me, found a seat that didn't seem to be too badly smeared with crumbs and soda stains, and pretended to be absorbed in a sheaf of Court of Appeals decisions that Laura had printed out of e-mail for me to read, while all the time my peripheral vision was scanning the car for the usual assortment of freaks and perverts.

19

I got off the train at Fifty-seventh Street and Seventh Avenue. The studio was a few blocks due north, but I toyed with the idea of a diversionary jaunt to the corner of Fifth, since it was such a beautiful afternoon. I thought of Holly Golightly and how she relieved her bouts of depression by visits to Tiffany's, on the theory that nothing bad could ever happen there. I could square the area and still be in time for class – Tiffany's windows, with Bendel's and Bergdorf's thrown in for good measure. Better than Prozac any day. Then I remembered the Warner Brothers store that expropriated the northeast corner and decided against the side trip. That giant souvenir shop had really brought the neighborhood down, I concluded, and kept on walking to William's loft instead.

The dressing room was empty when I went inside to change into my leotard and tights. It was rare that I arrived ahead of the regular students, most of whom lived and worked uptown, and I relished the moments of privacy and quiet at this end of the day as well. William was already in the studio, so I joined him for a series of stretches and bends, willing the tension and distress out of my stiff body as I tried to limber up.

'I didn't think you'd be here today, Alex,' he said quietly, in the calming manner that always put me at ease in his presence. 'I've been following the story about Isabella.'

'I think this is the best place for me to be. It really helps.' I was on the floor now, my back erect and the heels of my feet drawn up close to my body, as I tried to press my knees down to make contact with the wood. William walked over and began to knead my shoulders and neck, working the tightened muscles apart.

'I've got two tickets for the Kirov next week. I thought perhaps you and Bernard could use them. I hate for them to go to waste and I hope to get out of town for a few days by then.'

'We'd love them if you're not going to need them, Alex. That's very thoughtful. I guested with them once – nearly three decades ago. What a priceless week that was.'

'Must have been.'

'Bernard's dying to know if the police have any leads in the murder case. That you can talk about, of course.'

No wonder the neck massage. You can't ever get something for nothing, as my grandmother used to say. 'Nothing new.'

'Any rumors that Isabella was gay?'

That was a new one on me. 'That's never come up, as far as I know.'

'Phew. I mean after the furor over *Basic Instinct*, Bernard thinks the community would go wild if the killer turned out to be some crazed lesbian. Entirely too Hollywood.'

I laughed. 'Tell Bernard to relax. I think we're safe on this one.'

The dancers were beginning to filter in and warm up alongside us on the floor and at the barre. William went over to turn on his elaborate recording system, and the strong music of Beethoven's Fourth Symphony lifted me back to my feet and into the opening pattern of pliés and relevés in the standard numbered positions.

By the end of the hour I was physically drained – a perfect complement to my emotional condition. I dragged myself into the dressing room, showered in the tiny stall William had rigged up for his sweaty troupes, and put my business clothes on again to head over to meet Joan for dinner. I checked my answering machine from William's phone to make sure Joan had not changed or canceled our plans, but there were no messages at all, so I said goodbye to the stragglers and walked out onto the street.

When I reached the curb at the corner of Sixty-fourth Street and Central Park West, I was startled by the approach of a sleek navy limo that must have trailed me for the block and a half from the studio. The rear door opened and Jed stepped toward me, carrying an armload of long-stemmed yellow roses, my favorite.

'Please, Alex, you must let me talk to you. I know you're meeting Joan – just give me five minutes in the car and I'll take you wherever you're going.'

'It's over, Jed. I'm not interested in a post-mortem. And

I'm even less interested in creating a scene on a street corner.'

'Five minutes. I know you don't owe me anything, but I'd like you to hear what I have to say.'

I looked at the driver. It was Luigi, who usually drove Jed around town and who had always been a perfect gentleman to me. I still couldn't absorb Mike's theory that Jed was a killer, and I trusted that I was not in mortal danger as long as Luigi was in earshot. A smile formed on my lips, despite my company, as I toyed with the thought that the only thing Chapman and I hadn't floated was a conspiracy theory. He'd be livid that I got in a car with Jed, and ready to commit me if he let his imagination carry him to think that Jed and Luigi had conspired to do Isabella in.

I was tired enough to yield to the pressure and I bent to get into the car. Luigi began to draw closed the glass window that separated him from us in the backseat, but I put my hand up to stop him. 'Would you mind taking me to Sixty-fourth and Second, Luigi, to Primola? I'd like you to leave the partition open – you might as well hear all this.' I counted on the fact that I could at least embarrass Jed a bit in the process. Luigi had probably driven him to all his assignations anyway.

Jed grimaced at my suggestion, but was prepared to go ahead. He sat opposite me on the carseat, riding backward and trying to look me in the eye. 'I've called you dozens of times today and could never get through. Laura wouldn't take any messages from me, Joan won't help. I've left more on your home machine.'

Bullshit. Start with a lie, that'll really win me over. I just checked the machine and there was nothing on it, but why give him the satisfaction of knowing I even cared? I stared at the back of Luigi's head.

'Alex, I want to apologize to you. I have lied to you and I was unfaithful, but I think you'll understand what happened if you listen to the whole—'

'I've heard all I need to hear, Jed. This is one place where the details really don't interest me. Don't you see how painful this is for me?'

We were on the Park transverse now, right below the twinkling little white lights of Tavern on the Green, and dusk was fast becoming the darkness of a mild fall evening.

'I want you back, Alexandra Cooper. I love you and I want you back. I made a mistake – a stupid, selfish, pig-headed mistake. Are you so perfect that you've never done that in your life?'

'What was your mistake, Jed, betraying me – or getting caught at it?'

'You knew Isabella, you knew her far better than I did. She was relentless. She, she—'

'Don't make me vomit with this stuff. What was it, another stalker, Jed? Did she harass you?'

'You introduced me to her, you were there when—'

'I introduced you to a lot of people. Does that mean you had to play "hide the salami" with all of them?'

'Don't talk like your cop friends, Alex. It really isn't very becoming. You sound crass and vulgar.'

'Yeah, but it's a hell of a lot more direct than the crap you're trying to peddle.'

'You encouraged me to help her with her financial problems. "Call her," you said, "do what you can to help her."'

'You helped her all right. You apparently helped her into a shiny white coffin.'

'Stop that, Alex, that's a goddamn outrage, that kind of accusation. She begged me to come to the Vineyard, claimed she was desperate.'

'Tell it to the cops, Mr. Segal. Does your lawyer know you're about to incriminate yourself?'

'I'm not interested in the cops or my lawyer. I'm here to plead for your forgiveness. I never intended to get involved with her sexually—'

'Don't say the next line, Jed, leave me some piece of you I can still believe in. Luigi, I think he's about to tell me she raped him. Spare me this garbage, really. Did Isabella "make" you get in bed with her, Jed – did she really force you to make love to her? Please.'

Jed pounded his hand up against the roof of the car in disgust. 'It's always wisecracks with you, Alex. You won't even give me a chance to tell you what was going on, to tell you how I feel about you. Why do you think I'm here, why do you think I'm pursuing you like this?'

'You want to know what I really think? I think you're here because you're in a shitload of trouble, and if you align yourself with me, you're hoping I can convince Chapman that you're not a killer. You have lain in my arms and lied to me, Jed. You have made love to me *after* making love to Isabella in my very own bed . . .'

'That wasn't making love, with Isabella, that was—'

'Oh, forgive me, Jed. You made love to me after you screwed Isabella or f—'

'Alex, give me a chance to make it up to you.'

'I can't help you, Jed. I don't want to help you and I won't help you. I don't know whether you killed Isabella or not, but you sure as hell killed something inside of me. No life support, no resuscitation – it's dead, and I don't want to bring it back to life. Luigi, I'll get out at the light. No more calls, Jed, no more messages. Nothing.'

I was a block away from the restaurant when I got out of the car and slammed the door behind me. I stopped at the drugstore for a bottle of Extra-Strength Tylenol. While I ripped off the plastic seal around the lid and pulled the cotton wad out of the top of the container, I could hear the radio playing from the shelf behind the counterman. The raspy-voiced David Ruffin was leading The Temps through the classic 'Ain't Too Proud to Beg,' pleading for his sweet darlin' not to leave him. I swallowed hard and forced the three capsules down my dry throat, hoping they'd have some effect on my throbbing headache.

'*Com'e stai*, Signorina Cooper?' Giuliano greeted me as I entered the door at Primola and scanned the crowd at the bar for Joan Stafford.

'Fine, Giuliano, everything's fine. Is my friend here yet?'

'Of course, she's at the table. Follow me, please.'

As he led me to the corner, Joan saw me coming and stood to embrace me. 'No wonder he climbed into bed with a screen goddess. Maybe it takes a good friend to tell you how awful you look.'

'Thanks a million, Joanie. You sound like Mike Chapman. I'm beginning to get a complex.'

'How about a mental health day? Take tomorrow off and we'll go to Elizabeth Arden or Georgette Klinger – my treat. Facial, massage, pedicure, manicure – just a girls' day out. It'll make you feel good.'

'Maybe this weekend. Battaglia's going to be on me like a hawk. I have to show him I can do the work.'

256

'Listen, Jed called me three times this afternoon. I think he was driving around town looking for you – I didn't know what to tell him.'

'He found me. Not at the office, but coming out of my ballet class.'

The captain brought over our drinks. 'The usual, right?'

'Right. Joan, he's going to keep calling you, I'm sure. He wants to see me again, explain things, start over. Forget it. I don't need the aggravation. And furthermore, you can't believe a word that he tells you. Yeah, he tried to call the office a few times, but never told Laura he was waiting right outside for me. Tells you he's left messages on my home machine – not even my mother called today. He's a liar. He's scared and you can't trust a thing he says, so don't waste your time.'

I motioned for the waiter to come over. 'I'm starving. Know what you want?' Joan nodded. I ordered the tricolor salad and penne arrabiata, while she chose minestrone soup and a dish of linguine with white clam sauce.

'Basically, Joan, you have to be my Chinese wall. I don't want any information filtered through you from Jed. I'm not interested in his excuses or explanations. I know he'll try to use you, because he's manipulative and he knows where to find you. Whatever it is, I don't want to hear it, understood?'

'Yes, Madam Prosecutor.'

'I'm hoping that if I don't give him an ear, he *will* be forced to talk to the police. I'm in no position to listen to his story, and right now he won't cooperate with Chapman. So I don't know if he was on the island when Isabella was shot, and I don't know if he had anything at all to do with her death. But if he's got such an urge to

257

unburden his soul, let him do it at the squad, not to you or me.'

By the time our appetizers came, I had convinced Joan that I needed to talk about something else. We coasted through dinner as she caught me up on world news, a review of the latest Stoppard play that had just opened last week, and a description of what she planned to wear to the Literary Lions dinner, where she'd be feted for her recent Edgar nomination. Two double decaf espressos, a check, and we hailed a cab so she could drop me at my building while she went on to her apartment further uptown.

'Envelope for you, Miss Cooper.' Victor handed me the large manila packet that Chapman had dropped off as I passed through the revolving door. On the outside he had scribbled, below my name, 'Tonight's Final Jeopardy answer is Giuseppe di Lampedusa.'

I got on the elevator mumbling to myself, as I fumbled with the envelope's metal clasp, 'And the question is, who wrote *The Leopard*?' I ought to give that book to Mike sometime, I thought to myself, knowing he would love the fictional version of Italian history, portrayed through the story of the demise of an old aristocratic family. Inside, attached to the police reports, was a big yellow Post-it on which Mike had written: 'I didn't bet you on this one. Figured you'd know it. *I* thought it was a sexually transmitted disease. Leaf through these and I'll call you tomorrow.'

No light was flashing on the answering machine. Either my friends assumed that life was back to normal and had stopped worrying about me, or they had all reverted to the usual 'she's tough, she can handle it' mode. Either way it was sort of a relief, so I kicked off my shoes and put on a warm-up suit, then climbed on the bed to sort through the day's mail and read the correspondence that had been found in Isabella's home after her death.

LAPD Homicide Squad Report. Det. Reynoldo Loperra. Attached are pieces of stationery found on desk of deceased after search at request of Chilmark, Mass. Sheriff's Office.

My dearest Isabella,

I will first address your most serious concern regarding your forthcoming trip to Martha's Vineyard. Perhaps you are surprised that I know so much about your plans, but I must comment that you have been unusually careless in dropping broad hints that have come to my attention, and as you may realize by now, I am almost psychic in this regard. Should you have any doubts about that, perhaps our mutual friend can put your mind at rest.

There would be something sadistic about your mendacity and duplicity, cara Isabella, if it all wasn't so very mindless, and my concern about whether you would be a good candidate for psychoanalysis is because I fear it would reinforce a pernicious lasciviousness in you, which is quite inappropriate for a woman of your notoriety.

I know you have a strong ego, but I worry also that when you learn that you are not the only one who is capable of prevarication – that is, when you find that the woman he really loves is not your equal – not in physical beauty, not social status or material wealth, not even in professional recognition in her chosen field – the disappointment may be more miserable than the momentary pleasures of the flesh justify.

I am an ocean away and more than twice your age. I am confident, then, that you will not feel threatened if I tell you that my feelings for him are just as deep as yours, and so it is with profound respect for both of you that I caution you against the adventure you are undertaking so blithely.

Perhaps you will come to your senses – and send him on a plane to come and have some scones and a glass of burgundy with me. Better to love wisely than too well, and so on.

Best ever,
Cordelia Jeffers
Fellow, Royal Academy of Medicine

Maybe it was just the late hour but the letter made absolutely no sense to me at all. There were two or three others and I tried to skim through them to see if they were any more comprehensible. Was Isabella actually going back and forth to London to see a psychiatrist? There weren't any copies of envelopes attached to the reports so there were no postmarks to check for the mailing origin. The writing was sophomoric and pretentious, and I found it hard to believe that it could be the jargon or the wisdom of a prominent therapist. Was I the 'other woman' referred to in the letter? No match for Isabella Lascar, it's true – not her beauty, wealth, or fame, but certainly some recognition in my field. Was the mutual friend, in fact, Jed? More and more puzzles presented themselves instead of solutions, and I couldn't decide if someone had actually had the premonition that Isabella would be in danger if she kept her rendezvous with Jed.

I looked at my watch and saw that it wasn't yet eleven

o'clock. I dialed David Mitchell's number and was about to give up after five rings when he answered the phone. 'David, did I awaken you?'

'No, no. Alex?' He sounded reserved and rather cool. 'Anything wrong?'

'No. But I've got some letters here – letters that someone sent to Isabella, maybe a psychiatrist, and I was wondering if you could take a look at them for me.'

He hesitated before responding. 'Sure. Do you think it can wait until morning?'

'Oh, David, I'm sorry. I didn't even ask – are you in the middle of something?'

'Well, not exactly the middle, but I do have company and . . .'

'No problem. Let's make a date for tomorrow. That's fine.' Just because *I'm* Miss Lonelyhearts doesn't mean the rest of the world has to stop for me.

'Come on in for coffee at seven-thirty tomorrow morning. Bring the letters. I'm running at six-thirty, then a quick walk for Zac and I can give you as much time as you need.'

'And your company? This is kind of confidential. I think I'd rather wait and see you alone.'

'Gone with the first light of day, Alex. See you in the morning, okay?'

'Thanks.' I undressed, got into bed, and was asleep before I could even think about what the next day was going to bring.

The doorman rang my intercom shortly before seven-thirty on Wednesday morning to tell me that Dr. Mitchell was on his way upstairs and would like me to meet him in his apartment in five minutes. I had been up for almost an hour, getting ready to go to work and browsing through the *Times* for what seemed like the first day in more than a week. It helped greatly to put my personal situation in perspective to read that there had been yet another Ebola virus outbreak in Central Africa, a new Serbian uprising in a part of the Balkans I'd never heard of, and a recent discovery of mass graves containing hundreds of unidentified bodies in Guatemala. Humphrey Bogart was right: my problems don't amount to a hill of beans in a world as full of trouble as this one.

David was just unleashing Prozac after their walk when I opened the door to his apartment. The dog greeted me warmly and we played tug-of-war with her chewed-up rawhide toy while David went into the kitchen to get the pot of coffee he had set up before going out to run. She nosed her way into my hand and invited me to rub behind her soft ears, and I was grateful for her early-morning display of affection.

We sat at David's dining-room table and I spread out some of the papers for him to see. I began by summarizing the events of the week and trying to give him an objective overview of the cast of characters that was developing. As David studied the letters of Dr. Cordelia Jeffers, I glanced around the apartment, amused at the contrast in our decors. Mine was as utterly feminine as his was masculine, with every surface here bathed in brown, except those that were beige or tan. He had been a bachelor for too long and I instinctively began redecorating in my mind's eye as I waited for some kind of response to Isabella's bizarre correspondence.

'I suppose the police have checked this woman's credentials with the Brits.'

'I haven't heard any results on that yet.'

'I did some work with the president of the Academy when I was at Ditchley last year. I can call him today and try to get some information, but from the looks of these letters, I'd guess she's a fraud. This just seems like a lot of gibberish to me. Dr. Jeffers may be a bit senile and dotty, or else she's taken on the traits of one of her patients. She sounds more like someone in need of treatment than a physician. Can I hold on to these letters?'

I shouldn't even be showing them to anyone, I reminded

myself. 'They're my only copy, David. I'll Xerox them at the office and get a set to you tonight,' after I tell Chapman to get the lieutenant's permission to consult a shrink. 'But it would be great if you make the call to find out where this woman is and what kind of practice she has. Then we can interview her about Isabella.'

'I'll do that as soon as I get to the office, before they close shop in London for the evening. We'll talk tonight?'

'Yeah. Why don't *you* call me. I can promise you won't be interrupting anything.'

I hailed a yellow cab on the corner of Third Avenue and directed the driver to take me to the Criminal Court Building by way of the FDR Drive.

'Know where the courthouse is?'

'Yeah.'

Always a bad sign, it usually meant that the driver had a criminal record.

'You a lawyer?' he asked, looking me over through the rearview mirror.

Most cabbies asked that question when they picked me up or dropped me off in front of the building, hoping for free advice about their immigration status, moving violations, or arrests for assault.

'No. I'm going to court to testify. I was raped.' A surefire way to end the conversation and allow me to finish perusing the paper the rest of the way downtown, as the driver took another peek in the mirror to see what one of those looked like.

I was later than usual so the elevators and hallways were bustling with prosecutors and witnesses. A heavyset uniformed cop, pushing retirement age, stepped out of my way as I turned into the eighth-floor corridor. 'Hey, Miss Cooper. How ya doin'?

'Remember me? I had that rape case with you in '92.'

'Nice to see you. Sure.' I had only talked to a thousand or more cops about a thousand or more rape cases since then. Give me a hint.

Laura was at her desk when I walked in. 'You don't want to know who's been calling, I guess.'

'Not if it's more of the same from Jed.'

'Okay. There were a few others. Mercer just called. Said he was going out in the field and he'd try you again when he got back. They had a 911 call, something to do with the Con Ed rapist. Not a new case, just a possible suspect. Sarah needs to speak to you – she's got a question about a search warrant. And Elaine called from Escada. The suit you ordered came in. Can you get to the store to try it on?'

'Just ship it. I'll never get there.'

I started working on my third cup of coffee, called Sarah and several of the other assistants who had e-mailed for help, then spent some time responding to some of the mail that had accumulated on my desk. When I finished, I told Laura I'd be upstairs watching one of the newer members of the unit deliver his first summation. I took a legal pad and went to the trial part on the fifteenth floor, where I sat in the rear of the room to make notes for the critique I would do after the verdict came in on the case.

For the better part of an hour I listened to the defense attorney drone on about his version of the facts of the case. It was a date rape and therefore – automatically – a difficult trial. Sarah and I had prepared our newest recruit, Mark Acciano, for the problems he would have to confront before the jury. Most people considered this kind of case far less serious than stranger rapes, and trying to educate jurors during the course of the trial – if the ones with that attitude had not been identified and dismissed during the jury selection process – was next to impossible.

Unlike cases in which victims were attacked by armed assailants they had never seen before, the typical date rape involved two people who were together because they liked each other, and wanted to be in each other's company. Many psychologists called them 'confidence rapes,' because they occurred when a woman placed her trust in someone she felt she would be secure with, who then betrayed that reliance. While jurors tend to empathize with women who are raped by strangers, they are much tougher in these date cases, in which defense attorneys try to blame the victims for their participation in the events leading up to the sexual acts. The typical strategy is to attack the victim for every aspect of her lifestyle, from her manner of dress to her alcohol or drug use to her initial attraction to the defendant that must have meant that she 'asked for it.' They were ugly cases to try.

When the defense attorney sat down, Mark rose to make his closing argument. First, he marshaled all the evidence in the case, detailing every word and act that the complaining witness had described about her assailant during the course of the several hours he spent in her apartment when they had returned there after a dinner date. Mark was candid about the weak spots – how much liquor she had consumed, how much foreplay she had consented to – but firm about the fact that neither of those factors gave the defendant a license to force her to have intercourse with him. As Sarah and I had coached, he was graphic and emphatic about the defendant's threats, and about the force with which he had restrained his prey when she had tried to resist and escape his attack.

The victim's outcry had been prompt, which is somewhat unusual in many date rape cases when women are conflicted about whether to report the crime, fearful of not being believed. The medical record was a useful tool in this case, and Mark took the jury through it carefully. The fingermarks on the young woman's wrists and inner thighs corroborated her story about the defendant's application of pressure — no, she hadn't been beaten and bruised, but she had been held down against her will, and these marks did not support his story of tender lovemaking. The internal exam had revealed redness and swelling in the vaginal vault, with several very minor abrasions noted on the accompanying diagram, again inconsistent with the protection afforded by lubrication during consensual sex.

I was impressed with the construction of Mark's argument, and with the manner in which he made the jury confront the unpleasant details that established the elements of the crime. These were cases that had little to do with the business of a police investigation, but rather rose and fell based on the candor and credibility of the complaining witness. He placed that all before the panel of twelve jurors, some who nodded in agreement as he hammered home his strong points, some who sat stone-faced in their chairs, and some who appeared to be napping through all of the argument. He worked his way painstakingly toward his conclusion.

'. . . and I ask you to find the defendant guilty of the crime of rape in the first degree. Thank you very much.'

Mark had taken more than an hour for the delivery of his summation, and I smiled my approval to him as he returned to his seat at the prosecution table. The judge would now begin his charge to the jury, in which he'd explain the various laws that had to be applied to the facts in the case. I noted that it was after noon, so I slipped out of the courtroom and returned to my office, knowing that it would be hours before the jurors finished deliberations and reached a verdict in a case like this.

'Rod called. Wants to know if you'd like to go out for lunch,' Laura greeted me when I returned to my office.

'Please tell him I'm stretched for time – let's do it next week. And would you order me in a salad and soda?'

'Sure. Call Mercer at Special Victims. And Lieutenant Peterson at the Homicide Squad.'

I was excited when I picked up the phone to dial Mercer's number. We were overdue for a break in the serial rape pattern and I was hoping it had come.

'Special Victims. Wallace.'

'Any luck? Heard you went out on a call.'

'A bullshit run. Nothing.' Mercer sounded discouraged. 'Every time some pimply faced plumber rings a doorbell on the Upper West Side, somebody calls 911. Not our guy, not even close. It's a bad month to be a repairman – this poor slob was scared out of his wits. Took me two hours to calm him down. Then I had to call his old lady and explain the situation – make sure she understood it was all a mistake. Sorry for the false alarm. I'll be talking to you.'

Peterson was Mike Chapman's boss at the Homicide Squad, a tough old-timer who had worked Homicide most of his career, and knew the business better than anybody. 'Hey, loo, how've you been?'

'Pretty good for an old guy, Alex. Can't complain.'

'What do you need?'

'It's on the Lascar case. Mike's due in at four. I just called him to let him know what's been going on, and I thought you should know, too. Then we had an idea, maybe you could help us with.'

'Shoot.'

'Chief Flanders just called. I don't know the case as well as you do, but Mike says you'd understand what I'm talking about. First of all, Flanders got a hit on the photo ID of this Segal guy from the two sisters at the lunch place. That make any sense to you? Mike says it would.'

Butterflies began floating in my stomach and my spirits sank to a new low. It made no sense at all to me. 'Yeah, loo, it makes perfect sense. Go on.'

Now it was no longer speculation. And now it was no longer just a matter of infidelity. Mike had been right. Jed had been with Isabella less than one hour before she was killed. Despite all the indications, I had kept on hoping he had left earlier. I had refused to consider him a serious possibility as a suspect, but I had to come to grips with the reality of that fact. No wonder it was Peterson who made the call. Mike was too afraid I'd be shattered by the confirmation of that news.

'The next thing Wally says to tell you is that Burrell – I guess he's the ex-husband – has something to hide, too. Must've followed his wife from Boston to the Vineyard. Stayed at a hotel in Edgartown called the Charles Inn. Know it?'

'The Charlotte Inn. Gorgeous. Expensive.' Son of a bitch,

269

doesn't anybody believe in telling the truth anymore? Burrell shows up here to pitch me his case, then he looks me in the eye and lies. Interesting approach, I got to give him credit. Admit the gun possession, admit the fight in the Boston hotel. Just leave out the part that puts you within fifteen miles of the crime scene. Mike's right – they think we're all stupid if we're in law enforcement.

'Now that suggests two things to me, Alex. One is, he didn't go to the island planning to off his ex-wife. I think he woulda known to use an alias at the hotel. Even in the movies cops canvass hotels and motels to check the guest lists. But it doesn't mean something didn't set him off once he got there – maybe he saw her with the other man, maybe they had a phone conversation that made him crazy. He's in town, so we'll set up the interview and sweat him. It always helps to go in with a piece of information that he obviously doesn't think we have.'

I was still focused somewhere back on Jed.

'The rest is just local gossip. People who claim they saw and heard things all week. Someone in the post office says a woman was in asking directions to your place. Doesn't exactly remember what day it was. Could that have been Isabella or did you have other company?'

'I gave directions to Isabella a week before she went up there. But she could easily have left them behind or stopped in somewhere to check. Maybe she invited someone else over – I sure as hell didn't even know she had Jed Segal there.'

'Also, American Express confirmed the Chanel sale. Only thing is Segal bought the stuff in New York, on Saturday afternoon, after his European trip. Looks like he got it at a drugstore about two blocks from your place. Sorry. The good news was that he had purchased the Concorde ticket to Paris weeks ago, then he moved his departure back a day or two at the very last minute. So he hadn't planned the trip to the Vineyard for long. Well, that's today's report. Next thing, that FBI agent, Luther Waldron is in town. The feds had to make calls to get some of these guys to come to New York, which leads me to the favor we want to ask you.

'Mike doesn't want Waldron in on all the interviews tomorrow. Doesn't like the guy's style, doesn't think he knows anything about murder investigations, says he's no better than a Meter Maid. So Mike's trying to get as much done as possible *out* of Waldron's presence, okay?'

'Suits me fine.'

'Johnny Garelli – you know that name?'

'Yeah. Johnny Gorilla, she called him. The stuntman stud Isabella romanced for a few months. I only met him once.'

'Waldron got him to come into town for a sit-down tomorrow. He arrived on the red-eye this morning. Staying at the Gramercy Park Hotel. Mike thinks that if you called him and asked him to meet you for dinner this evening, you might be able to get more out of him than we could in a formal interview. Mike says Garelli likes broads better than he likes cops – I'm supposed to butter you up and say he likes blondes with great wheels – does that work?'

'No butter needed. You know this is the kind of assignment I love. Do I have to tell Battaglia?'

'Hey, you know me. If it was one of *my* guys did a thing like that without my permission, I'd wring his fucking neck. But in your case, don't you go off duty at 6 P.M.? I'm not asking you to get a pass from nobody to have a dinner date. It's nothing dangerous like Mata Hari. We have no reason to think he's the killer, but Mike wants to look at him 'cause he's got such a history of jealous squabbles with the deceased. We figure he'll bite if you call, one of yous'll pick a place, and Chapman'll be having a drink at the bar. Maybe you'll get some scoop, some juice he'll give you as a friend of Isabella's. Pick his brain – I guess I'm usin' that term loosely. Worst that can happen to you is you have a boring evening and a bad meal. Choose the restaurant, you might even eat good.'

'On the job, loo. I love it. I'll try to reach him. Tell Mike to call me when he gets in this afternoon. I'll really feel like a wallflower if he turns me down.'

'If he turns you down, Alex, I'll take you to Sheehan's for a steak.'

Ugh, the food at Sheehan's, a friendly bar run by the family of a retired Homicide cop. Great place to drink, but damned if I'd eat another meal there. That was incentive enough to put in a call to the Gorilla.

I got the number of the hotel from Information and asked the desk for Johnny's room. He answered the phone and sounded as though I had awakened him. I reminded him that we had met once at Mortimer's, expressed my less-than-enthusiastic sympathy for Isabella with exaggerated sincerity, and suggested that we might meet for drinks or dinner to commiserate about her loss. He told me he'd been napping because of his jet lag, and that he had a date with a dancer from one of the Broadway shows who couldn't meet him till almost midnight. Yeah, he'd be glad to do dinner with an old friend of Isabella's.

'Want me to suggest a restaurant, or do you know New York?'

'You got any problem with Rao's?'

'Only getting in. I adore it, but you'll never get a table for tonight.' A New York classic, but impossible to get into. The tiny place – four booths and a handful of tables – was one of the hottest tickets in New York, despite its unlikely location on the corner of Pleasant Avenue and 114th Street in the heart of East Harlem. It was one of the last remaining vestiges of the Italian neighborhood that once flourished there. Run almost like a club, regulars had their own tables for designated nights of the week and there was no room for reservations for unknowns unless every politician, actor, writer, and hotshot were marooned on the same remote island. Great food, no menus, and the most incredible jukebox in the city – light on Smokey, but lots of Sinatra and the Shirelles.

'Not a problem. Stallone told me I could have his table if I wanted it tonight. I was just about to give it up – this girl I'm being set up with doesn't get off till it's too late to eat. I'll meet you there at eight.'

Lucky for me. I get the good meal, and the showgirl gets Johnny Garelli for dessert.

When my lunch was delivered, I closed the door to the office and ate by myself, enjoying the solitude. It never lasted long.

The first knock on the door was Mark Acciano. I waved him in. 'What did you think?' he asked eagerly.

'Great summation, really good job. Thoughtful, thorough, impassioned. You gave it your best shot. Now you've got to let the jurors go to work – you've given them all the tools they need to reach the right result. The rest is in their hands.' We chatted about the case and I told him I would try to be with him when the verdict came in, to beep me when he got the call.

Then came Phil Weinfeld, aka The Whiner. He had two traits that made Sarah and me cringe every time he loomed in the doorway of my office. First was what we called the 'I knew that' problem. He'd call and urgently plead for ten minutes of my time, come over and present a hypothetical, and then ask for guidance. The ten-minute presentation never took less than half an hour, and at the end, when Sarah or I made a suggestion which obviously caught Phil by surprise, he'd say, 'I knew that.' Then what did you bother me for in the first place?

The other thing he was known for, much to the aggravation of most of his colleagues, was his insistence on seeking advice from eight or ten of us on exactly the same issue, without revealing that he had already consulted the others. We used to joke that if he got hit by a bus on his way home in the middle of the trial, the case wouldn't even need an hour's adjournment. There'd be at least a dozen of us who knew the facts every bit as well as he did who could pick up the file and carry on to the verdict. He had worn out his welcome with Sarah, who'd begin every conversation with him by asking, 'How many other assistants have you asked about this already?' If he'd been through it with half of the bureau, she'd point to the door and tell him to get lost.

'What's up, Phil?'

'Have you got a few minutes for a question, Alex?'

'A few.'

'I'm having a problem with the witness in the case that you assigned me in September, the woman whose old boyfriend came back to her apartment to pick up his clothes, and then beat her to a pulp when she wouldn't have sex with him? You know which one I mean?'

'Yeah.'

'Well, she canceled three appointments with me. Kept telling me that she didn't want to prosecute 'cause she still loved him. I was trying to work out a plea with his lawyer, figuring I'd rather take a misdemeanor assault than have him walk away with no record.'

'What's the problem?'

'She just called me in hysterics. Changed her mind completely. She went to a psychic this morning for a consultation. Didn't tell the psychic any of their history, nothing about the guy, and the psychic does her reading and says, "There's a man in your life who's very dangerous." She flipped. She's terrified. Now she wants to go all the way with the case.'

'You mean the ex puts her in the hospital with two fractured ribs, a loose tooth, a broken nose and a black eye, but it took a swami to convince her the guy is dangerous? Unbelievable. I'm sure she's sitting in front of the psychic with a huge shiner and her nose relocated next to her ear, and the genius figures out that a dangerous man hit her. Maybe we ought to put a psychic on the payroll to help with recalcitrant witnesses.'

'What should I do about the plea offer I made?'

'Withdraw it. If the schmuck was too stupid to take it and run, bring her in tomorrow while she's still hot to testify and put the case in the Grand Jury. Assign the arresting officer, even if it's his RDO' – regular day off— 'and I'll authorize the overtime. Indict him and let's get the felony instead of the misdemeanor. Be sure her order of protection is renewed.'

'Yeah, I know that. I'll take care of it.'

'Anything else today?'

'Nope – that's it. I'll let you know what happens.'

The rest of the day passed quickly with the usual array of cases and customers. Every time the phone rang I feared it would be Battaglia, and I played with the idea of asking him whether I should keep the meet with Johnny Garelli. But he didn't look for me once, and since I knew he would have been disapproving, I simply avoided having to deal with the issue.

Mike called me a little before four o'clock when he reached the squad. 'What a wimp you are,' I chided him. 'Couldn't even call me to tell me about the Quinn sisters making the hit on the photo of Jed, could you?'

'Frankly, I didn't want to tell you, you're right about that. You didn't seem to want to accept the obvious from the first time we talked about it.'

'Have you told his lawyer about the photo ID yet?'

'Nah. I just got in. I'll call him later. Meanwhile, the lieutenant tells me you've accepted our mission – gonna throw some moves on Johnny Garelli tonight. Did you find him?'

'Piece of cake. It's all set.'

'Where's the meet?'

'Rao's. Can you do it?'

'Way to go, blondie. We're both in for a good evening.'

'*You* can get a table at Rao's? I can't believe it.'

'No way. But I can get a seat at the bar. And once I'm in, the whole joint is so small I can scope it all pretty easy. Joey's aces, the best. He'll let me sit there all night, and Vic will keep my glass looking full.' The restaurant was owned by Joey Palomino – a real charmer, who not only ran the business, but also acted in a number of movies and TV series, usually playing cops and detectives. He was good to the industry luminaries who frequented Rao's, but just as nice to the guys who let him hang out at precincts and squadrooms to learn the ropes. And Vic was one of those astounding bartenders who would see a customer like me walk in – someone who wasn't likely to get there more than twice a year – point a finger at me, raise an eyebrow, and say, 'Dewar's on the rocks, am I right?'

'So what do I do, Mike? Johnny wants me to meet him there at eight.'

'I'll make sure I'm there at seven-thirty. I'll see if I can get Maureen Forester freed up from her bodyguard detail to go with me, so it looks like I got a date.' Maureen was one of the best detectives in the city, with the added advantages of being great-looking and having a superb sense of humor. 'We'll be at the bar.

'Nobody's expecting any trouble, but this way you'll have us at your elbow if the guy does anything jerky. Sit and have a nice dinner. See if you can find out what his relationship was like with Isabella near the end. So far, nobody we've talked to in L.A. has any idea where this goofball was the week of the murder. See if you can ease anything out of him.'

'What'll you do until then?'

'See what other information came in today. If I don't speak to you before dinner, you should let the Gorilla take you home from the restaurant. Then Maureen and I will come up for a nightcap when we see him pull away, and we can compare notes on the day, okay?'

'Yeah. See you later.'

I called Mark Acciano's office to see how the deliberations were going in his trial. His paralegal answered and explained that Mark was still in the courtroom. The jurors had asked for a lot of readback – most of the testimony of the complaining witness, which meant that at least one person, maybe more, were fighting on her behalf. That process alone would take several hours, so it was unlikely there would be a verdict this evening. 'Please tell Mark I can't wait it out with him tonight. I'm sort of working on something else. But my beeper will be on in case he gets a result sooner than I think.' I wished the team good luck and hung up.

Pat McKinney was standing in the doorway. 'I just got a call from Maureen Forester. She's bodyguarding that pros who's a material witness in a drug conspiracy murder case that Guadagno's on trial with. She says you've got an emergency – need a female undercover – that I've got to relieve her for the evening. Do I need to know about this?'

Shit. Not if I can help it. Oh, Mo – I wouldn't exactly have called this an emergency. 'Well, you know that pattern we're trying to break up – the Con Ed guy?'

'Oh, it's related to that?'

'Not ex—'

'You're not using her for a decoy or anything, are you?'

'No, of course not.' I wasn't lying, I was just stalling for an excuse. I think all the people who'd been testing my good nature all week had something contagious that I had picked up. Well, it was very unlikely that Pat would ever find out about my evening plans.

'Okay, Alex, you can have her but you're going to have to call around and get somebody to replace her on the bodyguard. My wife and I have theater tickets tonight, and I just don't have time to hang out here begging the squad commander for a replacement. It's in your lap, okay?'

'Fine.' Don't let your current state of despair get the better of you, Alex, I tried to tell myself. How does a sour, mean-spirited grouch like Pat get himself a wife who he can take to the theater at the end of a busy day, while I can't find a decent guy to save my life? Karen McKinney's a boring, computer science techno-nerd professor at Brooklyn College, but it still must be awfully nice to have someone to go home to and leave all this bad news behind.

I called Chapman at the office and told him what I needed. 'Pat dumped it back on me. If you want Maureen, I've got to get someone to bodyguard Mo's witness at the hotel overnight. Any ideas? Is she difficult?'

'Nah. We're just trying to keep her straight during the trial. Junkie. We call her the Princess. She's from the suburbs, very agreeable. Shoots up in her armpits so she doesn't leave any tracks for her old man to see. Easy to baby-sit – no problem as long as you keep her away from the stuff. I'll make some calls and have someone up there in an hour. Don't worry about it.'

My second line was flashing. Laura signaled that Joan Stafford was on the telephone. 'Can you believe how bad it is? Even Pat McKinney has more of a life than I do,' I moaned into the line.

'Little wonder, Alex. I'm thinking of having a Cooper family crest designed for you. A symbol of Athena, with a broken heart, and an inscription in Latin: "I sure know how to pick 'em."'

'Why? More from Jed?'

'Alex, he's going over the edge. Now he's calling *me* constantly. I love you dearly, but I've got a deadline with my editor and I'll never make it if I try to keep Jed at bay for you. I can't keep up with his calls. Maybe you should just hear him out for an hour tonight and get it over with. He can't understand why you won't respond to his messages.'

'Joan, there are no messages. He's manipulative and dishonest. Look, I'll speak with his secretary and have her tell him to leave you alone, but don't suggest for a minute that *I* see him. I'm busy tonight, working. You're an angel – I'll get you out of this one, promise.'

The last call of the afternoon was to David Mitchell. 'How's everything been going today, Alex?'

I'm not looking for a diagnosis of my condition, I just need help with the case. 'Much better, David, thanks. Got something for me?'

'Yes. I checked first thing this morning. There is no psychiatrist in England named Cordelia Jeffers, nor is there any record that there ever has been. At least she's not a licensed M.D., and there was never anyone by that name who was admitted to the Royal Academy.'

Curiouser and curiouser.

David went on. 'I'd like to look at the letters again, if I may. I'll probably have a few more questions for you after I do. Did you remember to make copies?'

I told him I'd make them right now and slide them under his door before my dinner date.

I closed up for the day and walked out of the office to look for a cab. The fall air was heavy and the thick clouds made an evening rainstorm likely. I grabbed a yellow on the corner of Worth Street and gave him my address. The inside of the taxi smelled like a corral for a herd of camels, and like so many of the new additions to the fleet of drivers in the past few years, the man at the wheel didn't seem to recognize too many words in the English language.

We attempted to make ourselves clear to each other by a combination of waving arms and grunts, but I yielded to the fact that I would have to stay on top of him for the entire ride to make sure he knew where I wanted to go.

'Here she is now,' I heard Anthony, the second doorman, tell the young delivery boy, who was barely visible behind the tall array of two dozen yellow roses. 'Miss Cooper, want me to send the kid up with you?'

'No thanks, Anthony.' I stepped to the table along the wall near the mailboxes and withdrew a pen and a twenty-dollar bill from my pocketbook. I removed the card, ripped up Jed's pathetic note – 'Please – I really need your help' – and gave the kid back the flowers along with the tip. I scratched on the envelope the words 'With gratitude for all you do,' relied on the old theory that anonymous giving was really the most generous form of the art, and directed the kid to New York Hospital, which was just a few blocks down the street. 'Sorry, this was a mistake. They were supposed to be delivered to the burn unit at the hospital. Just leave them there, at the nurses' station, okay?'

The young man didn't seem too annoyed, and I continued on my way upstairs. I heard Zac bark as I slipped 'Dr.' Jeffers's letters under David's door, and I unlocked my own apartment and went inside to change for my rendezvous with Johnny. No mail of any interest except a postcard from Nina and a request from the *Wellesley Alumni Magazine* for an update on my activities for the class notes. My schoolmates would be about as interested in my goings-on as I am in the news of their Zen weddings on hilltops in the Rockies, their inventive mothering styles, and the impractical topics of their postdoctoral theses. I ripped up the request and saved the notice to send in my annual dues before the end of the month. No messages on the machine, either, so I showered and selected a slinky black outfit to wear for dinner.

I was ready to go and called for a car service to take me uptown, as I waited for the Final Jeopardy question to come on, just before the seven-thirty close of the show.

The topic was world geography – Mike and I could split this one down the middle, but I figured he was already on his way to the bar with Maureen. The Final Jeopardy answer was: 'A town in France, famous for its tapestry, which was in fact an embroidered chronicle of the Norman Conquest.'

Alex Trebek began to go on about the tapestry not being an actual tapestry, but rather an embroidery made of coarse linen. I was sssshing him through the television screen as I tried to concentrate as hard as his contestants, who appeared to be as puzzled as I was. Alençon? Cluny? I probably would have bet my whole stash for the evening on a topic I figured I was pretty good at, but I was actually stymied by the time the stupid music of the jingle stopped playing. I made a last-ditch stab at Aubusson.

'No, I'm sorry. Aubusson is not the right answer,' Alex gently rejected one of the players who had come up with the same guess as I had. Player number two had just left her card blank, shrugging her shoulders and shaking her head. Player number three, an obese musicologist from Indianapolis with one arm and five children, surprised Trebek with the right question: 'What is Bayeux, France?'

'That's absolutely correct, Mrs . . .' I clicked off the television before I could hear how much money she had won and picked up the ringing phone at the side of my bed.

It was the polite, slightly Southern accented voice of FBI agent Luther Waldron, greeting me with a 'Hello, Alex, I never thought I'd find you at home tonight.' Well, I might ask, why did you bother to call me here then? But I didn't.

'Hi, Luther. I'm just on my way out the door.'

'Wanted to let you know I'm in town. I've arranged for some of Isabella's disgruntled suitors to be here for interviews.'

'Yes, so I've heard.'

"Course none of them look quite as likely as that character you had yourself mixed up with. That was certainly a shocker. Next time you get serious with somebody, you let me help you with a little background check, young lady.'

I'll just ignore that one for the moment. 'How can I help you, Luther?'

'Just thought you'd like to know I was in on this. Your Homicide guys may do fine with street criminals, but I'm not sure they know how to carry off the interrogation of Hollywood types, businessmen. You know, the more intelligent kind of suspect. I'm staying right on top of it.

'Couple of other items. Just tried to pass them along to Chapman, but he's out in the field. I'll brief him when I see him tomorrow.'

'What are they?'

'Well, for one thing, Burrell's back into the ice. Cocaine. We've got a snitch in Boston who says his main man made a delivery to Burrell's hotel room the same day Isabella checked out. You add that to his secret trip to the Vineyard, spice it up with his rage at her, and who knows what he did, without ever planning it in advance. We'll be talking to him before the end of the week, and I hear he's mighty nervous already.'

'What else?'

'One of our L.A. agents tracked down the local psychiatrists whose names were on the pill bottles in Isabella's bathroom. Three of them had been fired over the years for not giving her the ups and downs she wanted. The current guy seems pretty cool, but he's pulling all kinds of patient–doctor privilege stuff now. You know, he can't divulge things Isabella said to him because she was his patient. Claims he has no information about her that has anything to do with the murder anyway. Wants to confer with his lawyer first to find out, legally, whether the privilege survives her death. How can he know what's relevant to her murder without knowing half the details we know? The only thing he'd give up was that the lover she was talking to him about – sorry, but we figure that's Segal – he'd had an experience with a stalker, too. That's one of the reasons she was so comfortable with him. The shrink'll talk about Segal – says that *he* wasn't the patient, so there's no privilege with whatever things he told Isabella. He never met with Segal directly – just says Lascar told him Segal had also been stalked by some woman while he was running for political office. Did you know about that?'

'Yeah, we did.'

'We'll keep working the psychiatrist, Alex.'

'Okay, Luther. I've got to run.'

'Hey, got a couple of jokes for you, Alex. Heard them at Quantico the other day – right up your line of work, so I saved them for you.'

The guy just doesn't get it, I guess. 'Anybody down there tell you the one about FBI agents – about why each male agent has a hole in the end of his penis?' I asked him, cutting him off at the pass, before he had another chance to offend me.

'No,' he replied cautiously, 'haven't heard it yet.'

'So oxygen can get to their brains.' Have a nice day, Luther. 'See you tomorrow.'

I put out my lights and locked the door behind me as I went off to meet one more of the men who might have had a motive to take the life of Isabella Lascar.

21

I walked into Rao's a few minutes before eight, while Tina Turner was asking the gathering of diners what love has to do with it, and reminding me once again, as if the lessons of the last week had not been enough, that it was a secondhand emotion. There was no sign of the Gorilla, but I got a warm hello from Joey Palomino when I reintroduced myself to him and said I was happy to wait at the bar. I walked over and sat on one of the handful of stools, next to a very attractive black woman – Maureen Forester – who was sipping white wine, while her date – Mike Chapman – was working on what looked like a vodka and tonic.

The bartender was opening a bottle of wine at Woody Allen's booth, so I began to make small talk with the couple sitting beside me at the bar while I waited for him to return to take my order.

'I'll bet you twenty dollars you don't know the answer to tonight's question,' I said, leaning across Maureen and grinning at Mike.

'What's the subject?'

'World geography.'

'You're on.'

I knew I had a winner. I gave Mike the final answer, but before I could sit up straight, he came back at me with Bayeux.

'What'd you do, call your mother?' Mike's widowed mother was glued to the television most of the day and night in her little condo in Bay Ridge, and she was his shill when he couldn't count on seeing the show.

'No. I swear to God, that was an easy one.'

'Bullshit. How'd you know?' I couldn't believe it. And Luther's worried that Mike's too unsophisticated to interview a cokehead producer, an illiterate stuntman, and a cheating businessman.

He laughed. 'I was there in '94 – fiftieth anniversary of D-Day. Bayeux was the first French city liberated by the Allies. June 8, 1944.' Mike and his military history. 'Went with my uncle Brendan, who landed with the invasion force, remember? The only other thing in town is the tapestry museum. Had to take Aunt Eunice through it twice. Relax, blondie, you can pay up tomorrow.'

Vic came back behind the bar, shook my hand, told me he was sorry he couldn't remember my name but he was dead straight on the drink order. Maureen and I pretended to become acquainted while I waited for my host to show up. She complimented my outfit and thanked me, under her breath, for getting her out of the fleabag hotel where we stashed our recalcitrant witnesses during trials.

We three chatted about the music, the changing weather, and what the prospects were for the Knicks this season. About ten minutes later the door pushed open and Johnny Garelli stood in the frame, striking a pose and waiting to be fussed over by Joey. He was big and solid, as good-looking as the magazine photos, but with the most awful hair plugs dotting the front half of his head.

'Jesus, Mo, would you take a look at those implants? How'd she ever get in bed with that guy?'

'Now, now, now, Alex. You know better than that. A man's hair is like his penis – they get very sensitive about comments like that. I've had at least three domestics' – men who killed their wives '– caused by fighting over that kind of insult about hair. Be nice to the man.'

Joey and Johnny finished embracing each other, and I walked toward Garelli as Joey pointed in my direction. He had put us in the second booth – Woody had the best table, of course – and Johnny gave me the once-over as we made our way to our seats. I didn't think I was exactly his type, but at least my hair was my own.

'Nice of you to call. How'd you know I was in town?'

'Actually, one of the cops told me, when he was talking to me this morning. I've been interviewed by them a lot, too.'

'I forgot what you do. Are you in soaps? Acting?'

'No, I'm a lawyer.'

'Like a defense attorney, that kind?'

'Sort of.' Not exactly that kind, but then, he's not really an actor either, if you want to be truthful.

'D'you know Isabella for a long time?'

Longer than you, I thought to myself. 'About three years. I gave her some help back then, when she was starring in *Probable Cause*. We became friendly after that.'

Johnny and I reminisced for a while over our drinks, and by the time Vic brought him his second Ketel One martini, Joey was ready to take our dinner order.

'No menus here. You gotta tell Joey what you want.'

'Yes, I know.'

Rao's had the best roasted peppers I had ever eaten, so I chose them for an appetizer, while Johnny got both the baked clams and the seafood salad for himself. Joey suggested the shells with cabbage and sausage, and the lemon chicken. Johnny added another pasta and some salad, as if he had been pumping iron without eating for five days.

'So did Iz talk about me a lot?'

'She told me a lot about you, yes.'

'Good things, mostly?' he said jokingly. 'We had some kinda good times together, her and me.'

The English major in me winced. He may have been great in bed, but his syntax was as atrocious as his manners. He was shoving the bread in his mouth each time he came up for air, rinsing it down with the vodka.

'Did Isabella tell you how we met and everything? We was a hot ticket for a while.'

Enough about me, now let's talk about what Iz thought about me. This was going to be a long evening.

Garelli wanted to make sure I knew all about his career. The appetizers came and he inhaled his clams without missing a beat, taking me through his days in the Marine Corps. Stallone was his role model; he'd discovered Garelli when he got out of the service and cast him as a soldier of fortune in one of those blockbuster summer movies that I would have paid dearly never to have to see in my life. 'He was good to me, man, still is. Semper Fi.'

'Did you have to learn all that technical business about guns for the movie?' I asked, realizing as soon as I did that it was not the most subtle approach for the nature of the investigation.

His head was apparently thicker than his deltoids 'cause he didn't seem to get the connection at all. 'Are you kidding? Didn't Isabella tell you how I taught her to shoot when we were in Central America making that Clancy movie? Man, I grew up on that stuff, from G.I. Joe right to the Marines.'

'No, she just talked about your romance.' That had been nearly enough to make me question her sanity. I suppose I hadn't asked too many more details.

'We used to sit around at night, drinking and making love. There wasn't much else to do down there. I tried to teach her how to shoot. We'd set up the empty vodka bottles on a tree stump in the jungle and blast them to pieces. Some day – what do you call those guys – archaeologists? Someday, one of 'em will come along and do a dig right on that movie set. Iz used to say they'd think the Aztecs had invented Absolut, there'd be nothing but fragments of glass buried there.

'Then I could really make her laugh when I could nail one of them snakes, you know, like when they were moving? Man, she hated those snakes. Green mambos. Those jungles were full of 'em. She used to say she never wanted to see another snakeskin shoe or pocketbook in her life. I could spot those suckers as soon as they came out in the daylight to sun themselves and I could blast 'em in half while they tried to slither back into their holes. It used to be quite a game. Iz had a nice reward for me every time I killed her a green mambo.' He winked at me, so I was sure to know that Isabella was taking good care of Johnny's snake whenever he played sharpshooter.

To me it seemed like quite a skill. Not one that I wanted to master, much as I hated snakes. But Garelli had to be pretty good with a gun to hit that kind of skinny moving target.

Plates were exchanged for other plates, Maureen continued to ply the jukebox with dollar bills so that fine music constantly flowed out of it, and Johnny slugged vodka as if it were the last time he would ever have anything to drink.

'Why do you think the police want to talk to you?' I asked naively. 'Do you know anything about Isabella's murder?'

'Clueless, Alice, I am really clueless.'

I didn't correct him on my name. He was pretty drunk, and I guess his mind was on the dancer he was due to meet in another hour.

'They ran *me* through every conversation I had with her lately, wanted to know about the man she was with all week, wanted to know which of her lovers she'd fought with. I guess they'll do the same with you,' I suggested to him.

'Well, they'll get shit from me – excuse my language, sweetheart. She and me didn't see each other for weeks. We talked on the phone, she was some kinda tease, but if these motherfuckers think they're gonna dredge up my past and try to knock me outta the box, they got another thought coming.'

'You got a lawyer?'

'No way, man. I mean I got a lawyer back home, I got plenty of lawyers. But you walk into a police station with a lawyer, those cops *know* you did something wrong. I can go in by myself, tell 'em what they wanna know, and take the Fifth when I feel like it. I'm not payin' some sleazebag to tell me, "You don't have to answer that, Johnny." I been around the block a few times. No problem.'

Garelli was working the tortoni now, for dessert, and Rick had brought over a bottle of anisette to place on the table. The espresso was thick as mud and delicious, but Johnny cut his with the syrupy liquor, as though he needed more fuel. He lit a cheap cigar, leaned forward and eyeballed me. 'They ask you anything about me and Iz?'

'Yeah. They asked me some things, and I know they've been talking to a lot of other people about you, too.'

'They tell you what they know about me, I mean, besides me being like in the movies?'

'They haven't told me everything. I know they talked about your bad temper, your fights with Isabella—'

'Shit, that's nothing to talk about. That is zero, *nada*. You know these cops. They any good? Or are they complete fuck-ups, like the ones in L.A.?'

'I don't really know them. There's some jerk from the FBI who thinks he's running the show.'

'Yeah, Luther Waldo or something like that. Did they find out anything about you they didn't already know?'

Boy, am I the wrong one to ask. 'Yeah, actually, they did.'

'Something bad?'

'Very bad.' Put Tina on again, Maureen. Who needs a heart when a heart can be broken?

Now Johnny was puzzled. He had been convinced the meeting with the cops was going to be a complete cake-walk when he agreed to do it. 'D'you have something to hide?'

'I didn't know it at the time, Johnny, but it turns out that I did. Why, is there something you don't want them to know.'

I had started to confide in him, and he leaned further into my face to return the favor by trying to trust me with his secrets. 'I didn't have anything to do with killing Isabella – and, man, you know she coulda driven me to it – but I got things I don't want nobody to know about. We all do, don't we?'

'You bet.'

'They're gonna wanna know where I was the day she got it, right?' He was well oiled now and getting sloppy. 'Well, I got nothing to tell them about that. I'm not gonna ruin somebody else's life that's got nothing to do with their business, see?'

'Hey, Johnny, I'd be careful about lying to them. You know with credit cards and telephone bills and things that leave a trail of dates and records, it's stup— It's not too smart to lie about something they can check on as easily as that.'

He tried to absorb that for a minute. 'Well, I don't have to lie to them, I could just take the Fifth, right?'

'Well, not exactly.' I tried to explain the difference between being questioned by the police and being on the witness stand in a court of law. Forget about it.

I decided to try the direct approach. 'Maybe it's not all that tough, Johnny. Where were you last Wednesday? I mean, as long as you weren't on Martha's Vineyard I think you're absolutely right – it's nobody's business. Try your story on me – see how it flies. Isabella always trusted me.' That was a one-way street.

I smiled sweetly at him, and hoped it looked warm

and fuzzy as he stared back at me through his alcohol-filled haze.

He propped one elbow on the table and rested his chin in the palm of his hand. 'You know *The Tempest*?'

'Shakespeare?' The Gorilla and I are gonna talk Shakespeare tonight? The lieutenant won't believe it.

'No, not the movie. The boat, the yacht.'

'Oh, yeah. Sure. Sir Robert Ardmore's yacht. That one?' What unlikely shipmates: Johnny Garelli and British department store mogul, recently knighted, Sir Robert Ardmore.

'Yeah, Alice, that one. It's like an ocean liner. I don't know Ardmore, but you could say I'm a good friend of his wife.' Garelli smiled. 'When Iz dumped me, I thought I'd drown my sorrows in the ocean.'

Ardmore's fifth wife, a twenty-six-year-old stripper whose instep was reputed to be higher than her I.Q., had met the elderly billionaire when he was in Vegas, doing a site inspection for a series of shopping malls. He was still married at the time, and his fierce battle to retain the remarkable yacht – which had originally been named for his fourth wife – in the divorce proceedings led to its lavish rechristening as *The Tempest*.

'So you and Tiki Ardmore were together last week?'

'Obviously, that goes no further than this table, right? Her husband's got a lousy sense of humor, if you know what I mean. Really straight guy. Jeez, I've know Tiki since she was working the door at Morton's.'

I think Lord Ardmore and I could do very well together, sailing off into the sunset, faithful and loyal like a pair of cocker spaniels.

'Where was the boat?'

'I flew on board by helicopter when Ardmore went back

to London last Monday. I was in Easthampton, and the boat was cruising off Montauk, at the end of Long Island.'

Fifty-five miles from the Vineyard, as the crow flies.

'Well, at least you've got witnesses, Johnny. Crew, pilots, deckhands—'

'I got 'em all right, but one thing Tiki don't want is witnesses. Everybody who works for Ardmore is deaf, dumb, and blind, if you follow me. This marriage may be hard work, but it beats the shit out of the last two jobs she had. I can't burn her on this.'

'Did you put into port anywhere?'

'Are you kidding? Those dinky little islands can hold stinkpots and Sunfishes, but not a yacht the size of this one. *The Tempest* needs its own dock. Nah, last thing we wanted to see was other people.'

I guess Tiki Ardmore was a snake-charmer, too.

Johnny gave me a few more details about his shipboard adventure, and I was confident that there were enough people who could confirm or contradict his story, were his involvement really to become a major factor in the investigation. I don't know that I was any help to Lieutenant Peterson, but I would not have to eat again for at least a week.

The rain had started to come down heavily while we were eating dinner, and I was glad to see that there was a stretch limo waiting for Garelli at the curb. He left generous tips for Vic and the waiter, exchanged kisses on both cheeks with Joey, and asked me if I wanted to be dropped at my apartment on his way back to the hotel. Maureen and Mike had slipped out while Johnny was settling up his bill, and I saw their car parked just beyond the streetlight, as they watched me get into the rear seat before starting up their engine.

It was only a ten-minute ride down the drive to my place. Garelli leaned his head back against the seat cushion and let the alcohol do its work, while I played out the visions of a heli-copter or a speeding launch whisking him from *The Tempest* to the Vineyard, to kill Isabella, while Tiki Ardmore soaked in a bubble bath. The logistics of it were certainly possible, as any navigator could tell you. I had gotten the basics for Chapman and his team – they would have to go the distance.

I thanked Johnny for the meal and wished him good luck with Luther tomorrow, then I got out of the limo and waited in the lobby for Mike and Maureen to park and join me.

'You guys must be starved, watching me eat all that food while you just sat at the bar the whole time. I'll send out for a pizza for you.'

'One glass of wine and three bottles of Pellegrino water, just to keep our glasses looking full. I'll be running for the powder room as soon as you unlock your door,' Maureen responded.

'What d'ya get?' Mike asked.

'Nothing memorable. Has no use for cops, plans to lie to you guys tomorrow and stonewall you about where he was. Has a thing going with the wife of a billionaire, so he doesn't want you to know the truth and blow it for her by going public. And yes, in fact he was on the East Coast the week of the murder, cruising in the Atlantic Ocean on his personal "love boat," not too far from the Vineyard. He's a superb marksman, especially good at moving targets. Don't remind me that I've been fooled before, Mike, but somehow I don't think he killed Isabella. Too stupid to have actually formulated and carried out something that needed to be planned in advance like this murder. See what he tells you when he comes in to the office, but I don't think he's your man.'

We went into my apartment and I showed Maureen where to freshen up while I went into the den to call Steve's Pizza. It was only ten-thirty, so I called David Mitchell, too, to ask him to join us. 'I've got two detectives with me. Is this a good time to come by and talk things over with us?'

'It's great. Didn't you get my message? I just got home twenty minutes ago and suggested you call if you got in before midnight. I'll be right over.'

'Oh, I haven't even gone into the bedroom yet to check the machine. Glad it's still working. My mother seems to have given up on me this week. The door's open.'

Maureen called out to me from the bedroom. 'Mind if I use the phone to call my husband? You know how jealous he gets when I'm out dancing with Chapman.'

'Next to the bed, Mo.' Mike had gone through the Police Academy with Gene Forester, who left the job a few years back for a top position in corporate security.

David came in a few minutes later and the four of us positioned ourselves in the living room for an attempt to brainstorm with the information we had to date about Isabella's death. Mike had brought Maureen up to speed while they were sitting at the bar at Rao's, and David had spent some of his day considering the psychological aspect through the mumbo-jumbo of the correspondence found in Iz's apartment.

Each of the known suspects went up and down as possible perps in my view, depending on the hour of the day and the latest information. We filled David in on Jed's role and today's photo confirmation by the Quinn sisters, and I could see him watching me out of the corner of his eye to try to measure the effect of that news on my emotional well-being. Burrell had been an early consideration whom I had eliminated, but who now had reinjected himself into the mix with his deception and the fact of his drug delivery. Garelli was a long shot, but certainly within geographic range – and a great shooter. Whenever we thought we could narrow the field, a name like Freddy Weintraub, the felonious accountant, muddied the view.

'What's the likelihood that the killer is someone you've never even considered, someone whose name has never come into this yet? An unknown, a complete ringer?' David asked, directing his inquiry to Mike.

'Better than even, Doc. You know how low the clearance rate on homicides is if you don't break 'em in the first forty-eight, seventy-two hours? It's abysmal. We're starting with guys who knew her and may have had a reason to do her in – God knows how many freaks we never heard of who hated her. And then there's the simple fact that celebrities are fair game for more whackjobs than there are jail cells. Sometimes they just heckle and harass, other times they go for the gold.'

'So these aren't the only people to consider?'

'Nope. Just the first wave. Still a lot to do on these guys. If Segal's lawyer were smart and really wanted to give his client a shot, he'd tell us how and when his man left the island. There must be some way to prove that. The ferry's not much help. I've checked airport records by name and came up empty. But there's a couple of guys who paid cash on the 3 P.M. Cape Air flight. If he used an alias and no credit card, just 'cause he didn't want to get caught cheating on Alex, we might be able to clear him. Either he doesn't have that kind of alibi 'cause he was still on the scene when Iz was shot, or he's a horse's ass.'

'Or the lawyer's waiting for Mr. Green before he does any heavy lifting,' Maureen added as a possibility.

'Mr. Green?' David looked puzzled.

'Mean's Jed hasn't paid him yet. Sometimes, the defense attorney wants a big bundle of green bills up front, before he lifts a finger. Wants to keep the client on the hook a little longer, then the guy's *really* grateful when he's cleared,' I explained to David.

'*If* he's cleared,' Mike threw in, as a warning to me. No question that Jed was still Chapman's number-one suspect.

'Those letters mean anything to you, Doc? Did Alex tell you about the poem Isabella had copied into that script we found when we packed up her belongings? That also had "Dr. C." written next to it.'

'No, I don't think you mentioned that, Alex.'

At this point I couldn't remember whether I had or not. 'It was a few lines out of a Pope poem, David. The passage Iz had transcribed included the lines "Is it, in Heaven, a crime to love too well?" It looked like she thought this "Dr. C." had been the poet. I guess that's Cordelia Jeffers. Maybe it's got more to do with this than we thought.'

David tried to take us through his reasoning. 'Start with the fact that there is no psychiatrist named Cordelia Jeffers. I expect that no such person even exists, that it's a name assumed for the purposes of this particular correspondence.'

'Why?' Chapman liked to get right to the point.

'I don't know why, at the moment. But it's clear that the writer knew that Isabella was going to Martha's Vineyard, and it's even more clear that Isabella was not the source of that information.' He quoted back to us from the first paragraph, in which Jeffers commented on Isabella's trip, which she learned about quite indirectly. 'It's also obvious that she knew Isabella was going with a man – shall we assume Jed? – which is far more than you knew, Alex.'

'So if we want to know more about Dr. C., we're looking for someone who knew both Isabella and Jed, is that what you're telling us?' Mike asked.

'For openers, yes.'

'I thought I was the common denominator there,' I was quick to acknowledge. 'Perhaps there were one or two Hollywood acquaintances they had in common, but I was certain that there was no real link independent of me, except for friends of mine like Nina and her husband. Even Nina confirmed that she thinks this liaison only began a few weeks ago, when they ran into each other on the Concorde.'

'And the pretext for Isabella calling on Jed?' David asked me again.

'The fact that her accountant had been stealing her blind. Jed gave her the name of his man when we all had dinner together, and later on I urged him to follow up and make sure she was in good hands.'

'Yeah, but by the time she invited Jed to the Vineyard, the week before last, she had a new stalker, didn't she?' Mike went on. 'Did you tell David that Jed had been stalked when he ran for office? That's one of the reasons he told you he was so sympathetic to Lascar.'

'What was that all about, Alex?'

'I hardly know what to believe at this point, guys. When we first met, in June, one of the things Jed talked about when he heard I was a prosecutor was the time he'd been harassed. His version of the facts was that he shook hands with a young woman in a receiving line when he was running for the Senate and he couldn't get rid of her after that. Phone calls, letters, showed up everywhere he went, got on airplanes with him. Finally he had to go to the police to put an end to it.'

David addressed me in his soft, professional tone. 'Did Jed sleep with her, Alex? Did they have an affair?'

'For what it's worth, he denied they ever did. Of course, I wouldn't trust him from here to the kitchen now, but the first night I met him, when he told me the story, he had no reason to lie to me.

'In fact, he made quite a point of telling me that it played a big role in his divorce. The stalker actually called and spoke to Jed's wife. Tried to convince her that they *had* been having an affair – which didn't take much for his wife to believe. I'm so confused by him now I don't know what to believe anymore.'

'Do you know any more about this than you've just told me?'

'No, David. I don't. It's sort of like what happens to doctors. Every time you go to a cocktail party, people complain to you about their aches and pains and hope for a free diagnosis. Well, for me, it's the high crimes and misdemeanors they all unload on me. I listened to Jed's story, but he thought the situation had ended when he moved to New York and neither one of us dwelt on it. I guess it had a certain resonance for Isabella.'

'Alex' – David was in his most sincere mode now – 'Alex, would you mind if I talked to Jed about this a bit more? Perhaps something Isabella confided in him, because of his history with a similar problem, perhaps that will shed some light on these strange letters.'

Of course I minded. Mike leaped in over me. 'Hey, that's a great idea. His lawyer won't let him talk to us, but if you call him, as Coop's friend, I bet he'll be hungry to talk to you. He's screaming to get her back, Doc. That's a great angle to work with him.'

'How do *you* feel about it, Alex?'

'What difference does that make?' I could feel a good pout coming on.

Maureen came to my defense. She could see I was flagging and knew that I didn't want Jed to get his toe back in the door. 'Do what you gotta do, guys, but don't put Alex in the middle of it, okay? Cut her a break, will you? Where do you think this exercise in futility will get you?'

'I'm not proposing that there's any direct connection between Isabella's killer and Jed's problem, but it would certainly be interesting if they discussed the phenomenon with each other. He can tell us that, of course. *Very* interesting.'

Riveting. Ask him if they ever bothered to talk about me, while you're at it.

David tried to draw me back into the conversation. 'Alex, I'm sure you've come across this in some of your stalking cases. Obsessional love, delusional disorders – it's in all the forensic psych literature. Quite fascinating material. Do you detectives ever work with the *DSM*?'

'I've seen the book in Alex's office. Can't say I've ever used it,' Maureen replied. Chapman just shook his head.

'It's the forensic psych bible,' I explained. *The Diagnostic Statistical Manual of Mental Disorders*, weighty scientific tomes that detailed and outlined the elements and criteria for a mind-boggling array of psychiatric disorders, which guided doctors and lawyers through all the odd routes of affirmative defenses and excuses for criminal conduct.

'Yeah, I know it. "I killed my mother because I was born with very short earlobes and webbed feet and wasn't allowed to eat Cheerios for dinner; I skinned the cat because Uncle Harry never let me kiss Aunt Mary's ass after church on Sundays; I put the baby in the microwave because Jupiter didn't align with Mars and no one ever lets me do what I want to do anyway." Yep, for every violent crime there's a shrink with an excuse. I didn't know it all came out of one big book.' Mike's disdain for the psychiatric community was beginning to rear its head. 'What are we looking for here, Doc?'

'I'll have to do some more reading tomorrow. There's one category called obsessional love. Those are the cases where there *was* some kind of relationship between the subject and the victim – a love affair, a one-night stand, a "fatal attraction," if you will. The harasser begins a campaign to regain that relationship, or to seek revenge.

'The more unusual category is quite different. It's called erotomania and—'

'Erotomania? That sounds like something *I'd* like to catch.' Mike was clowning again, trying to get me to cheer up.

'In cases of erotomania,' David continued, 'there was never an affair or a romance between the parties – exactly like Jed told you, Alex. The stalker suffers from a delusion, the delusion that the man she fixates on actually loves her, even if she's had only the briefest contact with him. It's extremely bizarre.'

Maureen questioned him, 'Are you serious, that this is a

real disorder? The woman believes the man's in love with her – or vice versa, even though there has never been any kind of social or sexual interaction?'

'Exactly. It's a delusion that they are loved by another person. And other than that delusion, the patient's behavior is completely normal. In fact, these people are usually extremely intelligent. No other signs of mental illness or dysfunction.'

'Would you call Segal for us tomorrow, Doc? I bet he'd jump at the chance to crawl on your couch and talk to somebody about this, really.'

'Certainly, Mike, I'll call him. I don't think we can ignore that history of his in view of these references that Cordelia Jeffers makes, whoever she is. I'll leave a message for Jed at his office. Alex, you can jot down his number for me. And I'll pull some of the literature so we can find out more about the disorder. I have to take the shuttle to Washington first thing tomorrow – meeting with the Drug Czar about funding treatment programs. But I can see Segal in my office at the end of the day, and if that works with his schedule, we should know a lot more about whatever Isabella may have discussed with him by the same time tomorrow.'

'Great. I'll call the LAPD. They've actually got a special bureau called the Threat Management Unit – only one I know of in the country. Maybe they can pull up Segal's file and see if there's anything we should know about in it.'

I wrote down the CommPlex number and handed it to David as he left. Chapman answered the intercom and told the doorman to send the kid with the pizza upstairs. I sat and chatted with Maureen and Mike as they devoured their dinner, then sent them on their way home just before midnight.

I undressed, brushed my teeth, and started to get into bed, and remembered that I had a dog-eared copy of the *DSM* on the shelf with my reference books in the second bedroom, which I used as a home office. It was my habit to bring the old editions of penal codes and trial manuals here whenever the new ones arrived in my office, so I had a version to work with instead of carrying the oversized books back and forth each night.

The Diagnostic Statistical Manual was hardly bedtime reading, but I had put myself to sleep so many times with autopsy photographs and Emergency Room medical records that this would be relatively light fare. I carried the volume I needed back to my bed and climbed in, looking in the Index for Delusional Disorders.

The *DSM* noted a clear distinction in the two categories of behavior that David Mitchell had discussed. The more common was the one he referred to as 'obsessional love.' It was fascinating to read, because it seemed to have been written about Isabella Lascar and her kind of problem. The manual described the prototypical obsessional love victim as a 'sexy actress or bombshell' – that was our girl. In these cases, the women who became victims had prior knowledge of their harassers, usually intimate, and most of the stalking activity began following a 'love gone sour' relationship. The majority of the subjects – the stalkers – were male, who harassed with letter and telephone contact. Garelli and Burrell certainly fit the bill as soured lovers, and if she had told Jed he was just a one-week stand, he'd be in exactly the same category. I couldn't wait to show this stuff to Mike tomorrow afternoon.

It was impossible to plow through it all, with clinical examples and scads of footnotes, but it was Thursday morning already – exactly a week since I received the news of Isabella's death – and I had all weekend to research this material to see if it had any relevance to our work.

I skimmed down the pages to get to the related section on erotomania. If Jed had been truthful about his stalking experience, it appeared as though he and Isabella had been plagued by opposite aspects of a similar delusion. In cases of erotomania – unlike obsessional love – most of the victims were men, and most of the harassers were women. Like the situation Jed had described to me, the person stalked has had no relationship with the stalker, who is fervently convinced that the victim would return the affection – if not for some outside influence. Of course, I thought to myself, Jed's wife would have been the obstacle. The harasser kept calling his wife to tell her that Jed was unfaithful. Once she could get the wife out of the way, she was deluded enough to think the path to Jed's affection would be cleared.

No wonder Isabella and Jed had so much to talk about. It was really weird.

I wondered why I had never heard the term erotomania before, so I read on. 'Erotomania is the delusional belief that one is passionately loved by another.' But as recently as the third edition of the *DSM*, just a few years ago, there was no specific mention of the condition. It was only with the later publication of *DSM-III-R* – the one I was reading – that it was included as a specific category, as physicians began to document more and more cases of patients exhibiting this unusual conduct.

I was getting sleepy, so I decided to stop after the next

few paragraphs, which described the history of the original diagnosis of the condition. It was originally documented in 1921 by a French psychiatrist named G.G. de Clérambault and, therefore, named for him: de Clérambault's Syndrome, and referred to in the literature of the time as *psychose passionelle*. As I lay in my bed each of these last few nights, suffering from a serious bout of post-breakup depression, I longed for a malady with a fancy French name like this, and hoped some obscure footnote would drop a hint that would dignify my pathetic condition with a Gallic accent.

The early case descriptions were all quite interesting, as they typified the illness. The patients were usually women from modest backgrounds, while the male victims were generally from a higher social and financial status – executives, physicians, media figures. These otherwise sane women insisted they could provide evidence for their beliefs, in the form of signs from their love objects like 'meaningful glances, messages passed through news-papers, or telepathic communications.'

I had to admit my amusement at de Clérambault's first case analysis, comparing in my mind that victim – King George V of England – and the one I knew, Jed Segal.

The French psychiatrist wrote that one of his most dramatic cases involved a fifty-year-old compatriot who became completely convinced that King George was in love with her – although, of course, they had never met. She believed that British tourists and sailors were emissaries of His Majesty, sent abroad to declare his love for her. The deluded woman made several trips to London, and on one of them, in 1918, she stood for hours outside Buckingham Palace, waiting for a glimpse of her beloved. When at last she saw a curtain moving in a window, she interpreted this as a signal from the King. As she told all those who tried to bring her to her senses, 'The King might hate me, but he can never forget me.'

It was a merrier note on which to close the book for the night and go to sleep.

I reached for the light switch and took note of the still unblinking red light on my answering machine. It seemed to me that David Mitchell said he had left a message shortly before I got home from Rao's this evening, but then I remembered that Maureen had been in here using the phone to call her husband, and probably hit the rewind button by mistake. Tomorrow I would call my parents just to say hello, but for now I would give myself to dreams of some kind of *psychose passionelle*. Everything – even mental illness – sounded better in French.

C H A P T E R

The rain had stopped by the time my alarm went off at seven o'clock, and I opened the curtains to reveal a glorious October morning. It was Thursday, and I tried to remember what the day's line-up looked like in my red desk calendar as I showered and thought ahead to the weekend. I had planned to spend it with Jed, so I daydreamed instead about a whirlwind shopping binge, a haircut that would announce a new 'me,' and assembling a few of my girlfriends for a ladies' night out at an elegant restaurant.

I didn't feel like dealing with a yellow cab so I called a car service to deliver me to the office. I read my *Times* most of the way downtown while Imus kept me diverted on the radio, and I was pleased to note when I entered the building through the revolving door that Battaglia's car had not yet pulled into its reserved space directly in front of the office.

Laura was drinking her coffee down the hall with Rod's secretary and the phones were quiet. I turned on my computer and brought up the screen for e-mail to send some messages before starting on my response to the motions I had to file in the Reynolds case.

'Mind if I come in?' I looked up to see my old friend, Mickey Diamond, the veteran court reporter for the *Post*, standing outside my door. He had worked the courthouse beat for almost thirty years and was the revered dean of the school of the tabloid crime story. Diamond was tall and lean, with silvery hair and an irresistible grin, even when he was at his most offensive. We never ended a press conference on a rape case without his asking what the victim looked like, and even when Battaglia refused to give an answer, Mike would invent a description of his own. If he assumed the victim had been African-American because the crime had happened in a housing project in Harlem, she would appear in print as a 'raven-haired beauty,' and if the rape had occurred in a townhouse on the Upper East Side, the woman was invariably a blonde.

'Enter,' I said, trying my best to be cheerful, knowing that this visit was uncharacteristically overdue, given my tangential involvement in the death of a movie star.

'Anything new?'

'All quiet, Mickey. Nothing to report.'

'No, I mean, off the record.' Right. There was no such animal as 'off the record' for Mickey Diamond.

'I'm not kidding. I've got nothing for you, really.'

'Did you see "Page Six" today?' he asked, referring to the *Post*'s gossip column.

'Nope.' I hated to admit it, but I usually bought the tabloid because so many of the office stories were covered in it. The last few years, the Metro section of the *Times*, which used to be too classy to report on all the city's sex and violence, now read like the tabs on any given day.

'Johnny Garelli's in town for the Lascar investigation. Says he was at Rao's with an unidentified blonde last night. Probably a starlet or hooker. Thought maybe you'd know who she is, give me a scoop. Chapman and Peterson must keep you on top of things.'

Could he tell I was blushing? 'I'm out of the loop on this one, Mickey. Just a witness.'

He smiled that impish grin that usually worked on me. 'C'mon, it's really slow. Haven't you got anything for me?'

Unfortunately, the subject matter of my cases was prime fodder for Diamond's stories, and every available space in the tiny courthouse press office was literally papered with headline stories that he proudly called his 'Wall of Shame.' I had been a cover girl in more of those tales than I cared to count.

'Get out of here before Battaglia sees you with me and thinks I leaked something to you. Scoot.'

'Just give me a quote on the murder case, something I can use as an exclusive, please?'

'Are you out of your mind? I want to keep my job, I honestly do, Mickey.'

'Can I make up something, like how bad you feel about Isabella? I promise it'll be tasteful.'

I picked up my box of Kleenex and threw it across

the room at him, laughing at that prospect. Frequently throughout the last three or four years, before I could even ask Battaglia for permission to talk to any of the reporters about a case or an issue – a firm office rule – Diamond would have some pearls of wisdom, in quotation marks, attributed to me. Even the District Attorney had stopped berating me and come to realize I was not guilty but that Mickey had simply fabricated the statement, trying to keep it consistent with what he thought my views would be on a given subject.

'Hey, you owe me. My editor wanted me to do a story about you and Jed Segal. Even had a headline: "THE LEGAL MISS WHO MISSES KISSES," but I refused—'

I was out of my chair and making my way toward the door in a flash. 'I'll break your fucking neck if you even think about a story like that.'

'Easy, easy,' he said, putting his hands on top of his head, as if to shield himself from a strike by me. 'Don't be so sensitive, I was only joking.' He backed out past Laura's desk. 'City desk's working on an anonymous tip. D'ya hear that Garelli killed a guy once, when he was in the Marines? Not the enemy, I mean one of his buddies. Beat him into a coma over nothing – an insult the other guy threw at him. Guy died four months later in a military hospital. We're trying to check it out before anybody goes with it in print. Hear anything like that?'

'No, I haven't heard a word about it,' I responded, shaking my head in amazement. Not one of the things Johnny had chosen to confide in me, but that was hardly surprising.

Mickey left me with a last effort at a story line: 'Call me if you get anything decent. My imagination isn't as sharp as it used to be. I'm not so good at creative writing anymore.'

I called Mark Acciano to see how late the judge had kept the jury working last night. 'They deliberated till almost midnight, then he sent them to the hotel. Started again at nine-thirty this morning.'

'Could you get any sense of the split?'

'Nah. They all just looked tired and grumpy by the time he dismissed them. Impossible to tell what the problems were.'

'Any guessing from the court officers?'

Although it wasn't cricket, if the court officers liked the lawyers, they often reported back what they could hear of the arguments from their stations outside the door of the locked jury rooms. If the twelve were fighting like cats and dogs it was one thing, and quite another if eleven were ganged up against one.

'Not a whisper. I'm going up to sit it out in the courtroom. I'll let you know what happens. And, Alex, thanks a lot for your advice about the summation. I never would have thought to put all that detail in, but I think it helped a lot. Your notes were a godsend.'

'That's what I'm here for. Go get him.'

Laura buzzed me. 'Dr. Mitchell's secretary just called. Said to tell you he's going to see Jed in his office at seven-thirty tonight, and that you'd know what it's all about.'

'Yes, Laura, I do. Be right back, I'm going for a refill.'

I was on my way next door to the Legal Hiring Office, which kept fresh coffee going all day to impress the applicants who applied for positions in Battaglia's office by the thousands every year. When I returned with a steaming cupful, Laura was standing at the side of her desk. 'It's Mercer, I've got him on hold. It's urgent.'

I picked up Laura's phone. 'Yeah?'

'Coop, it's almost over.'

I had to think for a minute to realize that he wasn't talking about Isabella's case. 'What happened?'

'An attempt this morning. Two blocks away from the last hit. M.O. was identical – same approach, same description, same language. Woman lets the guy in the house, he's got the knife. Only surprise was that her husband was in the bedroom. The husband hears a commotion and comes into the kitchen, Mr. William Montvale gets so shook up he drops everything and runs out the door.'

'Wait, wait, wait. You're losing me. Who's William Montvale? The husband?'

'No, no, Miss Cooper. Stay with me. The man we have been looking for is William Montvale, otherwise known to the local media as the Con Ed rapist. Not only was this morning's attempt at a rape unsuccessful, much to the delight of the intended victim, but I am calling personally to tell you that the NYPD has solved this pattern, just for you, kid.'

'I know you're going to explain this to me, Mercer, right?'

'Make me a promise, Coop. No dates for the next seventy hours, okay? No champagne dinners, no trips out of town. As soon as I get my hands on Montvale, I'll be calling or beeping you, no matter what time of day or night, so you can run the line-ups and do the Q and A. Will that make you happy?'

'Delirious, Mercer.'

'Now, what you want to know is how *I* know the rapist

314

is William Montvale. Is that your question, Counselor? And the answer is, the usual brilliant detective work that you associate with me and my crew, with a dash of – ahem – shall we say, great good luck. Make that incredible good luck. The way most crimes are solved, Alex.'

'Tell me what happened.' My heart was pounding at the idea of catching this maniac and putting an end to his little reign of terror before any other woman was victimized.

'When the husband came out of the bedroom, Montvale was so flustered that he let go of his knife. He bent over to pick it up but the newspaper he was carrying in his back pocket got caught under the countertop and fell to the floor, too. Either he didn't notice or he was happy just to hang on to the knife, in case he needed it to fight his way out. By the time the couple called their doorman, Montvale had run down the staircase and out the rear service door. Gone.

'The people were so shaken they just sat in the living room holding on to each other till uniformed responded to the 911 call. That's when the first cops on the scene saw the *Post* on the kitchen floor and picked it up.'

'There's a scoop for Mickey Diamond. Most rapists prefer the *New York Post*. Hope his editor likes it. Go on.'

'Cop asks the couple if the paper was theirs. They say no. It had been rolled up to fit in the guy's pocket, so the cop unrolls it. In it, there's a letter from the New York State Department of Parole addressed to one William J. Montvale, inviting him to come to their offices at three o'clock this afternoon and bring his birth certificate as proof of identification. Seems he just got out of state prison in New Jersey, and they agreed to transfer his parole to New York, so he could move back in with his beloved mother.'

'Make my day – tell me what he did the time for in Jersey.'

'I'm trying to keep you happy, Coop. Your instincts were right all along. Four counts of rape, Bergen County. You just couldn't come up with him 'cause his priors weren't in New York. Got a release to early parole because he was in that treatment center in the Jersey system, you know the one I mean?'

'Yeah, Mercer. That one where they rehabilitate rapists. Then they send 'em back to us all cured and well behaved, like William Montvale.'

'This guy's a real pro. I'll find him for you, Coop, but then *you* got to put him out of business forever. Is it a deal?'

'Blood oath, Mercer. What's the plan?'

'We got a stakeout in front of his mama's place, but once he realizes he dropped those papers, I doubt he'll show there or at the parole office today. They're covered just in case. We got a team checking the Jersey prison files, looking for visitors' names, girlfriends, cousins, cellmates – anybody he might run to for a place to crash. Then we'll fan out to all the shelters and see if they got any "John Does" showing up today. You know I'll get his ass. Just stick with me and I'll hand you a lock-solid case.'

I knew he would. Nobody could do it better. 'I'm here, and I'll have the beeper on day and night. Whatever you need, just let me know.'

'I'll be in touch. Keep your fingers crossed.'

I called Rose Malone and asked her to tell Battaglia that we had a big break in the case, then told Sarah Brenner to be ready to cover me for the next few days in case I got tied up on the Montvale arrest. She offered to do my two witness interviews scheduled for the afternoon, knowing that it would be difficult for me to concentrate while I was primed to rush up to the Special Victims office the minute Mercer called.

My counterpart in the Bergen County Prosecutor's Office had been helpful to me in the past, so I reached out for him again and asked him to pull the closed case files on the suspect, just to see whether there was any other nexus to Jersey that might be useful. Don't cross the Hudson, I urged Montvale silently. I don't want to deal with the delays of an extradition proceeding – I just want to grab you here, let these women have a chance to confront you and put you behind bars till you outlive the ability to do this to anybody else.

Another lunch at my desk, this time consisting of a container of light yogurt and a seltzer. I checked Mercer's office every half-hour, but the entire squad was out in the field and the civilian aide who was handling the phones didn't know which end was up.

Shortly after two, Laura buzzed me to announce that we had a walk-in. The last thing I needed right now was a witness without an appointment, but that's exactly what I had. I couldn't pass her off to Sarah, whose hands were already full with my overflow. Angela Firkin had presented herself to the lobby security officer with a crumpled piece of paper that had my name printed on it, along with the address of the building.

I invited her into my office and seated her opposite me. 'How did you get my name, Miss Firkin?' I asked, as I took out a fresh pad to begin to make notes of our conversation.

'I called the crisis hot line, told them my problem, and they told me to come talk to you.'

317

'I see. Did anybody mention reporting to the police first?'

'I can't go to the police, Miss Cooper. I appreciate your seeing me without an appointment, but I was very upset and I just couldn't go to a police station. This is a situation about a man in an official uniform, and I'm just not comfortable talking to the police.'

'All right,' I said, after getting the pedigree information I needed, 'why don't you tell me what happened?'

Angela Firkin was a twenty-eight-year-old woman who lived alone in a brownstone in the East Eighties. She supported herself on disability insurance and a modest inheritance, but was unable to work because she had a long history of treatment for schizophrenia. 'I don't go out much, just walking for some exercise in the neighborhood, and getting my groceries. Almost everything else I do by mail order, by sending away for things.

'A couple of weeks ago, our regular mailman had a heart attack and we got a new guy. I have to see him a lot, 'cause some of the things that I order are too big for the mailbox. My book club delivery, my home shopping network things, you know.'

'Sure.'

'Well, this new guy started off fine. Then, one day, when he rang the doorbell to give me a package, he told me the Post Office had new rules. Said it was because of all the trouble the government was having with drug smugglers and, um, I think the word he called it was "contraband." He told me I had to open the wrapping in front of him, so he could see what was in the box. It was just a pair of cubic zirconia earrings I ordered for myself for sixteen dollars, so I showed it to him.

'A few days later, he did the same thing with my mystery book order, even though it had a return address and everything, from the book club.'

She was telling the story easily, in a coherent narrative, so I let Angela go on without interruption.

'Then the guy, his name is Oscar Lanier – it's right on his name tag – the guy comes back this Monday with another delivery for me. This time it's some pills, but over-the-counter stuff. From ABC Vitamin Company. I'm on a lot of medication for my – well, you know, my condition – but I also sent away for some vitamins. So Oscar says, "I have to search you before I let you have this package."

'I said, "What? I never heard of this before." He said, "New rules, I told you, new Post Office rules. I'm sure you're okay, but it's gotten very dangerous to go into people's homes these days. They're doing this to protect us."

'I felt kind of bad for him, I mean, I wouldn't want to go into a lot of apartments in this city. People with pit bulls and drug dealers and who knows what. So I stepped into the hallway, Oscar puts down his bag, and he starts to frisk me, like in the movies. But I'm telling you, Miss Cooper, he's running his hands back and forth over my breasts. I say, "That's enough, Oscar." And he gives me the package and thanks me a lot.'

I asked Angela how long the encounter took and exactly where and how the mailman touched her. She explained it all.

'Then he was back this morning. I'm telling you I never got my mail so early as this week. He's got a box for me, no return label. So he tells me it looks suspicious. I see it's got a postmark from Philly, and I know it's my cousin Muriel, sending me the sucking candies I like. She never puts a return address – in case there's not enough postage on it, she doesn't want it coming back to her. Wants me to pay it. But no, Oscar says he has to search me and then see the candy for himself. This time, he puts his hand inside my blouse and actually touches my breast. Can you believe it? I smacked him across the face and stepped inside and bolted the door. Never even got the candy.'

I asked some more questions and told Miss Firkin that I would like her to wait in our reception area while I called the Post Office.

'I already did that, Miss Cooper. No new rules. Oscar was full of baloney – thought he had an easy mark, just 'cause I like my packages. They don't have any new rules like that.'

I hadn't thought they were actually new rules, but I did want to check to see if Oscar was, in fact, an employee of the United States Government. Laura got Angela a seat down the hall and a cold drink, and I made my calls. Yes, there was an Oscar Lanier and indeed that was his postal route, although he was only a probationary worker at the moment. Just to satisfy my curiosity, I punched his name into the criminal justice computer network – AJIS – and within seconds, got the response that Lanier had a misdemeanor conviction earlier this year in Queens County. Not surprisingly, it was for sexual abuse.

My next call was to the head of the Special Victims Bureau in the Queens District Attorney's Office. I explained the story and asked her to tell me what the case was about. Fifteen minutes later, she called back to let me know that Oscar's previous job had been as an airport security guard at JFK. He was arrested after several women passengers complained that he took them out of line, into his office, and tried to do a body cavity search, looking for smuggled drugs. Fired, convicted, and rehired by the United States Post Office, all within the last six months. You couldn't make this stuff up if you tried.

I brought Angela back in, reassured her that this particular postman would not ring a third time, and told her that I would assign a female detective to work with her on the case. After she left, I made the necessary calls to arrange a temporary suspension of Lanier while we investigated the matter. It was almost five o'clock by the time I finished those details and attended to the rest of the paperwork on my desk.

Mark Acciano called to say that the judge would keep his jury only until ten this evening, and if there was no verdict by that time, he'd declare a mistrial. I tried to shore up his spirits, and told him I'd stick it out with him as long as there were no developments on the Montvale case.

Laura asked if she could leave a bit early to go to the dentist, and I told her I would get the phones myself. I sat at my desk, going through the pile of mail that had come with the afternoon delivery. Two demands for letters advising the Parole Board what position our office would take on cases coming before them next month, one request to lecture to a women's group at a college in Pennsylvania, and several offers to test software programs designed to expedite the preparation of lawyer's briefs were on the top of the stack.

Wedged in between the legal-sized envelopes that I had been opening was a small letter that appeared to be a personal note. It was stamped but had no postmark, and

I guessed that it had been delivered by hand. I slit it open with the narrow point of a pair of desk scissors and unfolded the page of single-spaced typed correspondence. It began with the salutation 'My dearest Alexandra,' and my eye flipped immediately to the bottom of the paper to see the closing that was identical to the one on the papers Isabella had received: 'Best ever, Cordelia Jeffers, Fellow, Royal Academy of Medicine.'

My thoughts scattered in a dozen directions. I was mad at myself for touching the letter and envelope, which may have yielded fingerprints if I had not smudged them; I wanted to have Mike or David or anyone else who knew the case sitting beside me as I read through the text; I wondered whether to march directly into Battaglia's office and tell him I was in over my head; and yet I couldn't stop myself from reading on.

My dearest Alexandra,

I debated about sending this to you at your office or your fancy apartment, but I didn't know if you'd notice it at home among the dozens of yellow roses that our mutual friend continues to waste his money on.

Sometimes, my clever girl, your actions do surprise me. Didn't you find it degrading, and I do mean thoroughly humiliating, to have him leaping into bed with that vacant slut, that Cleopatra-like whore you were stupid enough to befriend? And yet, thereafter you remained so desperate for his companionship that you accept rides in his limousine and let him try to wheedle his way back into your good graces. Deny him the help he seeks, he needs it not.

Like her before you, you will be shocked to find

that the woman he truly loves is not your equal – not in physical appearance, not social status or material wealth, not even in professional recognition in her chosen field.

As you know, women do crazy things in the name of love, and crazier still when they sense the beloved slipping away, becoming ambivalent.

Wasn't it the immortal Bard who said 'One may smile and smile and be a villain?' Keep that in mind and yield not to temptation.

Best ever,
Cordelia Jeffers
Fellow, Royal Academy of Medicine

I read it three times to try to make it make sense. How did this woman, this person, know the things she talked about in the letter? The yellow roses, my short ride across town in Jed's limo, his pleas for help these last few days, his betrayal of me with Isabella. I surely didn't believe in psychics, but could I have been unaware that someone was actually following me wherever I went? Not possible.

Then that paragraph that mirrors one in Isabella's letter, referring to the woman Jed really loves. Again, I was completely puzzled by its meaning.

Who was the beloved that Jed was slipping away from? Who was he becoming ambivalent about? Could this possibly be his ex-wife, now bitter about their estrangement? I had never even suggested that to Chapman. All I knew about her was that like many other women, she was unhappy in marriage and unhappier still in divorce. Why hadn't I asked more questions about her?

I called the guard at the security desk to see if he

remembered anyone leaving an envelope with him earlier in the day. He reminded me that the shifts had changed at four o'clock, when he had come on duty, and nothing except deliveries from Police Headquarters had been dropped at his station. I'd have to check with the day shift tomorrow morning.

Mike Chapman and David Mitchell needed to know about this letter at once. I called David's office and got the answering machine. I left a message, expecting that he would pick it up soon, since he was supposed to be there to meet Jed sometime within the next two hours, and I told him I would fax a copy of the letter to him before I left the office.

I tried Mike but he wasn't at the squad yet, so I hung up and walked down the hall to use the fax machine outside of Rod's conference room. As I walked back to my desk, I could hear the phone ringing and I ran to pick it up.

'We popped the motherfucker, Coop. We're in business.'

'Mercer? How'd you do it?'

'Seems like the last thing he did before he left prison was get himself an ATM card. A MetroBank cash card. I got that info from the prison this morning. I called the bank and told them to stop the card, figuring he had to get cash if he was gonna be on the run. He tried three machines, got a "Card not valid" printout. Picked up the courtesy phone and called the bank hot line. The branch manager told him to come in at four-thirty, after the regular banking was closed – at our direction – that there must have been a defect in the card. Manager called me back, and a few of us from the squad kept that appointment with him. It gives new meaning to the word "surprise."'

'That is fantastic. Where are you now?'

'Still at the bank. Listen, take your time. We'll take him back over to my office and process him.' Photographs, fingerprints, palm prints, background information. 'The boss'll start assigning guys to call the victims and pick 'em up for the line-ups. I'll chat him up, nice and easy, see if he wants to talk to my favorite prosecutor, tell her why he likes to do this shit to women. You go home, get comfortable – it's gonna be a long evening – and get yourself over to the office by seven, seven-thirty. Sound okay?'

'Perfect. I'll just go home and change, then be right there. Let me know if there's anything you need.'

'You got somebody who can work on a search warrant for his mother's place while you're up with us? See if any of his clothing, any of the women's jewelry's there?'

'No problem. I can phone it in when I'm over with you. It's all on the word processor in ECAB,' our early case assessment bureau, where whoever was on duty could help me through the evening's paperwork.

'And, Mercer? One more thing. Can you control your boss on this? *No* perp walk. Please, beg him for me. Not before the victims have a chance to see the line-up. Take him into the station house with a jacket over his head, will you?'

'You bet. See you later.'

Publicity on these cases could get out of control. Too often, police brass staged a scene taking a suspect in or out of the patrol car, resulting in the defendant's face being plastered all over the local TV and newspapers. For those victims who saw the 'perp walk' before they got to view a formal line-up, it often meant that defense attorneys challenged the propriety of the identification process, and the victim was barred from pointing out her attacker at the trial. We were too close to a great result to screw it up now.

325

I packed up all the supplies I would need to run the investigation from Mercer's office, left Laura a note telling her I might be late in the morning – depending on how long I had to be at the precinct throughout the night – and called Rose Malone. 'Is Battaglia in?'

'He's in a meeting, Alex. He's got the governor's Criminal Justice Coordinator in there. Do you want me to interrupt?'

'Nope. Just wanted him to be the first to know that we think we've got the Con Ed rapist. Tell him I'm going out on the case myself to do the line-ups and try to take a statement. He'll get a complete briefing in the morning.'

'Congratulations, Alex. He'll be really pleased. I'll put you in his book for lunch. I'm sure he'll want to hear all the details.'

'Thanks, Rose.' I hope I'm here in time for lunch. This kind of case could be an all-nighter, by the time we round up the witnesses and get the video team up to the squad.

My last call was to the video technicians. For most of the history of police work, statements or admissions made by suspects in criminal cases were recorded by officers in their notepads. Then for several decades, our office used stenographers who accompanied us on call and took down, verbatim, the questions and answers of an interrogation, to read back to a jury at trial. For almost twenty years in the Manhattan District Attorney's Office, we had developed a sophisticated unit of trained video professionals, who taped these critical sessions – always with the knowledge and consent of the accused – whenever a defendant was willing to participate.

This process eliminated the age-old complaint about police interrogations: that the cops coerced or beat the confessions out of the suspects. Instead, the video camera captured the entire scene. The defendant sitting calmly at a table in a detective's office, unshackled and unharmed, often munching on a doughnut and drinking a Sprite while the prosecutor repeated the Miranda warnings and got his informed consent to go ahead without a lawyer present.

I can remember the first time I went out on call with a cameraman, incredulous that any criminal would agree to film a confession to a crime and have it permanently recorded for use against him in the case. I read the guy his rights, showed him the camera, and explained its purpose. Instead of refusing to go forward, he sat up straight, combed his hair and reset his baseball cap neatly on his head for the movies, and spoke into the microphone as if it was his finest moment in the spotlight. I think that jury finished its deliberations in about twenty minutes. Guilty.

Bob Bannion answered the phone in the tech office. 'Great, I never dreamed I'd be lucky enough to get you tonight,' I said when he picked up. Bannion had started the system for us and he was superb at his work. He was a pro, with a keen, dry sense of humor, which helped get you through a long night in a squad room. Bob was also on call for any homicides or major cases that occurred in the next twelve hours, so I was delighted to try and wrap him up first. I explained a bit about the job we would be working on so he knew what to expect. 'Anything else cooking, or can I ask you to meet me at Special Victims by nine tonight?'

'I'm just on my way to film a crime scene. Multiple homicide in Alphabet City,' the Lower East Side of Manhattan, where the streets were named avenues A, B, and C. 'Looks like a couple of teens in a wild shoot-out. No arrests yet and nothing even close for tonight, but Rod asked me to do some interior shots of the apartment.' One of the valuable techniques Bob had developed was making videos of crime scenes as soon as they were discovered, so that there would be a permanent record of every detail in its place. The importance of objects or clues near a murder victim often did not become obvious until much later in the investigation, when detectives could refer back to their original relationship to the bodies or the evidence by looking at the video.

'When you're done there, will you come on up to Eighty-second Street? They'll be starting with the line-ups, so there's no need to rush. I'll beep you to call it off if he's not talking. The guy's a predicate, so maybe he's smart enough to keep his mouth shut. Give me a call if you get anything hotter than this, okay?' Predicate felons – criminals with records of convictions for serious offenses – often were savvy enough not to make admissions that would help sink them before a jury.

I ran out the door and had jumped into a taxi by the time I got to the corner of Worth Street, prepared to creep along the Drive uptown at the height of rush hour to get to my apartment. I brushed past the doorman, skipped the mailbox, waited with several of the neighbors to get on the elevator, and was inside my bedroom and stripping off my work clothes in seconds. I changed into a pair of jeans, a tailored shirt, and a blazer for the long evening of sitting on coffee-littered desktops and making notes while propped against dusty file cabinets. No need for a pocketbook – I clipped my beeper onto my belt and stuffed cash into my jacket so I could send out for food and soda for the crew working on the case throughout the course of the evening.

My turn-around time was less than twenty minutes. I

thought about calling David's office to see if he had studied the faxed version of Cordelia Jeffers's letter, but when I looked at my watch and saw that it was a few minutes after seven o'clock, I didn't want to risk calling just as Jed arrived to meet with him. Instead, I left a message on David's home machine, explaining where I would be for most of the evening and that I would try to reach him if I had any free time at the station house.

23

I went back downstairs and out onto the street, grabbed a yellow cab and directed the driver across the Eighty-fifth Street transverse to Columbus Avenue, and got out at the corner of Eighty-second to walk the short distance to the Twentieth Precinct. The uniformed cop at the front desk stopped me as I entered the building, so I identified myself to him and walked up the two flights to the Special Victims Squad, which had come to feel like my second home during the past few years. Every felony sexual assault that occurred on the island of Manhattan was referred to this little outpost of seasoned professionals.

When I reached the landing, I pushed open the heavy fire doors that separated the ugly brown-tiled stairwells from the dilapidated office space of the thirty-year-old squad.

The place was electric with the activity that accompanies a break in a major case. Detectives in every shape, size, and color had been pulled in from days off and borrowed from other details to help round up victims, witnesses, and the stand-ins or fillers needed to be the ringers in the line-up array with the defendant. Every shirtsleeve was rolled up, every collar was open, and the handful of ties I could see were unknotted and worn in the loose criss-cross fashion of the detective world.

'Hey, Wallace, Cooper's here,' I heard a guy I didn't recognize call out in the direction of the sergeant's office.

Mercer appeared in the door frame and waved me in. I started to offer my congratulations, but he talked over me. 'The captain is really pissed off. Stay out of his way.'

'At me? What did I do? I just got here.'

'He did *not* like your order about the perp walk. Thinks you're just doing that so that Battaglia can get the press release instead of the PD. He's mad at me for letting you know about it so early – didn't want me to call you till we'd wrapped everything up tonight.'

'What a fucking baby he is. I can't believe you gave me up on that. When is he going to learn that it's just the wrong thing to do at this point in the case? That'll be like the last pattern he messed up. Didn't want to call us for a search warrant so he gets the suspect to sign a consent. The judge threw out the whole thing, all the evidence – said once he was cuffed and asked for a lawyer, he couldn't consent to anything. C'mon, what's been going on since you called me?'

'First I had to accompany Mr. Montvale to the men's room so he could relieve himself. There's a fuzzy birthmark on his thigh all right, just to the southeast of his penis, the way Katherine Fryer had described it.'

'Great. Get a photo of it before he gets to Riker's and somebody tells him to paint it green.'

'Already done. Now, we've also got most of the people we need. The couple from the attempt this morning, they're here. We reached Miss Fryer. Detective Manzi just left to pick up the first victim, and the third one's on her way in from Westchester with her daughter. She moved out of town after the rape. I think we're only missing one. No answer at her house, so we may have to do her down at your office next week.'

'Everybody in separate cubbyholes?'

'Yeah. We're using the juvenile room and the detective squad on the second floor. None of the witnesses will see any of the others before the line-up. I'm telling you, you've got us all pussy-whipped, Cooper. We're doing this exactly the way you want us to,' Mercer laughed.

It was important that the victims who were going to view the array were separated before the identification process. In the old days, I had watched many of them cross-examined about the police procedures. When brought to the station house in the same patrol car or kept in the same waiting area, the conversation invariably turned to the only thing the women had in common: their assailant. 'What did your guy look like?' 'The man who raped me had a mustache.' 'My attacker had an accent.' 'No, I think mine was taller than that.' The defense could argue to the jury that the witnesses recollections were enhanced by each other's descriptions, and it became difficult to tell what each woman remembered before she talked with the others. It took three times the manpower to escort each one in individually, and every empty closet in the building became a holding place for a nervous witness before the procedure got underway. But it would all hold up in court.

'How do the stand-ins look?'

'See for yourself. You can take a peek in the viewing room. Glad it was such a beautiful evening – not like last night's rain. Lots of mopes hanging out on street corners who're happy to help out for ten dollars from the captain.'

Most of the time the cops scoured parks and playgrounds to find reasonable facsimiles of the suspects – similar size, weight, skin color, hairstyle. Drug treatment centers and homeless shelters were also good places for fillers, eager to get the ten spot for a guarantee that they wouldn't be arrested for a crime, even if they were picked out by the victim. A couple of hours' work, standing in the room with the perp and holding a number in front of their chests, and then walking out with the funds for a bottle of Thunderbird or a couple of vials of crack.

The squad had a regular line-up area, which consisted of two separate rooms, connected by a 'two-way mirror.' Montvale and five stand-ins would be in the larger one, with a couple of detectives standing inside the door to monitor his behavior and make sure he didn't say or do anything inappropriate. He would be allowed to pick his position – one through six – and each man would hold a large square sign depicting his number in front of his chest. All the men would be able to see as they faced forward was a large glass mirror, reflecting the image of the array.

Mercer, each witness, and I would be in the small room on the other side of the glass. We would take the victims in one at a time, darken the room, step them up to the glass and ask them to look at the men, who could neither see nor hear them. From our side, the mirror functioned as a window. Each woman would examine the array and tell us whether or not she recognized anyone in the room, and if so, what number identified him.

I stepped inside to check out the assembled group of skells. 'Nice going. I hope none of these guys walk out of here when I'm leaving tonight. Wait a minute, Mercer. Number three. Make him go to his locker and change out of his uniform pants and shoes, will you. It's a dead giveaway.'

In typical fashion, one of the fillers was a cop from the Twentieth Precinct. But once the Legal Aid attorney saw the photograph of the line-ups, he would argue that detectives had placed him there on purpose, still in half of his uniform, to make the selection even easier for the women.

Mercer yelled into the open door of the other room. 'Yo, number three. You got jeans and sneakers in your locker? The fashion director wants you out of those brogues and your nicely creased navy blue pants. Move it.'

'I tell you, he's as frightening-looking as those other guys you got off the street.'

'They can't all be as good-looking as I am, Cooper. You want to see Montvale?'

'Yeah. Might as well.'

We walked down the hallway, past the captain's closed door, and stood in front of the small cell which held a single prisoner. William J. Montvale was sitting on the narrow wooden bench that ran across the back wall of the barred area. His arms were crossed, his legs were outstretched and apart, and his face broke into a wide smirk when he saw us approach. 'Is this my district attorney, Mr. Wallace? The one you been promisin' me? You'll excuse me if I don't stand, won't you, ma'am, but I'm havin' myself a very bad day.' I had my look and turned to walk away, as Montvale called to Mercer, 'She's better-looking than that fat pig who tried my case in Jersey, but I bet she's no Marcia Clark. What d'ya think, Mr. Wallace?'

It was going to be a pleasure to send Montvale up the river.

In the background the phones were going like crazy. Some cop who owed a favor had undoubtedly leaked news of the arrest to a reporter and calls were coming in faster than they could be answered.

'Can we get this thing underway?' Mercer asked one of his teammates, who was coordinating the arrival of everyone we needed. 'I'd like to get these women out of here before the news trucks sit down at the door like vultures.'

'Ready to go. We're just waiting for you to get Montvale in the room.'

Mercer left me and went back to pull the defendant out of his cell. His wrists were cuffed behind his back and Wallace had one of his own enormous hands wrapped around the rapist's upper arm, leading him with a firm grip into the area with the five stand-ins. He was whispering in Montvale's ear, telling him – as I had heard him do so many times – that if he moved one motherfucking muscle or did so much as cross his eyeballs after Mercer uncuffed him and while those women were looking through the window, he could expect to be sporting a new asshole before the end of the evening.

While I stood outside the room, Mercer offered Montvale

his choice of numbers for the line-up. He selected the fourth position, and all of the other men switched the cardboard figures around at Wallace's order and held them on their laps as they were asked to sit in a row of chairs. The instructions were that upon command, the group would rise to their feet, each man would approach the mirror one at a time and face it directly before turning his profile to the viewer, and then they would return to their chairs and be seated.

Wallace stationed two of his teammates in with the prisoner, took several Polaroid photographs of the array to use for the pretrial hearing, and called to his sergeant to bring us the woman who had been attacked earlier this morning. I waited for her in the hallway outside the captain's office, then quietly introduced myself to her and explained the procedure that would follow.

'I'd like you to come into this room with me and Detective Wallace. Please don't be scared, we'll be right next to you. You're going to look at six men through a glass window. You can see them and hear them, but they cannot see you, I promise. We'll turn out the lights and I'll ask you to take a good, close look. I'd prefer that you don't say anything to us until after you've seen each of them up close. Then I'll just ask you three or four questions, and it will be all over. It won't even take two minutes. Are you okay?'

Mrs. Jeter appeared to be a few years older than I was. She was understandably tense and nodded in compliance as I went through the steps. 'Can't my husband be with me?'

Mercer was gentle and reassuring. 'In a minute, ma'am, we'll have you right back to him. But he's a witness, too, so each of you has to do it separately. I'll be right beside you. Nobody's gonna hurt you.'

She let us lead her into the small viewing space and I stood her near the window as Mercer switched off the lights. She gave a slight gasp: 'Oh my, it's so dark,' and reached out to grab onto my hand as she peered into the glass. I let her hold it and rested my other arm on her shoulder to offer comfort.

As the six rose to their feet and the first one walked toward the mirror, I could see Mrs. Jeter's eyes scanning the row. 'My God, I see him – it's number four. That's the man who was in my apartment this morning, that's him.' Her hand squeezed mine as though they were being crushed together by a steamroller.

She was perfect. She knew exactly who she was looking for and didn't even have to wait for the motley crew to parade in front of her one by one.

Wallace asked her to go through the rest of the process anyway, and to study each of the men as closely as possible. She did, but kept repeating, 'I don't have to – I know it's him.'

As Mercer took her out the door on the far side of the room, so she wouldn't intercept her husband or the women who had not yet viewed, she reached up and kissed him on his cheek, telling him how grateful she was that he had made the arrest so quickly. 'I'm a very lucky woman, I know that. And thank you.'

He turned and gave me a thumbs-up. 'The first hit is always the best. Nice and solid coming out of the box. We got him, Coop. Let's keep going.'

I backed out of the room and motioned to the sergeant to send Mr. Jeter up to us. An old uniformed cop who looked as if he could count the minutes to retirement and had been assigned to man the telephones walked through the rear of the squad. 'You had a couple of calls since you got here, Miss Cooper. I didn't know you was up here.'

'Remember what they were? Anything more pressing than this?'

'Nah. Kid from your office, Acciano, says he's got good news for you – a guilty verdict. He'll leave the details on your voice mail. And Chapman, Homicide. Says he knows what Final Jeopardy is tonight – something like that. Wants you to call him when you get home. He'll be at his office till 1 A.M. Lots of reporters asking what you were doing. That kind of thing.'

'Fine. Just hold everything till we're all done and I'll look for you on my way out of here.'

Mr. Jeter marched toward me, thrust his hand out to shake mine as we said hello to each other. He was feeling very proud of himself for having been able to thwart the attack on his wife. I started to describe the line-up but he cut me off. 'I've done this before. Mugged getting off work the year before last. Had to go to three of these before they caught the right guy. Take me in and let 'er rip.'

I re-entered the room where Mercer was already standing at the window and we repeated the scene. 'That's the little bastard. Number four. Right, am I right? Did my wife get him, too?'

Detective Wallace tried to steer Jeter's attention back to the full panel. 'We'd really like you to let each one of them come up here and—'

'Waste your time anyway you like, Wallace.' He stood still in front of the window and let the six men go through the motions, but shook his head back and forth the whole time. 'It's four. I just saw him this morning. I hope my wife wasn't too shook up to do this. Am I right?'

'Thanks, Mr. Jeter. We'll let you two back together now and Detective Wallace will explain all this mystery to you in about ten minutes. Then you can take Mrs. Jeter on home, okay?'

'Great. You give my regards to Mr. Battaglia, will you? This is the third time in six years I had a case with his office. He does a fine job. Met him once at a community meeting – very decent man.'

'He is, Mr. Jeter. I'll say hello to him for you tomorrow. Thanks for your help here.' I held the door open for him, ushered him out, and asked Mercer to get Katherine Fryer, the twenty-four-year-old illustrator I had interviewed in my office the morning after Isabella was murdered. Only one week had passed since that day, but it seemed like months.

Mercer went up to the fourth floor, where Fryer had been asked to wait, and brought her down to the viewing area himself. I recalled her extraordinary composure so shortly after her attack that day, and now felt the tremor in her hand as she extended it to meet mine. I asked how she had been doing as I guided her inside and repeated the instructions.

As Mercer reached back for the light switch, he mouthed something to me, which I realized were the words: 'Stand close.'

I moved in to Katherine's side as she advanced to the window and once again was glad for his advice. As she poked her head forward, nose almost against the glass, her knees buckled and she would have collapsed to the floor had Wallace not grabbed her at the waist and held her up. 'Sorry, sorry. I can't help it,' she murmured, trying to steady herself. 'He's in there.'

We both tried to soothe her and calm her down, but Katherine Fryer did not want to look through that window again.

'I really need you to take one more look. We're right here with you. Just tell us whether or not you see the man who attacked you last week, and the number he's holding, please.'

With great reluctance, the young woman pulled herself up and braced her body with an arm on each of us. She stared ahead for several seconds, then turned and glared at me. 'The rapist is holding the number four. I'll never forget that face. Now will you let me out of here?'

I nodded at Mercer, thanked Ms. Fryer, and stepped out for some air while the next two women were located and brought up, one at a time, in the same fashion. It was no surprise that each of the identifications were so positive. The Jeters' attack had occurred in their home only hours ago this very day. And unlike muggings on the street that take only two or three minutes to commit, the rapes that Montvale had committed kept him with his victims for extended periods of time. These women had been forced to experience him through every one of their five senses, and it was because of that lengthy, intimate exposure that I would be able to argue to the jury that these identifications should be more reliable than those made by victims of any other kind of crime.

The question for William Montvale's jury would not be how these witnesses remembered what he looked like, but rather, how they could ever forget the face of the man who so tortured them.

While Mercer made arrangements to get each of the witnesses home, the sergeant paid the satisfied stand-ins and sent them off into the night. I asked one of the guys on the team to take sandwich and drink orders and we called out to the deli on the corner of Columbus for a delivery. 'No beer till after all the work is done, agreed?' I asked, as I laid out the cash, noting that it was after nine o'clock as we moved into the next phase of the arrest process. Some of the guys grumbled but everyone knew there were still a lot of loose ends to tie up before the end of the evening.

'I'm gonna go in and try to warm him up for you, Cooper. The desk says your video man is downstairs. I told 'em to send him here so he can start getting set up.'

'That's good. I'll get on the phone and work on the search warrant. You certain he was living at his mother's place?'

'Yeah. That all had to be confirmed for Parole to approve the move to New York. Doesn't mean he hasn't flopped somewhere else a couple of nights. But if you look through the fives,' Mercer went on, calling my attention to the police reports known as Detective Division 5s, 'you can make a list of some of the items of clothing the women described and some of the jewelry he stole. Maybe even the knife.'

'It'll be drawn up and signed, ready to go so you can be at his mother's door at the crack of dawn.'

'When do we worry about DNA?'

'Nothing to worry about. At the arraignment, I ask the judge for a court order to draw a vial of Mr. Montvale's blood. If there were ever a case with probable cause, this one is it. Got the best serologist in the country right in the ME's office. They've got the blood from each of the victims already, to develop their typings to do the eliminations for the DNA results, and in a few weeks, that nail'll also be in Montvale's coffin.'

'I just want to place a few of these facts in front of him. Might help us get him to talk nice to you, Coop.'

It took me almost forty-five minutes to work through the application for a warrant by telephone to one of the rookie prosecutors who was manning the late shift in ECAB. There was a form in the word processor which made the conversation pretty easy, but there were a lot of details in Mercer's paperwork and I didn't want the detectives to have to go back twice. If Montvale's mother got smart, some of the things they weren't authorized to grab on the first trip might disappear by the time they returned with an amended warrant. We faxed the completed documents back and forth several times while I corrected the points that would be sworn to before a judge.

Mercer waited patiently until I was satisfied with the finished product. Then he signaled me to join him in the sergeant's office, where I started on my third or fourth cup of coffee, wide awake and tingling with the excitement of a good arrest and the rush of caffeine.

'Well, I've moved him along a little. When we glommed him in the bank, it was the usual "I-don't-know-what-you're-talking-about" bullshit. Then I unrolled his birth certificate and the Parole letter and stuck it up in front of his nose just now, and he mumbled something about making a mistake and knocking on the Jeters' door when he was really looking for his Uncle Louie's apartment. Of course, he doesn't have a fuckin' clue where his Uncle Louie lives. And I spent the last half-hour talking fingerprints, a little lecture about DNA, and then some yammer about everything the Jersey cops told me about his priors, and how similar they are to these cases.'

'Where'd that get you?'

'First he insisted that he was completely cured in that prison treatment center. Doesn't do that kind of stuff anymore. Likes women now, understands them better.'

'The therapist hasn't been born yet who can rehabilitate one of these predators. I once had a defendant who'd been treated in one of those programs tell me that if I broke the word "therapist" into two words, it forms "the rapist." How's that for rehabilitation, huh?'

Mercer went on, 'He saved the best for the last.'

Sergeant Barbero stuck his head in. 'You guys taking calls yet? These phones are wild.'

'Hold everything, Sarge. I want to see if he'll talk to Cooper.'

'What's the best?' I asked.

'After I laid it all out, I began to jerk his chain about how smart he was, you know, the ruse about Con Ed and talking his way into the apartment. Man, this guy is a sucker for having you tell him he's smart.'

It was odd what worked with different suspects – what approach would make them want to talk to you. The most unpleasant part of this process for me had always been sitting in these rooms, face to face with men who were capable of monstrous acts against other humans, and speaking to them civilly when the evidence of their guilt was overwhelming. Doing it, one hoped, to get even more information to use against them.

'I hit the button with Montvale. Enough times of complimenting him and he actually wanted to tell me how he did it. Not the whole thing, he's still not admitting the rapes. Says that till today he had never guessed wrong about which apartment he wanted to be in.'

I listened as Mercer went on. 'Getting past doormen is easy. He says you never have to wait more than an hour, even to get into the best buildings. Sooner or later, guy gets distracted by a couple of moving men, an argument with a porter or handyman, pain in the ass tenant who expects him to know what the temperature is today and what time it was when 14B and 6A went out to walk their dogs. None of that happens, the guy eventually has to leave his post to take a leak. That gets him in the front door and on his way upstairs.

'This is his favorite part. Montvale says his prime time is the middle of the day. He walks up and down the hallways, listening at the doors. If he hears the television, and the noise is a soap opera, it's a pretty sure bet you got a woman home alone watching the tube. Sometimes she opens the door and it's an old lady, so he's not interested. And sometimes there's extra baggage, like Mr. Jeter, so he usually just apologizes and walks away, saying he made a mistake. But he says the city is full of housewives and unemployed broads who are addicted to the soaps the way you and Chapman like your quiz show shit, and he thinks he can smell 'em right outside their doors. "Days of Our Lives," "All My Children," "General Hospital" – says they're a dead giveaway.'

'Thank goodness for watching American Movie Classics and reading great murder mysteries. Even when I'm home sick, I've never in my life seen a soap opera.'

'Anyway, that got him going.'

'Foolish question, Mercer, but did you read him his rights?'

'I told you how scared we all are of you, didn't I? You think I'm gonna risk your wrath over a little thing like that?'

'And no noise about a lawyer?' I asked. 'How'd we get so lucky?'

'If I were you, I'd get Bannion ready to roll right away. I don't know how long this'll last. Montvale knows the system better than we do – he's probably been in court more times in his life than you have.'

Mercer returned to the holding cell to continue talking with the prisoner while I sent a detective down to the lobby to help Bob Bannion bring his video equipment upstairs and get ready for filming a statement. I called the Deputy Inspector of the Police Department's Public Information Office and urged him not to allow Montvale to be photographed by the press on his way down to Central Booking, since we had other witnesses who had not yet had a chance to see an array, and his identification would be the key issue. The polite conversation became heated and, over my objections, it looked as if the inspector was headed to staging a press conference on the steps of the station house before I could even finish my work and get out of the way.

Bannion had cleared a place to set up in the sergeant's office. Montvale would sit behind the desk, and a huge wall clock over his head would show the court and other viewers that the sequence of the questioning – if the Q and A went as long as I hoped it would – had not been tampered with. He would face Wallace and me in the two chairs, our backs to the camera, which Bob had moved to the far side of the desk. As usual, I would ask the questions and Wallace would cue me if there were specifics about a particular one of the cases or details provided by a victim that only the assailant could confirm.

We were ready to go. I called to Mercer to bring Montvale into the room, and watched as he opened the barred cell and walked the sullen suspect down the hall to where Bannion and I were moving around the desktop letter trays and clutter to keep everything out of arm's reach. He took his seat and I took mine, three feet away from him, head to head, about to try to see how *he* described these hours of horror that so completely altered the lives of the women he'd encountered.

I repeated to Montvale what Mercer had told him about the video process and explained that I would begin the taping by telling him again, as Mercer had done hours ago, what his rights were. He leered as if he was looking forward to playing with the camera, and his smile broadened when Wallace leaned over and removed the handcuffs from his wrists.

'My name is Alexandra Cooper. I'm an assistant district attorney, and I am here with William Montvale and Detective Mercer Wallace of the Special Victims Squad, Thursday evening at' – I glanced up at the clock on the wall above Montvale – 'nine fifty-five.' I was putting the necessary heading on the tape.

'Mr. Montvale, I am going to ask you some questions about events that occurred in this county on a series of dates over the past six weeks, but before I do, I want to advise you of your rights.'

This is the part of doing interrogations where I always hold my breath and rely on whatever inexplicable phenomenon has made confession work so well for centuries in the ecclesiastical settings. Ignore what I am about to tell you about your legal entitlements, Mr. Montvale, and spill your guts to me. Tell me what you did. Every raw minute of it, so that you can pay for it for the rest of your miserable life.

'You have the right to remain silent and to refuse to answer questions, do you understand that?'

His head moved up and down, but he didn't speak.

'Mr. Montvale,' I pushed him softly, 'it would help if you spoke your answers aloud, instead of just nodding.'

'Yes, yes, Miss Cooper. I got it. Understood.'

'Anything that you do say tonight may be used against you later in court, do you understand that?'

'I certainly do.'

'You have the right to consult with an attorney before you answer our questions, and to have an attorney present during this questioning, as well as in the future. Do you understand that?'

'Loud and clear, Miss Cooper. I understand you.'

I was almost there. 'If you cannot afford an attorney, one will be provided for you without cost, do you understand that?'

'Yes, ma'am.'

'If you don't have a lawyer available, Mr. Montvale, you have the right to remain silent until you've had the chance to speak with one. Understand?'

'Yeah.'

'Now that I have advised you of your rights, just as Detective Wallace did, are you willing to answer my questions?'

The leer was still there. 'Try me. Let's see what you want to know.'

A wise-ass. I've been there before. Stay cool and he'll settle in. He'll be fine, just don't let him rattle you.

'Mr. Montvale, let's begin with this morning. I'm going to ask you some questions about what happened today, in an apartment at 246 West Sev—'

'Well, shit, Miss Cooper. I don't want to talk about that. I don't want to discuss that with you or your dumbass detective friend here.' Montvale's voice began to escalate as he rose to his feet and began pounding on the desk. 'I WANT A LAWYER. GET ME A FUCKING LAWYER.'

Mercer was around the desk and slammed the defendant back into his seat by his shoulders before I could even open my mouth again. 'Bannion, keep this video rolling,' Mercer shouted. 'Get every minute of this, so the judge can see how gently I treated this scumbag. You, Cooper, out of the room, now. NOW.'

I hesitated and Mercer screamed at me again. On my way out I was almost trampled by three other detectives who heard the shouting and ran in to give Mercer a hand. There was the sound of scuffling from the small room, punctuated by laughter from Montvale, who knew these guys were dying to land a few gut punches on him, but thanks to Mercer's quick thinking, the video was actually keeping him safe.

I was annoyed and deflated. I thought we had been so close to getting admissions to the string of rapes. They were not essential to a prosecution, just icing on this particular case, but I wanted to hear how it felt, from the rapist's perspective, to do these despicable things to other living beings.

I wondered if it was my approach that made him flip, as I paced back and forth in the filthy hallway. Sometimes these guys will talk to men, but not to women – and I kicked myself for not having had one of my male colleagues from the unit here as a backup to try to do the interrogation in case the suspect went dry on me. I knew Mercer would tell me not to take it personally, but whenever this kind of thing happened, I did.

'Hey, Coop, nothing personal,' Mercer said, as if on cue, when he stuck his head out of the room a few minutes later. 'Montvale had this one planned. He was no more gonna give you a story on videotape than I'm gonna give him a lobster dinner. He was just in the mood to play with you – a little variety in his day – for the last time in a very long while.'

He stepped out of the way as two teammates led the shackled prisoner out of the sergeant's office and back to his wooden bench. Montvale laughed out loud all the way down the hall, and I fought to hold my tongue so my comments wouldn't be repeated back to whichever judge we stood before together tomorrow morning.

Mercer had no time to deal with my long face and wounded ego. 'Stop feeling sorry for yourself, Alex. You got everything you need here, plus whatever we get from the warrant. D'you really think that a guy with that many felony convictions and so much state time behind him's gonna sit here and weave you some kinda tale of his exploits? You got a rock-crusher of a case, what more do you need? Now just take yourself outta here and get some sleep. I'll do the warrant first thing, then we'll have the arraignment by early afternoon and you can make the Grand Jury dates for next week.'

As high as I had let the adrenaline and caffeine carry me, as quickly did I drop when Montvale brought it all to an abrupt end.

'I hate it when they beat me,' I moaned in disgust.

'Beat you. How long you figure this guy's gonna spend in Dannemora? A hundred, a hundred-fifty years? That enough for you, or you want longer?' Mercer asked me.

'I'll take three lifetimes, consecutive. No parole.'

'Not likely that anybody's gonna parole Mr. Montvale early again. I bet they've got the editorials written for the morning edition already. Give it a rest.'

'I'm ready to pack it in,' I told him. 'Do you need anything else from me tonight? I'd like to get out of here before that press conference starts. Battaglia will never believe I tried to talk them out of doing it. Whew, those guys are stubborn.'

'I'm fine. Want me to call downstairs and see if they can free up someone who can take you home?'

I looked at my watch. 'No, it's not even ten-thirty. If there's anybody loose, I'll grab him. If not, I can get a yellow right on Columbus Avenue. It's still early.'

'Want the phone? Some privacy? You can use the sergeant's office – I'll close the door.'

'Mercer, I am going directly home. Not passing Go, not collecting two hundred dollars. Directly home. I'll return my calls from there. I'm whipped.'

'Thanks for coming out on this. I'll be in your office right after we hit his mother's apartment.'

Mercer picked up his case folder, escorted me to the stairwell, and held the door as I walked out. Most of the guys were too busy chowing down their hero sandwiches and uncapping bottles of beer to notice my departure, but I gave a general wave in the direction of the squad room and leaned on the banister as I plodded down the steep flights of steps to make my exit.

24

When I reached the ground floor, I could see through the glass partition that the lobby was swarming with activity. Men and women officers were beginning to trickle in for the late tour, and several uniformed cops were trying to hold reporters and cameramen at bay on the front steps of the station house.

I pushed through the door, lowered my head, and began to wind my way through the ranks of thick, uniformed bodies and around the side of the news crews. The reporters were listening attentively to an announcement from the desk sergeant about the fact that the Deputy Inspector would be speaking in a few minutes, and there would, indeed, be a photo-op of Montvale himself being booked at the desk.

Dammit. I kept walking and was only made by one cameraman as I reached the pavement. 'Hey, Miss D.A. – this your case?'

I shook my head in the negative and kept going, turning right to head to Columbus Avenue and the steady flow of cabs that I assumed would be making their way to nearby Lincoln Center for the after-theater pickups.

'Alex? Alexandra Cooper?'

My head lifted up at the sound of my name, and I saw Ellen Goldman step toward me from the front of the car she had been leaning against, at the edge of the precinct driveway, adjacent to the station house.

I smiled in relief. She didn't have a camera in her hand and she wasn't on a deadline for an 11 P.M. broadcast or a morning tabloid.

'The news of the case is all over the radio and local TV. My editor called me at home and asked me to get over here. We thought perhaps I could watch you do a line-up or something like that for our profile.'

I kept walking and her shorter legs tried to keep pace with my stride. 'Sorry, I could have saved you the trouble of coming out. I couldn't have let you up there – you might have become a witness in the case, you know, if you had been present for any of the crucial events, or the defense claimed you had seen or heard something important. Sorry. I wish I had known you were there – I could have told you not to waste your time.'

'That's okay. I kept trying to call upstairs but they wouldn't put me through to you.'

'I know,' I told her. 'My orders. Again, I apologize.'

'Don't be silly. That's the kind of job this is. You know we always keep trying. Listen, can I buy you a cup of coffee?'

'Ellen.' I stopped to face her, dropping my shoulders and letting her look at the dark circles I'd been growing under my eyes for the past week. 'Coffee? I think I've had half of El Exigente's North American supply in the last eight days. I don't want to be rude, but I just need to go home and get a decent night's sleep.'

I didn't mean to be as clipped as I was when I spoke to her, but I heard the edge in my own voice and I immediately tried to soften my response with a small bribe.

'There'll be an arraignment tomorrow, probably by mid-afternoon, and if you call Laura around eleven, I'll tell you exactly when to be in court, if you'd like to see it. Then, once the fireworks are over, it'll be a typical Friday afternoon – slow, I hope – and I'll give you an hour or so on the case and the investigation.' Battaglia wouldn't mind, I thought, because she's writing a piece that won't appear for months, rather than a story about this particular arrest.

Ellen obviously liked that offer and thanked me for it. 'Why don't I give you a lift home?' she countered warmly. 'Really, I won't pester you. I see how tired you are and I'll just drop you off and plan on seeing you and having all my questions answered in the afternoon.'

I hesitated and she seemed to sense exactly why. My reflexes were slowing down and she continued to speak. 'Don't worry about your privacy, Alex. I already know where you live. Remember, I dropped those flowers off for you the day after your friend was killed? You had canceled our first interview, don't you remember? I told you I've done my research – that's not the kind of thing I want to write about.'

I was relieved and, of course, her reminder was correct. It made me smile 'cause I remembered Mike's comment when

I referred to the sender of the flowers as a 'nice reporter,' and he told me that was an oxymoron.

'Sure, Ellen, that'd be lovely. As long as you don't think I'm abrupt for not asking you up for a nightcap.'

'C'mon. I understand. I'm parked right across the street.'

We checked the traffic and jaywalked over to the car she pointed out at the corner of the block. She unlocked the driver's side and my door latch popped up automatically. As I lowered myself into the passenger seat, I could hear someone calling my name from the front of the station house. 'Cooper, hey, Miss Cooper! Miss District Attorney!'

I could see in the rearview mirror that a couple of heads turned from the crowd of news people to see if I was somewhere in the vicinity. But I had already climbed into the car and was not about to walk back into that media circus without a pithy sound bite – the last thing Battaglia would want to hear from me anyway.

The voice shouted out, 'Cooper, call for you! C'mon back.'

Ellen put the key in the ignition and the engine started, but she looked over at me with concern before she set the car in drive. 'It's okay,' I told her, 'you'll have me home in five minutes and I'll return my calls from there. It's just a feeding frenzy with all those reporters at the precinct. I'll be much happier once I'm home. Let's go.'

25

I leaned my head against the backrest of the seat in Ellen Goldman's car, somewhat grateful that I had exchanged the adventure of a cab ride home in a fleet car with no springs or shock absorbers for the smoother trip in her later model rental that would simply cost me some chatter and forced girl-talk.

'What's the best way to get through the park from here?' she asked as we pulled away when the traffic light changed to green.

'South on Columbus. You can pick up the transverse on Sixty-fifth Street.'

I closed my eyes against the bright reflection of the overhead streetlights as the car moved down the avenue, and wondered whether Montvale's victims would sleep any differently tonight.

'Must be very satisfying to get someone you've been after for a while, isn't it?' Ellen asked.

I had hoped she would have had the good sense not to interview me on the way home, but her natural curiosity apparently took over. I reminded myself not to let my guard down completely and not to answer the question as though I were talking to a friend who could be trusted with the information. Yeah, I would say to Sarah or Nina or David or Mike, it feels better than you could ever imagine, and it is one of the great satisfactions of my professional life to know this bastard is going to spend the foreseeable future in a woefully unpleasant place where he can't hurt anybody else. But because I knew how a reporter could twist my words in print to make me sound like Torquemada or some man-hating witch, I simply said, 'Yes.'

Goldman made a left turn on Seventy-second Street and headed toward Central Park West. 'Don't you ever worry that one of these guys you prosecute is going to come back after you?' she queried.

I had been asked that question a million times, most often by my mother. That's not the kind of thing that keeps people in my business up at nights. 'That happens in the movies, Ellen. You can't let that drive you when you do this work. We'd never get anything done.'

'I read the clips about that case of yours that was just overturned on appeal. The serial rapist in Central Park – wasn't his name Harold McCoy?' she continued. It was the case I had just reminded Wallace about, in which the judge had thrown out half the evidence we had seized because the captain had refused to call us to get a search warrant. 'Does that mean he's out of jail now?'

'Don't remind me about him, Ellen. Yeah, Harold McCoy

is out. We get to retry him after the first of the year. But in the meantime, his brother posted bail for him and he's on the street.'

'I don't know how you do it, Alex. That would give me the creeps every time I go through the park. I'd be looking for him everywhere I went.'

'You think I don't? It's not even conscious at this point,' I told her. 'Certain places just evoke connections, memories – and they're not always good ones. It's ironic. I happen to think that Central Park is one of the safest places in the city. Look at the size of it, more than eight hundred acres. You've got more crimes committed in any two- or three-square-block area around the park every month than you have inside it. But when something does happen here, especially because it's so isolated at night, it's a legitimate public safety issue. It's awfully hard for the police to patrol a space like this.'

Goldman was driving east. She passed the guardhouse at the Dakota, and then continued straight on into the park. As soon as she entered the roadway, I realized her mistake. 'Whoa, I meant the transverse – the road that cuts through, from West to East. This is the long way,' I complained.

'Oh damn. I just saw this opening and thought it was what you were referring to. My fault,' she apologized.

The few extra minutes hardly mattered at this point. Instead of going directly across, this would lead us on the more rambling route down the West Drive and back up to the exits on the East Side. 'No big deal, Ellen. It's a prettier ride.'

The moon was full – maybe that had helped us catch Montvale, I thought to myself, if the cops were right about all the lunatics coming out under its spell – and

357

it would probably result in an overflow of business in my office tomorrow. Not the quiet Friday I had just predicted. The park showed itself brilliantly in the lunar glow, the foliage with its dapplings of yellows and auburns having replaced much of the verdant color of summer. The fallen leaves made it possible to see further off the road, into the beautiful park grounds, than you could when the trees were full of thick greens.

I was relaxed now, taking in the quiet view as we rounded the south end of the drive, and noting that the number of late-night runners and dog walkers tapered off as we left the areas of the park closest to the entrances and coursed up the Center Drive, almost smack in the middle of the two sides. Hard to believe this pastoral setting, with its fifty-eight miles of paths, was once the site of stench-filled swamps and pigsties. I enjoyed the tracks it provided for jogging, the lawns that hosted concerts I had attended with friends, and the cheerful zoo where I took my niece and nephew when they visited me in town.

But I knew better than most who loved its lush comfort the danger that could lurk in its bushes, the terrors hidden behind its trees and stone walls. I had enormous respect for the splendor it added to the city, and just as much respect for the power with which it controlled that gift.

We were past the Carousel now, almost parallel to the Bandshell, and nearing the fork that led to the first East Side exit at Seventy-second Street. Ellen knew my address, so it didn't occur to me to remind her to bear right at that point. When she missed the turn and veered off to the left, I groaned at the thought of having to circle around that long loop again.

'Shit, Ellen, you missed the turnoff.'

'Oh, sorry, Alex. I'm not that familiar with the park, especially at night. I haven't spent that much time in New York. I . . . I guess I just lost my bearings. It'll just be a couple of minutes. It's always when I'm rushing to do things right, if you know what I mean.'

I did. I guess that's why they always used to say most accidents happen close to home. I straightened up in my seat to try to observe the directions more carefully in order to get us back to my apartment as soon as possible.

Now we were traveling north again, on the portion of the road just beyond the curve that cuts off to the West Side at Seventy-second Street. I was watching the light from the sky dance on the small pond which was below me and off to my right, but was jolted back to attention when the car veered off the drive to our left and Ellen braked to a stop, almost flush against a large elm tree.

I had instinctively thrown my arms up against the dashboard to protect myself, but my head still smacked against the roof of the low car from the impact it made jumping the curb.

'Jeez, Ellen, take it easy,' I mumbled, shaking my head, as though that would clear the stars that started flashing in my eyes, and rubbing my neck, which already seemed to be sore. 'What happened, what's your prob—'

'I need to talk with you, Alex. You're going to get out of this car, and walk down that path with me—'

I hadn't looked up yet and I was massaging my temples with my fingertips. Everybody wants to talk to me except William Montvale, everybody wants to tell me their troubles. 'Ellen, this is stupid. If you'd like me to drive, I'll be happy to do it, but I'm not wasting another minute here . . .'

'Look at me, Alex. This is *my* investigation. I'm the one in charge now, and you're going to take orders from me.'

I lifted my head to try to see whether the words I was listening to bore any relation to the speaker or the circumstances I was in, or whether I had been knocked around in the car by that bad bounce so that I was truly a bit foggy. I was staring directly into the muzzle of a small handgun.

'Ellen, my God, Ellen – put down that gun and talk to me, tell me what you want!' My body had reacted immediately to the signals my tired brain was sending out, and I was shaking uncontrollably as I tried to shield myself from the pistol with my quivering hands.

'You're even more stupid than I thought if you haven't figured out what I want by now. You like everybody to think you're so smart – that's so important to you – but even I know the ridiculous mistakes you've made this time, and you're about to find out that *I'm* more clever than you are. Get out of the car, get out very slowly and stand right next to the door. This is not a joke – do it now.'

I looked at the gun again and remembered that Goldman had told me she had been in the Israeli Army – an elite antiterrorist unit. I had no reason to doubt her. The dark pathway in front of the car frightened me as much as she and her weapon did, and I had no intention of following her to a more isolated piece of turf.

'Let's talk right here, please, Ellen. I'll tell you whatever information you want to know. Whatever it is.' Where the fuck are the Park Rangers? I asked myself. Don't leave this car. Nobody's allowed to park off the roadway – it's a worse offense to the Rangers than a triple homicide. Keep her in the car and someone will come upon us, I kept thinking. Stay put.

'Get out,' she barked. She was out of her door, gun down at her side, and around the back of the car to me in a matter of seconds. I had thought about trying to climb over the console and into the driver's seat, but the model was too compact to do it quickly, and she had taken the key out of the ignition.

Ellen had an automatic light beam on the key ring which she held in her left hand, and she pointed it at my lock, which popped up at her command. 'I told you to get out of the car and I mean it, Alex, right now.'

'It doesn't seem to make any difference to me. I'm not moving. Either you shoot me in your car, which at least creates some problems for you, or you take me down into a park ravine and shoot me, God knows why. But I'll take my chances here.'

'Stop playing Clarence Darrow with me, Alex. I don't intend to shoot you, so get your ass out of the car and walk with me. We have things we need to talk about.'

My mind was trying to move more nimbly to process the words Goldman was speaking, while the rest of my body stayed taut in the presence of her pistol. Why was she holding me at gunpoint, why was she threatening my life, if she didn't intend to kill me? It made no sense, since I would obviously have to report this abduction to the police. Of course she was going to shoot me, so why give her the location of her choice? At least my body or my blood in her rented car would link her to my death. A wave of nausea swept through me at the thought of the possibility of those two words: 'my death.'

Goldman had seemed so sane and articulate and rational until moments ago, and now, so completely crazy.

'Walk down this trail with me, Alex. We just need to get a bit away from the road for a while, so we can discuss things.'

She had opened the car door and was nudging me with the short barrel of her gun, motioning me toward a narrow footpath leading downhill between a clump of trees and bushes. I stepped out, and let my blazer, which had been draped across my lap, fall to the ground. I didn't have enough possessions with me to make a track to follow, but surely it would be an identifying piece of clothing that would make someone look for me if I were missing. I fast-forwarded through every kidnapping case I had worked on and every dreadful story of disappearing people I had clipped from the tabloids.

'Pick it up, Alex,' Goldman chided me. 'I'll wear it. It's chilly, tonight. A little big for me, but it'll be fine.' She waited until I handed her the jacket and then put it on, one arm at a time, rolling up the sleeves to fit her shorter arms.

I scanned the area for signs of a jogger, a member of the Road Runner club, a homeless guy who'd have some kind of box cutter or object I could use to try to defend myself, but we seemed to occupy this little pocket of the park entirely by ourselves.

Goldman tugged on the sleeve of my shirt and pressed the gun into the small of my back. We started along the tree-lined walk and halfway down I stumbled on a piece of loose rock, falling backward and sliding another four or five feet, pounding my back against the stones and branches, and scraping my hands as I tried to break my descent. An involuntary screech let out as I fell and Goldman hurried to catch up to me, smacking me across the face with her free hand in punishment for the noise.

'It was an accident. I slipped. I'm not being difficult.'

'I thought you were so graceful,' she sneered, 'the ballet dancer. Ha! Get on your feet.'

I pushed myself up, wiping the pebbles from the abrasions that now covered the palms of both hands, but as I tried to stand it was obvious I had turned an ankle and couldn't put my weight directly on it.

'Keep going. Drag your damn foot if you have to, but move it over this way.' She poked me with the gun barrel to cross the paved sidewalk and moved me further downhill, near a weeping willow that was bent over, gleaming in the moonlit radiance of the lake. 'Under these trees, here. Now sit down. Does this place look familiar to you?'

How closely she had done her research was even more apparent now. We weren't more than thirty feet from the site of Harold McCoy's last rape, diagrammed on the front pages of each of the city papers when he struck the last time before his arrest eleven months ago. McCoy had brought his victim in from the other direction after he dragged her off her bicycle late one night, coming to this area from the north, near the Loeb Boathouse.

I couldn't tell which was throbbing more violently now, my head or my ankle. The former was urging me not to obey the command to sit, and the latter was eager to be relieved of my dead weight.

Goldman leaned over and seemed to be placing her gun in a holster on her ankle, hidden beneath the leg of her slacks. I lightened for a moment, thinking she had meant her statement not to shoot me, but closed my eyes in terror at the sight of the knife with the six-inch blade which she unsheathed and withdrew in the next gesture.

From her pants pocket she unrolled a small length of cord. 'Give me your hands. In front,' she demanded as she kneeled and wound the rope around my wrists, securing it with a knot that looked like some professional job – the kind that might have been taught to an army Special Forces recruit.

Talk, I kept telling myself. You've heard of victims who have talked themselves out of their situations. Offenders who can be reached and reasoned with, who walk away from the ultimate crime and leave their prey unharmed.

'Ellen, I won't run away, you don't have to tie me up. Please tell me what it is you want to know.' I tried to be forceful without letting the degree of desperation that I felt spill over into my voice.

'This is how Harold McCoy would do it, isn't it? This is his "signature," you were quoted as saying. Get them into the park, off the roadway, always near one of the bodies of water, trussed up like the pigs they are, and then cut them up.'

There was no place for me to recoil as she took the knife and slit a line across my jeans, right at the crease where the top of the thigh meets the hip. The thick denim material yielded like butter to the fine-bladed, sharp knife, and like a paper cut, I didn't even feel it pierce my skin until the stinging sensation began to smart and I looked down to see the oozing line of blood.

Ellen Goldman was laughing now as she saw the red stain creep onto the faded denim of my pants. 'I didn't even mean to cut you yet. I have plenty of time for that.'

Talk to her, I thought to myself again. But words didn't

come, and I didn't want her to enjoy the fact that I was in pain.

She went on. 'Don't you see how easily I could make it look like Harold McCoy did this to you? That he waited outside the precinct when he heard on the radio that you were there, then he forced you into the park. People would buy that, you know. The press would love that story.'

Was that her plan? To make it look like a copycat crime? Goldman had studied my cases and knew that Harold McCoy was out of jail. She could make it look like *he* had stalked me – his prosecutor, his nemesis – and taken me to his special place in the park and killed me there.

'No one would believe that, Ellen. People saw me get in the car with you.' I prayed that was true, as I said it aloud, although I had no more reason to believe it than she did.

'No one saw that – no one who knows me,' she snapped back at me.

'Yeah, but guys who know *me* saw us. That would destroy your game – someone would put it together.'

'But at least this time they wouldn't blame Jed. I never meant for that to happen, but *you've* got him in so much trouble – he's likely to be charged for a murder he didn't commit.' Ellen Goldman was raging now, and suddenly things were coming into focus for me.

'Isabella Lascar?' I asked her. I was incredulous. 'This is about Isabella?'

'No, no, no. Not at all. She was nothing. This is about Jed Segal.'

Crystal clear. The Final Jeopardy answer tonight is erotomania, and now I knew the question: 'What killed Isabella Lascar?'

Sitting before me was the person who had shot Iz through

the center of that magnificent head, and she did it because of an obsession with a man who barely knew her: Jed Segal. This must be the woman who had stalked Jed in California, a woman whose delusion had already driven her to kill. I was about to become Ellen Goldman's next victim, and I was struggling to call up the things I had read about her mental disorder – erotomania – before I fell asleep last night, hoping that something would trigger how to deal with this otherwise intelligent, functional human being.

The stillness of the night was cut by the shrill squeal of my beeper, ringing out high-pitched tones from its perch on my waistband. Ellen stood and reached down to rip the small black device from me, clicked it to the off position, and pressed the lever on the illuminated dial to see the caller's number.

'Who's looking for you? It's a nine one seven number – who is it?'

'It must be someone from my office. This happens all the time, Ellen. There must be a new case.' I tried to urge her to take me to a phone booth, sure that I could signal some kind of distress if I could get on the phone with Mike or Mercer or Sarah. 'They'll look for me if I don't get back to them soon. Please let us call in, and then we can walk away from this rationally, Ellen. Please? I'm through with Jed, we can—'

'Well, he's not through with you. Nor am I. Who is this trying to reach you now?' She repeated the nine one seven area code and began to recite the rest of the number to me.

It was Chapman's cell phone. He was somewhere in the field, roaming, probably in some joint having a beer and getting ready to hit on a girl at the next table, with no idea that I was sitting under a tree in Central Park with a lunatic. I lied to Goldman: 'I don't recognize the number. It could be from any squad. I'm on call tonight, all night. Let's just go on up to the street, we'll phone them back and you can listen to the conversation.'

Chapman had tried to reach me at the Special Victims office during the line-ups tonight and I had put off the calls. Maybe that was Mike trying to contact me as I was about to get in Goldman's car, when the cop was yelling to me from the steps of the station house. Of course, he must have spoken with David Mitchell after David's appointment with Jed at seven-thirty this evening. They had probably put some of this together tonight and wanted to tell me about it. Had they figured out that perhaps there *was* another connection between Jed and Isabella – that both of them were being stalked by the same person – one whom she wanted desperately, and one whom she desperately wanted out of the way? Maybe they had figured it out, but never dreamed she would be waiting for me as I emerged from the station house at the end of my long evening.

Goldman took the silenced beeper and stuck it in the pocket of the jacket.

'You're the woman who met Jed in California, aren't you?' I asked her as she loomed over me, looking around at the grounds above us, as though to see whether the loud 'beeps' had attracted any attention on the road or pathways.

Engage her. Do it gently. She's not crazy, the book says, in any other way. She just has this delusion about Jed. Apart from that, she's not odd or bizarre. I hope these fucking shrinks know what they're talking about. 'Didn't you meet him when he was running for the Senate, in California? You were in graduate school out there.'

Goldman cocked her head and looked back down at me. 'Why, did Jed talk to you about me?'

'Yes, yes he did.'

'Did he say I was crazy? Did he tell you he didn't want anything to do with me?'

Keep lying. They all do it to you. 'No, Ellen, he never said that.' Flatter her, tell her what she wanted to hear. Tell her that the unfaithful bastard really wanted her. 'I never had the idea he got to know you very well, but he used to tell me you came to all his speeches, his events – said you were very smart.'

She was thinking now, thinking about what I was feeding her, and whether there was any kernel of truth in it. It had to at least intrigue her, I told myself, that Jed had spent any time talking about her when he moved East. At least it kept her on her feet, with that blade away from me, as I sat in place, my body aching and my mind trying to give her some thread back to life.

'Jed was in love with me, you know. There was a time when we first met that he wanted to go out with me,' Goldman told me.

'I didn't know that.' Let her talk. Let her tell me any bizarre imagining that popped into her twisted brain.

'I'm not surprised he didn't tell you that. That's what got him in trouble with his wife.'

That and the thirty-six other women he had probably screwed behind her back.

'I know he felt terrible when the police arrested you in L.A.,' I said. Find out why *that* didn't make her turn against him. It's hard to believe anybody sane wouldn't give up after that.

'That wasn't *his* fault, Alex. Didn't he tell you that? His wife was insanely jealous. Every time he saw me at a rally or a cocktail party, the minute he wanted to make his way across a room to me, his miserable wife would get one of his aides to stop him. You were much luckier – he finally got smart enough to get rid of her before he moved to New York. *She* was the reason I was in jail until the end of the summer. They arrested me because she complained that I was harassing her.'

That explains a lot. No wonder Jed never mentioned anybody bothering him here, in New York, when we started dating in June. There was no interference from Goldman, that I was aware of, as of the last week. But obviously, her approach to me – which started before Isabella's death – was a pivotal part of it. I had never even asked Jed the name of the California stalker. It hadn't seemed relevant.

Goldman kneeled in front of me again. 'What else did Jed tell you about me, anything?'

Maybe this is part of my lifeline. Enough about you, Goldman must be thinking, now let's hear what Jed thinks about me. Use your imagination, Cooper. Fill her with whatever will fuel her fantasies of life with Segal. Keep talking to her.

'Well, yes, Ellen. You must know that what we had is over, ended. Maybe that's why he was talking about you so—'

'Don't lie to me, Alex, you know it wasn't over.'

'But for me it is, I swear to you. I can talk to him about you, I can arrange for you to be with him.' You two creeps really deserve each other, I thought. I'll even spring for the hotel room – just let me out of this deathtrap alive, please.

Why did Ellen Goldman think it wasn't over with me

and Segal? She knew about Jed and Isabella. She must have thought I would break up with him once I found out about it, too. Didn't she kill Isabella because that temptress, that irresistible goddess, stood in the way of her reunion with Jed? I wanted to remind her of that, to give my breakup with Jed more credence. And yet I didn't want to make her think of Iz – the rational part of her must have some consciousness of guilt for shooting another human being to death.

I tried it out on her gently. 'I – I broke up with Jed this week, Ellen. I'm not going to see him any-more.'

'That's what you say tonight, but I've heard him talk to you, I've heard him beg you,' she sneered at me.

Where? I thought. What could she have heard?

She went on. 'You still got in his car, didn't you? Accepted his flowers?'

The same observations that 'Dr' Cordelia Jeffers made in the letter that arrived today. Were those letters also a device of Goldman's?

'No, Ellen – I've ended the whole goddamn thing. It was much too painful for me. I don't want to be with Jed Segal and he *isn't* begging me to come back to him, I swear to you.'

'I'm the one who knows exactly what he's up to, and you'll fall for it sooner or later. You'll take him back, too, now that your competition – Isabella Lascar – is out of the way. I know you won't throw away everything he offers you. I'm sick of his pleading with you.'

'Don't believe him, Ellen,' if she's really spoken with Jed, I thought. Maybe he's told her, like he's told Joan and Mike that he has tried to reach me. 'He's telling people he's begging me, but I swear to you that he hasn't said a word to me.'

'That's because *I've* been picking up those messages, Alex. *I* know how he feels about you, and you'll give in eventually.'

'You've been picking up my messages?' My face distorted itself in puzzlement, as I looked over at Ellen, not believing what she had just said. 'You couldn't possibly have—'

She interrupted and seemed pleased to carry forward this part of the dialogue – an opportunity, it was dawning on me, to tell me how much smarter she was than I. My hands twisted and turned against the cord on my wrists as she showed off her superior intelligence, but it didn't feel as though I was making any progress.

She fixed her gaze on me. 'Did you know Lascar had a Filofax, you know, a date book and address directory?'

'Yes, I did.' Iz's bible.

'Well, I guess the stupid cops never knew it. At least, I never read that it was stolen, in any of the newspaper accounts of her death,' Goldman said.

That's because one of the smart things we do is to keep a few critical details away from reporters so we know when we're talking to the real culprit, Ellen. I knew about its disappearance before anyone else did, but it certainly hadn't been in the papers. 'No, I never read about that either. Was it with her, in my house?'

'No. It was right in her tote, on the front seat of her car. And now I've got it.'

I am looking at a woman who could kill a person she thought was in the way of her love object, and then step up to the bloodied murder scene and reach her hand in to

371

remove a diary from the car seat next to the warm body. I shivered at the reminder that I was being confronted by a professionally trained killer, who had learned her trade for a good cause and had thereafter been hideously derailed.

'Why did you want the Filofax, Ellen?'

'You know as well as I do that it would have every number and every detail I wanted. Most women keep their lives recorded that way these days – phones, faxes, birthdays, anniversaries, shoe sizes, maître ds, unlisted information. I knew she'd have numbers for Jed and for you – private lines, home phones, apartment locations – things I'd never be able to get from public directories for months. It was just an afterthought, but it was too good to walk away from.'

'Iz had all my numbers, of course, but she didn't have my answering machine code.' I hoped I wasn't risking an outburst by challenging Goldman, but this bit about the messages had me upside down. What was she talking about?

'I couldn't convince Jed how smart I was all those months. Maybe this will help him see it. You can't figure out how to pick up a message on somebody's machine? Ha. Wait'll I tell him.'

I was barely computer literate and completely mechanically dysfunctional. But I had never had a reason to give anyone else the code to pick up my messages.

Goldman loved to display her cleverness. 'Once I had Lascar's Filofax, the rest was easy. All these machines are the same. People like you only buy one or two models. You're like Jed – totally name brand, top of the line. You're Sony, Panasonic – the expensive models. Look at you once and it's obvious you're too materialistic to buy a discount, no-name item. That's just a guess, but it didn't fail me.

'Then you look at the instruction book for how they do the remote pickup. They're all basically alike. That's how I used to get all Jed's messages, from his campaign office in California. That's how I knew he was going to the Vineyard. Press three-three to see if there are messages. Press two-two-two to see if there are messages. Press seven-seven to see if there are messages. Try it a couple of times and you can figure out what brand of machine you're dealing with. His headquarters was a Sony. So is your apartment. Jed's is a Panasonic.' Ellen Goldman was puffing now, standing as though she needed to stretch her legs, and pleased with the demonstration she was giving me.

'I do have a Sony, you're right, but—'

'I know I'm right.'

'There's also a personal code you need to program in. How did you get to that?' Let her know how impressed you are with what she's done. Every time I thought I heard footsteps or voices in the distant background, the noise soon faded to quiet, blending in with the natural sounds of squirrels stepping on dry leaves or birds flapping wings as they landed on nearby branches. Cars whizzed by on the cross-drive from time to time, but the steady hum of their wheels suggested that none even braked at the sight of a car pulled in off the roadway. Lights from above in the apartment windows at the majestic San Remo were shutting off throughout the building as people all over the city were going to sleep, and my only companions were the scores of blue rowboats behind my back, beached on their sides and chained together near the boathouse.

'The Filofax,' Goldman said, smiling. 'There's always

stuff in that, if you've got half a brain.' So much for me.

She continued. 'People are too lazy to be subtle. Most of us use the obvious – significant dates, anniv—'

'But you didn't have *my* Filofax, you had Isabella's.' I wasn't playing coy – I simply didn't know what she had done to get into my code.

'That's all I needed. When Jed was in L.A., he used to use his anniversary as the code. A lot of married people do, especially the women. His was February eighteenth – two eighteen. I'm surprised he could remember it – it didn't seem too significant, given the state of his marriage. It was probably his wife's idea, you know, for the home machine. Here, in New York, I got his unlisted number from Isabella's book, then guessed he was using his birthday, now that he's divorced.

'For you, the birthday was my first guess. Never been married, no special anniversary date. Lascar had your birthday in her book, along with her other information about you. April thirtieth. Four three zero. You're probably stupid enough to use it for your banking code and all your other pin numbers.'

She had me there. Goldman was rapt in her own self-congratulatory explanation and didn't seem to notice that I was making headway against my binds. I wasn't free, but they were loosening.

'And you picked up messages from my home machine all week? And you erased them after you listened?' I had ignored Jed's protestations that he had called repeatedly, and I had been depressed that there were so few calls from any of my other friends and family. This was not the moment to find out who else had been intercepted and erased from my radar screen. No wonder Jed had been trying so frantically to get me and my network of friends to believe him. Goldman had found him again, had reapplied herself to the effort to attract him in the days after Isabella's murder, and he indeed was asking for my help these past twenty-four hours.

'If you're telling the truth about not wanting anything to do with him,' she scoffed at me, 'then you wouldn't have missed his calls, anyway. Pleading for forgiveness and complaining about me. Those things were bad enough. But telling you how much he loved you – that *you* were his golden girl, that Isabella was just a mistake, that he wanted to marry you more than anything in the world – all that made a mockery of what I had risked *my* life to accomplish. I didn't want you to hear any of them, if I could help it. Maybe he was getting that through to you some other way, but not with the messages *I* could stop.'

Ellen Goldman was intense now, concentrating her anger on me again. 'I followed him to New York when I got out of jail. I found him again. But he had become distracted because of you,' she said, with obvious disdain. 'I wanted to meet you, to see what you were like. So I arranged the interview.'

'Don't you really work for the *Lawyer's Digest*?' I asked, knowing that the Public Relations Office had vetted her before letting me set an appointment with her.

'What a joke,' she blasted back at me. 'I just said I was freelancing for them – I've never published anything in my life. I never finished graduate school. Your people were so hungry for good press about the office that once I told them how much I admired your work, I could have said I was writing for *Popular Mechanics* and they would have given me carte blanche. Nobody ever checked my credentials.'

My thoughts flashed back to the day after Isabella's shooting, when Mike brought me home to the apartment from the office, and Ellen had left flowers with the doorman. I had been so pleased to see them I had assumed Laura had given her my address. How easily I had been misled, to have commented to Mike then about what a nice reporter she was. Oxymoron, he had said.

'But why Isabella?' I asked her. 'I can understand you were mad at *me* for taking up with Jed while you were in jail, but Isabella Lascar?'

'All of a sudden, last month, I began to find out about his meeting her. I could deal with you, I was sure. There was nothing that special about *you*,' she said. 'I knew if I made him aware of me again, you wouldn't be in my way. But then when she began calling him and seeing him, here and in L.A., I knew it was a serious problem. I may be able to compete with you, but she was a movie star – people idolized her, adored her, worshiped her. He'd never come back to me as long as she was in his life. Once I learned they were going to Martha's Vineyard together, it just seemed so easy for me. I drove right onto the ferry, didn't need any reservations off season. Got up to your house easily – between the listing in the phone book and those locals in the post office who'd trust anybody – pulled off the main road, just like I did tonight . . . and waited. I was back on the boat within hours. I just never meant for Jed to get blamed for it.'

Psychose passionelle. I tried to recall more facts from my reading the night before. Ellen Goldman really believed that Jed loved her, that he would actually return her affection, were it not for some external influence. The person in jeopardy is not the beloved – she'd have no reason to harm *him*. The most likely recipient of the violent act, I had read, is the person perceived to be standing in the way of the desired union: Isabella Lascar. Get her out of the way and Jed Segal would be free to devote himself to Ellen.

And then, once she was dead, instead of turning his attention to Goldman, he tried to repair his romance with me. I wasn't interested, but that didn't lessen the annoyance of his calls and entreaties in her mind. For me, this was final jeopardy, too. Ellen was too impatient to wait for Jed's ardor to subside. She had seized the moment of my precinct visit this evening when she learned about it on the radio, and used the fact that it drew me through Central Park, to come up with a scheme. Kill me, in the style of Harold McCoy – who had a reason to want me out of the way – and it wouldn't look anything like the death of Isabella. Abduct and stab me to death, don't shoot another one. She was right – the tabloids would love it, and more importantly, no one would connect it to the death of Isabella Lascar.

How sadly ironic for me, to have spent a decade prosecuting men for crimes of violence against woman, and now to meet my peril at the hands of a woman. Perhaps that's what had me blinded in this case all along.

I thought of the lines of poetry scribbled in Isabella's manuscript, sent to her by Goldman, in the guise of the letters of 'Dr. Jeffers': 'Is it . . . a crime . . . to love too well?' Pope named it aptly – a most unfortunate lady. The crime was not the loving, but the murder.

I tried to give her more incentive to back off. 'Let's call Jed together, Ellen. Let's talk with him about—'

'I don't ever want him to talk to you again, don't you understand that? If you're out of his life, he'll come back to me. I know that.'

'I'm leaving New York. I'm going out of town this weekend. I – I won't come back till you work it out with Jed.' I'd go anywhere, forever, if you'd let me out of here. I was almost able to work loose my hands, but had no idea what I could do with them, against her weapons and her physical ability, if I were free.

'You're playing with me again, Alex. You won't leave for long. This is where your work is, you can't stay away.'

Shit, maybe they need a sex crimes prosecutor in Wyoming or Montana. Someplace without investment bankers and without erotomaniacs.

A man's voice from the top of the staircase on the Bethesda Terrace, to our south, broke the stillness. Both of our heads snapped in that direction, vainly trying to see who he was and where he stood, as he called out, 'Hey, girl, hey, pooch. You down there? C'mon back up here to me.'

A dog walker. Goldman tensed and held a finger in front of her mouth, warning me to stay quiet. I prayed whoever he was would venture down the steps to my hellhole.

'Hey, Zac. C'mon back up here. Zac? Zac? C'mon, let me put your leash on.'

David Mitchell? David and Prozac – was it possible?

My eyes were riveted to the top of the great staircase as David, snapping his fingers as though to attract a wandering dog, moved into sight, flooded in the full light of the moon.

'Hey,' he called out again. 'Anybody there? Anybody see a Weimaraner loose around here?'

It was impossible to know whether he could see Goldman

from his angle, but I was certain that he wouldn't be able to tell that I was seated below her on the ground. She didn't speak. I assumed that she hadn't recognized him, but she had done so much research about me that I couldn't be sure she hadn't checked my building and neighbors as well.

'Yes,' I screamed out at the top of my lungs, and she swung around to stick the tip of her knife against the back of my neck, without uttering a sound.

David started down toward us at a trot. 'Great,' he was enthusing, 'which way did you see her go?' He was still acting as though he were simply looking for a lost dog, so it was impossible to tell if he had anyone else with him, or if he had identified the sound of my voice.

He was coming at us too quickly now, and I feared that Goldman wouldn't let him intrude on our session without penalty. I could feel her body leaning over, from behind me, and although she was out of my range of vision, I was afraid she was going to make a move to reach for her holster.

'David,' I screamed out, 'she's got a gun.'

I lurched forward by my own motion and pulled one hand out of the rope. But it was my left hand, and as I broke away from Goldman's grasp, I was useless to do anything to disarm her with it. My right one was still entangled in the cord. As she dropped the knife to the ground and reached for her pistol, four or five dark figures ran down the steep incline and the staircase heading for us, as David dropped to his knees in place.

I could hear Chapman's voice yelling orders from somewhere in this small charging force. First at me, to stay flat, and then at the others to move in slowly, and next at Ellen to throw down her gun.

A shot rang out from just inches above my right ear and

I looked for a place to shelter myself without success. I had no idea who Goldman was aiming at, but if she chose to focus her attention on me again, there was no way she could miss.

Someone on Mike's team had apparently been waiting for Goldman to shoot first, and fired back in our direction. I flattened myself on the ground, my face crushed against a sharp rock – my left arm out to the side and my right one pinned beneath me.

Chapman shouted at her once more: 'Drop it!'

Goldman fired again and again. I ached so badly from every bloodied joint and bruised skin surface that I wasn't sure I would know if a bullet struck me or not.

Seconds later, I heard footsteps approaching Goldman from the rear – a crunching on the dry leaves as someone ran down the slope from the north. She must have heard the sound as well, since she swung herself around to point her pistol in the direction of the man coming in behind her. But he got a shot off first, and she screamed as she dropped backward, her body falling across my own.

The gun was still in Goldman's hand as she lay writhing in pain, her body cushioned against mine. I couldn't tell where she had been hit, but her legs were still twitching and kicking like a frog on a dissection table in a high school biology class.

I didn't know whether to try to wrest the weapon from her grip, but within moments the cops were on her, and I was relieved of that decision.

I could see, from my limited angle of vision, that the shooter was the first to get to us, landing on her right arm with his foot and bending down to take the small pistol away from her as he pressed her elbow against the rocks with his heavy boot. I didn't know who the guy was or whether I would ever lay eyes on him again, but I was certain I would be in love with him for the rest of my life.

Goldman was coughing and crying at once, and in an instant we were surrounded by six or seven other men, Chapman and Mitchell among them. They were all talking over each other, as two of them lifted her off my body and David leaned in to help me raise myself up from my awkward position on the ground.

'Where's she hit?' I heard someone ask, while Mike got to his knees in front of my face, questioning me – at the same time – 'Are you shot?'

I rolled onto my back, biting the corner of my lip to prevent myself from crying, and shook my head in the negative.

'Looks like the gut,' was someone's answer to the question about Goldman, and the men carrying her between them started up the pathway to the street. Another guy was on a walkie-talkie ordering two ambulances – stat – to meet us at the pavement above the Bethesda Terrace.

David was on one side of me, asking where I was injured and checking my vital signs. He pressed my shoulder back against the ground as I tried to sit up, cradling my head in place with his sweater and stroking my hair to calm me, telling me not to try to talk yet. Chapman was on my other flank, working his cell phone, telling someone – probably his boss – where we were and what had gone down. He reached for my right hand, inspecting the abrasions and rope burns that covered its surface, and I grabbed him back, squeezing as hard as I could and holding on to him, because it was so much easier than saying anything aloud.

'Just rest for a few minutes,' David urged me.

'Listen to your doctor, Coop. We'll explain it all later,' Chapman said, laying the phone on the ground and trying to muster up something that resembled a smile.

I closed my eyes, keeping hold of Mike's hand and attempting to make myself breathe more evenly. The noise and commotion of people running up and down the incline continued to swirl around me, and I relished the sound of sirens coming closer and closer to the roadway above.

Within minutes, two EMS workers came pounding down the staircase, carrying a stretcher which they placed beside me on the ground.

'Which one we got here, the perp or the victim?' one asked.

'You got the victim,' Mike said, rising to his feet and flashing his badge at the pair. 'She's a prosecutor,' he went on, summarizing the story in a couple of sentences. 'VIP treatment – or else she's likely to drop a dime on you.' My mouth curled up in a grin as he used police lingo for ratting someone out.

'I'm a physician,' David added, 'I'd like to ride with you. She's my friend.' He began to describe his observations of my condition as they gently lifted me onto the canvas.

'I don't need this, really. I can walk,' were my first words as they carried me toward the staircase.

'Relax, blondie. You're going first class. You're *my* case now – I make all the decisions,' Chapman replied.

It wasn't exactly *Notorious*, but I was every bit as grateful as Ingrid Bergman must have felt as my saviors swept me up the grand steps toward the waiting ambulance.

26

It was almost 5 A.M. by the time I was comfortably settled into a nightgown and robe, sipping some warm, exotic combination of herbs that was prepared for me by Joan Stafford's Asian housekeeper, after David had refused my request for a double Dewar's. He had called Joan from the Emergency Room of New York Hospital, when I admitted that the only way I could get any sleep during the next few days was in the care of a friend I could trust.

Mike had known the triage nurse in the ER from years of working the same midnight shifts. She had taken me into an examining room after the domestic stabbing and before the alcoholic who cracked her elbow tripping off a curb. By the time the resident came into the cubicle to inspect me, the nurse had wiped all my scrapes with

383

alcohol, determined that the wound on my thigh was too shallow to need stitches, and ordered that a set of x-rays be taken to make sure the injuries to my ankle were not serious. The doctor finished the once-over and prescribed some medication for pain and sleep.

Ellen Goldman had been taken to a hospital on the West Side. Mike was smart enough not to tell me which one, although I overheard him phoning the captain to say that her condition was critical but stable when she got out of surgery shortly after four, about the same hour of the morning I was released from the Emergency Room.

Mike and David drove me to Joan's apartment, where she had dressed to meet us in the lobby. 'I didn't think you could look any worse than you did when we had dinner on Tuesday, but you've reached a new low, girl. We'll get you back in shape,' she said as she embraced me, preparing me for what I would see when I got up my nerve to look myself over.

She lived in a eight-room duplex in one of the most elegant buildings in Manhattan, and her guest bedroom, overlooking the East River, was plumped and fluffed for my arrival, like a soft aqua-toned cocoon, ready to shield me from the real world. I spent a few minutes checking myself out in the bathroom mirror, appalled by the number of lacerations and marks that criss-crossed my cheeks and neck, and the variety of bruises that had swollen and discolored my slender fingers and hands. I changed into Joan's lingerie and velvet robe, and descended to the library, where she had poured a brandy for herself, David, and Mike.

'Anybody want to tell me what took you guys so long?' I asked, directing my question to Mike. I screwed up my face at the first swallow of the tea, which was sour and tasteless, so Joan came to sit beside me on the thick arm of my lounge chair, offering me a mouthful of her Courvoisier.

'Next time I call you, don't tell me you can't take the call,' Mike fired back at me.

'In the middle of a line-up? The first time you called, right after I got to the Special Victims Squad, nobody said it was urgent.'

'Well, it wasn't – then. I hadn't spoken to David yet. After I started to get information from him, I called back twice. Got some old hairbag who didn't seem to know what was going on. Finally, when we put most of it together, I called there frantically, telling them to find you and get you back upstairs to take the call. That's when the desk sergeant told me you'd gotten into a car with a woman.'

'Start over,' I said. 'Tell me how you figured it out.'

David started to talk, describing his meeting with Jed. 'He showed up in my office a bit earlier than expected, at seven-fifteen, eager to tell me – to tell anyone who would listen, I think – what had been going on. I asked him to describe the details of the case of the woman who had been stalking him in California – he said her name was Ellie Guttmann—'

Mike interrupted him. 'Yeah, I had already gotten that from the Threat Management Unit during the afternoon, when they pulled up Segal's case for me in Los Angeles. I just had no way to connect it to Ellen Goldman then.'

'Jed insisted to me – and I believe him, Alex – that he never had any kind of relationship with Goldman or Guttmann, whichever is her real name.'

'It's Guttmann,' Mike broke in again. 'I checked with Immigration. Israeli passport.'

Joan had joined in the hunt. 'After you guys called me

from the hospital, I checked her name in Nexis, on my computer. Just territorial on my part – I couldn't believe a writer had tried to kill you, Alex. There must be fifty Ellen Goldmans with published articles in the last year alone. My guess is that it was a pretty safe alias, close to her real name, if anybody was going to try to check out her press credentials and see if she had ever written anything before.'

David went back to his story. 'My secretary had pulled some of the recent publications on erotomania. I read them on the shuttle yesterday, and then Jed and I went over the information. He had never heard whether there was a diagnosis in Goldman's case, but it's true that Jed's wife was the complaining witness. He had wiped his hands of the matter once the police locked her up, and he was moving East.'

'No diagnosis was made, according to the LAPD,' Mike reported. 'They had an easy conviction for aggravated harassment, based on the telephone records of her calls to Segal's home and office, and the letters to his wife. Just a lock-up, no psych report.'

'Ellen Goldman is a classic case. I read Dietz, Zona, Sharma – all the current experts on the subject.'

'What's a "classic" erotomaniac?' I asked.

'To begin with,' he responded, 'most of the subjects of the disorder are women, young women – like Ellen Goldman – in their early thirties. Their victims are male, usually older, and usually men of a higher status, socioeconomic class – or even an unattainable public figure, like a celebrity or politician. Jed fit every one of those categories when she first encountered him in California.'

We were all listening attentively. 'It's interesting, too,

that almost half of the subjects studied were foreign-born. Again, like Goldman. And a lot of them adopt different persona that they use for writing letters to their subjects, because they're so smart and articulate – in this instance, the Cordelia Jeffers correspondence.'

'How long before they give up this delusion?' Joan wanted to know.

'With other obsessions, so-called "simple" obsessions,' David told her, 'the subjects only made contact for less than a year. With erotomaniacs, these episodes have gone on for ten or twelve years, with repeated efforts to keep in touch with the man. They make phone calls, write letters, stalk their subjects at home, in offices, on airplanes, in hotels – you name it. They are convinced – that's the delusion – that if they can get the obstacle, the other woman, out of the way, the man they're obsessed with will be united with them and able to declare his love.'

'Wasn't Jed aware of any of this, with Isabella? Didn't it ever occur to him that Goldman was her killer?' I wanted to know.

'Absolutely not,' David said. 'When Goldman got out of jail, there was an order of protection still in effect by the court. She was not allowed to have contact with either of the Segals. And she was otherwise sane enough to avoid them at first, knowing that would land her back in jail.

'So she didn't bother Jed when she first got to New York last month. At least, not directly – not that he knew about. There was enough publicity about his move to find his office at CommPlex, after the Senate race. But I'd have to guess that she spent more of her energy finding out about you, once she learned you were dating him. Was that fact ever in the newspapers?'

'Yeah, Liz Smith did an item in her column,' Mike added, '"SEX CRIMES CRUSADER DOES SENATE LOSER," or something like that. That's how she knew about you. We figure she found out about Isabella by intercepting some of Jed's messages on his voice mail at CommPlex. He said she did that all the time when he was in California.'

'She had her eye on you, Alex,' David continued, 'trying to figure how long you would last with him. Then along came the ultimate antagonist, in the form of a Hollywood goddess: Isabella Lascar. *You* were a mere mortal, but Isabella was serious competition.'

Ellen and I apparently had that much in common.

'But I thought Jed and Isabella had discussed their stalkers with each other?' I queried aloud, remembering that snippet of conversation with him.

'Yes, that's true, in general,' David told us. 'But it had never occurred to either one of them that they were being harassed by the same person. Isabella was a celebrity and had been exposed to a lot of unwanted attention, as you know, Alex. When she started to get hang-up calls at the hotel she didn't know what their source was, and the letters from Cordelia Jeffers were a complete mystery to her. She never divulged their exact contents to him – and Jed thinks that's because she knew how guilty he felt about betraying you.'

'When David called me tonight after he finished his meeting with Segal, he asked me to come over to his apartment to talk to him about the interview. I got there about nine, with Joe Duffy,' one of the other guys who worked the squad with Mike. 'Up to that minute, I was still convinced Segal was the killer.

'But David said Segal could prove his alibi – that his

lawyer had the Cape Air ticket receipt that would show he was already on the plane off the Vineyard by the time Iz was blown to bits. Just that his lawyer is playing hardball 'cause we haven't released the exact time of her death yet. He doesn't want to show us the plane ticket till we tell him time of death.'

David was nodding his head in support of Mike's information.

'The reason Jed was leaving messages for you all over, Alex, was that Goldman finally began to dare to get closer to him. Finding Isabella's Filofax was a gold mine for her, and made it much too easy. It had loads of information about access to Jed, as well as to you. Not only was she erasing the messages he left you,' David explained, 'but she waited for him outside his office these last few mornings – not to make contact, but just to see him. That's typical of the disorder.'

'So who figured out that Ellen was the killer?' I looked from David to Mike, but both shook their heads.

'We didn't exactly figure it out,' Chapman said. 'When David told me about the reappearance of Jed's stalker, I asked him to make a call and get her description. Jed told us what she looked like, even mentioned the accent, and told us she was driving a white Celica, with rental plates.

'I gotta say, Alex, my thinking was like yours. It never occurred to me a woman was the killer. I was so sure it was Jed – or some other jilted lover boy.

'But by the time David and I had gone over all the stuff about erotomania, and how the person most in danger is the one in the middle, and Jed's insistence that he was leaving messages that you weren't getting – we just assumed *you* were in danger, whether or not it had anything to do with Isabella Lascar.'

'So why did you call me back at the precinct, you know, the last call?'

Both David and Mike hesitated, before David answered. 'Actually, it was Jed's idea.'

I was stonefaced, but David went on. 'When Mike told me to call him and get the description of the woman, Jed pleaded with me to make you understand how dangerous he was afraid she could be. Once he saw her here in New York – knowing how she had plagued his wife – he was afraid she'd start to harass you next. He didn't think murder, but just an embarrassment you didn't need, with the public nature of your work.'

'I called them to tell you not to go home alone,' Mike said, 'and to make sure Mercer got a patrol car to get you to your apartment and then down to your office in the morning, just until we could find this woman and identify her. But I couldn't get Mercer on the phone. And it didn't become urgent till the guy on the desk told me you were fine – you had just gotten into a car with some woman up at the corner. A white car.'

'Dammit, nothing like this ever happens to me,' Joan said.

Mike went on to describe that he had called his office for a backup car to meet him at Fifth Avenue and Seventy-second Street. He planned to go over to the West Side, near the Special Victims Squad, and see if people on the street had seen or heard anything that would give him a lead. He requested that headquarters put out an alert in Manhattan North for a white Celica with two women traveling in it. Then he and Duffy started out of David's apartment – and David insisted on going along.

Chapman and the backup team met eight minutes later at the Fifth Avenue entrance to the park and started on the cross-drive to the West.

'Like Mercer always says, detective work is ninety-nine percent genius and one percent luck,' Mike reminded me. 'I'm whipping through the park like a tornado on the Seventy-second Street crossroad, then Doc in the backseat screams out that there's a white Celica pulled in under a tree on our right side. I braked, made a U-turn and parked across the way, in front of the Bandshell. We all fanned out, and David offered to do the ruse about the dog – figured you'd either make his voice or the dog's name. Best thing *you* did was warn us about the gun. I knew we had a whackjob, but I still didn't guess that she was the shooter.'

'Talk about blindsided, I'm the one who got right in the car with her,' I said quietly, wondering how an intelligent human mind like Ellen Goldman's could go so singularly off-track.

'What hurts more, Coop,' Mike questioned me, 'your feelings or your neck?'

'At this point it's about even,' I told him, smiling for the first time in hours.

'She'll stay with me for as long as her doctor wants her in town, and then, I'm taking her away for some tropical sunshine,' Joan announced.

'This isn't a great time for me to go—'

'Hey, you think there won't be any perverts left in town for you to handle two weeks from now? You think they're gonna go out of business while you take a break, Cooper?

Give it a rest – you're the only person I know who isn't gonna be outta work in the foreseeable future.'

I wanted to keep my three friends around me and talking to me for hours more, despite my exhaustion, until the daylight poured in through the windows over the river. I wanted to put off my dreams for as long as possible – dreams that would inevitably be haunted by delusion and betrayal, murder and death.

Keep talking, I said to myself, keep talking. It had worked with Ellen Goldman, maybe it would hold off my nightmares as well.

'Did Alex ever tell you about the first case we had together?' Mike asked Joan and David, as I shifted my body in the comfortable chair and rested my head against the pillows, watching for the sunrise.